BOUND FOR
SALVATION
BOOK TWO

KENDRA LEIGH

Published by Evoke Publications

Cover Art by Kendra Leigh
Copy Editing by The Polished Pen
Formatting by Tugboat Design

ISBN: 978-1-910713-03-7

This is for M... my real life salvation.

CHAPTER ONE

Despite living in the most densely populated city in the United States, I'd spent the majority of my life alone. Emotional isolation as a child had left me reluctant to share my space, in a physical sense, as an adult. Until recently, I'd cocooned myself in a private world, believing it would protect me from the ravages of reality. In fact, less than six months ago, I would have rather had hot, melted wax poured into my eyes than spend every living second with another human being. But that was before I entered the world of Ethan Wilde. And now, for the first time in my living memory, I wasn't alone.

Ethan's trip to London had taught me that being alone is actually very different to being lonely. The physical distance had tested our relationship, making us doubt its resilience, but we'd learned that despite the miles that had lay between us, our hearts had remained entwined. Our feelings wouldn't change regardless of space and time.

This hadn't, however, prevented us from making up for the impingement of both since Ethan's return from London.Even though it had been a week since he'd been to the New York office, he'd chosen to spend Monday working from home. For a large part of the day, we'd sat at opposite ends of the Petrie sofa, each with laptops across our knees, our legs outstretched with feet touching to maintain constant contact. Exchanging frequent meaningful glances and smiles, we'd made love with only our eyes, communicating in a silent, unspoken language, which only he and I would understand.

For the remainder of the week, we managed to tear ourselves away from each other, if only during working hours. Staying in constant touch by text during the day, and spending our evenings talking and laughing and making sweet, decadent love. Our bond was growing stronger by the day, our desire and need for each other consuming us both like a drug—a drug that was more necessary than the air we breathed.

And so I'd gone from the girl who'd refused to share her space with anything other than her late, beloved goldfish, to someone who quite happily and eagerly, yet unofficially, cohabited with another human being. Ethan not only kept my world rotating by simply existing in it, but actually made me feel so much more comfortable in my own skin than ever before. The fact his super-sexy, fuckable body was almost permanently attached to it was clearly the principle reason, but there was more. It was odd, but when I was with him, I could swear it was easier to breathe. Almost like a hard, painful obstruction had been removed from my chest and suddenly there was space for oxygen.

Now I gazed at Ethan across the breakfast table, rolling these thoughts around in my head and munching on fresh fruit and yogurt. He was totally engrossed in the morning newspaper, so I took full advantage of the opportunity to study his striking face.

The muscles of his perfectly angular jaw were flexing furiously, as they often did when he concentrated intensely. I gazed, mesmerized by his impossibly blue eyes flittering back and forth across the page as he read. The light shining through the vast windows emphasized the rich honey tones of his mussed up, sex hair, making me want to thrust my hands into it and tug him close to dip my tongue into his full, sensual mouth.

"You're staring," he muttered suddenly, disturbing me from my daydream. His eyes remained on the page he was reading, his expression indiscernible.

"You're right," I replied simply.

Folding his newspaper and placing it on the table, he leaned across the corner toward me. "Why?"

Shifting, I leaned so that the tips of our noses were almost touching, our lips only inches apart. I could feel his warm breath on my face and smell the intoxicating scent of... Ethan.

"Because you fascinate me... and because I can," I said mischievously, tossing his own words back at him.

Smiling a sexy smile, he angled his face to kiss my lips softly, his tongue lapping gently against mine. The effect was immediate, the flesh at the apex of my thighs heating as he deepened the kiss, his eager mouth and increasing desire unmistakable.

"Fuck, Cinders. What it is you do to me." He pulled away, shifting uncomfortably in his seat, attempting to readjust himself. "Christ, I'm achingly hard for you right now." Glancing at his watch, he groaned. "And as I haven't got time to bend you over this table and bury my cock inside you, it looks like I'll have to remain that way all day."

"I may not give you much choice if you continue to talk dirty to me like that." I bit down on my lower lip, my brow flickering in challenge.

"Oh, Angel, you dirty, dirty girl." His lips kinked into a sexy smirk. "You're completely insatiable. It's barely an hour since you climaxed delectably into my mouth." He licked his lips. "Mmm, see, I can still taste you."

"I didn't realize my orgasms were limited."

"You and your sassy mouth." His gaze shifted to my pouted lips, his darkening eyes betraying his arousal.

"Want to fuck it?" I breathed, throwing down the gauntlet some more.

My words caused him to wince, as if in unendurable pain, his eyes squeezing shut for a beat before snapping open. "Yes," he hissed through clenched teeth. "Hard and quick—swallow," he instructed as he pushed himself to his feet and swiftly unfastened the zipper on his immaculate, navy suit pants, unleashing his impressive, swollen cock. Stepping back, he perched his backside on the edge of the table, his hands curling over the lip, grasping it securely.

Feeling triumphant, I shifted quickly, moving to arrange myself in between his legs and lowering to my knees. "Hold on tight," I breathed seductively.

As I took him into my mouth, I glanced up through my long, dark lashes, my eyes settling on his beautiful chiseled features, where very soon I would watch while he lost himself inside my mouth. And every last drop of pleasure would be proportionately mine—because I was the reason for his undoing.

Ethan pressed the button for the basement and the elevator door slid closed. A sinful smile lurked at the corner of his lips as he eyed me sideways. Suddenly, his smile faded into a thin, serious line, his brow scrunching as he peered closer to scrutinize my face. Then using his pointy finger to swipe at the corner of his mouth, his eyes motioned to point at my lips in a gesture which said I should mirror his actions.

Horrified, I turned to the mirror expecting to see the remnants of his arousal at the corner of my mouth. It was clean.

Throwing his head back, he began to roar with laughter. "Sorry, baby, I couldn't resist."

"Well, I'm glad I'm a good source of entertainment as well." I glared at him, feigning shock and offense. "For a moment there, I thought you kept me around to merely empty your balls."

His smile fled, chased away by a look of utter mortification. "That's not what you really think, is it?"

Trying but failing to remain impassive, I beamed a smile. "Jokes! Sorry, baby, I couldn't resist."

"Christ!" He rolled his eyes in relief and pulled me into a tight embrace. "You mean so much more to me than sex and entertainment, baby. I promise."

"Really?" I pushed for compliments.

"Really."

"Like what?"

"Well... let me think... Oh, I know, you can cook."

My mouth mimicked an *O*, as I pushed him away and punched him playfully in the arm. "Yeah, yeah. Jokes, I know."

The elevator reached the basement garage just as he wrestled me into a tight embrace moving in to nibble at my ear. We looked up giggling to find Jackson waiting by the car stifling a smile. He opened the rear door as we approached, and we slipped into the luxury of the back seat.

"Let's go out to dinner after work tonight," Ethan said brightly.

"Okay, yeah, I'd like that. I'll meet you back here though. I'm only going in to the gallery for a couple of hours, and then I thought I'd hit the gym or take a run in Central Park. I can freshen up and change for when you get home."

Unease suddenly ghosted his expression. "I'd rather you went in the gym, I don't want you out running alone. Jackson can pick you up in a couple of hours and bring you back here, unless you wanted to go to the gym in your block. Which reminds me..." He flipped open his brief case and dug out two set of keys, handing both to me.

"New keys for your apartment. There's a spare. Jackson had a new security door fitted and there's a brand new CCTV system installed. It includes the corridor leading to your door as well as inside your apartment. It's all safe and sound if you wanted to spend some time there."

I stared down at the keys in my hand and winced, as if the metal had burned my skin. The hairs on the back of my neck prickled as an involuntary shudder ran down my spine. I hadn't been back to the apartment since the break-in, and in truth had absolutely no desire to. All that came to mind when I pictured the place was...

"Angel?" Ethan startled me from the disturbing scene manifesting inside my mind. "If it makes you uncomfortable, we can go together."

I nodded, half smiling, and then something else occurred to me. *Maybe he wanted some space.*

"Do *you* want me to spend some time there?"

"Well, only if you want to, and only if it includes me." He narrowed his brow thoughtfully. "I'm not trying to get rid of you, if that's what you're thinking. I've had the keys since Monday but was enjoying having you around. I love having you at my place. I just know how you feel about your apartment and understand if you need to spend some time there, is all." He reached out, tucking a stray strand of hair behind my ear.

How I felt about my apartment, I thought sadly. I shrugged it off and smiled again as the car pulled into the sidewalk outside the gallery.

"I think I'd prefer we went together," I said in answer to his earlier question.

"Okay, well we can take a quick look before we go for dinner. Check everything's in order, grab the mail."

Feeling only slightly better about the idea, I nodded and smiled encouragingly, not entirely sure if it was Ethan I was attempting to reassure or myself.

After I waved goodbye, I stood outside the gallery staring again at the keys in my hand, and suddenly I had an idea.

Pushing open the door, I shouted out to Jia who stood talking to Alice at the reception desk. "I just need to dash out to get something, I'll be back shortly."

"You only just got here, bitch."

"I know—I won't be long."

"Bring coffee!" I heard her shout as the door closed behind me.

An hour and a half later I had exactly what I wanted.

Ethan stood distractingly close as we rode the elevator up to my apartment later that day. He gazed down at me through hooded, slanted eyes, an all-too-familiar yearning on his face.

"You look amazing, as usual." His fingers traced over the bare skin of an exposed shoulder. "I love your style."

I wore a brown, loose-fitting, mini-dress with flared sleeves and a scooped off-the-shoulder neckline. It was adorned in multicolored paillettes that produced a variety of whimsical patterns. I teamed it with bronze strappy Giuseppe Zanottis, and I felt glitzy but casual.

Ethan had changed into slim-fit jeans and T-shirt with a navy blazer and desert boots. He looked hot. And felt hot, as his wandering fingers slid down to the hem of my dress and glided up my inner thigh to the thin lace of my panties, brushing gently against my sex. I bit down on my lip to silence my involuntary gasp and stepping back out of reach, raised my brow with stern admonishment. As hot as he was, there was no way I felt relaxed enough to make out in an elevator, especially the one ascending to my apartment.

"Are you turning me down, Cinder-fucking-rella?" The expression on his face was something between shock and vague offense.

"Only for now, Charming, calm down. And calm him down," I said, poking the rigid bulge behind the zipper of his jeans. "It's not the time or place."

"Since when does fooling around in a public place bother *you*?" He studied my face some more, and somehow things seemed to fall into place. He reached out to stroke my cheek, his frown softening. "You're worried about going inside, aren't you?"

I cut my gaze, hoping to hide what I felt was frailty.

"Baby, it's okay. It will be fine, I promise."

As the elevator door slid open, he took my hand and smiling reassuringly, led me down the hall to my new security door.

Swiftly, I placed the key in the lock, turned it, and opened the door. Ethan stepped inside first, taking care not to make a big deal of our entry. I followed, trying my best to act casual, but like metal to a magnet, my focus was immediately drawn to the breakfast bar where Ponyo had lay slain and lifeless. Of course, now it was cleared of all debris, just a clean, polished surface remaining, and for one foolish moment, I found myself hoping it had been a huge mistake and Ponyo would be swimming happily around her luxury bowl. But when my gaze shifted across the open-plan lounge to the coffee table, I found the space bare, all trace of her vanished, and my heart sank again.

Ethan followed my gaze. "Jackson had everything tidied away. He hasn't missed anything. I thought it was best."

I nodded approvingly and began to wander around the room.

A strange sort of eeriness lingered heavily in the air, an unfamiliarity settling around me like a thick layer of dust. It was as if I was seeing it for the first time. I felt at odds with the place, disconnected and disquieted in the way I felt on the rare occasions I'd been back to my father's house—a place I'd grown up in. I raised my hand to smooth the hairs that had risen unbidden prickling the back of my neck.

Ethan followed me in silence as I moved down the hall to the bedroom, unnecessarily realigning objects of no importance for no particular reason. Finally, when I thought I'd given it a reasonable amount of time, and could bear it no longer, I turned to Ethan and said, "I'm famished. Let's go get dinner."

Tilting his head to the side, he eyed me suspiciously. "Would you like to come back here later?"

"Not especially." I kept my reply brief and made my way back through to the kitchen to collect my purse. "I mean there's not much point really. I don't have any groceries in or—"

"I could ask Jackson to collect some essentials if you wanted."

"No, Ethan, it's fine. We'll just stay at yours—for now—please."

"Okay, baby, that's okay. I don't want to push you, but I don't want you to be afraid either. I want you to feel comfortable here."

"I know, and I will. Which is why I want to give you this." Thrusting my hand into my purse, I pulled out the spare key he'd given me earlier and handed it to him. "Because I want *you* to feel comfortable here too," I added.

A shy smile ghosted across his lips. "That's your spare key."

"No... that's your key. If you want it."

"Of course I want it. I thought you'd never ask." His smile widened as he reached out and took the key from between my fingers, pulling with it the key ring which I'd kept carefully hidden in the palm of my hand—the gift I'd run out to buy earlier that day.

"You've attached a key ring. That's pretty," he said turning it all ways to try and decipher what it was. "What is it?"

I smiled wryly, having fully anticipated the question. "It's a… a sort of symbolic representation."

"Of what?"

"Me."

He looked puzzled. "How so?"

"Well, you need the other half for it to be a complete representation. Here, lay it down flat." I patted the kitchen work surface and retrieved my own key from my purse, laying it down next to his. The two key rings were a perfect mirror image, each part identical but reversely arranged. I watched as Ethan's expression changed from one of puzzlement to a smile of comprehension.

When placed together, the two pieces suddenly morphed into one single recognizable image. In fact, the only thing that gave them away as separate individual items was the tiny, almost imperceptible fracture that had been created by placing them together, and which now ran straight through the center. The representation was unmistakable— the reassembled pieces formed a pair of silver diamond encrusted angel wings surrounding a beautiful red gemstone cut to the shape of a heart.

"You once said I was a broken angel and that you wanted to mend me. The heart enfolded by angel wings represents me and the way you complete me. Separated, I'm broken. But as long as you're with me, I'm whole—and I'm mended. You mend me, Ethan."

His eyes, deep pools of blue, were suddenly swimming with awed devotion. Curling his fingers around my jaw, he drew my face to his and leaned his forehead lightly up against mine. His breath was hot against my lips, his eyes blinking to quell the misty moisture I caught just a glimpse of.

Freshly composed, he cleared his throat. "You have no idea what your words mean to me. I know it's hard for you and this…" His eyes darted to the symbols of my affection lying unified on the kitchen counter, that were, for now, the only way I could express my innermost feelings for him. "This is beautiful. *You* are *so* beautiful. Thank you, I'll treasure it the same way I treasure your heart."

Smiling shyly, I pressed my lips gently against his. He responded with the lightest, most featherlike brush against my mouth and then paused, as if figuring out the best way to convey the thoughts transpiring in his mind.

"What you said, Angel… about me mending you… I want more than anything for you to be whole, and if I can be the one who helps you, it will be the most gratifying and jubilant accomplishment of my entire life."

"But that's what I'm trying to tell you. You do mend me. I am whole."

"Not entirely, baby. Not yet." He cradled my face in his hands, as if his gentle touch put emphasis on the caution and care that went into his words. "You've come such a long way. But I still see the demons that you battle every day. The way they torment you. The way they hunt you down while you sleep and terrorize your dreams. Only you can truly banish them forever. I'll do whatever I can to give you the strength and support you need to finally lay them to rest. But you have to trust me to let me guide you."

Despite my assertion, I knew with every inch of me that he was right. I could keep on papering over the cracks forever, but one day I'd have to realize it wasn't a permanent resolution. Ethan couldn't mend me completely until I finally conceded to just how fragmented I was.

"Yes, that's what I want more than anything. You do give me the strength I need. I trust you. If you show me the way, I'll try my best to follow."

His eyes widened, seemingly stunned by my willingness to accept his invitation. "Really, you will?"

"Yes."

"Okay." His expression was suddenly alight with a plan that was clearly hatching inside his mind. "Well let's start with dinner."

"'Dinner'?" I puzzled.

"Yes. At Eden."

I inhaled slowly and deeply, attempting to assuage the fluttering nerves which were eating my belly from the inside out. My appetite had vanished the moment Ethan had suggested eating at Eden, and even the gorgeous aromas permeating the air weren't enough to kick-start its return.

Adam was nowhere to be seen, no doubt hard at it in the kitchen, knowing him. The hostess, whose name I think was Andrea, recognized me immediately and ushered us past the queue to a table.

Unusually, I paid little attention to the fluttering eyelashes of the waitress and the way other female diners appeared to hanker after my man. As a rule I would dish out a death-stare, issuing a warning somewhere on the lines of "don't-even-fucking-look-at-him, bitch," but tonight I was too busy scanning the restaurant for any signs of my toxic family.

An initial survey didn't turn up any nasties, so I thanked my lucky stars and took the seat at the table which afforded me the best view, and, therefore, ample forewarning should any show up.

"Okay?" Ethan's voice was steeped in concern as I merely nodded in response. "Shall I order for us?" When words continued to fail me, he reached across to squeeze my hand. "Relax, Cinders." I looked at him, smiled, and took a deep breath.

The pan-fried sea bass with citrus dressed broccoli and crushed new potatoes was delicious, and slowly I began to unwind, a modicum of my appetite returning. I looked to find Ethan regarding me closely from across the table, a look of amusement adding a glow to his savagely handsome face.

"What?" I asked, feeling suddenly self-conscious.

"You look as if you're watching a very intense tennis match," he said, doing a quick demonstration of me oscillating my eyes between door-to-street and door-to-kitchen.

I shook my head, laughing at his impersonation.

"If you need me to help you relax, I know of a very private storage room not far from here," he nodded his head toward the stairs.

My cheeks flushed as I recalled our very first encounter, how we'd eye-fucked each other from across the room with such burning intimacy it had resulted in mind-blowing, shelf-clawing sex in one of Adam's upstairs storage rooms. The flush wasn't a result of embarrassment, but from feeling completely horned-up by the memory.

"Not private enough," I muttered through clenched teeth, squirming to relieve the sudden ache between my thighs. "I cannot believe we did that."

"I can—and I'd do it again and again if I knew it would lead to this. To us."

"Me too—without a second thought. My life changed forever that night, and I'm in no rush to get my old one back, thank you very much."

His sexy dimpled grin spread from one ear to the other. Reminiscing about the storage room incident was clearly having an effect on both of us.

Out of the corner of my eye, I saw Adam threading his way through the diners towards us, and I felt myself tense, my libido deserting me instantly.

"Hey, Angelica. It's great to see you. Where've you been hiding?" He bent to kiss me on the cheek. He looked handsome and every bit the restaurateur in his navy pinstripe suit, white shirt, and red tie, and suddenly I was filled with affection for him.

"Hey, Adam. Yeah, I know it's been a while. How are you?"

"I'm good, Sis." He turned curiously to Ethan.

Ethan stood up to greet him, a slightly guarded look replacing the playful one from the moment before.

"Adam, I'd like you to meet Ethan Wilde, my boyfriend. Ethan, this is my brother Adam."

"Oh." Adam's jaw fell open in shock as he turned to Ethan and shook his hand. "Well, that explains why I haven't seen you in a while. It's good to meet you, Ethan."

"Likewise, I've heard a lot about you—and the restaurant. You've got a great place here," Ethan replied politely.

"Oh, thanks. We aim to please. How *was* the food?"

"Fantastic," both Ethan and I replied simultaneously.

"Well, good." He held a finger up to one of his staff, who appeared to be in a tizzy about something, gesturing that he'd be one minute. "Listen, I'm sorry I can't stop and chat, but it appears I'm surrounded by incompetence."

"It's fine, don't let us keep you. We can see you're busy. It was good to finally meet you," Ethan said, reaching across the table for my hand and giving it a squeeze. I nodded in agreement.

"And you, Ethan. Don't be strangers. And dinner's on the house." Ethan looked like he was about to protest, but Adam held up a hand. "Please, I insist." He clasped my arm affectionately. "I'm happy for you, Sis," he muttered so only I could hear.

"Thanks, Adam. See you later."

Just as he was about to walk away, he paused to glance at his watch. "Oh, just so you know. Aaron and Dad said they were calling for a drink—they're due any time." My face fell, my mood plummeting along with it. Adam shifted uncomfortably, smiled an apologetic smile, pivoted, and walked away toward the kitchen.

As the speed of my pulse accelerated and my palms grew clammy, I turned my gaze to Ethan. He considered me carefully, as if processing my reaction before taking both my hands in his.

"If we stay, you get this over with and you're not worried every time you want to come here to see Adam. But if you prefer, we can leave. One step at a time. We'll go at your pace."

"Mmm." I frowned and puckered my lips to the side, trying my best to give the impression that I was at least mulling over the options. "Let's go."

Grabbing my purse, I pushed hastily to my feet before he could remonstrate. Thankfully he followed my lead, and looking only slightly thwarted, placed his hand at the small of my back to guide me through the restaurant toward the exit.

As we rounded the dining area into the bar, I stopped dead in my tracks. We were too late. My father had just entered the restaurant, Aaron following closely behind him like a slightly larger shadow. They were laughing and making small talk with a man and his wife, who they were evidently acquainted with.

When our eyes met, my father's smile faded to a straight, impassive line, like our running into each other was rather bothersome and ill-timed.

Well, ditto, asshole. You're not the most idyllic end to my day either.

Ethan sensed my immediate unease through the taut rigidity of my posture and stroked my back encouragingly. "Okay, baby, we've got this," he muttered into my ear as he steered me purposefully forwards.

I mustered a half smile as we approached, trying my best to still my fretful, wringing hands and sudden erratic breathing triggered by the toxic fumes which seemed to emanate from their presence.

My father's gaze flicked from me to Ethan and a slow, disturbing smirk settled on his face. "Angelica, what a delightful surprise. And who have we here?" he asked, eyeing Ethan with relish.

"Um… uh," I faltered, completely blindsided by his seemingly sincere greeting.

"Ah, Angelica made a friend," Aaron jeered, his tone spiked with contempt.

Christ, he might as well have poked Ethan with a stick. As expected, I felt him bristle beside me, so I shifted my weight, nudging closer to him and raising my hand to his hip. Squeezing firmly, I prayed that my touch would be enough to hold him back, but the heat was already coming off of him in waves.

To my utter surprise, my father held up his hand in rebuke, halting Aaron in his tracks, the action stunning him even more so than me. At best, my father would usually overlook Aaron's goading, even incite it, but he would never inhibit it. Ethan shifted, his hand sliding pointedly around my waist in a statement of solidarity. I held my breath.

"Dr. Lawson," he said with self-assured authority, holding his hand out to my father. "I'm Ethan Wilde, Angelica's boyfriend."

I let out my breath slowly.

Aaron's smug face dissolved like melting wax as recognition dawned. The name Ethan Wilde was evidently familiar to him, and his reaction made me chomp down on my lip to refrain from laughing aloud. But it was my father's reaction which had me reeling with astonishment. A full-on, delighted grin spread across his lined but handsome face.

"So the rumors are true. How wonderful. It's an honor to meet you, Mr. Wilde." He returned the hand shake, his tongue rolling over Ethan's name as though he were savoring the feel of it. "Angelica, darling, why didn't you come and tell me the good news yourself? I had to hear this from Claudia Miller."

Darling? He'd never called me darling in his life. Who was this man in a mask that looked a lot like my father, but sounded nothing like him? I stared at him in disbelief, as did Ethan and Aaron.

"She says you met at her wedding," he went on oblivious.

Wrong.

"I'm so glad I had a hand in your... union."

Wrong again.

Of course, I wasn't about to set him straight, especially considering the exact nature of our first encounter. Ethan and I just sort of smiled and nodded, but remained noncommittal. For a brief second, I thought I saw a trace of annoyance in my father's eyes, but he made a swift recovery and continued to simulate enthusiasm.

Aaron, who was obviously bewildered and unable to stomach my father's gusto any longer, grunted some excuse and shuffled away to find Adam. As he passed, he leaned in to my ear. "I give it a month— tops," he scoffed nastily.

"Go choke," I offered in return. Fortunately the exchange seemed to go unnoticed by Ethan, who was dubiously assessing my father's disposition.

"So, you two must have been together, what a couple of months? I hope you made a good impression on Ethan's parents, Angelica, and that you did the Lawson family name proud."

I felt Ethan stiffen again, could sense his simmering annoyance as he struggled to tolerate my father's blatant phony attentiveness.

I held my breath again as Ethan began to answer for me.

"Actually, my parents haven't had the pleasure of meeting Angelica yet. They're out of the country on an extended vacation. But I am certain that she will do *herself* proud when the time comes to meet them. I know *my* parents will love her." He turned and offered me the widest smile. "How could you not?"

"Indeed," my father breathed in a state of bemused joy. The remarks that Ethan had shrewdly alluded to had either gone over his head or he was choosing to ignore them. Whichever it was, it hadn't affected his mood. He looked positively happy—and on the other hand, eerily subversive, as though an intriguing but conniving idea was gradually occurring to him.

"You must accept my invitation and accompany Angelica to the charity dinner next week." Oh my God, I had completely forgotten about that. "I'm sure she's told you about it. The Lighthouse Project raises money to help young people with either drug addictions of their own, or who are growing up in drug abuse environments. We provide rehabilitation programs to help them and their families find freedom from drugs."

Ethan raised his brow graciously. "A very worthy cause. I'd be delighted to," he enthused. He was playing my father at his own game, although I was yet to fathom what that was. "And you must allow me to make a donation in return for the privilege of having Angelica on my arm. It will be worth every cent."

"How wonderful! That's incredibly generous of you. The charity will be profoundly grateful, thank you."

My father was delighted, utter joy practically oozing from his toxic pores, and for some stupid reason, I couldn't help the flood of happiness which enveloped me. My father was standing in my company—and he was smiling with pleasure. I wasn't a fool, I was aware that Ethan's wealth and how lucrative it would be to know him was playing a large part in my father's sudden predilection. But if I could bring him something he could approve of, something to embrace, maybe it would just give me an in, an opportunity to gain the two things I craved. Acceptance—forgiveness. I felt quite giddy at the thought.

"Well, it's been a long day, we really must go." Ethan placed his hand on the small of my back to guide me out of the restaurant. "It was a pleasure to meet you, Dr. Lawson."

"The pleasure was all mine," my father practically purred. "And please, call me Harley. Goodnight, Ethan. Angelica." He nodded his farewell.

Jackson was waiting outside, as usual, and as I climbed in the car and shuffled across the rear seat, I was still unable to shift the buoyant smile from my face. Ethan climbed in next to me.

"Fucking two-faced, phony fucker," he blurted angrily the moment Jackson closed the door. "I wanted to ram my fist into his devious fucking face. What a fucking performance." He shook his head, his hands running through his hair in irritation.

The cold truth hit me like a sledgehammer, chasing away the ludicrously short-lived optimism I'd had no right to feel. Ethan stared at me, the realization that I'd dared to hope hitting him just as hard as he watched my smile evaporate.

"Oh, baby, please tell me you didn't fall for that heap of crap," he pleaded desperately. "For Christ's sake, the dollar signs were flashing in his eyes. He was practically rubbing his hands together."

Suddenly feeling incredibly foolish, I cut my gaze to focus on the road as the car pulled into traffic. Ethan grasped my hand and shuffled across the seat toward me.

"Angel, look at me." He reached out, taking hold of my chin between thumb and finger, turning my face to search my eyes.

"Only for a second," I admitted, blinking to banish the disappointment which loitered gloomily underneath my long, dark lashes. "Just for a brief, crazy second. I know it's absurd, but I thought that if he likes you, he might begin to see me differently. Or at least pay enough attention to see that maybe, one day, he might. I'd love—just for a solitary moment—to be the cause of his happiness instead of his misery." Feeling stupid, I turned back to the window.

"Oh, baby. I don't think it's absurd for you to seek approval from your own father, just maybe a bit... naive to expect that you'd find it. Not because you don't deserve it, but because he's a jerk-off, and it's futile to even hope. And for the life of me, I'll never understand why you feel you *need* his approval. He's not worthy of you. You should believe in yourself, look at what you've achieved without it. See the person you've become. And he's not miserable, Angel. He's a fucking sadist who gets off on making you miserable."

I turned back toward him and snuggled under his arm, tilting my chin to gaze up into his beautiful eyes. "I didn't realize he made you this mad."

"I'd put a bullet through the bastard's head if I thought I could get away with it—and if you wouldn't hate me for it."

"I could never hate you," I said wholeheartedly. His lips moved in a halfhearted smile, but I could tell he was struggling to quell his anger. "Why can't I see through him like you can? You had the measure of him straightaway, even played him at his own game."

"Because I see him for what he is. And you could too, if you wanted. I threw the money at him to show him how transparent I thought he was. To cut out the unnecessary preamble and sucking up—predictable son of a bitch. Were you expecting an invite to this charity thing?"

"Yes, actually, I'd just forgotten about it. It's the only time I can guarantee a call from my father, when there's an impending charity event. And the only time he treats me like a human being—publicly at least. He likes to give the impression he's an accomplished father, the head of a united and doting family, who come together effortlessly to fight for the good cause. I'm sure it's the only reason he hasn't disowned me altogether… because it wouldn't *look* good."

"See, you do see through him. You just need to divest yourself of this irrational need to make amends in order to receive acceptance. It's nonsense."

I nodded, all too aware that what he was saying was true, but as usual, finding the subject too intense and exhausting to discuss. Ethan must have sensed me withdrawing and changed the subject.

"Have you finalized your selection for the exhibit?"

I smiled at his tact and uncanny ability to read me. "Yes," I answered with enthusiasm.

"And does the series have a title?"

"Yes." I laughed again, this time with irony. "The Essence of Hope and Optimism."

CHAPTER TWO

I woke the next day feeling strangely relieved, like a weight had been lifted from my shoulders, but couldn't quite figure out why. Conflicting thoughts about last night's events mashed my head. My father's bizarre and rare cordial manner bothered me some. In times gone by, I would have jumped out of bed and performed cartwheels across the floor in some deluded notion that I was finally making headway with him. But my feet were planted firmly on the ground with all things in perspective, thanks to Ethan's shrewd ability to see through him like a pane of glass.

So why didn't I feel squashed in the way I usually did when my hopes had been dashed—and why this strange sense of release? Unable to arrive at a feasible conclusion, I decided to file the puzzle in the already overstuffed box marked "I'm-fucked-if-I-know-what-to-make-of-this," and toss it to the back of my mind.

Ethan was in his office when I got up, so I spent an hour in the gym and then showered quickly. I made a light breakfast of granola and fruit for me, and Ethan's usual omelet, then called him into the kitchen.

"You haven't forgotten I promised Abby that I'd go to the spa with her today, have you?" I asked before biting into a strawberry.

He groaned. "Fuck, I was just making mental plans of my own. Watching you eat that strawberry like that makes me want to do wicked things to your mouth."

I took another bite, this time snapping my teeth together rather viciously.

"Ouch." Ethan pursed his lips before adding rather hopefully, "You know you don't have to go if you don't want to."

"I do." I smiled sweetly to take the sting out. "It will be nice to hang out with Abby for a while. I can get to know her better, and I've never been one to refuse a massage and a facial. Besides, it will help me to relax before Damon's party tonight."

"Okay, well as long as you're happy. I have some work to do today anyway. Just make sure you let Jackson know when you're ready and take this with you." He produced his wallet, opened it and handed me a credit card.

"Christ, E, I'm not taking that. It's *my* spa day."

"And it's *my* body that you're off to indulge. If it's going to be pleasured in my absence, I'm making damn sure I have a hand in it, in whatever way I can. I want to be responsible for every bit of gratification your body experiences." He smiled wickedly and added, "Besides, it's one of our own spas, so it comes back to us in one form or other. Please let me treat you, baby."

"Okay, thank you." I leaned in for a slow, seductive kiss. "But on one condition," I said, biting my lip mischievously.

"Name it."

"You let me treat you before I go."

His lips curled at the edge slowly, his eyes dark and hooded. "What did you have in mind, Cinderella?"

"Well, first, I thought you could show me the wicked things you want to do to my mouth. And then when my pussy's nice and sweet and wet, I thought I could wrap my legs around your neck and let me do the same to yours. We could finish with you sinking balls deep inside me with a good, hard fuck." I arched a barely visible but challenging brow.

He sucked in a deep breath through clenched teeth. "Christ, woman, what are you waiting for?" Pushing swiftly to his feet, he grabbed my hand and tugged me toward the bedroom.

Several hours later, I stood examining my reflection in the mirror and smiled, feeling happy with the way I looked. After a fun and relaxing day at the spa with Abby, I felt pampered and rejuvenated. For the party, I'd selected a chic deep-red cocktail dress coated in twinkling, sequined adornments of the same color. The plunging V-neckline accentuated my not excessive but moderate assets while the knee length hemline gave it a classy, elegant flair. Sheer illusion panels ran down the length of the sides of the dress, creating a unique figure-flattering look, but making it virtually impossible to wear even the skimpiest panties without being noticeable.

I observed myself for a moment, contemplating the problem. The panel was only narrow, but any amount of visible panty lines would be a total fashion-fail, and I was certain that wearing panties would draw far more attention than if I didn't. Because of the plunge, I wasn't wearing a bra, so I may as well ditch the panties. *Mmm, how would Ethan feel about that?* I wondered. A wicked smile crept onto my lips. What Ethan doesn't know won't hurt him.

I made the final touches to my makeup: dark, smoky eyes, exaggerated lashes, and a rosy-red pout. My dark mahogany hair was styled in a dramatic side part and brushed into a tight chignon to the side of my neck. I applied a smidgen of ridiculously expensive scent—a gift from Ethan, created especially for me at a fragrance boutique in London—to my pulse points, slid on my shimmering strappy heels, and went in search of him.

As I passed the office, I could hear him talking on the phone and not wishing to interrupt, I decided to wait in the lounge. One of Ethan's favorite tunes was playing on the sound system: Arctic Monkeys' "Do I Wanna Know?" I took two glasses from the cabinet and poured us both a glass of crisp white wine as I moved casually to the music. As I was returning the bottle to the chiller, I felt the warmth of Ethan's heated gaze trickle seductively over my skin, and I knew he was behind me.

As I turned, our eyes met, both of us taking our own private moment to absorb, in total awe, the sights before us. He wore a beautifully tailored black-metropolitan silk striped suit and black dress shirt. His hair had that sexy tousled look, charm and raw sex appeal simply oozing from his pores.

As his eyes slithered provocatively over my body, his lips parted, his eyes growing dark and lust filled. "You are beyond exquisite, Angelica. Turn." He made a twirling motion with his finger. I did as I was told and began to rotate on the spot. "Slowly," he breathed. "I want to appreciate you entirely."

When I completed the turn, he held his hand out and tugged me toward him, bowing his head to graze my neck gently with his lips, inhaling me. When he straightened, his eyes were closed and he was biting down on his lower lip.

"You are so fucking hot, baby. You steal my breath away. I thank God every day for bringing you into my life. I will never tire of gazing at you, of inhaling your scent. You're my very own slice of Heaven."

Smiling shyly, I leaned in for a gentle kiss.

"I want to give you something," he said suddenly.

I cocked a brow suspiciously. "You'll have to wait, E. As much as I love the idea, we'll be late…"

"Not that, you naughty girl, this…" He laughed, reaching for a drawer in the kitchen and retrieving a red leather box from inside. Scrawled across the top in elegant gold writing was the word *Cartier*. My heart skipped a beat as I glanced nervously from him to the box and back again. I took the box tentatively from his proffered hands, my fingers drifting lightly over the sumptuous leather.

"Well, open it, then." His voice sounded slightly breathless with nerves.

I took a deep, hungry breath of my own and lifted the lid.

Inside was a pair of long-drop white-gold earrings with three heart shaped diamonds and a matching bracelet with thirty equally beautiful diamonds, also cut to the shape of a heart. Both pieces were exquisite, flawlessly finished and tastefully elegant, and I couldn't help the sudden thought that they would have coordinated with my mother's pendant perfectly.

When I could finally tear my eyes away from their shimmering, lavish beauty, I glanced up to see a look of pure pleasure dancing in Ethan's perfect eyes. He was studying me, trying to gauge my reaction, and it occurred to me how excited he was to give me such a gift, how he'd even probably tried to second guess my response.

"Well?" he asked quite anxiously. "Do you like them?"

For a moment, I was speechless, glancing between sexy, smoldering eyes and sumptuous diamonds, my mouth gaping in awe.

"Ethan... I love them, adore them, but... they must have been absurdly expensive. This is way too extravagant a gift."

For a second he seemed aghast by my comment. "Nonsense. There will never be a diamond in the world too exorbitant to be worn by you. I want to smother you in diamonds. Here—" He took the box from my hand and taking the earrings, then the bracelet, fastened them both in place. When he finished, he stood back to admire the effect before guiding me to the mirror. "See? Perfect."

The diamonds twinkled, throwing back the light of the room, just as my mother's pendant had done, and a hard lump formed in my throat. My gaze flickered to Ethan's reflection in the mirror where he stood behind me, his dazzling blue eyes catching glimmers of light as if in perfect harmonious correlation with the diamonds, and suddenly my heart swelled with absolute adoration for him.

"They *are* perfect. Just like you, Mr. Ethan Wilde. Thank you so much." I spun around and flung myself into his arms.

"It's you who's damned perfect, woman." Cupping my face, he closed his mouth over mine in a demanding, tongue-entwining kiss. My body responded instantly, a low groan bursting from my lips. Suddenly, he pulled away in a determined attempt to maintain some self-control and taking my hand, strode briskly toward the foyer and the elevator.

"We'd better leave before that dress of yours ends up in shreds on the bedroom floor," he snarled, pressing the button to call for the elevator.

As we waited, his gaze flittered over me again, a trace of unease edging its way gradually onto his face.

"What?" I asked, perplexed.

With a single fingertip, he reached out to toy with my earring, and then with a delicate, almost weightless touch, trailed a path down my throat, along my clavicle, and down over the swell of my bosom to the exposed hollow between my breasts. His touch was sensual, searing, awakening every nerve ending in my skin. My nipples jutted out, erect and sensitive as they pushed against the fabric of my dress, and as the elevator door slid open, I made a move to enter, afraid that if I didn't, we wouldn't make it past the foyer.

Ethan put his hand out to stop me, a question playing on his lips. "I don't suppose you'd consider wearing a wrap or a jacket?" he asked warily.

"What? No," I snapped. "Why?"

He rolled his eyes, as if reluctant to have to explain. "Angel, your tits look like something straight out of every guy's wet dream. They're... fleshy and round and delicious and the way the light casts a shadow in the valley between them will make everyone with a dick wonder what it would be like to have it nestled between them, and it will make me want to kill every single one of them."

I blinked several times, struck dumb for a moment by Ethan's bizarre notion that everyone saw me the same way he did.

Slowly, his beseeching expression dwindled, smoothing out to resemble one of hopeless resignation. "You're not going to put a jacket on, are you?"

I shook my head, but smiled apologetically to ease him through it, and entered the lift. He sighed, raising his eyes to Heaven, as if in silent prayer, and followed me inside. As the door slid closed, I turned to the reflection in the mirrored wall behind me, raising a hand to finger the dazzling diamonds. The action of raising my arm suddenly exposed the side of my dress, completely revealing the semi-transparent panel to a jaw-hanging Ethan.

"Oh fuck," he stuttered, making an unusual gulping sound. "Your dress is virtually see-through, Angel." He motioned with his hand down his side, indicating the area of the dress he was referring to, as though I might not be aware of it.

"Yes, Ethan, I know," I said slowly, as if to a child, "and so should you, as I gave you a 360-degree twirl less than ten minutes ago."

"I didn't notice it was see-through in the muted light. Oh fuck," he repeated his earlier profanity as his eyes wandered down the length of the dress, absorbing every detail. "Please tell me you're wearing panties." His tone was suddenly terse, as if he'd reached the threshold of his tolerance.

My cheeks heated slightly as I cut my gaze and shook my head contritely.

"Oh fuck. Angel, *everyone* will know."

"Calm down. No one will know. Some may wonder—but aside from you and me—no one will know." I soothed him like a child on the verge of a tantrum.

"Angel, it pains me enough that people look at you at all. But in that dress, they will be leering at you and envisioning what lies beneath. It *will* drive me insane, or to murder, or both."

"Ethan, it's a slice of material, barely an inch wide, which is *almost*, but not entirely, see-through." I paused, hoping for a sign he was about to give in—nothing. I had one last try. "No one will even notice, E."

Still nothing—just an impossibly arched eyebrow which said, "Really? You think?" I hadn't convinced him.

Suddenly, I thought of the way he'd gazed at me with those loving, adoring eyes when he'd given me the jewelry, and my stomach twisted with guilt. I sighed, defeated. "Would you like me to go back and get changed?"

Relief and surprise flooded into his eyes, his expression suddenly softening. "You would do that for me?"

"Yes, of course—if it's going to upset you this much. I just thought you'd like the dress."

"Oh God, I do, but... so will everyone else."

"But I don't belong to everyone else, E. I belong to you. I only care what you think."

"Really?" He smiled warmly.

"You really have to ask?"

He shook his head and looked me over again. "It's more than an inch. It's at least two."

I shrugged. "So am I getting changed?"

For a second, he didn't speak, just continued to scan me, contemplation evident in his riotous eyes. Then, raking a hand through his hair, he took a deep, soothing breath and leaned over to press the button for the ground floor. "So help me God, if anyone looks at you in the wrong way—in any way..." The elevator began its decent. He closed his eyes. "Fuck, what am I thinking? 'Course they're going to fucking look."

I bit my lip to stifle my amusement. My poor, beautiful Ethan.

When the elevator door opened, Ethan took me by the hand and led me through the foyer and outside to where Jackson stood by the car waiting for us. When he spotted us, he nodded politely and opened the rear door.

"Mr. Wilde, Miss Lawson." His eyes widened as he turned to observe me properly, his mouth curling up into a smile of appreciation. "May I say how splendid you look this evening, Miss Lawson?"

I was about to thank him when Ethan snapped, "No, you may not. Thank you, Jackson."

Instead, I smiled a small, apologetic smile and climbed into the car. Ethan closed the door after me, turned to exchange a few words with Jackson, and walked around the back of the car to climb in the other side.

Jackson reached inside his jacket for his cell, turning away from the car while engaging in a brief conversation with whoever was on the other end.

"What did you say to him? Who's he speaking to?"

Ethan hitched a brow. "Questions, questions." I mirrored his expression, ensuring he knew I expected an answer. "I was reaffirming the importance of security for tonight. There will be a lot of people in attendance. Jackson is informing Simon and Carl of our impending arrival. They'll be there to meet us."

Jackson hung up the call and after climbing into the car, pulled out into traffic.

"Is all that really necessary? We will be inside Damon's apartment, after all."

He narrowed his eyes in frustration. "Have you forgotten that you had your apartment broken into last week? And some sick prick with a death wish has been stalking you?"

"No, of course not. But how long is this going to go on for? Is that what you and Damon went off to discuss yesterday?"

"Yes, he needed to understand why I was stepping up security, so I told him about everything that's gone on. Plus, I wanted to see the guest list, so he emailed it over this morning."

"E, you have to relax—about the dress *and* the security, or we won't enjoy ourselves and there will be little point in going," I snapped, feeling pissed about the unwelcomed reminder of recent, dreadful events. I still choked up at the thought of Ponyo's horrific demise.

He frowned. "I'll try and relax about the dress, but your safety is paramount and non-negotiable." He took my hand and gave it a squeeze. "Let's just leave it now. I don't want to fight."

Neither did I, so I relented and returned the squeeze.

The party was in full swing when we arrived. As arranged, we were joined by Simon and Carl at the entrance to the building and escorted up to Damon's apartment. The elevator opened into a foyer and an apartment similar in size to Ethan's, but the furnishings and design were very different. Dark wooden floors and furniture ran throughout the living areas, which were designed in a color scheme of creams, beiges and browns while subtle lighting concealed in the ceilings and coves created a soft ambient effect. The place had a rich, luxurious, and homey feel to it.

The minute we walked through the hall and into the large lounge area, we were accosted by Abby and her friends, Alisha Miller and Jess—the small, curvy blonde, who I recognized from the pillow fight in the pool house. All three looked slightly tipsy already, and it didn't go unnoticed by Ethan, who snatched the champagne glass from Abby's grasp, a look of blatant disapproval furrowing his brow.

"What the hell, Abby. Take it easy with that stuff. It's still early."

"Oh, don't be so stuffy, Ethan. It's a few glasses of champagne, no biggie." She slapped his wrist and boldly took back her drink. He relinquished it reluctantly, shaking his head.

"Oh. My. God," Abby exclaimed, giving me a full tip-to-toe once-over. "You look freaking amazing, that dress is *so* to-die-for."

Alisha joined in, gushing and gaping with admiration, while Jess watched the scene play out silently, seeming self-conscious and shy in comparison to her friends.

"Pfft, what there is of it," Ethan stated, still mildly disapproving but smiling with it.

"Ignore him, he's grumpy." I rolled my eyes. "And thank you, girls, you look amazing too. I see you went for the silver-gray dress. Abby, you look stunning. It was the right choice for sure," I said, referring to the dress I'd helped her pick out for the occasion.

"I know," she squealed, spinning around in a circle so the smooth, silky material floated around her. "Although, it was your influence that sealed it, and judging by your own selection, I'll definitely be coming to you for fashion advice again." She giggled and hugged me.

"Anytime." I smiled, inwardly wondering what the hell I'd let myself in for.

Ethan pulled me to him, kissing my forehead. "Come on, let's find Damon and get a drink."

Abby cocked her head to the side. "Aww, you two are *so* the perfect couple." She pouted, as if we were a couple of fluffy bunnies in a pet store. As we began to walk away, her expression changed, turning first to stunned surprise and then a wide grin of utter glee.

"Wait," she shouted. She closed the gap in a few steps, leaning in to whisper in my ear. "Are you… uh… wearing anything… underneath, I mean."

Flushing, I glanced at Ethan, whose frown and rolling eyes implied he knew exactly what Abby was asking.

"Of course," I feigned incredulity and pulled on his hand to urge him away from the exchange. As we walked away, I turned discreetly and imparted a sly wink to Abby, who giggled and winked back, thrilled to be in cahoots.

"I told you people would know," Ethan said through gritted teeth as we made our way through the blanket of people in Damon's vast apartment. He took two glasses of champagne from the tray of a passing waitress and handed one to me.

"And *I* told you people would wonder. However, the fact remains, that the only ones who really know for sure are you and me. So suck it up, Wilde." I clinked my glass against his and took a sip of the mouth-watering, ice-cold fizz.

He raised a brow at my quick-witted admonishment, a smirk forming on his lips. "You're so fucking sexy when you're cheeky, Cinders." He leaned in close to ensure he wasn't overheard, his warm breath stroking seductively against my ear. "But let me warn you. Any more lip from that sassy mouth of yours, and I'll waste no time in finding somewhere to hitch that fucking dress up around your waist. Then I'll bend you over and fuck you until you beg me to stop. At least there won't be any damn panties to get in my way."

The victorious smirk sidling its way onto his lips suggested he expected to have shocked me, but instead the threat was an instant turn-on, and for a second I wished I was wearing panties. The exposure caused the clingy fabric of my dress to swish against my naked sex, and Ethan's debauched words just added fuel to the red hot embers of my fire. What I wouldn't give for him to bend me over right now and…

My expression must have reflected my thoughts entirely, because Ethan's gaze grew wickedly dark, his smirk hot and sinful. He shook his head slowly in amazement. "You dirty, dirty girl," he murmured.

"Mmm, aren't I just?" I replied errantly.

He snaked an arm around my waist and pulled me against his hard body, our lips only inches apart. His sweet breath on my face heated my blood, making me radiate from the inside out and warm, slick moisture to pool between the lips of my bare sex. How is it we could be in a room full of people and in one miraculous moment feel like we'd transported to a world where only he and I existed?

"Can you two keep your hands off each other just for one fucking minute?" Damon was suddenly by our sides and tearing us involuntarily from our intimate moment.

"Hey, happy birthday, Damon." Ethan grinned at his brother, reaching up to inspect his hair. "Any gray ones yet, Bro?"

"Says the guy with the bed-head," Damon retorted, making sarcastic reference to Ethan's messy, just-fucked-looking hairstyle. "I may have been unlucky when I inherited dad's genes in terms of hair color, dude, but I was also the one to gain the Wilde's impressive architecture."

"Oh, please," said Ethan, laughing, "you're such a comedian."

We all laughed and Damon turned his attention to me.

"Happy birthday, Damon." I reached up and kissed him lightly on the cheek, making him grin arrogantly at Ethan, whose smile transmuted to a snarl.

"Another one in the bag, dude. I'm finding it hard to keep score these days," he teased. "Thank you, Angel, and man you are looking hot tonight. Way too hot for this guy here, babe."

I shook my head and smiled cautiously, my eyes on Ethan. "Oh, I doubt that. But I'm a one-man woman, so I guess I'll never know."

Ethan gazed at me with adoration.

"Yes, I can see that." Damon pouted, feigning disappointment.

"And I think that makes us equal." Ethan grinned at his brother.

"Okay, you guys, I get it. I'll leave you to mingle—or not." He clapped Ethan on the back and began to walk away. "Oh, Angel, one-man woman or not, I expect a dance later. Think you can tear yourself away for long enough?"

"I'll see what I can do," I laughed.

"Attagirl." He winked and wandered off in the direction of a group of attractive women, his utmost flirty grin plastered all over his face.

"I swear to God, if he was any other guy..." Ethan said, smiling after him.

"He just likes to tease you, E. Let's be honest, he's pretty damn good at it."

"Don't I know it."

"Why hasn't he got a girlfriend?" I asked, wondering why somebody hadn't snapped him up already.

"I suspect he's got several. Let's just say, Damon prefers to play the field a bit. The one-woman man act really isn't his thing."

"He's a player, you mean."

Ethan shrugged. "He has his reasons." A look of melancholy briefly ghosted across his features as he stared after his brother, but before I could question, he laced his arm around me and began to guide me through the crowd. "C'mon, I want to show you off, introduce you to a few people."

An hour or so later, I'd been introduced to several lovely people, all of whom both Ethan and Damon had business dealings with but knew socially as well. He'd nodded an acknowledgement to numerous others or simply said, "Hey," without pausing to speak to them— many of whom I'd noticed were attractive blondes who all appeared to assess me with frosty, scornful glares. I simmered gently with curiosity, but didn't question. After all, being with a man like Ethan Wilde was bound to create lustful envy in other women; I could do little to prevent it. They could look all they liked—touch and it was a different matter.

Or so I was about to discover.

We were standing chatting with a man named Edward Hale—an architect who did a lot of work for Wilde Industries—and his wife Claire, when Ethan wandered off to replenish our drinks.

As I spotted him moving back toward us, armed with a fresh bottle of champagne, an arm reached out from the crowd of people and grasped his elbow. I couldn't quite see who the arm belonged to, but it was definitely female, tan and toned with overly-long, painted fingernails.

Ethan reacted with objectionable surprise as he glanced briefly, but uncomfortably in my direction, before maneuvering out of my line of vision.

My skin prickled possessively, my senses on full alert. Unable to prevent curiosity from getting the better of me, I attempted to reposition myself in order to see who the seemingly disembodied limb belonged to.

Edward Hale had struck up a conversation with another man, and Claire had been expressing an interest in my work, saying she would love to attend my forthcoming exhibition. Feeling incredibly rude that I could no longer concentrate on the conversation, I promised that I would send her an invitation and excused myself.

Gradually, I made my way toward Ethan and his unidentified female companion, approaching cautiously in order to gain a good view. I wanted to assess the situation before I decided whether or not I should join the party. She wasn't unattractive—a slim and busty blonde—but I couldn't ever imagine her being described as classy. No, something about her definitely screamed *trash*.

Ethan was listening to something she was saying, a look of blatant irritation marring his handsome features. She was talking animatedly at him, as if vaguely affronted by something he'd said. As I drew closer, Ethan glanced my way, and on noticing my approach, muttered something to her and began to move away. The long talons reached out again, gripping his arm firmly to prevent his departure. Unease tore through my bones like an unrestrained and frenzied twister. I didn't know who this woman was, but she had her hands on my man, and I didn't like it one bit. This was one party I was definitely due to join.

Ethan paled as I drew up beside them, but offered me a wary smile. "Angel," he greeted.

Trashy blonde turned to meet my eyes, a combination of shock and anger on her face. Her menacing glare scanned the full length of my body, absorbing every detail.

"Is this her?" she hissed.

Ethan cleared his throat nervously. "Um, Angel, this—"

I held a hand up to quiet him and smiling the widest, sweetest smile I could muster, I turned to trashy blonde.

"Hi, I'm Angel Lawson… Ethan's girlfriend." I paused to allow the word *girlfriend* to penetrate her thick, sun-exposed skin, and then continued. "I have no clue who you are—much less do I care—but you appear to have your grubby-looking hand on my boyfriend's ludicrously expensive suit." I pointed with distaste at her hand, wrinkling my nose as if her touch were soiling the material. "I suggest you remove it." I smiled, meeting her eyes again. "Now."

Her narrowed eyes exuded resentment, but my words impacted enough for her to drop her hand to her side. A glance at Ethan's face told me he was stuck somewhere between being stunned and amused.

"Girlfriend?" she snorted scornfully. "Whatever, honey. You, me, and at least a half dozen others in here. Now if you don't mind, Ethan was just about to explain why he hasn't returned my calls when he's usually so eager." Her hand flittered up to the lapel of Ethan's jacket where she began to play with an invisible thread.

Anger bubbled inside me.

Ethan shook his head in disbelief, an amused snarl curling the edge of his lip. "Lucy, you've just met the reason why I stopped returning your calls. Now take my *girlfriend's* advice before you embarrass yourself." He pushed her hand away in frustration.

I glanced around the room until my eyes found Jackson's and as anticipated, his ever vigilant gaze was aimed directly at us. I nodded discreetly and without hesitation he began to make his way toward us.

Trashy blonde, who I now knew as Lucy, bristled, affronted at Ethan's words and tone. "She's not even your type. Since when do you do brunettes?" She glanced at me and sneered. "You must know blondes are a *lot* more fun."

"Oh, sweetie." My smile oozed condescension, my tone mocking like she was a small child who had just said something stupid, but cute. "*You* must know that's just a polite way of saying blondes are easy."

I turned to Jackson who had joined us—much to Ethan's confusion—just in time to hear the last comment. Struggling to stifle a smile, he waited patiently for instruction. Ethan, decidedly less contained, was now blatantly grinning.

"Ah, Jackson. I was wondering if you'd do me a favor and take the trash out." I wrinkled my nose in disgust at Lucy. "I know it's a dirty job, but someone's got to do it."

His nostrils flared as he choked back his amusement. Ethan, clearly less inclined and no longer able to hide his, almost choked on his laughter.

Lucy blushed furiously, her eyes widening as though she were about to explode. "You bitch." She took a threatening step toward me only to be stopped abruptly in her tracks by Jackson, who stepped in front of her, gripping her firmly, but discreetly by the arm.

"Don't make a scene, miss," he warned.

With a disdainful smirk, I thanked Jackson before turning to thread my arm through Ethan's and casually walked away. As we reached a set of folding glass doors opening on to the terrace, I glanced back over my shoulder in time to see the scorned busty blonde being escorted through the foyer doors, an annoyed and confused, leggy redhead trailing not far behind her.

Ethan and I wandered into a quiet corner of the terrace, his expression a confused mishmash of amusement and utter shock.

"Well, Miss Lawson, that's a side of you I've never seen before."

The power of speech had temporarily eluded me. The anger and adrenaline, which had surged through my body, empowering me moments before, suddenly depleted, leaving me drained and slightly shaky. I took a steadying, replenishing breath and shuddered as I regained my equilibrium.

"I've never shown that side of me before. I didn't know it existed. I was just so angry when she put her hands on you." I shook my head, just as stunned by my behavior as he was. "I think you bring out the worst in me, Mr. Wilde."

"Well, if that's the worst of you, I sure as shit hope I see it again. You're a foxy little minx when you're jealous, Miss Lawson. Sexy as fucking sin. And the way you brought Jackson in was classic. It brought a whole new meaning to his role as *The Man*. You were amazing," he laughed.

"You're not mad?" I asked.

"Mad? I'm as horny as hell, woman!" He spoke a little too loudly, causing a few people to turn and stare curiously.

I burst out laughing and he grabbed me by the hips pulling me toward him. The steely extent of his erection pushed against me and the effect it had was immediate and somewhat intensified by my brazen panty-deficiency. I placed my hands on the flexing muscles of his upper arms and pushed him back. He gaped at me in puzzlement.

"Not so fast, Mr. Wilde, I have some questions."

"I thought you might." Rolling his eyes, he released me and took a step back, hands in his pockets, head to one side. His eyes gleamed wickedly and a crooked smile played on his lips. He looked sexy as hell and I wanted him. However, I needed to remain astute, so I ignored the wanton yearning inside me. I could satisfy that particular craving later.

"Who is she and why the hell was she here?"

"Her name is Lucy and I haven't got a fucking clue why she was here. Damon didn't invite her; she must have come as someone's plus-one, because I saw the guest list and she wasn't on it."

I frowned nervously. "I got her name, Ethan. Who is she to you? Did you date her before me?"

"Date her? Christ, no!" He seemed adamant in his answer.

"So why would she expect you to call her?"

He sighed in defeat, a grimace settling on his face. "I screwed her once or twice. Is that what you want to hear?"

The comment stung like a slap to the face. The thought of that grubby-looking slut with her hands on my man made my insides coil in jealousy and disgust. "Not particularly, no," I said when I found my voice. "Well, which is it, once or twice?"

"I really can't remember, Angelica. It wasn't of much consequence."

I was sure he could remember, but I was glad he'd spared me the gory details; I didn't really want to know. "I'm not stupid, E. I realize you have a past. What I don't know is how colorful it is. The trashy blonde implied she was one of many. Is it possible I'll be forced to exploit Jackson again this evening?"

His face fell as he glanced at the floor anxiously, and I could tell he was deliberating about how honest he should be. I cocked an eyebrow to make it clear I knew what he was thinking.

"There are a couple of familiar faces, but it won't happen again, I can assure you."

I closed my eyes, mentally kicking myself for asking. There were some things you were better off just not knowing. It totally explained the frosty glares I'd experienced tonight, at least.

"And these *familiar faces*—were they just a screw?"

"Yes."

"Why didn't you date any of them?"

"Because I didn't have the time or the inclination." He sighed, becoming frustrated with my questions. "Have you finished?"

"Not quite." I refused to be deterred. "So why date me? And why are brunettes not your type?"

He shook his head and laughed. "I knew you'd pick up on that. You know why you… I tell you often enough. You are right for me because of who you are and how you make me feel. It has nothing to do with the color of your hair. But if we're being pedantic, as you are the one I want to be with and they're the ones whose names I can barely recall, I think it would be more accurate to say that blondes are definitely not my type."

I smirked, mentally punching the air. "Good answer, Mr. Wilde."

"Have I passed your inquisition?"

"I'll let you know by the end of the evening."

"Mmm, well, maybe it's best if we call it a night now. It's driving me wild knowing you're completely naked under that dress. I need to be inside you."

Moving forward he closed the space between us, our bodies within a hair's width distance, but instead of trying to touch me, his hands remained tucked firmly inside his pants pockets. Mischief played on his mouth as his tongue ran smoothly but discreetly over his lower lip. Suddenly, through the material of his pants, I felt his fingers press against me, moving to gently graze my sex. The contact was unexpected, the wanton gasp of pleasure hissing from my lips causing Ethan's face to light up with amusement. I stepped away from him, and his wicked smirk reluctantly traded places with a sulky frown.

"Not a chance, Mr. Wilde. Besides, I promised your brother a dance."

"You have got to be kidding. You can't dance with my brother, especially with no panties on."

"Wanna bet?" Flashing him an alluring smile over my shoulder, I sashayed away.

CHAPTER THREE

The party had reached that time where the majority of people were sufficiently inebriated enough to quit worrying about how much they'd drunk and what effect it was going to have on them in the morning. The less dedicated had long since departed, leaving mostly diehard party goers to devour the champagne and hard liquor.

Damon and I shimmied around the dance floor to Robin Thicke's "Blurred Lines," deliberately teasing Ethan. Damon loved to get one up on his older brother and I—on this occasion—was inclined to take advantage of the fact, if only because of my petty jealousy over the trashy blonde, whose name I refused to use.

I smirked cheekily over Damon's shoulder at Ethan, who stood sipping a glass of champagne, looking moderately pissed off.

"Am I still getting the evil eye from my big brother?" Damon asked with glee.

"Mmm, how did you know?"

"Because I can practically feel the blood dripping down my back from the daggers he's throwing my way. I may need hospital attention before the night is through." He swung me around so he could flash a playful grin in Ethan's direction. "Oh man, has he got it bad. This is so much fun."

I laughed causing Ethan's frown to deepen.

Just then he was joined by a woman with extremely long black hair and flawless skin, possibly Middle Eastern. She was exquisitely beautiful. They appeared to be making polite conversation, like that of two people who were unacquainted. I tried to soothe my inner green monster with the consolatory notion that at least their unfamiliarity meant she wasn't another former screw. My skin prickled in contention, nonetheless. I needed to rein it in. As much fun as I'd had earlier, I rather preferred to keep the new ball-busting Angel in her box for the rest of the night.

Damon was saying something about how good I moved and how he was certain I should dance professionally. A complete overstatement, of course, but my attention was now so entirely drawn to Ethan and the mysterious beauty beside him that I didn't bother to comment.

Ethan glanced up at me, smirking as he said something to the girl—a compliment, I could tell, because she lowered her head and flushed coyly. That now-all-too-familiar, low, growling, pang of jealousy bubbled away in the pit of my stomach. Glancing my way again, he slowly cocked an eyebrow, a smug lopsided grin hijacking his perfect face. He was playing games with me. He was jealous because I was dancing with his brother and this was payback. How fucking childish.

Smirking back, I began to wiggle my hips provocatively to the new tune that had begun playing. Jason Derulo singing about talking dirty—how appropriate.

"Angel...?" Damon urged, seeking an answer to a question I hadn't heard.

"Oh... yes... sorry... what?"

"Your dress?"

"What about it?"

He smirked playfully. "Well, I probably shouldn't ask—"

Oh my God. My underwear—or lack thereof. "Then don't," I interrupted him quickly.

Damon looked stunned. "No, you're right. Completely inappropriate. Forget I even asked."

I nodded and then shook my head. "You didn't."

"No, you're right, I didn't." He stopped dancing abruptly and released me. "Go on. You're dying to get back to him, I can tell. I hope I'm lucky enough to find what you two have one day." He looked toward Ethan and added, "Smug bastard. Look, he's only talking to her in a desperate bid to make you jealous."

Flushing, I glanced over at Ethan, who was overtly lapping up the attention he was getting.

"And it's working," Damon added, grinning.

I shrugged unapologetically, leaned in, and kissed him on the cheek. "Happy birthday, Damon."

"Thank you, Angel. Go on, go get your man."

In a second he was gone, whisked away by one of his countless admirers. I turned, about to make my way over to reclaim my man, when a dark-haired man appeared in front of me. At a guess, he was mid-thirties, and although not unattractive, wasn't my type at all.

"Hi," he said enthusiastically, proffering his hand. "Would you do me the honor?"

Before I knew it, he'd whisked me into a tight embrace and began to dance around the room with me. Shocked, I looked over to Ethan, whose expression was now stone-faced, his beautiful companion instantly forgotten.

"I'm Tom."

"Oh, um... Angel," I reciprocated politely.

I wasn't really bothered who he was, preferring instead to get back to Ethan, but part of me also wanted to play my man at his own game. So I danced on.

"I know," he said matter-of-factly.

"Sorry? Know what?"

"Your name."

Oh. Strange.

I smiled, but was more interested in Ethan's reaction, his frown informing me he was positively pissed. Dancing with his brother was one thing, but this raised the game way beyond his comfort zone. The girl by his side spoke to him, and he answered with a forced smile before diverting his attention straight back to me, his eyes narrowed in an admonishing glare.

"You're here with Ethan Wilde," the stranger said. "Been together long?"

"Awhile."

My answer was terse, but I was still distracted by Ethan and his changing expressions, trying my best to determine his mood and how much more I dared get away with before he stomped on over to reclaim his woman. Even from across the room, I could see that his eyes were growing darker, clouded with fury and… what else? A look I recognized, but for a moment couldn't place. Another glimpse of it and it came to me. He was aroused. His jealousy was actually turning him on.

Oh fuck.

That look in his eye sent a shock wave of exhilarating energy straight to my groin, and if I knew my man, I was in for a punishment fuck of the kind I thoroughly enjoyed.

"*Enough.*" He mouthed the command across the room with an unyielding, penetrating glare.

Who was I kidding? He didn't need to stalk on over to take back what was his. He could project his authority from right where he stood. Claim possession of me with one single word and one single look. Just like the night we met, I knew exactly what he wanted; I was impossibly attuned to him and impossibly turned on because of it.

I needed to go to him.

"I'm sorry…" I stuttered, stepping away from the stranger. "It was nice to meet you… um… Tom, but I'm afraid I have to go. Thank you for the dance."

"Of course." He nodded, fixing me with a lewd, unsmiling stare. "The pleasure was all mine, Angel."

Ewww, creepy.

Smiling politely, I turned in time to see Ethan mutter his excuses to his now puzzled companion. His melting, red-hot gaze collided with mine across the space dividing us, causing my skin to prickle with anticipation as we wordlessly conveyed our carnal intentions. Almost imperceptibly, he nodded toward the corner of the room where a staircase led to a second floor—a silent instruction to follow him.

Again, memories of our first encounter came bubbling to the surface of my mind. Oh, we'd been here before alright, and the rush was overwhelming.

Just as I was about to head for the stairs, the stranger called after me.

"Oh, Angel?" Glancing over my shoulder, I noticed a change in his expression, one which now hinted of sorrow or even pity. "Sorry to hear about your fish."

What?

I frowned, astonished by the remark, my mind wandering briefly to how he could possibly know about Ponyo and resolving that he must be a friend of Damon's. I wanted to ask him, but the pull of Ethan was too strong. I was aroused to the extreme, sodden between my legs and precariously devoid of my panties. So instead, I simply nodded my appreciation and headed off toward the staircase.

Ethan paused at the foot of the steps to be sure I was shadowing him, and with one hand in his pocket, casually ascended the stairs. I followed at a distance, the way he'd followed me on the first night we met, and as I reached the summit, I caught sight of him disappearing into a room at the end of a wide corridor. The noise from the music and chatter faded into a distant hum as I made my way down the hall, my heart hammering rhythmically against my chest as excitement built up inside me, just as it had that night. The door to the room stood slightly ajar and tentatively, I reached out to push it open.

The room was in darkness, but the brightness from the hallway cast a muted light into the room, enough so that I could just make out a large, silver, Las Vegas pool table. It was a games room. Suddenly, the chrome lights above the table flicked on, drawing my attention to the high quality, smooth, black cloth covering the table. *Wilde* was scrawled in gray writing across the middle. The rest of the room remained in the shadows.

I entered the room slowly, a quick glimpse revealing, among other things, a foosball table, a pinball machine, and several vintage arcade games. A proper boys-with-toys room. I couldn't see Ethan, but his presence was indisputable, like an electrical force field charging the space around me, exerting his force without any tangible contact.

Behind me, I heard the sound of the door closing, the key turning in the lock. A combination of apprehension and exhilaration sped through me, a shiver chasing a trail up and down my spine, continuing down and under to my naked, clenching sex.

Suddenly, there was a noise from behind me, somewhere to the left in the corner of the room. The sound of a dime being pushed into a coin slot and the whirring of mechanics—a jukebox. I didn't turn around. Ethan's imprecise location, the unfamiliar surroundings, the uncertainty of what was about to happen, all seemed to exacerbate my arousal beyond reason, and everything south of my navel began to pulse.

From the jukebox came an instantly recognizable tune: Placebo, "Running Up That Hill," and with the resounding beat, the recollection of a prior conversation when we'd deliberated whether orgasmic ecstasy felt the same for a man as it did for a woman and how fabulous it would be to trade experiences. The song selection alone was enough to have my knees trembling.

Without warning he was behind me, his breath on the back of my neck, hot and full of sinful promise. His nose brushed my earlobe gently, his intoxicating scent soaking into my senses as he pressed his body up against me. At my lower back, I could sense the unmistakable presence of his longing. His cock throbbed and pulsed through the restraining fabric of his suit and the urge to push back against it was impossibly tempting. But instead I stepped forward and climbed gracefully onto the pool table. Using the frame of the overhead lights, I pulled myself to a standing position and slowly turned to face him.

His expression was one of pure carnal need, his eyes dark as bullets and exuding desire. "You've been bad, Cinderella," he growled seductively. "Very bad."

"Yes…" I paused, my breath becoming shallow, my body quivering with excitement. "Yes, I have. So I guess you'd better punish me."

My words seemed to strike him, his eyes screwing shut to absorb the hit. When he opened them his heated gaze trickled down my body. "Open your legs. Wide," he ordered.

I did as I was told, moving my feet as far apart as my dress would allow.

He nodded once at the red twinkling fabric sheathing my trembling body, and lowering his voice to a deep husky tone, rasped, "Now show me."

Immediately, I released the light above, splaying my hands, one on each thigh, and slowly inched up my dress. Ethan stood with his hands in his pockets, observing me through heavy, lust filled eyes, his lips slightly parted, breath hissing through clenched teeth. The dress slithered up gently, caressing my thighs until it reached the summit, the hem barely concealing my sex. His chest heaved with eagerness and expectation, his tongue snaking out to dampen the lips of his hungry mouth.

With deliberate precision, I slid my shoes along the ledge of the table, opening my legs wider still. Darkened blue eyes darted back and forth between my face and the apex of my thighs, mentally urging me to reveal what he desired the most.

Finally succumbing to his demand, I inched the dress up over my hips to my waist.

"Holy shit." A gasp of awed appreciation hissed from his lips.

I smiled a slow, victorious smile as I observed my lover's yearning, how he thirsted for my body—to taste it, to savor it, to devour it. He wanted me like I wanted him, like I craved him.

Slowly, I lowered into a kneeling position, my hands on my thighs pushing my knees as far apart as I could comfortably, until my pulsing sex fell directly in line with his vision. His awed gaze fixed on the treasure in sight, his hands reaching to stroke a leisurely path from my knees, up over my thighs, toward my sex. My sex trembled beneath his touch as his fingertips trailed softly over the needy flesh, spreading the moisture around my clit, teasing and massaging. He parted my lips with his thumbs, displaying me fully, his expression one of exalted admiration. This extraordinary curiosity he had to study my every detail was beyond arousing and never failed to affect me.

"You have the most amazing pussy," he crooned as his thumbs slid over the tender bud. "Slick and hot and dripping." His tongue snaked out, flicking against my clit.

I gasped, throwing my head back, my hands reaching behind me to support my weight while I thrust my hips toward his hungry mouth. His hands slithered around to grip my buttocks, tilting me up toward him, his head lowering as his mouth closed over my throbbing pussy. His hot, wet tongue lashed out and plunged deep inside, licking and tasting, devouring me completely.

My moans of utter pleasure echoed around the vast space as I bucked against him, grinding myself against his fervent mouth, my body swirling effortlessly and violently toward climax. His tongue was relentless, whipping hard against my clit, his fingers digging into the flesh of my ass as he thrust his tongue deeper inside. He released a hand, the other holding me firmly against his mouth, and then frenzied fingers plunged into me. They delved and searched, spreading and rubbing, as his mouth continued to consume me as though I were his last meal. He gasped and groaned, the primal noises barely scraping past the extent of his desire.

My body went rigid and as I held my breath, a sudden surge of heat coursed through my veins. My body shook and shuddered uncontrollably as my climax exploded into his mouth. I screamed my pleasure as he extracted every earth-shattering drop of ecstasy from my seemingly never-ending orgasm.

Wildly aroused eyes bored into mine as he released me, his hands plowing into my hair to tug me to him like an untamed beast. His sinful mouth, moist with the soft luster of my juices, clamped over mine, claiming me with a need that was fierce and unrepentant, our tongues entwining to share the taste of my arousal.

"You are mine, Angel." He pulled back, gasping out the words, panting and breathless.

"Yes."

"Say it," he demanded.

"I'm yours, Ethan. Only yours."

Through my abating tremors, I was vaguely aware of him unfastening his pants, shoving them down past his hips, and grasping me by the waist to lift me down from the table.

"Promise me you'll never allow anybody else to touch you—not ever." His hands gripped the back of my head as he held me firmly, hot breath against my mouth, his fixed gaze predatory, yet imploring. "It would be *so* much more than I could ever take."

"Never," I whispered, stunned by the depth and intensity of his emotional plea.

In one swift move, he turned me to face away from him, bending me over the table and pushing my legs apart with an almost violently urgency. Gripping my hips, he pulled me back, angling me so my ass was pushed out, presented, and on offer. Then he guided himself toward my slick opening.

"Aahh," he screamed as he lunged into me, thrusting his hips as he pulled me back onto him.

I cried out with almost unbearable, burning pleasure, accepting the fullness of him inside my clenching channel. Slowly, he retracted before driving back into me again and again, his hips gyrating, pelvis bumping against my ass cheeks, sending me spiraling toward another rapidly building orgasm.

My muscles tensed and contracted in preparation and pursuit of the highest hedonistic pleasure, until I could hold on no longer and my orgasm ripped through me, flooding my body with blissful, decadent joy. My sex pulsed and pounded around Ethan's throbbing cock as I reached my release, the impact causing him to increase his impetus. Harsh sex words grated gutturally from his throat and with one last wild, unapologetic thrust, he finally abandoned himself to euphoria and erupted, spurting hotly inside me.

A low, incomprehensible groan rumbled from within as he collapsed his front to my back, his breathing ragged as he purred contentedly into my ear. "I own you, beautiful Cinderella."

I smiled a blissful, enraptured smile. "And I you, Charming. And I you."

"I'll never be able to shoot a game of pool in here with a straight face again." Ethan tucked himself away and fastened his zipper. "Damon will think I've lost my touch, but how in the hell will I pot a ball straight, when all I can envision is me feasting on your delectable little pussy."

Grinning jubilantly, I smoothed down my dress. "You've no one but yourself to blame. It was you who dragged me in here."

"Oh yes, by your hair, kicking and screaming—I remember."

"Your eyes ordered me to follow you, and I did."

"Yes, because you know better than to defy me. And if you hadn't misbehaved—yet again—you wouldn't have needed ordering in here to be taught a lesson. You are mine and mine alone. You needed a reminder." Grabbing my wrist, he pulled me toward him.

"Well, if that's what happens when I misbehave, I can't promise it won't happen again."

"Such a dirty girl, Miss Lawson." He reached up to smooth the escaped strands of my previously immaculately styled hair, but failed miserably by getting distracted, resorting instead to nibbling my earlobe.

I pushed him away playfully. "Stop, before someone catches us. We've been gone way too long already," I scolded. "Here, hold this for me." I handed him my compact mirror to hold steady for me while I teased my blatantly-just-fucked hair back into some semblance of a style and applied lip gloss.

"What am I to do with you, Mr. Wilde? You and your jealousy. Look at the trouble it gets us in." I shook my head in mock disgust.

"You're just as bad," he pouted. "Who was that fucker anyway? I wanted to kill the cheeky bastard putting his hands on my woman."

"Oh, I thought you knew him. He knew you," I said, taking the mirror from him and popping it back into my purse.

His playful mood fled instantly, his shoulders tensing, brow furrowing. "What do you mean? What did he say?"

"Not much." I paused to cast my mind back. "Just that he already knew who I was, and that I was with you. And he asked how long we'd been together."

"Anything else?"

I shook my head. "Oh, wait. Yes, actually, something really strange, a bit creepy, in fact."

"What?" he urged impatiently, his frown deepening.

"He said he was sorry about my fish."

The blood drained from Ethan's face instantly, his eyes darkening with anger and some other unnamed emotion. "Fuck, Angel, why didn't you tell me?" Grabbing my hand, he rushed toward the door, unlocking it swiftly.

We ran down the corridor and down the stairs to the great lounge where the party was still in full flow.

"What are you doing?" I asked, baffled by the sudden urgency.

"Trying to find the fucker!" he yelled, frantically scanning the room and nodding an instruction to Jackson who hastily made his way toward us.

"Boss?"

"Jackson, get Simon and Carl on the elevators. Nobody leaves until

I say, and then meet me in Damon's office. I'll explain then."

"That's him," Ethan said, freezing the screen on the CCTV monitor a few minutes later. He had just relayed the details of my encounter with the strange guy to Damon and Jackson, and now we were studying a shot of him standing alone sipping a glass of champagne. Damon and I were also in the shot in the midst of our dance. "The bastard's watching her. Who is he?" He aimed the question at Damon.

"Haven't got a clue," Damon shook his head. "Never seen the guy before."

"I thought you had this under control, Damon. If he wasn't on the guest list, how the fuck did he get in?" Ethan snapped angrily.

They both looked up at Jackson, who looked furious. "I'll speak to the others," he said, stalking out of the room.

Ethan scrawled through the CCTV footage some more. It showed the stranger entering the elevator car and leaving about thirty minutes earlier, around the same time Ethan and I had been *playing* in the game room. He pulled out his cell and pushed speed dial. "He already left. I want all of you in here, now."

I assumed the call was to Jackson, and from his tone, he was severely pissed at both him and his team. In fact, everyone seemed pissed, at themselves, at each other, and I didn't have a clue what the hell was going on. It was time to ask questions.

"So, if neither of you know the guy, how did he know us? And how did he know about Ponyo?"

"Good question," Damon said gravely.

Ethan was deep in thought, a distinct look of unease etched firmly onto his face. It was a look I'd come to discern easily of late; the bunching jaw muscles were a dead giveaway. My stomach twisted suddenly as a new thought occurred to me.

"Do you guys think he was the person who broke into my apartment?"

Neither Ethan nor Damon spoke and other than exchanging a brief glance, kept their eyes fixed on the image on the screen. "But I don't understand. Why would someone I've never met do something like that?"

Still nobody spoke.

Jackson, Simon, and Carl entered the room and took a look at the image on the screen. Carl was the one to speak. "I remember him. He arrived with Miss Abby."

Ethan and Damon exchanged a stunned look.

"That's not possible. Abby's been here most of the afternoon. When was this?" Damon asked doubtfully.

"An hour and thirty, two hours, max. She left with a girlfriend and about five minutes later returned with this guy." He pointed at the screen. "That's why I didn't check him off the guest list. She seemed to know him, so I just assumed…" His voice tailed off as he realized his mistake and all eyes turned on him.

Whoa, talk about atmosphere. The temperature in the room suddenly seemed to plummet to something arctic. Jackson pressed his fingertips to his forehead and shook his head in utter disbelief while Damon swiftly left the room declaring he was off to find Abby. Ethan, red with rage and practically shaking, looked as if he was about to blow a fuse. He turned to Jackson.

"Deal with it," he hissed.

"Yes, boss." Turning to Carl, who seemed to have turned a funny shade of green, he added, "Let's go."

Oh, what does that mean?

Suddenly, I felt sorry for Carl. I frowned questioningly at Ethan who shook his head, dismissing my unspoken enquiry into Carl's welfare, clearly too angry to even speak. Moments later, Damon returned minus Abby and looking none too pleased.

"Where is she?" Ethan snapped at him.

Damon held his hands up to calm him. "She won't come because she knows you're angry, but she told me what happened." Ethan shook his head impatiently and Damon continued. "Okay, long story short: Two of her friends had a fight, one went to leave. She went with her in the elevator to try and talk her round. Our guy got into the elevator as she was about to come back up, called out to her by name to get her to hold the elevator. She says he spoke to her like he knew her, made out like he was some old friend of mine, but because she couldn't place him and didn't want to be rude, she pretended to know who he was. He told her how she'd transformed into a beautiful young woman since he saw her last, linked her arm getting off the elevator, laughing and chatting—you get the picture."

"Sly fucker!" Ethan raged, pacing up and down.

"Yep," agreed Damon, sitting down at his desk to study the camera footage again. "I'll arrange to get this fine tuned, get a clearer image." Pausing, he turned to look at Ethan. "Don't worry, Bro, we'll find out who the fucker is. Break his fucking neck myself if I have to." He offered me a consolatory wink, and I half frowned, half smiled in return, unable to really focus on anything other than Ethan's fury.

Color had drained from his face, the muscles in his jaw working furiously as his features creased into a tight ball of concern. I could almost hear the whirring sound as his mind worked through the endless possibilities of what all this meant.

Somebody was out to unnerve us. At least, that's what I hoped their objective was. Anything more sinister was too scary to even contemplate. But the loaded look on Ethan's face told me that was exactly what he was doing. Driving himself mad with endless questions, which I knew would begin and end with: Who is the intended target? Was it was him or me—or was it him through me? Whatever the answer, the horror remained the same. I could see it there on his face as plain as day and the reality made one more thing certain. The emotion that had seemed to consume Ethan when we first realized there was a problem back up in the game room, the one I couldn't quite pinpoint at the time was now staring me right in the face.

It was fear.

Ethan poured amber liquid into two glasses and handed one to me. Why did everyone reach for a shot of good quality cognac in times of worry?

The liquor was warm and soothing as it slid down my throat, but the aftermath of the potent liquid was like a back draft of fire, shocking my senses and causing me to take a sharp intake of breath. Wow. Maybe that was why. It soothed your nerves while at the same time gave you a metaphorical slap in the face to keep you on you on your toes.

The journey back from Damon's had been traveled in silence, both of us in quiet contemplation as we reflected on the evening's events, trying to make sense of why and who and what it all meant. My head was filled with a thousand questions, but I wasn't sure which one to start with, because I was finding it difficult to process the muddle of information into any form of logic. Finally, I decided on a question I knew Ethan could answer.

"What did you mean when you told Jackson to deal with it? Deal with what?"

Ethan sipped his cognac as he stared pensively at the twinkling nighttime lights of Manhattan through the glass wall in his apartment. "Carl, of course. Errors of that magnitude cannot be overlooked."

"You fired him?"

"Yes. Well, Jackson did."

"But on your orders," I spat accusingly, surprised by his lack of tolerance. "Ethan, it was a mistake anyone could have made."

"Mistake?" He looked incredulous. "It was negligence—career fucking suicide in his line of work. What if that fucker had pulled a gun on you, or a knife? That mistake could have cost you your life, or mine, or anyone else in that room. Carl has been given the best training money can buy. There is no room for error in our security team, Angelica. I won't take chances with your safety. He fucked up, he's gone—end of," he shouted angrily.

His words seemed to tug the floor out from under me, the blood draining from my body at the mere thought that the intruder could have possibly been violent. "You really think it's that bad? I assumed he was just some freaky guy out to piss us off for some reason. But you don't. You actually think he's out to harm one of us. But why? Do you know something I don't, Ethan?"

His expression smoothed as if suddenly realizing how alarming his words may have sounded, and rushing over he took me into his arms. "No, of course not. I'm sorry, baby, I didn't mean to scare you. You're right. It probably is just some dickhead trying to get under our skin. I'm just saying that until we know for sure, I don't want to take any chances. And ensuring we've got the best security team around us is the best place to start." Taking my face in his hands, he kissed me, his beautiful, blue eyes glistening as they brimmed with genuine, earnest devotion. "Nothing is more important to me than you, Angel. You're my life now. I love you."

I averted my gaze, unable to face the hope that I knew I'd find burning from Ethan's as he searched my face for a response to his words. The depth of my feelings for this man went way deeper than I could have ever thought possible. My heart felt as if it might actually burst apart at the seams, so crammed with feelings of need and passion for him that it was an actual physical pain. I knew by now, without any degree of doubt, that these pure, raw emotions could not be anything other than love.

So why couldn't I tell him? Why was I so afraid to surrender to these unfamiliar emotions? I willed myself to relinquish my fragile heart, to give it up entirely to this man who sought it so badly. My eyes returned to lock on his as I reached out to gently stroke his face, my fingertips running softly over his full lips. Tears sprang unbidden to my eyes, as the words I longed to say, and was certain he wanted to hear, remained frozen, unspoken on the edge of my tongue. When my lips parted to speak, Ethan leaned in, covering them quickly with his and kissing me softly.

"It's okay," he murmured quietly, leaning his forehead against mine.

"I'm… trying." I stuttered the inadequate words out feebly. *I'm trying? Really?*

"I know." The lines of his mouth curled up into a heartening smile, but the smile didn't reach his eyes. His eyes couldn't lie—and the disappointment there was unmistakable. "Come on, let's get ready for bed. It's late."

When I emerged from the bathroom, Ethan was already changed into his dark gray lounge pants and looking delicious. I slipped my shoes off and began to unpin my hair, allowing it to fall loosely around my shoulders. Ethan stood leaning against the doorjamb of the dressing room watching me.

"Need a hand?" he asked as I reached around my back to find the clasp on my dress.

"Mmm, please."

My failure to reveal my true feelings to him, yet again, was still preying on my mind, and I was scared beyond belief that my cowardly reticence would eventually push him away. Shifting to stand behind me, he gently gathered my hair, draping it over one shoulder to run a gentle trail with the tip of his nose down the length of my neck and inhaling deeply.

"You looked *so* sexy tonight. I could barely take my eyes off you," he breathed. "The only trouble was neither could anyone else. Including my brother."

Disapproval laced his tone as he slowly unzipped my dress, pushing it off my shoulders, allowing it to pool on the floor at my feet. His fingertip brushed lightly down the length of my spine, sending a tingle of awareness straight to the juncture at the top of my thighs. I shivered.

"Cold?" he asked, snaking his hands around to my breasts to tug at my erect nipples.

"Aroused," I replied seductively, knowing deep down inside that because I couldn't tell him how I felt about him, I would do my best to show him in the only way I knew how.

Stepping out of my dress, I retrieved my moonlight-gray chemise from the closet and slipped it over my head. The satin fabric clung to my body, accentuating the curve of my breasts and rigidity of my nipples.

His lust-filled eyes shone with a glint of amusement as they traveled down my body appreciatively. "Are you trying to distract me?"

"From what?" I asked innocently, knowing full well he was referring to his comment about Damon.

"From our conversation."

I sighed. "Damon just enjoys winding you up, E. Just ignore it, don't fall into the trap. Damon is no more interested in me than I am in him."

I squeezed past him and walked into the bedroom to turn down the bed, catching a glimpse of a frown on his face as I went. Although I was certain it was an innocent remark, I'd decided not to mention Damon's almost-but-not-quite enquiry regarding my underwear—or lack thereof. A decision I was now certain was a wise one.

"Are you kidding, he was practically drooling. There wasn't one guy in that whole place who wouldn't have fucked you given half the chance. Christ, come to think of it, I think even half the women did."

I laughed and shook my head. "Where do you get this shit from, E? Honestly, you're deluded to the point of crazy."

"Yes, I think crazy's pretty accurate—crazy about you." He made his way to the other side of the bed. "You make me crazy. Very crazy. Especially when you flirt with other guys."

I halted in the midst of plumping pillows and gaped at him in disbelief. His mouth was a still, impassive line, making it difficult to figure out whether he was playing with me or deadly serious.

"Now you're the one who must be kidding. Not only did I have to stomach the trashy blonde's inflated tits and ego, I then had to endure you practically throwing yourself at some long-legged, dark-haired beauty. Did you get her name, by the way?" With an obstinate shrug of my brow, I hugged the pillow in my arms, my expression as poker faced as his.

The edge of his mouth flickered with amusement and something which vaguely resembled triumph. He was reveling in my jealousy. Turning, he sat down on the bed, his back to me to purposefully conceal his enjoyment.

"Yes, I did, actually. Ayesha—pretty name, I thought."

I could sense him laughing at me, and suddenly I had an overwhelming, impulsive urge to teach him a lesson. Glancing down at the pillow enfolded in my arms, I took it firmly in both hands and raised it above my head. "I do believe you're laughing at me, Mr. Wilde," I giggled, as I brought it down with a thud directly in the center of his shoulders. He stilled. "Not so funny now, huh?"

The seconds ticked by as I waited for a reaction, and slowly he began to turn, his eyes wide with utter shock. "Did you just strike me with your pillow?" The question was drawn out deliberately slowly, as if to emphasize the threat in his tone.

I swallowed hard. Then, mustering up an air of casual arrogance, I hitched a brow, a slow, sexy smirk tugging at the corner of my mouth. "Yeah, I did. So what are you going to do about it?"

His mouth fell open aghast, but his eyes brimmed with elated joy. In one swift move, he scrambled over the bed toward me and grabbing a pillow, took a haphazard swing. I backed up just in time to avoid the blow and took another swipe, this time landing it squarely in his face.

Oh shit! Now I was going to get it.

Swiftly deducing it wasn't a great idea to hang around, I fled, bolting out of the bedroom, down the corridor, and launching myself through the doors into the huge open space of the living area. Ethan was close at my heel, whirling his pillow in my direction. Having caught a couple of minor blows to the arm and shoulder, I finally made it to the dining table, which thankfully formed a barrier and some much needed sanctuary.

We faced each other on opposite sides of the table, gasping between giggles to regain our breath.

"'What am I gonna do about it?'" He repeated my question, his voice filled with playful excitement. I nodded, sticking my chin out boldly.

"Oh, Cinders, you are one hell of a brave, but naughty, naughty girl. I didn't realize how on the edge you liked to live until tonight."

What was it about him calling me naughty or dirty that tweaked my horn button? My teeth scraped suggestively over my lower lip as I squirmed with increasing excitement.

Catching my expression, his eyes narrowed, taking on a wicked, sinful quality. "I hope you know that when I catch you, I'm going to fuck you hard in all sorts of unimaginable ways so that in the future you think twice before being so unmanageable and badly behaved." He nodded once to add weight to his threat.

"Oh, I see." My entire body flushed with desire, every muscle below waist level clenching deliciously at the mere thought of his lewd, suggestive intentions. "Just so we're clear, what bad behavior might you be referring to?" I was buying time to think, all the while moving slyly around the table away from him, trying to create enough distance to make a dash for it.

"Oh, Angel, baby, where do you want me to start?" He shifted his direction, pivoting in an equally crafty attempt to head me off at the top of the table. "Let's see. One: going out in public and refusing to wear panties. Two: flaunting the fact in a very hot, but obvious dress. Three: dancing provocatively with Damon while devoid of said panties and wearing the very hot but obvious dress."

I began to move backwards and forwards, oscillating between directions indecisively. Ethan replicated my moves, changing course each time I did, all the time rhyming off the list of my very naughty misdemeanors.

"Four: turning me on by being *very* sassy to a former fling in a *very* public place, then making me wait to fuck you. Five: driving me so wild with jealousy that I had no choice but to very shamefully lead on an innocent and very pretty girl for no other purpose than to even the score. Six: being a horny bitch who is clearly so greedy for sex that you completely neglected to identify an intruder and potential assailant. Seven: assaulting me with a pillow. And finally, Miss Lawson: for being too... fucking... sexy."

We stood motionless, trying to guess each other's next move.

"That's a hell of a list." I was panting now, excited from the thrill of the chase and Ethan's masterful, domineering tone.

"Yes, Angel. One *hell* of a list."

"And you've decided that fucking me hard in all sorts of unimaginable ways is a fitting punishment to what? Deter me from misbehaving in the future?"

"Uh huh."

"I see. There's just one problem, Mr. Wilde."

"And what's that?"

"Your methodology is flawed."

"Oh, I doubt that," he said with an amused and arrogant frown. "Though, I'm happy to discuss any concerns. Why don't you tell me what's on your mind, Angel."

"Okay. Well, I see your approach to dealing with my 'bad behavior' more as a... reward-based incentive as opposed to punitive." Dipping my chin, I peered through long lashes while biting down on my lower lip seductively. "And based on the fact that I'm actually a bit of a badass who loves nothing more than to be fucked hard, I think it's almost certainly destined to fail."

He shook his head slowly, his eyes narrowing with a wickedly hot look. "You're a dirty... dirty... girl."

I squealed and ran, but he was faster this time, and I knew I wouldn't make it to safety. Instead, I halted, spinning around to face him and taking a desperate swing in his direction. The pillow skimmed his arm, the weight of it tipping me forward enough to take the full blow of his vengeful aim on my left shoulder. I retaliated quickly, swinging my pillow low to knock him off balance.

We giggled like children in the middle of the room, ducking and swerving, taking swing after swing. Finally, overcome with laughter and exhaustion, I slumped, incapable of taking even one more swipe. Ethan took advantage, grabbing me by the waist and whirling me around.

We didn't hear the sound of the elevator or the approaching footsteps in the foyer amid our juvenile jollity. In fact, the first time we realized we were no longer alone was when we heard the grating sound of someone clearing their throat.

Startled, we turned in unison, our focus shifting toward the sound to seek the source of the intrusion. Standing in the doorway to the foyer was a woman. She was dressed elegantly in a dark, expensive looking trouser suit with an overly-large purse hanging from the middle of her arm. Her strawberry blond hair was styled into an immaculate, sharply-cut bob, perfectly framing her pointy, but very pretty face. Her skin was unusually pale, alabaster-white with the perfect amount of pink, rosy blush on her cheeks and lips, and her eyes were a pale icy blue. Despite her sweet appearance, she seemed to have a supercilious iciness that simply oozed from her aura.

I loathed her instantly.

"How sweet," the woman chuckled, though her expression was devoid of all humor. Her stony gaze rested on me, boring into my soul like a red-hot poker. "And who might this be?"

The first thing that struck me was her very polished and refined English accent. There was no question of her background—she was an extremely cultured, well-educated individual.

The second thing was the expression on Ethan's face.

Initially, I thought he may be about to collapse. Every drop of blood had drained from his face, leaving him sickly pale and shrouded in an avalanche of complete horror. His usual strong and powerful built frame was slumped, sagging and heavy, as if trapped under a cumbersome weight.

"Wh… what are you… doing here?" Ethan finally stuttered, his words barely a whisper.

Her gaze turned to him, smug and appraising. "I thought I'd surprise you, Ethan, darling." Her expression froze in sudden distaste. "Have you put on weight?"

Who the fuck was this bitch?

My initial bafflement melded into irritation at this woman's rude intrusion. "Ethan, what's going on? Who is this woman?"

He said nothing, just continued to stare at her.

"Who am *I?*" she sneered, repeating my words as though she were calculating their absurdity. "Mmm, you might well ask."

She turned to Ethan and began to walk into the room toward us. As she shifted from the doorway, I was shocked to notice Jackson standing behind her, surrounded by what was clearly her luggage and looking hugely contrite. He glanced at Ethan, trading a look as they communicated silently, but his eyes never reached mine.

What the hell was going on?

"Ethan, darling, you appear to have lost your manners. How rude," she scolded, addressing him as if he were a wayward child, then walking directly up to him, kissed him lightly on the cheek.

It was as if he hadn't noticed. He stared right through her into the space beyond, as if numb from shock—traumatized even. She turned to me, but didn't approach. Instead, she eyed me up and down scornfully, like I was something unspeakable stuck to the bottom of her shoe.

"Let me introduce myself. Although, forgive me if I don't shake. I'm Rebecca Staunton—Ethan's fiancée."

CHAPTER FOUR

My head felt like it had been used in a game of racquetball, my ears pounding with the sound of rushing blood. I felt dazed and unfocused, my vision hazy, as if staring through a windshield awash with rain. But still I clambered through my mind of hopeless sanguinity, grasping at the tiniest grain of hope I could find, and concluded that this either had to be some mad, seriously unfunny joke, or any second now, I was going to wake from one of my crazy dreams.

But I didn't wake up in a fevered sweat, and nobody delivered the punch line. I wasn't laughing and neither was Ethan—he just stood there, inanely still and disturbingly mute.

"Jackson, you can put my things in my room and unpack them and then you're dismissed." Rebecca Staunton waved her hand in a sweeping motion to Jackson, who instantly began to collect her luggage and disappeared off into the corridor, looking somewhat relieved to escape.

Even in my dumb stricken state, it struck me how subservient they both appeared to be, as though she were some high superior being who wasn't to be defied. She strode with exaggerated grace toward the kitchen and set her purse down on the breakfast island before continuing in what immediately stood out as an incredibly grating, pretentious voice.

"I could really use a glass of champagne, Ethan, darling. The flight was wretched. And *do* pick your friend's jaw up off the floor. You know how I despise clutter."

Friend? Fiancée? What the fuck?

I spun around to face Ethan.

"Ethan," I hissed, attempting to command his attention. "Ethan!" My tone was harsher this time, an urgent plea for him to dash away the doubt and fear that was clawing its way into my heart like a rabid beast.

With a seemingly vague awareness, his eyes flickered to my face, but didn't connect with my gaze. They appeared clouded over and heavy, as if too full of shame and humiliation to look at me. Panic suddenly consumed me as my unimaginable fears moved swiftly toward reality. Why wouldn't he look at me?

"Ethan, what the hell is going on? What does she mean, 'fiancée'? Speak to me, goddamn it," I yelled, my voice swelling with frantic desperation.

Still, he didn't move, didn't speak—not even a flicker.

"Oh dear. It seems somebody's not been entirely honest." The bitch-from-hell resumed her bid to bulldoze her way into my life. She waved a finger, making a *tsking* noise. "Ethan, what have I told you about making sure your friends understand the situation? It's imperative, darling, if only to avoid tantrums like this. You know I can't abide tantrums."

To hell with this. I turned on her.

"What the *hell* are you talking about? Understand *what* situation?"

She rolled her eyes at me. "You're not terribly clever are you? Mind you, they never are—Ethan's *friends*. I must confess, though, you're not entirely what I expected. Not as... obvious as the others and not blonde." She seemed to find this amusing as she weighed my horrified expression. "Oh come now, surely you didn't think you were the first?" She flashed me a condescending look of sympathy. "Ah, bless. Sweetie, Ethan's had lots of friends. It's okay. I'm not angry. He has my full permission. I know how... bored and fidgety he gets. He has his needs. But *I'm* here now. So why don't you be good girl and run along."

My blood boiled, rage whirling through me like a thunderstorm after a heatwave. I glared at Ethan, praying and hoping that any minute, he would declare she was a deranged lunatic ranting a complete load of bullshit on some sort of rambling invective and throw her out.

But nothing.

Enraged, I swooped up the discarded pillow from the floor and smashed it into Ethan's face, desperate to rouse him from his dumbstruck stupor. He gasped as if I'd splashed him with cold water, his eyelids blinking in rapid succession, until finally they came to rest on my face for the first time since the she-devil's rude and untimely entry.

"Well?" I raged.

Although he was looking at me, his gaze was unfocused, his mouth set in a grim and fathomless line. He swallowed hard, then whispered, "She's not my fiancée."

I held my breath at the first glimmer of hope, nodding to urge him to continue, to tell me how deluded this woman was. Above the noise of my battering heart, I heard the she-devil muttering something about the ludicrously large diamond ring she had on her finger—which I'd homed in on the second she uttered the word fiancée—but I tuned her out. I'd heard enough from her. I needed to hear from Ethan.

"Go on!" I ordered him to continue.

His skin had turned a peculiar shade of gray, his mouth downturned as if any second he was about to vomit. "Angel, you have to listen to me..." The words were almost a whisper, like what he was about to divulge were a high-priority secret for my ears only.

Oh God! Oh no! My psyche screamed at me.

"Angel? Oh, I thought it was Angela, silly me. Well, it's quite sweet, I suppose, in a... an American sort of way. " Somewhere in the background the she-devil yapped persistently like a demented, needy poodle. I continued to ignore her and glared at Ethan.

"I'm listening, Ethan." I held my breath.

"Ethan!" the she-devil yelled at him. His head turned rapidly toward her, reacting instantly like an errant child to a parent. "I'm hungry and tired, darling, *do* get rid of her." It was an order.

"Is it true?" I asked quietly, suddenly feeling hopelessly out of control of what was unfolding before me.

His eyes bore into me, beseeching and pleading with earnest desperation. For what? My understanding? Pity? Forgiveness?

In that moment, I knew it was over. This man who stood before me, who had become my reason for living, was a stranger. Everything that was my life only ten minutes before was shattered into a billion untruths. Turning, I bolted for the bedroom, pulling jeans, a sweatshirt, and sneakers from the closet and putting them on. I grabbed my purse, cell, and keys and ran back down the corridor to the lounge.

Ethan hadn't moved. He remained frozen like a statue, staring at the floor. The she-devil was sauntering around with a glass of wine in her hand, like the motherfucking Queen in-situ.

"Finally," she muttered caustically.

Without pausing, I ran past them into the foyer, fumbling for the button to call the elevator. As the doors slid open, I heard Ethan approach behind me.

"Angel, please, you don't understand," he pleaded, his voice still a furtive whisper.

Ignoring him, I stepped into the elevator and turned to face him.

"Please, wait. Let me get Jackson to take you home. I don't want you to leave alone."

His words crashed into me like a wrecking ball. My life had just been torn apart. There were a million things he could have said to instill some hope into my dying heart, and he was expressing concern about my travel arrangements?

Gathering all the strength and bitterness I could muster, I leaned forward and pressed the button for the ground floor. The words resonated from me as I forced them vehemently past the pain of my shattering heart. "Go to hell, Ethan."

I have no memory of the cab journey from Ethan's apartment to mine. In fact, the first time I became aware of anything was when I slid my key into the lock and my skin began to prickle with fear. I'd been back to the apartment only once since Ponyo, and I hadn't been alone; I'd been with Ethan. I knew that the locks and door were new and highly secure, but the feeling I used to get when I unlocked my door—like I was walking into a pair of safe, warm arms—was gone. Now the only emotion I could identify with was fear. I was afraid.

Cautiously, I pushed the door open and flicked on the lights. Immediately, my gaze zoomed in on the breakfast bar where the reflection of shimmering golden-orange had flickered conspicuously in the cold steel blade of the knife. Shaking my head, I took a deep breath and briefly closed my eyes, hoping to divest myself of the haunting image. When I was as composed as I was likely to get, I stepped inside and closed the door behind me. Slowly, I began to move around the room, attempting to reacquaint myself with the place, trying desperately to gain a glimpse of the fondness and connection I used to feel for my home. I shivered, the chill of desolation seeping into my bones. It didn't even smell the same. It smelled stale and unlived in, and empty.

I felt empty.

I trailed my fingertips over the tabletop where Ponyo's bowl once sat, wishing with all my heart that she were there to nuzzle against the pad of my finger, to offer me comfort in the way that she used to. Suddenly, a rush of bile rose to my throat and I bolted for the bathroom, making it just in time to empty the contents of my stomach into the toilet bowl. I wretched until I was dry heaving, my stomach muscles cramping painfully. When it was over, I pulled myself up and staggered over to the washbasin to splash my face with cold water.

When I opened my eyes, I stared into the mirror at a face I barely recognized. The light had vanished from my eyes, leaving them hollow and dejected—dead. In that moment, the familiar pain of loneliness speared through my heart, gouging and slicing it into a million pieces. I sank slowly to the floor, bringing my knees close to my chest and clasping them to me in a futile effort to ease the agony. And as I cradled myself in my arms, I began to rock back and forth uncontrollably, an unearthly, feral wail thundering from within me to penetrate the silence.

I don't know how long I remained there on the floor. The concept of time had upped and deserted me long ago. At some point, I dragged my aching, sobbing body into my bedroom and opened the closet. Once inside, I closed the doors firmly and burrowed my way underneath the hanging garments, curling into a fetal position on the floor.

All I could see when I closed my eyes was Ethan's face, bleak and fearful, pinched with guilt and shame. I could still smell the scent of him on my skin, and I longed for the feel of his arms around me, grasping me to him possessively, his hopeful eyes desperate and hungry for my love. His words from earlier echoed abandoned around my head.

Nothing is more important to me than you, Angel. You're my life now. I love you.

Desperate to flee from the torturous agony that was annihilating me, I willed myself to sleep. And the last thing I remember thinking as sleep, hopelessness, and the yearning for peace descended was the vague hope that I would never wake.

My eyes squinted at a long, narrow streak of light squeezing itself through the crack of the closet door, and a fresh wave of despair swooped down to envelop me. I unfurled my stiff, aching body and crawling on hands and knees, slowly emerged from the closet.

I used the bathroom quickly, relieving myself and brushing my teeth to wash away the unbearable, god-awful taste that coated my mouth. Glancing briefly at my red-rimmed, swollen eyes, I splashed water on my face, grabbed my purse, my leather, studded biker jacket, and left. I couldn't stay here a moment longer.

It was early—six, six-thirty at the latest, which meant I'd slept for less than four hours. I bought coffee from a street vendor and seeing nothing and nobody, began to walk aimlessly with no clear destination in mind. Eventually, I found myself in Central Park, looking out over the pond on Gapstow Bridge. For some reason, I always felt myself drawn to this spot when I felt my most forlorn. Like somehow it could offer me some semblance of solace.

All concept of time had yet again deserted me, having no value or significance. When I realized I was exhausted, I stopped to rest, sitting cross-legged on the grass and staring unseeing into space. I don't really remember thinking about anything. It was as if my body was awake, but my mind had shut down to preserve my sanity. I vaguely recall the incessant buzzing of my cell from the bottom of my purse, which I now know only ceased when the battery finally died.

Eventually, when the light began to fade and my body began to shudder with cold and the pain of misery, I got to my feet and began to walk again. I needed to sleep, but had no clue of where to go. I couldn't face my apartment, and there was no way I was going to Jia or Adam. I couldn't bear the endless questions. There was nowhere and no one to go to.

By the time I turned the corner to my street—too exhausted now to even try and think—I'd resolved that I had no choice but to endure my apartment. But as I approached, I noticed a familiar car parked up outside. The man pacing the sidewalk while talking into his cell was also very familiar. It was Jackson.

Swiftly, I stepped into a doorway, my heartbeat thudding so violently, I could feel it resounding inside my mouth. If Jackson was outside, I was fairly certain Ethan would be inside. I couldn't face him, couldn't face *it*—the reality that our relationship was a sham. I didn't want to know, didn't want to talk about it. Christ, I didn't even want to think about it.

Ten minutes later, I'd checked in to a hotel and after putting the *Do Not Disturb* sign on the door, I locked it, kicked off my sneakers, and crawled into bed. Within minutes, I'd fallen into an exhausted, tumultuous sleep.

The room was crammed full of affluent people, everyone dressed in their finery and moving with overstated elegance. Although, I could see that people were chatting and laughing, clinking glasses and dancing to a beat, there was no sound. Instead, there was a deathly, eerie silence, as though I were watching a movie without volume.

An increasing sense of unease bled into my bones as I made my way through the crowd of unfamiliar faces. I felt noticeably out of place, vulnerable and exposed, and for reasons I couldn't interpret, people appeared to be regarding me with loathing and disgust.

I felt a tap on my shoulder and startled, I spun around to see a man. His dark, almost black eyes were malevolently cold, his lip curling into a malicious snarl.

"Sorry to hear about your fish," he spat viciously.

The silence broke and everybody began to laugh hysterically, the volume suddenly unbearably loud, almost deafening. Fear gripped me as I turned and began to hurry away from the man, but the crowd closed in to form a barrier in front of me, preventing me from moving forward.

"You don't belong here," shouted a tall, busty blonde. "Somebody take out the trash."

The laughter grew louder, everybody pointing and sneering. A sudden, sharp pain seared through my chest, and I raised my hand to rub at the discomfort. Something didn't feel right; it was warm and sticky, and when I looked down I noticed a large, bloody hole in my chest. I gasped in fear as the pain became unbearable, my head feeling fuzzy, and my stomach inside-out with wooziness. Desperate for somebody to help me, I scanned the crowd, and suddenly my gaze found a familiar face.

Ethan stood in the midst of a crowd of doting, blond women, their long, claw-like nails stroking him with adoration. There was blood all over his shirt and mouth, and he was holding something out to the strawberry blonde next to him. She laughed with exaggerated delight, the pretentious sound tinny and distant as it echoed around the room.

"He's had his fill, sweetie, you can run along now."

An evil smile slithered slowly across her face as her eyes lowered to look at the thing he was holding in his outstretched palm. Suddenly, Ethan looked distraught, his expression a blanket of shameful regret as he stared pleadingly into my eyes.

"What have I done?" he asked the strawberry blonde, his horrified gaze darting between me and the thing he held in his hand.

"It doesn't matter," she said flippantly, unmoved by his distress. "She doesn't need it anymore. Look at her—she's dead."

I gasped in horror, choking for breath as realization finally dawned. The thing that lay bleeding in Ethan's hand—was my heart.

I woke drenched in sweat, gasping for air and clutching at my heart. It took me a few moments to remember where I was, my mind grasping at fragments of my dream until dread filled me once again with the knowledge that reality was an even bigger nightmare.

Dizzy with the need to vomit, my head throbbing with pain, I staggered to the bathroom and fell to my knees. I dry-heaved into the toilet, coughing and retching until the pain of convulsions finally subsided, and I crawled on my hands and knees back to bed.

I flitted in and out of a conscious and unconscious hell for the rest of the night and well into the next day. At some point, I turned on the television, flicking it onto the Disney Channel in the futile search for distraction. And in a desperate bid to quell the unrelenting nausea, I tried nibbling on the complimentary cookies. By eight-thirty in the evening, the walls were closing in and inexorable loneliness seemed to sheathe my heart in a layer of ice. I didn't know what to do, where to go, the feeling of helpless uncertainty crushing down on my chest like I was suffocating.

Thoughts of Ethan were hammering on the door to my mind. I'd kept them at bay and refused them entry for as long as I could manage. I longed to hear his voice, soothing me, telling me he loved me, and to feel safe with his arms around me in a tight, protective embrace. But I knew I wouldn't—couldn't—because he wasn't mine. And the knowledge was sheer agony.

Once again, I'd been deceived. I'd been fooled before, by my ex, James, when I was confronted by a wife I had no idea existed. And here I was again. Except this time it was a billion times more painful. Because this time, I'd let my guard down; this time I'd invested emotion and trust and fallen helplessly and irrevocably in love.

In love with a man who was betrothed to someone else.

I began to piece together the confusing enigma that was Ethan's vile and dirty little secret. The woman he'd kept hidden from me, hoping that miles-upon-miles of ocean would conceal his deception. Two different women—two separate continents.

Is that what he'd hoped to achieve, what he'd had planned all along? To have me here and her there? To keep us a secret from each other forever? And then she turned up out of the blue—bam—secret's out. While these thoughts tunneled angrily like sewer rats through my brain, something from that blurred encounter suddenly struck me.

I must confess, you're not what I expected. That's what she'd said. Rebecca Staunton had been fully aware of *my* existence.

She'd also implied there'd been other *friends* like me. Like Lucy, the trashy blonde. Oh Jesus, was that it? I was just the current fling he'd been granted permission to have? Someone to scratch his itch when in New York, while the real holder of his heart was at home in London?

71

But he'd said he was done with London. Is that what he meant when he said his love affair with the city was over, or was she the love affair? Maybe that's why he went back to London, to end it, and that's why he was distant and aloof while he was there. He was with her. But then why wouldn't he have told me?

He told me he loved me. Did he, or was that a lie too?

Hell, I was so confused. So many unanswered questions, all of which I wasn't even sure I wanted to know the answers to. I wished I could talk it through with someone, but the only person I'd ever opened up to was Ethan. I needed him. I wanted him. Briefly, I thought about calling Jia, and then realized my cell was dead and I didn't know her number by heart. Apart from Ethan's, there was only one other number I knew from memory. Without over thinking it, I tentatively picked up the hotel phone and dialed.

The male voice that answered sounded annoyed that he'd been disturbed. I hesitated, unsure if I should speak or hang up.

"Hello?" he repeated. "Who is this?"

"D-daddy?" I stuttered feebly. There was silence at the other end. I heaved a deep breath for courage, my heart beating so loud against my chest I was sure he would hear it.

"Daddy, it's me."

"Speak up."

"It's me. Angelica." There was another excruciating pause while I waited for him to speak.

"What is it, Angelica? What do you want?"

"Um... I... I just wanted to talk."

"Talk?" He sounded baffled, amused even. "I see. Well, you should call Audrey. She can tell you if I have a window available over the next couple of days."

Fresh tears welled up in my sore and swollen eyes, brimming over and trickling down my cheeks. "I... I wanted to talk now." Shit, I was pushing my luck.

He sighed impatiently. "You have two minutes. There's a

documentary I want to see. Time starts now, Angelica." I could picture him observing the minute hand on his wristwatch to ensure we didn't go any longer than my allocated time. I felt rushed and panicked, not giving any thought to what I might say.

"Well, it's… it's me and Ethan. It's over." My voice broke on the final two words as I finally acknowledged the truth. There was more silence at the other end.

"And you're telling me this, why, exactly?"

I stifled a sob. "I thought you liked him."

"Oh, Angelica," he laughed. "You always did have a proclivity for melodrama. I should have known you would fuck it up, but I expected you to hold on to him for longer than five minutes." He sighed with irritation, a trace of resignation in his voice. "You were punching above your weight, girl. You should be grateful he gave you the time of day at all. Stop sniveling!"

His tone made me jump, and I covered the mouthpiece with my hand to smother the sound of my sobbing.

"This had better not affect his donation or his attendance at the charity dinner."

The charity dinner! Mother of Christ, I'd forgotten about that. Of course, Ethan had been right about my father's objectives that night at Eden. He'd had his eye on the money, he'd had no interest in me or that Ethan had made me happy. Why would *he* care that it was over? What the fuck was I doing?

I said nothing, remaining outwardly silent while inside I was screaming.

"Right, well if that's all, my documentary's starting. Oh, before you go—one question." He paused. "Did you love him?"

I faltered, completely astounded by his deep and direct inquiry. "Yes," I whispered as a fresh wave of grief prevailed.

"Good." I sensed his smile radiating down the phone line as he sighed triumphantly. "Losing someone you love hurts like a bitch, doesn't it, Angelica?"

The line went dead.

"No! No! No!" I screamed hopelessly into the phone. "You fucking bastard. Even now you throw it at me. Even now, when I'm lost in hell—when I need you. Even now..." I sobbed with anger and grief and utter despair.

I charged around the room like a crazed animal, tearing the sheets from the bed and the pictures from the wall. I picked up the complimentary tea and coffee tray and flung it against the mirror, shattering it into tiny pieces, scattering anything and everything which wasn't fixed to the wall. Finally, distraught and exhausted, I sank to my knees and wept uncontrollably.

When security pounded on my door a few minutes later, I opened it a fraction, explaining in a quiet voice that I was sorry I'd caused a disturbance and assured them it wouldn't happen again. They eyed me suspiciously and warned me that the police would be called if they heard another peep.

Thirty minutes later, I'd drunk the entire contents of the mini-bar, thrown it all back up, and curled up on the floor in a desperate search for oblivion.

When I awoke at six-twenty the next morning, it was with steely resolve. I'd spent the last forty-eight hours trying to claw my way out of my own mind, but if I was going to survive this latest... blip in my life, I needed to get up and get a freaking grip. Because that's all it was—a blip. Christ, I should know, right? I mean I'd had enough blips to know one when I saw one. Trouble was I should have seen this one coming long before it hit.

I'd been a fool who deserved to crash and burn. Someone like me should know better than to believe being loved could ever be a possibility—especially by someone like Ethan Wilde. My father had spent the majority of my life telling me why I was unworthy of love, and of course had been eager to remind me as recently as last night. He was right. And if I'd backed off from Ethan when he left for London—when I realized I was falling for him—I wouldn't be sinking in shit now.

I would face Ethan, let him have his predictable say. It would be interesting to hear how the bastard planned to justify his treachery, if nothing else. And then I would move on with my life, alone. I didn't need him, I didn't need anyone. No one would ever hurt me again.

The tumultuous anguish and confusion of the last few days had left me wrung out, detached and emotionless. My heart had grown cold once again, deprived of its capacity to beat, like the lifeless piece of meat lying dead in the palm of Ethan's hand.

After paying for the damages and apologizing profusely for a second time, I checked out of the hotel shortly before seven. Then, wrapping my new found resilience around me like a suit of armor, I made my way across town to my apartment.

As anticipated, Jackson was camped outside in wait. He jumped out of the car as soon as he spotted me, his face a picture of shock as he took in the sight of my shabby, disheveled appearance. I was wearing the same clothes I'd left Ethan's in two nights ago and hadn't showered or brushed my hair.

"Angel... Miss Lawson. Christ, what happened? Are you alright? Where've you been?"

I didn't answer his questions, I just watched as he reached predictably into his inside jacket pocket, retrieving his cell to call Ethan.

Suddenly, I recalled the way the way he'd avoided eye contact with me the other night, the way he'd jumped to Rebecca Staunton's every command. It had been excessively obsequious and it stank of betrayal.

"Can I ask you a question, Jackson?"

"Yes, of course."

"That night in the coffee shop, after the break in, when we were talking about Alex... You inferred I was worrying about the wrong person. You knew, didn't you?"

Contrition settled onto his handsome features, his eyes flickering briefly to the ground, before returning to fix me with a penitent gaze. It was all the answer I needed.

"Is he inside?" I asked impassively.

"No, he's out looking for you. He's beside himself with worry."

I shrugged with blithe disregard. "How long do I have?"

"I have to call him now, Angel." His voice was laced with sympathy and regret, all earlier formalities dispensed with. "Ten minutes, at best."

CHAPTER FIVE

I gazed in bewilderment at the stranger in the mirror as I brushed my teeth. My hair was tangled and unwashed. Dark circles surrounded my red-rimmed eyes, too large for the hollows in my pale, haunted face. Turning away in disgust, I stripped naked and climbed into the shower. The steaming hot water cascaded over my tender, aching body, cleansing and soothing me, both physically and spiritually.

When I emerged, I towel dried my hair and put on my robe, knowing I had only seconds to spare. As if on cue, I heard a commotion in the hallway before Ethan burst through the door to my apartment, frantically shouting out my name.

He appeared in the doorway of my bedroom from the hallway as I entered from the bathroom and stared transfixed, his eyes wide with fear. The look of torment and suffering etched on his usually seamless face reflected that which I felt, and my heart constricted at the sight of him. His face was pinched, pain and misery evident in every crease and curve of his beautiful features. His bedraggled hair and bloodshot eyes revealed a state of turmoil and sleepless nights.

The transformation was devastating. He stood before me, a mere shadow of his usual assertive, confident self, and suddenly my mind reeled with conflicting emotions. I hadn't expected this. I'd imagined him shameful—remorseful even—that his deceit had been exposed, but this was an image of a broken man. Broken like me.

Part of me wanted to run into his arms and kiss away the anguish and the hurt, and the other wanted to scream at him, pound my fists violently into his chest. I did neither. I just stood, rooted to the spot, incapable of any reaction.

"Angel," he gasped in shock as his eyes moved, scanning every inch of my body and face, almost as if he were examining me for injuries. "Are you okay, are you hurt?"

"'Am I hurt?'" I asked incredulously, shaking my head. "Are you fucking crazy?"

My response made him flinch, recoiling as if from the force of impact, his expression shocked, almost offended by my tone. "I meant physically."

A sudden surge of anger hurtled through my blood. "No, Ethan. I am *physically* unharmed. Nobody attacked me and I didn't throw myself under the wheels of a car—more's the pity," I said the last part under my breath.

He frowned, seemingly unsure of what to make of the comment. "Where were you? We've been searching everywhere?" His tone was chastising, like I'd just gone off shopping and carelessly lost track of time.

"Look, Ethan, you lost the right to check up on my whereabouts a few days ago. What do you want? I need to get to work," I snapped as I began to tug a brush through my hair.

"*Work*?" He said it as though I'd just informed him I was off to the moon.

"Yes, work. I have a living to earn and an exhibit to organize."

"Jia has it all under control."

"You've spoken to Jia?"

"Of course, that's where I thought you'd gone. She's been worried about you too."

"Well, thank you all for worrying about me, but it wasn't necessary. I don't know whether you've noticed, but I can look after my fucking self. I'll ask you again. What do you want?"

He started toward me, arms outstretched, a please-forgive-me look on his face. I cast him a warning scowl, holding my hands up in a back-the-fuck-off gesture.

"Please, Angel. I just need to talk to you, I need to explain. Let me make you some tea and we can sit down and—"

"*Tea?*" I hissed. "*Tea?* I think you're getting me confused with your English Rose, dahhling," I scoffed in a mock English accent, viciously adding, "Since when did I drink fucking tea?"

"All right, coffee, then. What does it matter? And why are you cursing so much?"

"Oh, I'm sorry, does it offend you? Not quite the eloquent, Cambridge University etiquette of the stuck-up, supercilious bitch you're engaged to? Well fuck you, Ethan. And get the fuck out of my room while I'm dressing. You took the last glimpse of my naked body two days ago, you son of a bitch."

He glared at me, his mind slowly absorbing the reality of the destruction his betrayal had caused. Had he really expected me to fall into his arms, pathetic and forgiving and willing to take him back in whatever capacity he could spare? Christ, he was more deluded than I was.

Reluctantly dragging his tragic gaze from mine, he backed up slowly and closed the door. I heaved in deep breaths of air, trying frantically to make sense of this muddled mess, and to regain the rigid indifference I'd promised myself. I didn't know what to make of Ethan's raw and exposed emotions, but I needed to protect myself and remain strong.

I took my time, dressing with careful consideration in a black leather, box-pleat mini-skirt, a white silk blouse, and ankle boots. For some reason, I believed my outfit would empower me, embolden me to behave with a confidence I didn't feel. Leaving my hair to dry naturally, I applied simple makeup—a touch of blush, mascara, and nude gloss. I pulled on my denim jacket, pushing the sleeves up and folding the cuffs of my blouse over the top. When I looked back at my reflection, I knew I'd disguised my emotional state-of-mind well. Old habits really did die hard. The broken angel had been eclipsed with a cool, unemotional, moody mask. I was badass-with-attitude and back in control.

When I emerged from the bedroom, Ethan was pacing the lounge nervously. On the breakfast bar stood two steaming coffees in to-go cups, and a bag of what looked like various bagels and pastries. My stomach lurched at the sight of food, taking me briefly back to a time in my life when I would frequently starve myself as a form of self-punishment. When I could no longer endure the hunger pains, I would binge, stuffing myself with food until my stomach could tolerate no more, and then the purging would begin, completing the wretched, vicious cycle that was my penance.

Ethan stopped in his tracks, examining my appearance, a muddle of longing and concern etched in the creases of his frown. "I sent Jackson for these. When did you last eat?"

I shrugged and picked up a coffee, taking a cautious sip. The heat was soothing and the sweetness awakened my taste buds, causing an audible, involuntary growl to rumble from the depths of my belly.

"Christ, Angel, you're starving. You must have dropped five pounds, at least. Eat something for fuck's sake," he ordered, pushing the bag toward me and raising a threatening eyebrow in the event I put up a fight.

I took out a pastry, tore off a corner and put it into my mouth. It tasted delicious and I suddenly felt famished. A look of relief settled onto his face, as if my willingness to comply was somehow a sign that my resolve was thawing. But he was mistaken. I ate, not because I was told to, but because I wanted to. As if to bolster the fact, I pushed the rest of the pastry to one side.

"You have five minutes to say what you came to say." I glanced at my watch. "Time starts now."

"Where were you? Where did you spend the last couple of nights?"

"That's none of your business, Ethan. The clock is ticking."

"You weren't with Jia or Adam, and Dylan said he hasn't seen you around Paddy's Bar, so where were you? Tell me," he demanded.

"You checked with Adam?" I asked, horrified.

"No, Jia did. Please tell me you didn't go to that dickhead, Jean-Paul?" He looked sick.

"Ethan, you really are not in a position. You have four minutes remaining."

"You're not going to tell me, are you?" His tone was immersed in fear and exasperation.

"Three minutes, fifty." I was completely unrelenting.

"Goddamn you, woman." Frustration crumpled his face as his hands raked through his hair. Then, as if resigning himself to my cold, uncaring manner, he shrugged. "Fine. I'd better be quick, then." He took a deep breath to compose himself and began.

"I met her six years ago. There was a… an unfortunate incident, and we found ourselves thrown together. As a result, we fell into a relationship—well, more of an arrangement, really. It was purely one-sided. She wanted to be with me; I was obligated to her. I suppose it suited me for a while. I didn't have the time or inclination for full-on romance, and she was a convenient… companion to accompany me to social and formal gatherings. She understood the arrangement, knew I would never commit romantically to her. I made it perfectly clear."

I opened my mouth to speak, a ton of questions rattling through my brain, but I didn't want to appear interested so I kept quiet and let him go on.

"I won't insult your intelligence by telling you we never had a sexual relationship. We did, but it was few and far between. It wasn't the basis of our relationship, just when… necessity compelled. I didn't see her like that, wasn't in the least bit attracted to her, so I had flings—lots of them—all of which were purely based on sex. They weren't a threat to her position in my life, so she accepted them."

God, did I really want to hear this? *Lots of them. Great.* I was getting the picture, and quickly realizing that facts relating to Ethan's former sex life were hard to stomach.

Attempting to conceal my discomfort, I moved toward the terrace doors, opening them to let in the cool, welcomed air. Ethan followed, leaning up against the doorjamb beside me. His close proximity was difficult to ignore, so used to reaching out and touching him that I had to fold my arms across my chest as a reminder to keep my hands to myself. He went on.

"About a year ago, I started to worry that she was becoming too dependent—seeing the relationship for something it wasn't. And lo and behold, I'm finding myself at family gatherings being introduced as her boyfriend. The icing on the cake was when she made a big deal of having Christmas dinner with her folks and turning up with an engagement ring on her finger. She told them this elaborate fairy tale of how I'd proposed to her at midnight on Christmas Eve. When I confronted her about it, she didn't understand what the big deal was, said she was 'simply giving me a push in the inevitable direction.'"

Shit, she sounded completely insane.

"I tried to end it, but… well, she made all kinds of threats."

I frowned questioningly, but he didn't expound and I didn't want to appear concerned enough to ask so I didn't.

"When my father became ill and needed me to take over here, it gave me an out, the opportunity to create the distance I needed. I thought that eventually, over time, she would just move on." He shoved a hand through his hair, exasperation palpable. "But she was like a fucking stray cat—give it a saucer of milk and it just keeps on coming back. I couldn't get rid of her." His tone had changed, tinged with something deeper than frustration now. What was it? Fear? Hate?

Suddenly, he turned to me, his countenance steeped in anguish like a little boy lost, his eyes squeezing closed to shield himself from the pain. When he opened them they were glistening with an abundance of emotion, and I felt my heart begin to thaw.

I must stay strong, I told myself. *Remember the lies, the deceit, the pain that weakness causes. Protect yourself.* I cut my gaze, afraid that seeing his pain would be my undoing and I would crumble.

"And then I met you." His voice was hoarse, strangled by emotion. "I knew the moment I saw you that night in Eden that you were meant for me. I was drawn to you—bewitched by you. What happened that night, the way we… connected. At first, I'll admit, I thought it was pure sexual desire. The only form of sentiment I'd ever experienced before had been communicated to my brain through my dick. But when you just took off without even telling me your name, I was terrified I'd never see you again. I couldn't get you out of my mind. It became an obsession to find you, and when I did, you didn't seem interested, and it scared the shit out of me. My feelings scared the shit out of me.

"When you agreed to go out to dinner with me, I was elated—cloud-fucking-nine, Angel. If you'd turned me down, I honestly don't know what I would have done, other than pursue you until it was the death of me. I quickly realized that my feelings for you were way beyond intense, something way beyond anything I'd ever encountered.

"I wanted to tell you about her. But that night here on the terrace—when you told me about your ex, James, and the surprise visit from his wife—I could see how much guilt you felt when you realized you'd unwittingly contributed to that woman's misery. That the idea of stealing another woman's man was abhorrent to you. And although mine and Rebecca's relationship was nothing like that, I knew you wouldn't see it that way. You'd have run for the hills, Angel, and I couldn't risk losing you."

Suddenly, the urge to cry was overwhelming, a combination of anger and sympathy causing a painful lump to form in my throat, because he was right. I would have run.

I moved further out onto the terrace to look out over Manhattan, where I could discreetly rub away the pain in my chest and swallow back the threat of tears. A moment later he was by my side.

"I was standing here the first time I knew, without any shadow of a doubt, that I was in love with you, Angel. When I looked out and saw the world as a brighter place—just the way my mom said it would be."

I couldn't speak, couldn't even look at him. I knew that if I did, I would fall helplessly into his arms, because everything he was saying was the truth. I knew, because I'd felt it, too—in this very spot—and I'd seen it in his eyes. He did love me.

Perhaps everything could work out after all. I mean what he said made sense—was building toward a reasonable explanation for this nightmare we were in. But I couldn't afford to let my guard down yet. Couldn't afford to hope that by the end of this story, the nightmare could have ended, and the she-devil would no longer exist in our lives. So I held my tongue and allowed him to continue.

"For a while everything seemed like it was going to be okay. You and I were going from strength to strength. Rebecca had been quiet and I thought she was finally getting the message. And then she began calling again. She was relentless, the woman was taking obsession to another level, and I knew I had to fix things."

Suddenly, I remembered the storm I'd seen brewing in his eyes on the countless times I'd witnessed him rejecting calls from his cell. Those calls were her. Shit. Why hadn't I questioned it at the time?

"So I went to London to end things, permanently. Hammer it into her deluded fucking head. The relationship had only ever existed in her mind anyway. I told her that my life was here now, that I wouldn't be returning to live in London, and to forget about me.

"But I wasn't getting anywhere—the woman's insane, refused to even listen. And then that whole thing happened here with you and that fucker Debree, and I just needed to get back to you. I was finding it difficult to even attempt to put your mind at rest about Alex, because I knew that I'd been less than honest about the real reason for my trip to London. I *was* hiding something from you, just not what you thought. We were drifting apart because of the distance and the uncertainties, and I was desperate to close the gap, so I made a mad dash back here. I admit it was stupid to believe that it would all just go away, but I didn't think for one minute she would turn up here the way she did.

"When I went to London to end it, I didn't tell her anything about you, because I didn't want her believing you were the reason it was over. She needed to realize that she and I were not going to happen, regardless. And I was scared she would seek her revenge on you if she knew of your existence, and even worse if she realized I was in love with you.

"I know I handled it badly when she turned up that night, but I panicked—torn between wanting to explain things to you and terrified of demonstrating my feelings openly in front of her for fear of repercussion. She assumed you were a fling and it was best that she continued to think that.

"So, there you have it, the whole grim account. Angel, you have to believe me when I say that the only reason I didn't tell you about her was because I knew you wouldn't understand the nature of our relationship, and you would have left me. If I'd tried to explain, you would have assumed I was a heartless bastard who just used women for convenience, and I honestly thought with time she'd just move on."

When I still didn't say anything, he reached out tentatively and touched my arm. I flinched away from him, still too confused by my emotions and the complexity of this whole damn saga to think clearly. Of all the explanations that had run screaming around my head the last couple of days, this wasn't one I could have even made up. I mean Ethan Wilde was a powerful man, right? But he couldn't get rid of skinny little English girl with a crazy and apparently unwelcomed fixation? Something about this story just wasn't sitting right.

A sudden need for answers engulfed me, and I knew there was one particular question I needed to ask before I could even begin to make any sense of it all, or dare to think that we could come through this nightmare. So I took a breath and found my voice.

"Has she gone?"

At first, I think he was startled that I'd spoken at last, and then he absorbed the question. His cheeks started to color, his eyes darting away from me to the floor and back again, as if deliberating how to reply. His hesitation alone was enough, I had my answer.

"Why?" I spat. "Where is she?"

He had the grace to back up, to step away from my impending fury.

"Um…" He half laughed as he fidgeted nervously. "Probably out spending my money, I shouldn't wonder. That's what she's been doing ever since she arrived."

"How dare you?" I hissed at him. "You come here with this pathetic, far-fetched tale of why you deceived me, and then have the audacity to tell me she's out topping up her pompous wardrobe with your credit card. Why? If what you're telling me is the truth, then why haven't you put the crazy bitch on a plane with a one way ticket?"

"Angel, it's not as simple as that."

"It's as simple as you want to make it, Ethan." Suddenly, something snapped inside me. "Okay, if you won't do it, I will. There is nothing I would like more than to stick it to that arrogant, supercilious bitch. Come on, we'll go now. I'll explain it all to her." I turned and headed back toward the door. In a second he was behind me and gripping my wrist.

"No! No, Angel." Panic was raging through him, the blood draining from his face once again.

"Why? What are you afraid of?" I snatched my arm away.

"Just let me deal with this my way. She'll go, I promise you that. But this has to be handled carefully or—"

"Or what? What is she going to do, throw her diamond encrusted toys out of her horse-driven pram? Your way clearly isn't working, Ethan. She needs to be told."

"No, Angel. I said, no! You have to trust me on this. It's best that she thinks you were just a fling like all the others, or she'll never let this go. She needs to believe you're history."

His words hit me like a blow to the chest. "Oh, I see. That's what all this is about. You expect me to swallow this utter bullshit about trying to get rid of her and agree to be your bit on the side. That way you can keep us both sweet, am I right?"

"No, of course not." The notion appeared to horrify him, his deep-seated frustration now virtually tangible. "I came here, primarily, to make sure you understood the situation, put your mind at rest. Reassure you that I'm not with her in the sense that she told you I was, and that it's you I want to be with. I love you, Angel. What I'm asking is for you to please give me some time. Allow me to deal with her in my own way. And I know it's a big ask, but—to wait for me."

God, this was a complete head-fuck. Part of me was convinced he was playing me, and the other half said I was being wholly unreasonable. I couldn't get my head around it.

"But I don't understand why. If you want to be with *me*, why can't you just tell her? It's as simple as that."

"No, it isn't. Angel, please." He plowed his hands into his hair, raw with exasperation and weariness.

And then I saw it.

"My God, you're afraid of her." Suddenly, his fear was unmistakable. "Yes. Shit, why didn't I see it before? The way you behaved when she walked through the door of your apartment has had me baffled, but now I see it. She terrifies you. Why?"

"You don't know her like I do, or what she's capable of."

"No, I don't. So tell me."

"She's volatile. Her behavior's erratic to say the least. She needs careful handling... Christ, you really don't need to know the ins and outs of her."

I laughed at this preposterous remark. "Don't treat me like a fucking child, Ethan. She seemed to know all about *me* when she arrived unannounced to wreak havoc in my life, so you can damn well... Wait a minute." I paused, trying to work my way through the scraps and slivers of insufficient information I'd been thrown. "How *could* she have known anything about me? You said you didn't tell her anything when you were in London, but I distinctly remember what she said about me not being what she'd expected, and some other smart-assed comment about thinking my name was Angela."

A brand new wave of dread seemed to wash over him as he stared at me wide-eyed, his jaw muscles bunching beneath his cheeks. What wasn't he telling me?

He opened his mouth to speak and then hesitated, as if struggling to get the words past his throat. "Somehow, she figured out I was seeing someone—you—when I was in London." When he paused again, it was if he were gathering courage. "She must have hired someone to snoop around here. Put the frighteners on you."

"What do you mean, frighteners?" I frowned impatiently, unsure as to where this was going.

"I swear, I didn't know, Angel, but this is exactly what I'm talking about. She's unpredictable, and frankly, I don't know what lengths she's capable of going to if someone stands in her—"

"Didn't know what?" I cut him off, mid-sentence. "What did she do?"

He took a step back, like he was seeking space to figure out whether it was best to be honest or to wriggle out of answering me.

"What did the crazy bitch do, Ethan?" I yelled at him.

A hopeless, bleak expression invaded his features as he swallowed hard. "I think she may have organized the break-in here."

My jaw went slack, my mouth dropping open in horror. "Ponyo?" I whispered in disbelief.

He nodded cautiously. "I think the intention was to go through your stuff, find out who you are—an intimidation exercise. Maybe, Ponyo was a last minute casualty of her twisted cruelty. I think the guy at Damon's was the one she hired to do it."

The horror of his words hit me like a train, the initial shock morphing into a sharp, fiery burn, as I tried to assimilate what he was telling me. The guy at Damon's was the one who'd broken into my home and violated my safe haven. The one who'd killed Ponyo. Hugging my arms around my body, I attempted to soothe the inward shiver of disgust which crawled like an army of insects over my skin.

Suddenly, I was flooded with uncontrollable rage. I hurled myself at him, pounding my fists against his chest. "You! This was all because of you! Get out!" I hissed, pushing him toward the door.

His pale features filled with shock and despair as he struggled to defend himself against my flailing hands, moving backwards precariously through the doors into the lounge.

"Get out!" I raged, pushing him through the room toward the door. "You knew it was her. Knew she was the one responsible for making me afraid in my own home, for murdering my friend—and still you have her in your home." The words tore through my throat like acid. "I hate you for this, for what you've done to me. You've brought me to my knees, cut me open, and exposed me, leaving me vulnerable to fuckers like her. It's your fault I'm back in the closet, your fault I can't breathe anymore. Get out, go back to that crazy-fucking-whore; she's welcome to you. I should never have let you near me. You said you wanted to fix me, but you've made me weaker than I've ever been. Get out. I've had enough misery in my life without you bringing me more."

"This isn't just about you, Angel. If you stop playing the victim for one minute, you might be able to see that," he yelled.

I froze. *Victim?*

The word stung with ultimate insult. Piercing through me like a red-hot sword, slaying every remaining ounce of faith I had left in him. And suddenly, my heart was icy cold—frozen. And it was far, far easier to endure.

When I spoke, it was with calm, cold brutality and for the first time in my life, I felt like my father's daughter. Innately evil.

"Victim?" I let the word sit there for a second or two, watching as he screwed his eyes closed in regret at what he'd said. "Oh, rest assured, Ethan, I've spent my very last day as a victim. Nobody will ever get the chance to hurt me again. I want you to leave now." Slowly, I turned and walked toward the door.

"Angel, I'm sorry, I didn't mean that. I'm overwrought, desperate for you to understand. Please, we can work this out, I promise you."

"I don't care anymore. I want you to go."

"But what about us?"

"There *is* no us. It's over. Done—finished."

"No. You're just saying that to hurt me, because you're hurting."

"I'd have to care to want to hurt you, and I don't." I opened the door and stood aside for him to leave.

"Why are you so cold?" he whispered.

"Because I'm dead inside. Cold and dead and evil."

"You're wrong, you're not evil. You're a heavenly angel—my Angel."

I laughed. "No, *you're* wrong. I'm no angel. I'm a killer—a sinner. And Heaven is no place for sinners. I always said I was bound for Hell—this is my due penance. And do you know what? I'm okay with that. I'm tired of seeking happiness. I don't care anymore."

"No, don't say that, I beg you," he sobbed, slumping to his knees and shaking his head. "You have every right to seek happiness, Angel. I can make you happy."

"No, you make me weak. It's over, Ethan. It never should have begun. Please go."

"I'm not going anywhere until you listen to me. Please, you have to listen."

"Fine. I'll go then." Striding over to the breakfast bar, I picked up my purse and turned on my heel to leave.

"No, don't go, please. I need you." The emotion in his voice was gut-wrenchingly raw as he pleaded unrestrained, his words hoarse and trembling as they rattled hopelessly from his shattering body. "I love you, Angel."

The words hung heavily in the air between us, huge and desperately tempting as they endeavored to thaw my frozen heart. But it was too late. There was nothing left in the void of my chest where my heart used to be. Just tiny fragments of shattered dreams.

I turned slightly, just enough to glance over my shoulder in Ethan's direction, but I couldn't meet his gaze. I knew that I wouldn't speak if I did. The words that left my mouth were cold and resolute, devoid of all humanity, and would resound in my head for weeks to come.

"But I don't love you, Ethan. I don't love you."

CHAPTER SIX

J ackson was waiting dutifully outside when I emerged from
my building stone-faced, my emotions firmly encapsulated
somewhere within my damaged and fragmented soul.

"Get him out of there," I instructed.

Jackson responded with a nod, his eyes filled with sadness and
disillusionment. As he turned to enter my building, I called out to
him again. "Jackson." I paused, and then, "Take care of him."

I walked the streets of Manhattan for an indeterminate amount of
time, the haunting echoes of Ethan's sobbing and my parting words
causing me to die a thousand deaths with every step I took. And then
I did what I've always done. I closed the door to the pain and slipped
into a masquerade made of self-preservation.

Eventually, I found myself at the gallery, which appeared in relative
calm considering I had an exhibit opening in two days' time. I keyed
in the password on the entry panel and entered the sparkly white
foyer. Our receptionist, Alice, a petite blonde, was on the telephone
and on seeing me enter, simply raised her hand to wave. Off to the
right was the main showroom, consisting of several small sectioned
off display areas, each of them adorned in contemporary photography
by various artists. To the left of the foyer was the exhibition space,
which—if everything was going to plan—would currently showcase
my work.

I wandered through the archway into the long, narrow room, which, using white divider walls, had been constructed to form a zigzagging corridor. The partitions made up an entrance, a course with abrupt alternate left and right turns, a sharp turn at the end, and an identical zigzagging walkway running parallel to the first, which led to the exit. The idea was that the display could be appreciated gradually.

Some artists preferred to display sporadically so people are able to amble through their work leisurely, but I liked to ensure all of my work was seen so tended to favor a meandering arrangement.

Frank and Joe—the two portly, gray-haired brothers we hired to erect the displays—were in the corridor hanging the few remaining photographs in the sequence. I threaded my way through to survey my work.

Usually, I expressed myself through a theme when I exhibited, the subject generally relating to a particular place, an atmosphere, or an object of thought. Quite often, though, my work was inspired by my prevailing state of mind.

On this occasion, I'd wanted the fundamental theme to convey optimism, hope, and positivity—to reflect the mood and emotions I was feeling at the time. The arrangement was made up of titles, such as, *It's the Little Things that Make You Smile*, and *Random Acts of Kindness*.

A man stopping and getting out of his car on a busy Manhattan street to help a bewildered old lady across the road; a small boy offering his ice cream to a homeless man; a woman helping a struggling mother to carry her child's stroller up the stairs from the busy subway.

The shots had been captured over time—years in fact—on the few scattered instances I'd indulged in such sanguine emotions. They'd been archived and waiting for a time when they could collectively reflect the way I felt. I'd thought—when I'd selected them—that now was the right time. That finally these images would give credence to what was taking shape in my life. Evidence of inner peace and happiness—of hope.

Now they felt all wrong.

"Stop!" I yelled suddenly.

"What is it, Miss Lawson?" Joe asked, wiping a fine sheen of sweat from over the top of his upper lip.

"They're all wrong. They'll have to come down."

They gaped at me in a, you-have-got-to-be-kidding fashion. "But these are the ones Miss Huang told us to—"

"Angel, is that you?" Jia's concerned but angry voice hollered from the direction of the foyer, interrupting Joe. A moment later, she stood before me, hands on her hips, lip curled into a growl. "Where the *fuck* have you been?"

Joe and Frank exchanged a cowering glance.

I ignored her and turned back to them. "I'm sorry, guys, but they'll have to come down. I'll let you know what I plan to replace them with."

Jia glared at me in disbelief, upturned hands outstretched, her what-the-fuck face oozing disapproval. I said nothing, just strode past her down the corridor to the office. Distantly, I heard her muttering something to Frank and Joe, and then she followed me into the office, closing the door behind her.

"What has that arrogant prick done to you? Look at you! Where the fuck have you been? I've called and called. Why haven't you been answering your cell? That fucker said you went missing on Saturday night. I've been going crazy. He said some ex-whore of his had turned up and called dibs on him. What the fuck is going on?" She finally stopped for breath.

"I'm sorry you were worried, Jia. I'm here now and I'm okay. Me and Ethan…" I paused, trying to work out what I wanted to say and deciding it wasn't much, added, "It's over. I don't want to talk about it."

As if to underscore the finality of my words, I sat down at my desk and turned on my computer to open up my files. Somehow I had to rescue this exhibition. It would be easier to cancel the whole thing, but not very professional, and to be honest I needed the distraction.

"Okay… whatevs. As long as you're all right," Jia said eventually.

Oh! Diplomacy wasn't usually Jia's thing when it came to me; I'd expected a full-on interrogation. I mean, where the hell would I start? The truth was a complete mind-fuck. Besides, if I had any chance of keeping my sanity intact, I definitely couldn't risk talking about it. Not yet anyway. Grateful that I'd been granted leave to explain further, I attempted a smile and turned back to my computer.

"What's with Huey and Dewey?" Jia asked, hitching her thumb in the general direction of Frank and Joe.

A smile twitched at the corner of my mouth, almost succumbing to Jia's charming and comical analogy between Frank and Joe and two of Walt Disney's mischievous, animated Quack Pack.

"I'm changing the display. It's not working for me. I've got a more appropriate theme in mind."

Jia understood the way my mind worked, and how my photography ultimately mirrored my mood. She blinked a few times, absorbing what I'd said. "Okay… your prerogative, you're the boss, after all. Although…" She paused to glance at her watch. "You couldn't be cutting it any finer."

"I know, but I'll deal with it. I have the time."

A furrow appeared between her immaculately-shaped eyebrows as she regarded me with concern, but again, she elected not to delve into my psyche and instead sat down at her desk. "I'll get on with the rest of the arrangements, then. Leave you to it."

I nodded gratefully.

"Angel. You know I'm here, right?" she added with gentle concern.

A hard, painful knot formed in my chest, my hand reaching instinctively to rub it away. Then nodding again, I turned back to my work.

Having worked tirelessly until almost midnight, I finally succumbed to fatigue, put on the alarm, and closed the gallery door, locking it securely behind me. I don't know whether I was surprised or not to find Jackson waiting in the car at the curb. He jumped out when he saw me emerge, a cautious but hopeful look on his face.

"What are you doing here, Jackson?" I asked wearily.

"Just following instructions, Miss Lawson."

"Drop the formalities, will you? I'm too damn tired."

After a slight hesitation, he dipped his chin to eye me warily. "He's worried about you, Angel. He just wants to make sure you're safe."

The now-familiar bubble of anger began to resurface. My safety had only become questionable since the she-devil decided to break into my apartment and murder my fish. An act of atrocity both Ethan and Jackson had vowed faithfully to avenge. Oh, betrayal had a loathsome stench.

"Well, I'm no longer his concern, so you can tell him that as long as he keeps his psycho bitch out of my face, I'll be just fine."

"It's just a ride home, Angel. It's late, I'm not comfortable leaving you here."

"I don't need babysitting, Jackson. I've been looking after myself since I was six years old. You think I had someone to hold my hand before he came along? Well, I didn't, so either back-the-fuck-off, or I'll get a restraining order. How does that sound?"

My words seemed to sting as his handsome face crinkled into an expression halfway between being wounded and disapproving. Without waiting for a response, I turned and began to walk briskly away, the anger fueling my momentum. I could hear a vague muttering as he spoke into his cell, updating Ethan of the situation, I guessed, and awaiting instruction. As I turned the corner, a discreet glance over my shoulder confirmed what I'd already predicted. Jackson was shadowing me on foot from a distance. I shook my head in exasperation. To hell with him. If he wanted to roam the streets of New York at practically midnight, who was I to argue.

Despair hit me anew the moment I put my key in the door—dread of the cold, desolate void that lay beyond. I unlocked it swiftly and flicked on the lights, my eyes immediately drawn to something lying on the breakfast bar. My heart thundered into my mouth as flashbacks of a cold, glinting, steel blade came unbidden to my mind. I shook my head, dispelling the image and closed the door firmly behind me.

As I stared again at the object across the open-plan room, I realized instantly what it was. My pounding heart plummeted. Stark realization slowing it to a meager, sluggish beat. I glanced down at the item clutched in my fisted hand, my fingers slowly unfurling to reveal the other half of the object which lay on the surface across the room. Slowly, I moved toward it, placing the two halves together, side-by-side, and immediately a recognizable shape took form—the figure of a heart surrounded by angel wings.

The ache in my chest grew duller—heavier. I rubbed at it briefly. Then, pulling the two halves apart, hastily flung mine to the bottom of my purse, the other—firmly attached to the key I'd given Ethan—in the kitchen drawer, along with various other useless, discarded items. The representation was no longer intact, no longer symbolic of what was once my healing soul. Like me, it had been torn apart. Once again, I was a broken angel.

I took a quick shower, the scalding hot water melding perfectly with the scorching tears spilling relentlessly down my face, making them all the more easy to deny. Then dragging the pillow and comforter from my bed, I slid open the closet door and burrowed my way to the back, cocooning myself in the small, protective space.

Alone in my own private hell.

On Wednesday, I made a fleeting visit to the gallery, staying long enough to make sure everything was on course for the exhibition opening the following day, but not enough time for Jia to ask too many questions. Frank and Joe were busy with the modifications to the display, and Jia had the rest of the arrangements well in hand, so I decided to go walk-about with my camera.

By two o'clock I hadn't taken a single shot. Nothing had inspired me, and although I'd grown up with the frenetic pace of New York, suddenly it seemed to drain me. I couldn't recall the last time I'd eaten or drank anything, and when I spotted my hands trembling, realized I was in desperate need of a sugar rush. I dove into the nearest Starbucks, grabbed a large caramel macchiato, and on spotting an available seat—a rare thing in New York—at a bench facing the window, I decided to take the weight off my aching feet for a while.

As I sipped my coffee, I stared unseeing and unthinking through the window overlooking the busy street. Passers-by were a mere blur of colors and shapes flitting in and out of my field of vision, indistinguishable and insignificant. Afraid that sitting still would lead me to think, I blocked out all cognizance of the incessant and raucous noise of traffic and chitchat around me, choosing instead to conjure the image of an infinite blue ocean.

I could almost hear the sound of gentle, lapping waves when I was torn from my reverie by a soft tap on the window. It took a moment for me to stir, but eventually my vision cleared and focused on the face looking back at me. Emerald green eyes gazed warmly into my deep brown ones. They crinkled attractively at the edges with a smile that continued on to a pair of full lips, opening to mouth a single word. *Hi.*

For the first time since Rebecca Staunton entered my world, annihilating it beyond recognition. The first time since... Ethan. I smiled a full-on genuine smile.

Hi, I mouthed in response.

For a few seconds, we gazed at one another with warmhearted, remembered fondness, and then picking up my purse and camera, I made my way outside to Dr. James Foster.

Apart from Ethan, James was the only other man I'd ever felt any affection for. It was very different to the intense passion which had ruled my feelings for Ethan, but my initial, instinctive reaction told me I still held a torch for him.

James was ruggedly attractive in a way that exceeded regular handsomeness. With piercing green eyes, short, light brown hair, and stubble, he was lean and strong and stood around six foot. He was dressed casually in jeans and a deep red hooded top and looked amazing.

We stood on the sidewalk smiling at each other, and after a beat stepped into a warm, but slightly awkward embrace. Neither one of us seemed to know the right thing to say—after all, in our last conversation, over a year ago, I'd told him it was over between us. The grim recollection of why I'd ended it sprang suddenly to my mind and my smile faded.

James recognized the look in an instant and swooped in to recover the moment. "You look incredible," he breathed enthusiastically.

I frowned, looking down in dismay at my clothing selection. An A-line denim mini-skirt hanging limply from newly acquired bony hips, a navy-blue silk shirt tied at the waist, and calf-height biker boots with cashmere socks peeking out of the top. Not my most glamorous look.

"Do you... wanna go somewhere?" he asked cautiously, gesturing over his shoulder with his thumb in no particular direction.

I nodded and we headed off down the street.

A few minutes later, we entered a small Italian bistro on East 20th Street, not far from Gramercy Park. The restaurant had a cozy, intimate vibe with an old wood-burning stove and exposed brick walls. The only other two occupied tables were deeper into the restaurant, near the open kitchen, so we opted for privacy and took a candlelit table near the window. We ordered some wine from the elderly Italian waiter. Although, I wasn't sure how much of it I would be able to consume on an empty stomach.

The silence stretched between us, almost comfortably, as we searched for the right way to begin.

"So—there you were. Sitting all alone, shining and radiant, like a beacon out at sea. Question is—does your light serve as a signal of welcome or of warning?" His question was candid but casual, his head cocked to one side, eyes filled with humor. I'd forgotten just how analytical and to-the-point James could be, and the reminder made me smile again.

"I'm here, aren't I?" I said simply.

"Yes. You are. It's a big old place, New York, and yet here I am, back in town for barely a week, and it's you I bump into. Fate or chance?"

I shook my head and giggled. "Definitely chance, I'd say. I see you don't change. You're as off-the-wall as you always were."

He pouted, doing his best to feign offence.

"So, are you back in town for good, or is it a fleeting visit?" I continued, wanting to maintain the flow of the conversation.

He smiled, his eyes narrowing as he tried to read me. "For good. I think."

"You think?" He simply nodded, so I continued to pry. "I heard you moved to Boston. So what, that didn't work out?"

"Ah yes, Boston." He gave a half laugh. "Boston was good, for a while. Rachel has family there. Rachel's my wife, but then you knew that, right?"

Oh. I'd often wondered whether she'd ever told him about our meeting. Suddenly, I worried where this conversation was going—the last thing I needed was to be scrambling around in drama that was dead and buried long ago. I breathed deeply, seeking strength and motivation for the inevitable discussion.

"Yes, I know about Rachel. She had the courtesy to pop into the gallery one day and introduce herself—which was super weird, considering I didn't know she existed."

"Why didn't you tell me?"

"Excuse me? What, so now you're calling me out for being deceitful and dishonest? You lied to me for the entire eight months of our relationship, James."

"I know, and I'm sorry. Trust me, if I could change things…"

I suddenly decided that I no longer cared about why he'd lied. It was old news now and the least of my worries, so I let it go and answered his question.

"She asked me not to tell you, and I thought I owed her that. And she was right. It was far less complicated that you didn't know. Which is why I don't understand her decision to tell you herself. How long have you known?"

"Oh, well that's the funny part. She told me about her little visit to warn you off about three weeks ago, right after she told me she was leaving me for another guy."

My eyes widened in shock. "Oh... Right back atcha, huh?"

"Yeah, karma's a bitch, aint it? Thing is, I was more pissed about finding out the truth of why you'd ended it than I was about her leaving me."

I didn't know what to say to that. I wasn't sure whether I felt sorrier for him or for her. So I just muttered, "I'm sorry things didn't work out for you both."

"They were never going to work out for us, Angel. It was over between me and Rachel before I even met you. I just wish I'd had the balls to end things with her then. There hasn't been a day gone by that I've not wished I'd have handled things differently. I was going to tell you about her, I was just waiting for the right time and it never seemed to come. But I was going to leave her, Angel."

"Well, I'm glad you didn't. I couldn't have lived with myself if I'd been a part of that. I was never up for stealing another woman's man." *Despite that fate seemed to have that in store for me.* "What we had was good, James, but not worth throwing away your marriage."

"It would have been worth it to me," he said in a hurt, quiet voice, which seemed to gain strength when he added, "but I suppose you've answered my question, at least."

"What question?"

"I needed to know if that was the only reason you ended it, because she asked you to. It's always haunted me why you changed your mind about us so suddenly."

Christ, how was I going to answer that? I wasn't even sure about how I felt now in my current fucked-up predicament, never mind how I felt about something that happened over a year ago. In fact, I didn't know shit anymore. So I answered as honestly as I could.

"Yes. That was the only reason—at the time. But, I don't know,

James, people change. And over time, I've come to realize that we probably wouldn't have worked out anyway."

"I think we would have," he blurted without hesitation.

Anxiety was building inside me again. I didn't need this right now. "Well, we'll never know, will we?" I snapped.

Flinching from my response, he glanced away, trying to conceal his wounded expression behind his glass as he tilted it to his lips to take a sip.

"So, where are you staying?" I asked, quickly trying to move on.

"Why, are you offering me a place to crash?"

"No," I half laughed.

"I rented a place not far from here. It's no penthouse, but it will do for now, until I work things out."

I nodded.

"How's the gallery? Christ, how's Jia? Did you get her on a leash yet?" We both laughed and I knew we were back on safe territory.

We chatted for hours, ordered pizza, and chatted some more. I'd forgotten just how funny James could be and realized that it must have been his ability to make me laugh that had drawn me to him in the first place—that and his ridiculously handsome face. He had a knack for making me smile, and when I smiled, I felt better about myself. Spending time with him had been a breath of fresh air and a tonic I so desperately needed.

He ordered mixed ice cream with marshmallow and chocolate toppings, in the largest glass the restaurant had available. We spooned some of it to each other and fought over other bits, having fun—like old times. And for a while, I forgot about my shattered soul and even found myself selfishly wishing I could just spend lots of time with James and laugh my way to a time in the future, when it didn't hurt quite so much to think of Ethan.

James put down his spoon and pushed the glass across the table toward me. "You win. You get to finish it. I can't eat another thing." He sat back in his chair and gazed at me.

Grinning jubilantly, I tucked into the remaining ice cream at the bottom of the glass—the chocolate bits. His green eyes sparkled with warmth and humor in the candlelight as he watched me, and for a few minutes neither one of us spoke. I watched as he scraped his fingers through the stubble on his chin in that old familiar way of his, and for a moment I could almost feel the burning sensation it used to leave behind on my chin when he kissed me, and then on the delicate skin of my inner thighs when he pleasured me more intimately.

I blinked to chase away the image, surprised that I'd allowed my mind to conjure it. Deep down, I knew that if James had walked back into my life a few months ago—before Ethan—I'd have welcomed him back with open arms. The original attraction was still there, the old feelings were still there. But now? Post Ethan? I knew now that James could never be enough, that it could never work. There would never be another man alive who would make me feel the way Ethan had. Nothing would ever be the same again.

The realization settled resolutely in my soul like a block of unmovable cement. I glanced at my watch. It was almost eight o'clock. "They're going to start charging us rent if we don't get out of here."

"You're right. Where did that time go, huh?" He waved to the waiter and gestured for the check.

A few minutes later we were outside on the sidewalk.

"I'm glad we ran into each other. I had fun," I said, feeling slightly awkward as I wondered how we were going to end this.

"Me, too. So… we could do it again, maybe?" His tone was hopeful but cautious. My mouth twisted wryly, in a not-so-sure-that's-a-good-idea way. "Oh, come on, you said you had fun. What are you doing this weekend?"

My heart almost flatlined, filling with dread as I suddenly remembered the charity dinner. "Oh, I've got one of those awful charity events for my father."

James knew very little about my childhood, but enough to know that my father and I didn't exactly have a conventional relationship, and there was definitely no love lost between us.

"Need a date?"

I frowned. "No, James, I don't need a date. I don't even want to go."

"Then don't. Do something with me instead."

I shook my head apologetically in response. "I really must get home. I've got a busy day tomorrow."

"Let me see you home, then." He stretched his hand out to flag a cab and one pulled over to the curb.

"No, it's fine, really. I've got it."

"Okay, if you're sure," he sounded deflated. He waited a beat then, "Can I call you?"

"I'm not sure, James. It's not a great time for me."

Disappointment drifted into his features like a shadow, his eyes losing that twinkle of hope, which had been growing steadily brighter throughout the evening, and suddenly I felt the urge to hold him.

Stepping forward, I flung my arms around his neck, pulling him toward me in a tight embrace. James responded swiftly, enfolding me in his arms, face nuzzling into my hair to breathe me in. My eyes misted over as I snuggled into the affection I hadn't realized how much I hungered for.

"You smell the same," he breathed against my neck before angling his face to look at me. "You're so beautiful, Angel. Even more so than I remember. I need you to know that I never stopped thinking about you. I'm so sorry I fucked things up, and I'm so sorry I hurt you."

I released him and shaking my head, placed a finger across his lips to silence him. It was done now, and it wouldn't do either of us any good to rehash it. As I reached out to open the cab door, he raised his hand to mine, halting my progress.

"Wait." His tone was earnest—the word insistent, as if that moment might be his last chance to say what was on his mind. I frowned at him questioningly and waited.

"*I* know." The words were barely a whisper.

I shook my head in confusion. "You know what?"

"You said earlier that we would never know how things might have worked out between us. But *I* know. I know it would have worked—because I know I was in love with you. I was in love with you then, and I'm still in love with you now. And I think you feel the same."

Oh fuck. I did not want to hear this. Not now—not ever.

"No, you're wrong, James," I said rather too harshly. "I'll admit, at the time, I thought what I felt for you could be love, but… it wasn't—because I know what that feels like."

My words seemed to hit him like an icy breeze, his gaze cutting instantly to the ground and when he spoke, his voice was hoarse with disappointment. "Who is he?"

"Who *was* he," I corrected. "It's over now, so it doesn't matter."

Suddenly encouraged, he looked up to search my eyes for any sign of hope. "So there is a chance for us. We could see what happens, see where it takes us. Spend some time getting to know each other again. There's no one standing in our way this time. Angel, I want this, I want you. Give me one last chance."

I shook my head slowly. "We had our time, James." Reaching out, I took his strikingly handsome but defeated face in my hands and kissed him lightly on his lips. For a brief moment, he responded, the tenderness of the kiss a confusion of regret and acceptance that what it meant was goodbye. Then, stroking my cheek gently, he stepped back to open the cab door.

As the car pulled away into the night, there was one thing I was sure I'd learned from the day's events. One thing I was absolutely certain of: I was irrefutably and irretrievably in love with Ethan Wilde. And I didn't know how the hell I was going to make it go away.

CHAPTER SEVEN

Staring blankly into space, I sat at my office desk nursing a mug a coffee that was almost certainly cold. I'd arrived hours ago, but couldn't seem to muster the energy or enthusiasm to venture out into the gallery to check how things were coming along. My exhibition was due to open in just over an hour, and I couldn't have cared less.

Guests would arrive, champagne would be poured, canapés would be eaten, and all I wanted to do was curl up in a ball. Misery, along with sleeping on the floor of my closet, was taking its toll on my body. I'd woken that morning feeling more disconnected than ever. Like my mind was floating above me somewhere in a dense fog, unable to fully awaken, and my body was progressively failing because it was unable to function without it. Joints and muscles that I didn't even know existed, ached almost virally. I felt drained, exhausted, and in pain.

My chance meeting with James had left my thoughts and feelings even more jumbled. At times, I'd found myself questioning whether the encounter had been real or just another surreal dream. His declaration of love had knocked me for six. Mainly, because I now knew, without any shadow of doubt, that the craziness I felt for Ethan was undeniably love. Love to the deepest, most heartrending, soul-puncturing degree—and it wasn't just going to go away as I'd hoped.

My unseeing eyes suddenly focused on the charity dinner tickets, which lay on the desk in front of me. The thick ivory card and gold embellished font seemed elaborate and unnecessary. I picked them up and thumbed through them. There were three, one each for both Ethan and me and one for Jia. Jia had accompanied me to events involving my father, providing moral support, since I'd known her and I'd seen no reason to change that, so had purchased a ticket for her as well.

A wave of nausea washed over me, settling in the pit of my stomach as a hard, knotted ball of anxiety. As if I didn't dread these damned events enough, without the added torment of my current state-of-mind and the uncertainty of whether Ethan would show or not. I didn't think I could bear the pain of seeing him if he did, but by the same token, couldn't bear the counterattack from my father if he didn't. There was, of course, one simple solution… Fuck the whole thing off. Without further reflection, I leaned over and threw them in the trash.

"I take it we're not glamming it up tomorrow night, then?" Jia leaned against the doorjamb from where, it would seem, she'd been watching me.

"I can think of easier, less painful ways to spend the evening. A sharp blade and a hot bath should do it," I spat callously.

A fine indentation appeared in the usually flawless space between her brows, making me instantly regret my outburst. I hadn't been a good friend to her of late. I'd shut her down and vetoed every attempt she'd made to talk through my problems with me, telling her only the minutest snippets of information. Divulging my feelings and fears, well… it just wasn't the way I worked. I tended to compartmentalize my emotions, lock them up in an unused section of my mind to ultimately fester.

"Sorry," I said contritely, raising my hand to rub at the tension in my neck. "I'm not myself. I know I haven't been much use to you around here lately. I'll get my shit together, I promise." I pushed to my feet and smoothed down the black silk material of my jumpsuit. It was a simple but stylish design, wide-legged and backless with a halter neck.

"Where do you want me?"

"Sit the fuck down, bitch. I've got this shit in hand." She pushed a glass of champagne at me, which I felt was safe to sip, as she'd virtually force fed me a fine Chinese meal she'd ordered in about an hour earlier. I sat down and took a grateful sip, savoring the icy effervescence on my tongue, before the bubbles slid down my throat to explode like popping-candy in the depths of my belly. It felt warm and soothing.

"You know, I can handle things here if you want to take off," Jia said cautiously. "I mean… I'm not saying you should. Only if you can't face it, I'll just… make something up. I'll say you got sick."

The idea was tempting. I'd wished so many times over the course of the week that I'd never agreed to showcase, but who the hell had heard of an exhibition opening where the photographer didn't show—except when they were dead.

"No. Thanks, but I should stick around." I pushed to my feet again and walked past her in the direction of the exhibition area. "I'll go run my eye over things."

It was the first time I'd wandered through the twisted corridor to look over the completed display since changing the theme. Suddenly, the prospect of viewing an interpretation of my own state-of-mind, up there in black and white print, where anyone could glimpse through the windows of my tortured soul, was disconcerting, at best.

The showcase began with some of my very early work, before I'd even realized how much the images I chose to capture revealed my mood and inner feelings. A few years ago, when I turned twenty-one and had finally gained access to my inheritance, my father—suddenly having no further financial responsibility for me—had celebrated by packing my bags. So, with only my own rules to abide by and nowhere in particular I needed to be, I'd taken off for a while and driven cross-country.

Initially, I'd embraced the freedom. Being lonely while living among familiar faces could be horribly oppressive, but the trip had soon led me to the stark, daunting reality that I was just as lonely, only now I was alone all by myself.

The pictures, which now lined the walls of the makeshift zigzagging corridor before me, reflected that realism. Some were of landscapes, largely taken when I'd driven through the Great Plains. It'd seemed like a place where time was endless—a place that didn't lead anywhere, just broad, flat land and vast infinite bleakness. In one, I'd captured the image of a lone tree standing in the midst of miles upon miles of nothingness. It stood exposed and vulnerable, its branches reaching up beseechingly at the thunderous sky looming ominously overhead, like outstretched arms begging for mercy.

And then there were several images of buildings—an array of desolate, neglected, ramshackle houses, factories, and warehouses. All had been abandoned to survive against the unpredictability of nature, but all had sustained it. Despite their neglected, beat-up appearance, the cracks in their walls, their unstable foundations, they continued to stand, categorically refusing to collapse and crumble in defeat.

Alongside them were more depictions of hopelessness, doom, and isolation. One was of a simple passageway, a door standing half-open at the end. It had been taken inside a derelict house, the walls encasing nothing but sadness and gloom. There was no clue as to what lay beyond the door, just darkness and emptiness, and fear of the unknown.

Then there was the homeless woman—the image a far cry from the humor of the two men with the newspaper on a Central Park bench. She was crouched in a shop doorway, head bowed, clutching her knees for comfort. The hopelessness in her eyes told of a lifetime of misfortune and a future of uncertainty—nowhere to go and no one to turn to.

The final picture in the series had been shot at ground level. The image followed a set of seemingly infinite railroad tracks into the mouth of a dark, foreboding tunnel, with no promise of light or that the darkness would ever come to an end.

A novice would see a bunch of depressing snapshots. But those among us with a psychoanalytic eye would no doubt be handing me their therapist's contact details. Collectively, the images were a statement. The words in bold, shouty capitals and underlined appeared to yell, "Take a peek at my fucked-upness everyone, because I'm no longer able to hide it." Maybe I didn't have the capacity to divulge my fears and feelings verbally, but these images spoke louder than words ever could.

"Happy?" Jia muttered, popping her head around the corner.

I cocked a brow, my mouth twisting wryly. "Evidently not."

The sound of the buzzer at the front entrance broke through the tension. The exhibit didn't officially open until six and it was only five-twenty, too early even for the waitstaff. Jia moved to the foyer to get a better view of the door.

"Shit!" she hissed, moving back out of sight. "It's that fucker, Wilde."

My heart barreled into my mouth, my head suddenly swooning from the frantic, racing speed of my elevating pulse.

Ethan was here.

For the first time since I'd left him alone in my apartment, I knew exactly where he was. I was terrified, yet for some unknown reason, I also felt a surge of hope blooming in the depths of my awareness.

"See what he wants and get rid of him, but tell him I'm not here," I whispered breathlessly.

Hurriedly, I ducked behind the partition walls of the meandering corridor, knowing that the screens would keep me out of sight, but not out of earshot. I heard the door chime as it opened and some vague mumbling, before the sound of footsteps moving swiftly through the foyer and into the exhibit corridor.

"I told you, she's not here. What do you want, Wilde?" Jia demanded.

"I need to speak to her. I thought the exhibition opened tonight. Where is she?"

His husky, familiar voice curled around my frozen heart like a blanket, the effect like that of an electric defibrillator attempting to restore it to its normal rhythm, pumping back the life that had miserably drained away. A sudden aching need developed in my chest, the pieces of my shattered heart stirring from the mere proximity of him as he drew closer.

"I'm not sure," Jia answered impatiently, "she said she might be back later. I'm overseeing the exhibit."

"What are these? These images aren't the ones she selected…" His voice faded out. He was looking at the photographs. I'd discussed the original theme with Ethan on several occasions, giving him a significant insight into what my display would include. Any fool could see that the pieces on display did not denote the subject matter we'd discussed.

"No, *The Essence of Hope and Optimism* was shelved. Funny enough, she wasn't feeling it. Ya know? The whole *life's a bowl of cherries* shit. So she revised—can't think why." Jia's tone oozed sarcasm.

"And this *is* what she's feeling?" he asked quietly.

A few moments passed.

"Yeah," Jia finally answered. "This is what she's feeling. The series is entitled *Broken*. Tell me, Wilde… what do you see when you look at them?"

What the hell was she doing? I'd told her to get rid of him, not engage him in a full-blown, analytical conversation about my fucked-up art. My heart was hammering so damn loud, I was sure he would hear it if he came any closer.

Ethan was silent. I sensed him moving slowly down the corridor toward me, quietly perusing the photos. Then I noticed a slither of light shining through the tiny gap between two sections of the divider walls, where they'd been hinged together to form a diagonal slant in the zigzag formation. I shuffled silently down toward it, repositioning myself to peek through the narrow space into the corridor beyond.

After giving Ethan a minute or so to respond, Jia continued.

"I'll tell you what I see, shall I? I see one screwed-up little girl whose been abandoned in the dark, alone, to fend for herself—again. That's what these shots tell me. And you know what else? I'm staring at the motherfucker who put her back in that bleak, despairing place she thought she'd finally crawled out of."

Holy fuck, is that really who I am? I glanced down at myself in horrified shame that I should be so blatantly consumed with self-pity. *Is that what everyone will see?*

A flicker of movement in my peripheral vision drew my attention back to the gap in the wall, and suddenly he was there, right in front of me, only the divider wall standing between us. His physical, touchable form charged my body with sensory overload, and I began to tremble. The energy which seemed to emanate from his aura was so powerful I could almost feel his touch and smell the scent of his skin. I wanted him—needed him so badly in that moment that I thought I might actually die if I was denied him.

And then I saw his face.

Pain was etched into every curve and contour of that usually flawless face, contorting it with pure, raw emotion. If Jia thought you could see into my tortured soul though the images I took, you only needed to take one look at Ethan's face to see that his agony mirrored mine unequivocally.

A sudden intake of breath gasped noisily from my lips, so taken aback by the sight of him. His eyes widened in shock at the sound and then began to dart about, frantically seeking out the source of the noise. Finally they settled on the tiny opening, his gaze narrowing in an effort to see through the gap. I knew that he wouldn't be able to see me, as I was hidden in the shadows, but he'd heard me. And he sensed me as I'd sensed him. He was so acutely aware of my presence, his gaze locked—unseeing—into mine. A rush of sorrow and remorse flooded his expression, his lips trembling as they parted to mouth silently, *I'm sorry.*

Sorry?

Oh! The agony I'd seen on his face wasn't evidence of his broken heart, as I'd first thought. It was acknowledgement of his guilt and regret that he'd broken mine. What I saw delineated in his flawless face was pure pity.

"Well, have you nothing to say?" Jia's accusatory tone broke the excruciating silence.

Without a second's delay, I moved, swiftly emerging from my hiding place. I needed to put a stop to this pitiful fiasco. "That's enough, Jia!" I warned, entering the corridor. And then in a more gentle tone, added, "Give us a minute, will you?"

"What the hell, Angel, he needs to see—"

"Leave it, Jia! He doesn't need to see anything. They're just pictures, they don't *mean* anything—much less what I'm *feeling*. They were taken years ago, for fuck's sake. Now, I know Mr. Wilde is a very busy man, so let's give him the opportunity to say what he's come to say and then he can go. I'm sure his *fiancée* must be wondering where he is."

Ethan flinched, physically taking a step back from the impact of my words.

"Have it your way." Jia turned on her heel, moving off in the direction of the office.

I turned to meet Ethan's gaze, drinking in the sight that I'd missed until my body physically ached. Even through his anguish, he was exquisitely beautiful. He was dressed casually in slim-fit jeans and a crumpled T-shirt—that looked like it had been slept in—with a black leather jacket and chukka boots. His scandalously sexy hair had that artfully mussed-up look and his beautiful, vivid blue eyes bore into mine with an expression I no longer dared to try and interpret. I looked away quickly, knowing that I would dissolve if I didn't.

"How are you?" His voice was soft and raw, the weight of his penetrating gaze burning a hole through my heart as he studied me intently.

"I'm good. I'm fine. Busy," I shot at him. "What is it you want, Ethan?"

Suddenly, he seemed to harden before my eyes, withdrawing to a psychologically safe distance and pulling on a layer of indifference to rival mine. Crossing his arms over his chest protectively, he pivoted on his heel and began to pace up and down.

"It's about tomorrow night—the charity dinner. I don't know how he got a hold of it, but your father is aware of... of our separation. Apparently, he approached Rebecca with a personal invitation to the dinner. I'm assuming he wants to make certain I'll stick by my word regarding the promise of a fat donation."

I don't know whether the searing pain of being stabbed in the back came more from the verification that Rebecca was still very much in the picture, or my father's relentless betrayal. Either way, I was all out of words so I said nothing, just pointed my chin at him in cold indignation.

He waited a few seconds, and when I didn't respond, he went on. "I'm informed that Rebecca plans to attend with or without me. I'm afraid I have no control over what she does, nor do I care," he added quickly, "but I wanted to forewarn you that she's going to be there."

The muscles in my face flinched with the effort to contain my emotions, but I still didn't speak.

"Angel, I want you to know that I'll happily decline the invitation if you wish. But I didn't want to just not show—and have you suffer the backlash from your father."

My throat was dry and tight, restricting as if the fingers of a fisting hand were closing around it. I swallowed hard to ease the pressure and opened my mouth to speak. My voice was smaller than I intended it to be, and the energy it took to form the words was immense.

"Do what you want, Ethan. I'll endure the consequences and survive, whatever—I usually do. But it was polite of you to consider me, thank you. Was there anything else?"

For a moment, he seemed to examine my eyes and face, as if he were seeking for something more than what my words had offered. And for one horrible second, I worried that my mask had slipped and he was peering into my soul. When defeat finally settled onto his features I knew he hadn't found what he was looking for. In silent dismay he shook his head.

"Goodbye, then, Ethan."

He blinked and without another word, turned and left.

I didn't wait for the door to close before I spun around and stormed down the hall to the office, a sudden rush of anger fuelling my defiance. Crouching down next to my desk, I scooped the charity dinner tickets out of the trash, and threw one on the desk in front of Jia.

"Looks like Cinderella's going to the ball after all," I declared.

Jia gazed at me with a combination of relief and awe, and something else—it was as if she hadn't seen me in a while and my sudden arrival was a pleasant surprise. She smiled and glanced down at her watch. "Well, you'd better get the hell out of here before anyone arrives. Get an early night, because tomorrow I want you looking like one hot bitch who's ready to turn some heads. You need to sass it up, girl."

Without a second's hesitation, I nodded, picked up my purse, and made for the door.

"Oh, and... Angel? Good to have you back."

"Oh, I'm back, alright. I've been screwed over for the very last time." I blew her a kiss. "I'll see you tomorrow."

Outside on the sidewalk, I dipped my hand into my purse and retrieving my cell, scrawled through the directory until I found the number I was looking for. My finger hovered above the call button for a brief, uncertain second before pressing it quickly in case I changed my mind. The person at the other end answered swiftly, their voice a blend of hope and pleasant surprise.

"Angel?"

"James... About that date..."

CHAPTER EIGHT

O n Friday, I shopped until I was ready to drop. Choosing the right evening gown for the night's event was crucial. As Jia had suggested, I planned to turn heads and had spent an obscene amount of money in order to do it.

James had been stunned, but overjoyed to receive my call. I'd apologized swiftly for my aloofness the night before, explaining that running into him had taken me by surprise, and that maybe I'd been a bit hasty when rejecting his offer to be my date for the night. He'd laughed and said he'd be stoked to accompany me and would pick me up at six-thirty.

Okay, so it wasn't the exact truth. Changing my mind about seeing James again had been an impulsive decision, and admittedly, one which had been influenced by the unexpected actions of others. But sometimes, acting on a whim was fate's way of telling you which direction to go in—especially when your head was royally fucked, which mine apparently was. Maybe, I was supposed to be with James and we'd been thrown back together for a reason—I'd forget about Ethan in time. Or maybe I was just being plain selfish and manipulating the situation to suit me.

Jia had once said to me, "Angel, in life you can either be the statue or the pigeon—you choose." Well, I was tired of being crapped all over. It was my turn to be the goddamn pigeon.

Not wanting to rush things, I'd arranged to meet James in the lobby. Although my apartment wasn't the sacred haven it used to be, having someone in my living space so soon after Ethan seemed way too—intimate.

When the elevator door opened into the lobby, I was momentarily teleported back to the night of mine and Ethan's first date, when I'd done exactly the same thing and met him in the lobby. For a second, I could have sworn it was Ethan standing there, looking debonair in his fine tux and bow tie, and had to blink a few times to see that it was James.

He gazed at me adoringly, and I smiled warmly in return. He was just as dashing and well-groomed as the Ethan in my fleeting fantasy had been, but the effect was altogether different. There was a notable absence of electrified fluttering deep within my core when I looked at James. And yet the mere memory of seeing Ethan standing there had stirred an instant, heated arousal. A stab of disappointment ensued, but I was careful to avoid wearing any evidence of it on my face.

"You look... amazing. Actually, no, amazing just doesn't do you justice, Angel." He flashed a face-splitting grin in my direction, and I couldn't help but respond in the same way, jubilant in the knowledge that I'd achieved the effect I'd been hoping for.

Despite the mingling of dread and anxiety that'd had my stomach wringing itself out for the most part of the day, I felt confident and resolute and freaking sexy. The dress was a floor-length curve-kissing design with a slashed neckline and an up-to-there side slit. The delectable bronze colored fabric draped down my back, pooling just above the crack of my butt, creating an ultra-sensuous backless style with the rest of the fit and flare skirt flowing fluidly to the floor. The warm, bronze metallic shimmered in the light, reflecting in the browns of my eyes and hair. The result was downright foxy.

My hair was swept up at the sides to create height and then teased into dramatic tumbling curls, which spilled over my shoulders and down my back. I'd completed the look with dark smoky eyes, exaggerated lashes, and nude glossy lips. In my ears, I wore simple pearl studs, but no other jewelry.

"Why, thank you very much. You look pretty hot yourself, splodge," I said, smiling.

At first, he looked taken aback, surprised that I'd referred to him by the pet name I'd given him when we were together, but then he relaxed, smiling at the familiarity. Splodge referred to a small, fingerprint sized birthmark, which nestled snuggly between his hipbone and treasure trail, and resembled an irregular shape, which I'd once described as a splodge.

James took my hand and grazed my knuckles with a gentle kiss. "Come on, I've got a car out front." He turned and offering me his arm, led me outside to a waiting town car.

We made small talk in the comfort of the car on the way to the opulent, seven hundred room hotel where the event was being held. All the time, I tried hard to focus on my breathing, taking long steady breaths, in and out, in my attempt to remain calm. In a matter of minutes, I would be in the same room as Ethan, Rebecca Staunton, and my father, all at the same time. But for some reason I couldn't place, I felt abnormally strong and determined.

We emerged from the car and moved swiftly through the camera flashes of the assembled cluster of press, wanting to avoid any unnecessary attention. These events were usually the only time I was acknowledged in the public eye as Dr. Harley Lawson's daughter— probably because it was the only time he acknowledged me, period. We crossed over into the splendid lobby, done out in Italian marble and handwoven carpets, and made our way through the crowds of people to the reception room impressively designed with trompe l'oeil panels and gilded crown moldings.

The moment we stepped inside the room we ran right into my father, brothers, and several members of the press. Adam's eyes found me immediately, a wave of relief flooding his face. He'd clearly been trying to stave off the photographers and my father's wrath until I arrived. Aaron smiled smugly and glanced down at his watch in a what-time-do-you-call-this fashion.

"Ah, here she is. Angelica, a moment for the press." My father smiled a sweet, but incredibly false smile as he waved me over to the group.

"I'm sorry, James." I felt bad about leaving him alone so soon. "I promise I won't be long."

"No worries, I'll grab us a drink."

I joined the group and turned toward the flash of the cameras, pasting on my best fake smile.

"Thank Christ, I thought you weren't coming," Adam whispered in my ear. "I thought the old man was going to blow his stack."

"So, what's new?" I muttered.

"Don't antagonize him, Angelica," he warned.

In response, I offered him a sideways glance of disgust. When had I ever needed to do anything to fuel my father's anger? The fact that I merely existed infuriated him. But I didn't say this, because Adam was already over it and quickly added, "And what the hell happened with Wilde? He showed up with someone else."

Although I'd known to expect it, I still felt the blood physically drain from my face. I realized that I'd half hoped Ethan wouldn't show; it would make this whole debacle so much easier. But he was here—and he was with *her*. And I was with James. That was the game wasn't it? The game of take what you want, do whatever you please, and to hell with whoever you hurt in the process? The game everyone had been playing, but me—until now.

Suddenly, something caught my eye. Jia had secreted herself in amongst the press, using her petite stature to stay virtually unnoticed, but as was the intention, I'd spotted her easily. Her thumb and finger were in her mouth spreading her lips wide across her face. The gesture said, *smile for the camera, bitch,* and it was just the push I needed to spur my momentum. I did as I was told, and with renewed resolve smiled a false but face-splitting grin.

A few minutes later, I separated myself discreetly from the group, escaping quickly while my father was still busy talking to the press.

Grabbing Jia, I made my way over to James, who stood waiting patiently by the bar holding two ice-cold flutes of champagne. I took one gratefully and downed over half of it, relishing the soothing, emboldening heat of the alcohol.

"Jia, you remember James. He kindly agreed to be my date tonight." I smiled as I watched her attempting to conceal her surprise. I'd told her the briefest details about my bumping into him, but hadn't warned her that I'd invited him along as my date. For some reason, I'd kind of worried she might try and talk me out of it.

"Oh." Her expression implied she was processing this new revelation, and after a beat decided she approved. "Okay, yep, smart move." Turning to James, she eyed him with an austere warning. "You're on my shit list, Foster, be very fucking wary."

"It's nothing less than I expected—or deserve. I promise I'll be on my best behavior. Oh and it's lovely to see you again, Jia. You look amazing."

"Hmm." For the moment, she seemed placated by his outward remorse, helped no doubt by his added flattery. "Well, I'm aware of how hot I look, actually, but it's nice that you point it out."

We laughed, amused by Jia's bullishness, but I had to admit she did look stunning in a shimmering, figure-hugging, electric blue number. Even with fantastically-high killer-heels, she still only came up to my shoulder. If you didn't know Jia, you would be tempted to reach down and pinch her cheek, or pull her into a bear hug and pat her on the back. But those who possessed even the slightest knowledge of her knew better than to try.

Something about the way her smug smile slithered off her face, to be replaced with hostile indignation, as she stared beyond me over my shoulder warned me of Ethan's approach even before I felt his touch.

The warm skin of his hand melted into the curve of my naked, lower back, and my body responded without warning. Suddenly my breath was uneven, my pulse racing, as waves of scorching lust and desire bloomed within me. I'd yearned for the feel of his skin against mine, and just for a second, I closed my eyes to savor his touch. That touch alone possessed me like nothing I could have ever imagined, and like a drug it left me craving like an addict for more.

"Angelica." His voice was low and husky, his tongue seductively caressing my name.

I shot Jia a silent request to remain quiet and turned my face toward him. Ethan regarded me closely, his sculpted, sensual lips set in a hard impassive line. I gasped, struggling for breath at the sight of him, taken aback, yet again, by his unmitigated, devastating beauty. The familiar, intrinsic connection between us was immediate, like his physical form was somehow an extension of mine that had been crudely severed—the close proximity making it almost impossible to refrain from reaching out and grasping what was mine. Would he ever fail to have this effect on me?

Reluctantly, he tore his gaze away from mine to glance around the group. His eyes flicked fleetingly over Jia, who mercifully held her tongue, before coming to rest suspiciously on James. "Aren't you going to introduce me, Angel?" Ethan probed, his eyes boring into James.

Blood roared noisily in my ears as my pulse rate elevated. I took a cautious sip of champagne to dampen my rapidly drying mouth and inhaled deeply hoping to control the tremor in my voice that was certain to betray me. "Yes, of course. I'd like you to meet James... Dr. James Foster." Ethan's eyes widened in instant, horrified recognition of the name. "James, this is Ethan Wilde. He's... he's someone I used to know."

Ethan paled and pivoted to face me. "May I have a moment in private?"

I took a moment to absorb the look on his face. The tight bunching of his jaw muscles betrayed his anguish, and I almost reached out to smooth and soothe away the ache.

And then I saw *her.*

Rebecca stood a few feet behind him, a look of fury and frustration marring her prissy, upturned features. One look at her filled me with vehemence.

I pointed my chin toward her, my expression dripping with pure loathing. "Something tells me you don't have a moment to spare. It looks like you're being called to heel."

"Ethan. Come," Rebecca demanded in a starchy voice, right on cue.

Ethan's expression transformed the second he heard her repugnant voice. He glanced sideways in her direction, but without looking at her—a savage snarl akin to a ferocious, menacing dog formed on his lips. It was a look I'd never seen on his face before. The look of a man who'd been stretched to the limit of his endurance. He glanced once at James, then at me, pivoted, and stalked gracefully and silently away toward the dining room. Rebecca scurried after him, like a rat gnawing at his ankles.

My knees buckled slightly, unseen beneath the fabric of my dress. The altercation had left me drained, and I felt the overwhelming urge to crumple to the floor. I glanced at Jia, who was glaring gob-smacked but admiringly at me, and then at James whose expression was unreadable.

"It looks like we're moving into dinner. Shall we?" he suggested, offering me his arm. I took it gratefully and we walked through to join the other diners.

After briefly checking the seating plan, we took our place at the table. Alongside Jia, who sat to my right, and James to my left, nine other people were seated at our table, most of whom were money-rich professionals or socialites. An old colleague of James's was seated at the same table with his wife and immediately engaged him in a conversation. I heaved a sigh of relief. At least it would buy me some time to think of a reasonable explanation for what had just happened.

The deep rumbling of my father's exhibitionistic voice grated on my frayed nerves, and a glance over my shoulder confirmed that he and both of my brothers were seated at the table directly behind me. I shuddered, cringing with the almost physical burden of their close proximity.

Mustering the courage to glimpse around the room, I found my gaze drawn directly to Ethan's. Much to my dismay he was seated at the table to our immediate left, directly in my line of sight. Desolate blue eyes gazed hopelessly into mine. Unable to turn away, I stared back, trying to read him, but there was nothing. He looked empty, blank— almost dead behind the eyes. He blinked a few times, refocusing, as he was drawn grudgingly into a conversation with the man who was seated next to him.

I turned my attention to Rebecca sitting to his other side. She shot me a venomous look before she too joined the conversation. She spoke animatedly, her expressions and overstated hand gestures seeming exaggerated and false. *Who was she performing for?* I wondered.

The meal was served and I poked at my food, paying little attention to my tablemates. I nodded and smiled at the appropriate moments and spoke only when necessary, ensuring my answers were brief but polite. Jia and James appeared to be keeping everybody amused, which meant that mercifully little attention was paid to me.

I took the opportunity to study Rebecca Staunton. Her strawberry blond hair had been kinked into deliberate springy curls, which appeared to bounce the more hyperbolic she became. She wore a vibrant fuchsia-colored dress with an asymmetrical bodice and single embellished shoulder strap. More floral adornments wound around the apparel, running all the way through the ruffled skirt. The overall effect was—busy.

Jia giggled and nudged me. "Is *that* what all this fuss is about?" She nodded toward Rebecca for the sake of clarity. "So, what is it she thinks she's got that you haven't, apart from the obvious uncanny resemblance to Bo-Fucking-Peep? Because whatever it is, she's pissin' in the wind, I'll tell you that for nada. I mean, it's evident she doesn't look in the mirror very often, or she wouldn't have ventured out looking like she just stepped out of a nursery rhyme—that dress is a fucking car crash. And don't even get me started on the hair."

I puckered my lips and made a wincing face. It was a low but justified blow, and I couldn't help the smile which ghosted across my lips.

Jia continued to rant. "If I were to give the bitch some advice, I'd tell her to take a close look at Wilde's face and ask her what she sees when he looks at her."

I turned my head to study them, trying to see what she was seeing. "What do you mean?"

"Hatred," Jia continued in my ear, "pure, unadulterated fucking loathing. If you don't see it, bitch, you've gotta be blind. And pretty fucking stupid too, if you don't see the grief on his face when he looks at you. The only other person I've ever seen looking so dejected and completely broken—is you." She halted when she saw my look of astonishment, adding quietly, "Just sayin'."

Turning my attention back in their direction, I studied them, trying to make sense of what she was saying. I tried to look past the guilt and pity I read in his expression when he looked at me, tried to acknowledge the tension in his shoulders as they turned slightly away from her in revulsion. But I couldn't. Because if what she said was true—if he hated her—why didn't he put an end to all this? Why didn't he just send her away?

"I know he fucked up," Jia went on, "but look at him, would you? The guy's shackled to a freaking beast."

I couldn't have put it better myself, and strangely took some comfort knowing Jia could see it as well. It meant my judgment of her wasn't being influenced by sheer jealousy. "He must see something in her or he wouldn't be with her. I don't know, Jia. Every time I close my eyes, I see the two of them together. Maybe that's it. I know sex is important to him, maybe he just can't say no to her."

Jia almost choked on a sip of wine. "Are you shitting me? He'd sooner chop off his own dick than risk losing you by letting someone else take a ride on it—especially that mess." She nodded toward Rebecca. "I'll admit, at first, I thought he was just another red-hot billionaire with too much money and a hyperactive nut sack. But I've seen the way he looks at you—and you're killing him, bitch."

Her words were like an ice-cold splash in the face. "It's not up to me though, Jia. If it was me he wanted, he would have told her and sent her packing, but he hasn't. He's different with her, weird, like he's scared of her or something."

"Well, maybe he is. One thing's for sure, what you see there isn't a relationship, Angel. Not a conventional one, anyway. I don't know what it is, but there's something else going on with those two. Maybe you should hear him out."

Suddenly, my frozen heart twisted with guilt. He'd tried to explain what was going on that day at my apartment, but I'd pushed him away—didn't want to hear it. I'd told him I didn't love him and the lie had been crushing me on the inside ever since. What if there was truth in what he'd told me that day? What if I should have trusted him to deal with it in his own way, like he'd pleaded with me to do?

"What if it's too late? What if I'm too late? What if I've pushed him too far?" I glanced guiltily at James and wondered for the hundredth time about the state of my sanity. "What have I done, Jia?"

"Nothing that can't be undone. You've both made mistakes."

I shook my head. "I don't know."

"Angel, what are you afraid of? Okay, so you got burned and it hurt like hell—but you're not dead."

She was right. Everything she said was right. I'd feared hearing him out, because I was afraid of lies, afraid of being hurt, afraid of being with him because I was afraid of losing him. But I wasn't dead. Being afraid wasn't the thing that was killing me. The pain of living without him was. The pain of living without him had made me wish I was dead. And that was far worse.

"Fight for him, Angel. Give him a reason to buy her a ticket on the next flight out of here. Show him you love him."

"*Love?*" I gasped. She'd used the word so effortlessly.

"Yes, *love*. That's what I see when I look at the two of you."

"I thought you always said love was for pussies?" I snapped.

"I changed my mind. I now think it's the asswipes who don't give love a chance that are pussies. Yes, it's a scary thing to entrust someone else with your heart, and they might fuck up a few times before they get the feel of it. But it can't kill you. So don't blow it, bitch. You deserve to be happy more than anyone I know."

She grabbed her purse and slid her chair gently away from the table. "It looks like the speeches are about to start." She nodded in the direction of the stage, where my father and several others had gathered. "And frankly, your old man spouting shit about how much he cares about other people's misguided kids, when he can barely remember your name, could well make me hurl. So if Selena Gomez comes looking for me, tell her I'm at the bar." She winked and pushed to her feet.

"Jia?" I grabbed her arm as she was about to leave. "Thanks."

"That's what I'm here for, bitch." She shrugged and slinked away.

I gazed over at Ethan and my frozen heart began to thaw. For the first time, I dared to peer through the murkiness and confusion in my mind, allowing myself to see his despair. He *was* broken. I'd just been too wrapped up in my own misery to see it. But was I brave enough to surrender to my feelings for him? To compromise my heart and embrace my love for him? I'd spent years bolstering the damage caused by rejection, making myself resilient—could I afford to become vulnerable again? And what if Jia was wrong? What if he was just riddled with guilt and that's what was written all over his face. If I concede, could I be exposing myself to more pain, more hurt—more rejection? Christ, it was all so confusing, my thoughts and feelings were in tatters.

Suddenly, I became vaguely mindful of someone talking to me, dragging my awareness back to the table.

"Angel?" James urged me from my musings.

"W-what? Sorry, what?" I blinked and turned to look at him.

"I was just saying what a talented photographer you are." His brow furrowed as he observed my faraway expression. "Are you okay, babe, you seem a thousand miles away?" As he said the words, James reached out and closed his hand over mine, bringing it to his lips to graze it with a gentle, meaningful kiss.

My gaze flew to Ethan, afraid that he may have witnessed the intimate gesture. I knew how jealous he could be, and my own instinctive reaction to preserve his feelings had left me in no doubt where my heart belonged. It was well and truly devoted to him. The look of horror and doubt on his face corroborated my fears. It was a look that said I'd betrayed him in the worst possible way. His pain was etched in the downturned curves of his beautiful lips as he mouthed the words, *please, no.*

Without a second's hesitation, I snatched my hand away from James and looked down at the table, my face burning with shame and regret. What was I doing? Why had I brought James here? What was I thinking? How could I have got this all so wrong? It was bad enough that I'd used James for my own selfish reason, falsely building his hope that there could be something between us again. But even more, the idea that I'd inflicted unnecessary suffering or torment on Ethan was utterly abhorrent to me.

Suddenly, an eerie shiver ran down my spine and my body stiffened, as if I were responding to an approaching threat, like an animal sensing imminent danger from a predator. I was about to turn to see what had caused the reaction, when I realized someone was standing at my shoulder.

Rebecca bent down toward my ear, her proximity so close she was practically leaning on me. A sweet, repugnant smell emanated from her pores, making my stomach roil, and as she began to speak, I could feel the heat of her breath against my ear.

"You appear to have become something of an encumbrance to my fiancé." Her condescending tone had my teeth on edge. "And frankly, that causes me a degree of irritation. For some reason, the silly boy thinks he may have misled you and has asked me to give you something as recompense for your, um… disappointment. Use it prudently, create some distance between you—a new start, a new city, perhaps. It's not a request. " She paused for a few seconds, no doubt for impact, and then thrust something into my hands—a folded piece of paper. Then leaning in further, to ensure she wasn't overheard, added, "Actually, I think the gesture is rather excessive. I know people who will rape you and leave you for dead for a fraction of the cost, but I suppose we can call that *Plan B*. Now, be a good girl, take this extremely generous gift and disappear—or I *will* make that call."

The air caught in my windpipe as I gasped, appalled by her savage words, her vile threat sickening me to the core. She straightened and glared down at me with such venom and malevolence, I could feel myself physically recoil. She sniggered, pivoted on her heel, and sashayed as innocuously as she could manage back to her table.

Silence fell around the room and all attention turned to the stage. My father walked confidently up to the podium, tapped the microphone, and cleared his throat. I stared down at the folded piece of paper in my trembling hands, my heart thudding loudly against my chest.

"Ladies and gentlemen…" Dr. Harley Lawson began his speech.

Slowly, I unfolded the piece of paper. It was a check, made out to me, and signed by Ethan. The amount was for five million dollars. Scalding tears pooled in my eyes as I tried to breathe past the hard, burning lump searing my throat. I stared down at the check, trying to absorb the enormity of its significance. What I held in my hands was a payoff—Ethan's ultimate betrayal. And it was so much more than my heart could bear. My body began to shake and without warning, an audible sob escaped from my throat.

"What is it?" James put his hand on my arm. "Angel, what's wrong?"

"I… I need to leave. Now," I stammered, and without waiting for a response, I flung my chair back and pushed to my feet. My blundering haste caused my glass to tip over. It rolled to the edge of the table and tumbled to the floor, shattering into tiny pieces. The noise in the silence of the room was thunderous, and all eyes turned to stare at me.

My father halted mid-sentence. "What the…?"

I turned and fled, racing out of the dining room and through the hallway into the corridor, leaving the stunned silence behind me. My pace was slow, hindered by my dress and heels and my trembling legs, and as I turned a corner, I noticed the door to an empty room standing open. It seemed to beckon me, so I stepped inside the door, leaning flat against the wall in an attempt to calm my shallow, ragged breathing.

"Angel!" Ethan rounded the corner entering the room, his eyes blazing questioningly into mine. "What happened? What the fuck did she say to you?"

"This!" I smashed the hand with the check against his chest, forcing it into him. "This is what she said, you bastard. If you wanted me gone, you should've just said. I don't need your fucking money—your pity alone makes me sick."

"What the fuck are you talking about?" he spat, grasping the check from my hand and staring at it incredulously. Suddenly, rage enveloped him. "I didn't write this!"

"Oh? If you look closely, you'll find your signature right there at the bottom."

"I *didn't* write this, Angelica. Why would I?"

"Why would you have a fiancée that you didn't tell me about?" I pushed my hands against his chest, trying to shove him out of my way. "You're a liar. Everything you've done and said is a lie. Get out of my way, Ethan," I shouted, my anger exploding like a rocket from the scramble of confused emotions inside me.

"No, I won't," he yelled, gripping me by the wrists, his fingers biting painfully into my flesh as he pushed me back against the wall. "Why are you doing this to me, Angel?"

"Why am *I* doing this to *you*?" Holy fuck, was he for real?

"Yes. Why did you bring him here? Why?" His words were bitter and accusing, and for a second I had no clue what he was referring to.

And then suddenly I realized—he was talking about James. I'd just been smacked with five million dollars' worth of betrayal and he could barely contain his fury because I'd brought a date.

"Did you fuck him, Angel?"

"What? N-no, of course not!"

"I don't believe you! I think you let him touch you!"

"No!"

Suddenly he released one arm, his hand sliding possessively to my breast. "Did he touch you here, Angel?"

"No!"

"Here?" He crushed his body against me, his thick erection pushing through the thin fabric of my dress to press covetously against my sex.

Despite the roughness of his touch and the thick layer of hurt and anger that surrounded me, I was suddenly overwhelmed with desire and the hot, burning need for him. I felt my body respond instinctively, my hips thrusting forward to meet the demanding jab of his eager cock. His hand shifted suddenly, releasing my breast and reaching up to grasp my face. Suddenly, his mouth was on mine, his tongue delving inside, deep and needy. The kiss was violent, claiming me—possessing me, and then he pulled away leaving me gasping, breathless, and desperate for more.

"Did he kiss you like that, Angel?" The words came out slowly, strangled with brutal emotion.

I shook my head as warm, salty tears spilled from my eyes and trickled gently down my face. My throat was tight, causing my answer to come out hoarse and scratchy. "No, Ethan. I swear to you."

Something unnamed flashed in his eyes before he closed them and leaned in toward me, his forehead against mine as he grappled for composure. When he spoke his tone was gentle but resolute. "I believe you, Angel. I believe what you tell me... because I believe in us. I believe you... because I saw the truth in your eyes."

He pulled back slowly, but only enough to allow him to look into my eyes. Then, running the pad of his thumb gently over my swollen lips, he reached up to place his palm firmly against my cheek, preventing my gaze from leaving his.

"Now look into my eyes, Angel. I see your truth—now you see mine. I *did not* write that check. Why would I do anything to push you even further away? Every day since you left me, I've clung onto the tiniest shreds of hope that you'll come back to me. That hope is the only thing that's kept me alive."

Something suddenly snapped inside me, realization striking like a bolt of lightning. Consumed with wild, violent fury, I snatched back the check and slithered from his grasp.

"Angel, what… where are you going?"

"There's something I need to do."

Unable to focus on anything or anyone, other than my goal, I rushed from the room and down the hallway, back in the direction I'd come. As I rounded the corner, Rebecca was striding down the corridor toward me, a menacing, unhinged look in her eyes.

"You stupid, gold-digging whore. What, five million isn't enough for you? You had to cause a scene?" She glimpsed swiftly over my shoulder to the end of the corridor where Ethan had emerged and was stood rooted to the spot. She immediately reined in her anger, her outward demeanor calming the instant she laid eyes on him.

Mine didn't.

I slammed the flat of my hand into her chest, in much the same way as I had with Ethan, only harder, forcing her back and pinning her against the wall. "No!" I hissed viciously. "Five million is *not* enough. There is *no* amount of money large enough to keep me away from him or him away from me."

Her eyes narrowed, burning into me with hatred. "Plan B, then," she whispered with a sneer.

"Angel, leave it," Ethan yelled down the corridor toward me.

Ignoring him, I tightened my grip, laying the length of my forearm against her chest with the full weight of my body. Then lifting my chin boldly, I whispered, "Bring it the fuck on, bitch. I'll take my chances, and I'll be waiting for you."

Rage boiled inside her, her milky white skin taking on a deep red, furious glow. "I'm going to make sure they fuck you up so badly, you'll think you're in Hell."

At that moment revulsion for that woman consumed me—a

loathing so intense and complete that it burned into my soul with the sharp, bitter corrosiveness of acid.

"I'm tired of hearing your whining, prissy little voice." I screwed my hand into a fist, crumpling the check within into a tight ball. Then raising my arm, I shoved it viciously into her sadistic mouth. "Why don't you keep this—because there is *nothing* you can show me of Hell that I haven't already seen." I used my thumb to give the paper one last shove, just deep enough to make her gag, and then released her.

She buckled, coughing and spluttering as she expelled the remnants of the check onto the floor. I spun to walk away, almost crashing straight into the flurry of rage that was my father.

"What in God's name do you think you are doing?" he bellowed. "Not content with making me a laughing stock, you're now attacking my personal guests."

I was in no mood for my father's relentless rounds of persecution, so I moved to walk around him wordlessly, my only form of response an exasperated glower.

He grasped my wrist, halting my progress, his fingers biting painfully into my flesh. "You always were a waste of fucking air, Angelica."

"Take your fucking hands off her!" Ethan's voice roared from behind me.

Swiftly taking advantage of the moment, I tugged my arm free and ran full pelt down the hallway toward the foyer, loosely aware of the ensuing chaos I'd left behind in my wake. But all I could think of was breaking free of the conflict and confinement and finding my escape.

When I pushed through the door and ran down the steps, James was waiting for me.

"There you are—I was worried." He opened the rear door of the town car and I clambered inside, sliding across to make room for him.

He climbed inside next to me and the car pulled out.

"Are you okay?" His voice was a tender, reassuring caress and suddenly guilt gripped me by the throat, choking back my response.

"You should have warned me he'd be there."

I turned to him as tears welled in my eyes again. "I'm so sorry, James. I—"

"Shh, no." He shook his head and took my hand in his. "You don't need to explain."

"Yes, I do. I shouldn't have taken you there. It was unfair and cruel of me. I don't even know what the hell I was thinking—"

"Angel, please, you really don't have to explain. You don't owe me a thing. Like you said, we had our time. I had my chance with you and I'm the one who blew it."

"It doesn't excuse my behavior. James, I… I used you."

He nodded on a shrug, his smile instantly assuaging my shame. "Well, maybe I deserved it. I think I owed you, after all. It's that motherfucking karma, come back to bite me on the ass again."

I smiled, grateful for his understanding and compassion. "Maybe you did deserve it a little bit." Laying my hand against his cheek, I leaned in and planted a chaste kiss on his lips. "You're a beautiful man. I hope beyond belief that you'll find happiness, James. And although I'm deeply ashamed of what I did tonight, I'm glad that we had this time to…"

"Settle the score?"

I shrugged in assent. "At least now I won't have a bitter taste in my mouth when I remember us. Instead, I'll always look back on us with fondness."

"Me too." He nodded on a smile. "And anytime you need a date, you know who to call. I mean, I'd fight for you now if I thought I'd get anywhere. But any fool can see where your heart belongs."

He was right. Amidst the car crash of emotions that were vying for position in my heart—the anger, the hurt, the fear—there was one that far outran the rest. My love for Ethan Wilde.

"What will you do?" James asked.

"I'm not sure I know," I answered honestly, turning to gaze through the window.

The truth was it didn't really matter how I felt. I could fight for Ethan all I liked, but unless he fought for me—for us, it would amount to nothing. Our relationship wouldn't survive an intrusion as destructive as Rebecca without a battle. And if Ethan wasn't prepared to wage a war, if he didn't stand up to Rebecca, what chance did we have? I didn't know what hold she had on him, but I knew without question it wasn't love. In fact, although I didn't claim to understand it, I was certain it was hate.

"He loves you—if that helps. That much is obvious."

James's words gave me hope. And as I recalled Jia's words of wisdom over dinner, and Ethan's words, when he'd admitted hope was the only thing keeping him alive, I began to believe for the first time that maybe we were big enough to beat this nightmare. Just like the whirlwind rollercoaster ride at the onset of our relationship. If we were both on board, we could conquer anything. Couldn't we?

With a hopeful but heavy heart, I resolved there was nothing I could do but wait and see. If Ethan was ready to take this journey, he would come to me. Until then, I'd have to patient.

We sat in silence, and after a while, the car pulled into my street, coming to a halt outside my apartment block. The driver got out and opened the door.

"Would you like me to come up?" James asked warmly.

I shook my head. "No. But thank you."

"Promise me one thing, Angel."

"What's that?"

"If it doesn't work out—hold on. It will get easier in time."

"What will?"

"The pain of a broken heart."

Suddenly, I felt despair hit me again, because deep down, I knew that what I'd experienced of it so far was crushing me, and I wasn't sure how much more I could endure.

"How can you be certain? How do you know?"

He kissed the back of my fingers. "Trust me, Angel. I know."

CHAPTER NINE

By the time I opened the door of my apartment, I was so emotionally and physically drained, I wasn't even sure which way was up. Sleep beckoned me, but the thought of spending another night on the floor of my closet was enough to have me searching my cupboards for a shot of something potent enough to dull the ache.

I found a bottle of vodka and was just wondering how much of it I would need to drink to crash on the sofa, when there was a faint knock at the door. I froze—my heartbeat hammering against the wall of my chest as Rebecca's sadistic threat resounded in my head. *I know people who will rape you and leave you for dead.* The knock came again, and I made my way slowly and silently toward the door and waited, straining my ears for any sound. It came again, louder this time, and I found myself scanning the room for something I could use as a weapon.

Suddenly, a loud thud hammered once against the door—the sound of a fist or a kick, and an exasperated curse, "Fuck!"

The noise startled me and I cried out.

"Angel?" A hoarse voice croaked from the other side of the door. I recognized the deep gravelly tone instantly, and without further hesitation, unlocked the door and heaved it open.

He was here.

I gazed at the man I loved with every inch of my being, standing in my doorway, his hands holding on to either side of the frame for support. Our gazes locked for the longest time, a question I couldn't pluck up the nerve to ask burning in my eyes.

Why are you here?

Was he here to take that journey with me, to fight for everything we'd built, to fight for me, for him—for us? I searched his expression for an answer, sucking in a deep breath of relief at the sight of it staring back at me. A desperate plea for permission to return to my life burned longingly in his eyes. Unable to tolerate the distance between us any longer, I nodded my assent and flung myself unashamedly into arms.

He grasped me to him tightly as I wrapped my legs around his waist, gasping great heaving breaths of his scent into my lungs, as if I'd been starved of him for far too long. Thrusting his hands into my hair, he held the back of my head and gazed into my eyes like I was his entire reason for living.

"Angel." He took my mouth, kissing me with the ferociousness of a dying man taking his last breath. Our teeth clashed briefly before his tongue pushed violently into my mouth to find mine, and then he was sucking and lashing at me in desperation.

"Angel, baby, my baby…" With my legs still wrapped around his waist, we stumbled inside and he kicked the door closed behind us.

"Wait," I cried. Suddenly, I was terrified. Terrified that I would give myself over to him once again, only for him to tell me it was over and that he couldn't be with me. "Wait, Ethan, please!" I pressed my hands against his straining biceps in a futile attempt to suppress his growing passion.

"Don't push me away, Angel. Please, I can't bear it anymore," he sobbed, catching my wrists and stilling my movements.

"But I'm afraid, Ethan. I'm terrified."

"Terrified? Of me?" The idea seemed to shatter him.

"Terrified of losing control—terrified of *losing* you. If this isn't real, if you can't be mine, completely mine and only mine, then you have to tell me now and I'll walk away. I'd much rather that, than be the one who's left behind again."

"I never left you for a single minute, Angel, and I never will, I promise. You're the one who left—you pushed *me* away."

"I didn't have a choice. You were leaving anyway. It was always just a matter of time."

"Why are you so sure this is doomed, Angel?"

"Because I don't deserve you. Giving me your heart and then snatching it away is God's punishment."

"You're so wrong, baby. My heart's never belonged to anyone but you. This isn't God's work, it's the Devil's sent to try us. But we will defeat him, Angel. And we'll defeat her—together. I'm so sorry for what I've put you through. Please give me a chance to put it right, I beg you. Please, just accept that we're meant to be. Let me in, baby, just feel it."

"I'm afraid." Tears coursed down my cheeks.

"Don't be afraid. I won't let you go, I promise. I'd die before I ever let you go again."

Electricity hung in the air between us, sizzling and crackling as our bodies buzzed with pent-up emotion and passion. I stared deep into his scorching blue eyes, misted with raw emotion and the irrefutable promise of his heart. Desire surged through my body, pooling in the depths of my core and my pulsing, longing sex.

Desperate to fill the aching void between us, I nodded urgently. "Yes. Take me, Ethan. I'm yours."

My words were his undoing, his voice raw with pain and relief as he sobbed, "I love you, Angel."

My frozen heart began to melt, and as my tears fused with his, the deep-down fear that I would never touch him again began to wane.

"I love you so much," he said again, but this time the words faded away inside my mouth as he kissed me, plunging his tongue inside and claiming me as his.

Pinning me to the wall with his hips, he found the slit in my dress and pulled it open and up, exposing me from the waist down. The tautness of his bulging cock fought, restrained against the fabric of his pants as he pressed it against my soaking cleft.

"I want you so badly, my body aches, Angel." He grasped at my panties, pushing his thumb through the delicate fabric and tearing them from my body. I gasped, wildly turned on by the hint of violence.

Swiftly, he sank to his knees and I braced my shoulders against the wall for support. Laying the flat of his hands along my inner thighs, he slid my legs open, gazing in awe at my sodden, pulsing flesh and tilting forward, closed his eyes, inhaling me deeply.

"Oh, baby, the sight of you, the smell of you—I've missed you so fucking much."

"Please, Ethan," I begged, desperate for him to soothe the almost painful building ache of desire.

At last, his fingertips grazed over my clit and down to my slick opening. My body quivered in the luxury of his long anticipated touch, as he began to rub my slickness over my heated sex the fingers of both hands spreading me. The feral moans and look of pained appreciation on his face was impossibly arousing.

"So wet. My Cinderella's so fucking wet." He sank a finger inside me. "Aahh, and hot, you're red-hot inside for me, baby."

A second finger slid inside, rubbing and massaging my sweet, aching spot. The pad of his thumb on his opposite hand began to rub in a circular motion over my clit, torturing me mercilessly as I began to pump my hips shamelessly against his fingers, my whole body tensing and burning with building pleasure.

Suddenly, he withdrew his fingers making me cry out, bereft and aching for more. He gazed up at me with red-rimmed eyes, full of pain and regret and yearning. Then, leaning forward he plunged his tongue inside me. I thrust my hands into his hair, gripping it tightly in bunched fists and moved against his mouth. Ethan continued to rub my clit with the pad of his thumb, thrusting his tongue inside me again and again, fucking me with his mouth until I could hold on no more.

"Come for me, Angel. I need to see you—to feel you—to taste you," he sobbed.

Every inch of my body tensed as the shock waves of my impending orgasm spread like the flames of a raging fire from my core and out, flooding my blood and organs. My rigid, trembling muscles clenched desperately around his decadent lapping until I exploded, coming uncontrollably into his hungry mouth. I cried out, screaming his name and sobbing through my ecstasy as the orgasm rolled on and on, singing through my veins.

My body sagged from the exhausting intensity of my climax, and instantly, Ethan was on his feet enfolding me in his arms. He carried me effortlessly across the room to the sofa, and set me down, my backside on the edge of the seat. His gaze never left mine as he shrugged out of his jacket and knelt between my open thighs.

Weary, but hungry for more, I reached down to unfasten his button and fly, eager to hasten the flesh-to-flesh contact that I'd been craving like a drug. I pushed his pants down past his hips, releasing his thick, hard cock, which fell heavily into my palms. He groaned at the feel of my touch, an almost painful, guttural noise grating from his throat. The sound was so deeply erotic that I thrust my hips toward him, desperate for his hot, hard length to penetrate me.

Folding my hands around him, I squeezed him into my fists, sliding up the length to the tip of his cock to run my thumb through the ridge and over the head. I groaned loudly when he quivered from my touch, the pressure of my thumb releasing a warm surge of pre-cum. Then, keeping him firmly grasped in one hand, I brought my thumb to my lips and suckled the juice of his arousal deep into my mouth. Ethan moaned and inched forward on his knees as I guided him toward my yearning entrance.

The head of his throbbing cock nudged against my clit as I nestled it between the folds of my quivering flesh. I spread my legs wider and folded them around him, pressing my calves to the back of his thighs in a vise-like clinch. Then, taking his exquisite face in my hands, I smoothed my thumbs through the tear tracks, attempting to erase the misery which seemed to haunt his perfect features. He mirrored my actions before resting his forehead against mine to gaze lovingly into my eyes.

"Please don't be afraid, baby. I would rather die than live without you—without this. Our connection is like a drug to me. I want to possess you as you possess me." He breathed heavily, in short, sharp gasps, his arousal and pure, raw emotion evident in every breath.

"Then never allow anything to tear us apart again. Promise me, E. Promise me that the only thing that will ever come between us is death itself."

"I promise you, Angel. With every breath in my body, I promise you."

I could feel the pulsing throb of his cock waiting eagerly in the shallow entrance of my sex. His eyes were on fire, dark and fervent—almost as black as bullets as he waited for my consent to enter me, to take me so completely and wholly that I would belong to him forever.

"Give yourself up to me, Angel," he pleaded. "All of you. Let me get lost in you...and let me take you with me."

The pounding of his heart against my chest reverberated through my body, and my melted heart suddenly began to beat. It was as if the rhythmic pulse of his had restarted mine. A heart that had shown no vital signs since the last time he'd held me. Life flooded into my veins and arteries, and my body took a long awaited breath. It was all the evidence I needed. Without this man, my life would fade away completely. I would no longer exist. Without him, I couldn't breathe.

Fresh tears began to flow softly down my cheeks as I nodded my consent. "Yes. Take me, Ethan. Take all of me. Now."

Slowly and gently, he sunk into me, every thick, throbbing inch claiming me as he pushed deeper and deeper. My breath caught, a gasp hissing through teeth, still shocked by the extent of his mass stretching me and filling me. Our eyes never strayed from one another, both of us choosing instead to observe each other's distinct, carnal and emotional experience as we finally reconnected.

His hands slithered to my buttocks, bracing me as he pushed deeper inside, deeper than he'd ever been, until I'd engulfed every morsel of his enormity. The depth and intensity of the penetration sent a sharp sting of sweet agony throughout my core, becoming a sensual, soothing caress as he slowly withdrew to the tip. He glided back inside easily now, the smooth, slippery slickness of our combined arousal building into a symphony of sweet, decadent pleasure.

Carefully, he pushed his hands inside my dress, sliding it up and over my head, leaving me naked but for my shoes. Tossing it to the side, he ran his hands back down my arms and down my sides, his touch appreciating my curvature, his eyes consuming me with adoring reverence. His gaze shifted, dragged reluctantly from mine to look down at my heavy, swollen breasts—his hands following suit to cup and knead, pulling and elongating my nipples.

He began to move in leisurely, deliberate thrusts as I rocked my hips forward to meet him. His hands and fingers continued to play skillfully with my breasts and nipples, sending sharp, agonizing pleasure straight to my sex. I clenched my muscles tightly in response.

"That's right, baby. You hold on to me. Grip my dick like that with your tight, sweet pussy. Squeeze me, Angel."

His sinful, libidinous language drove me wild, and I propelled forward, clenching my muscles around him. Reaching out, I gripped hold of his shirt, yanking it open so the buttons popped and scattered in various directions. The gesture excited Ethan, a frenzied and wild desperation taking possession of his eyes. He shrugged out of the shirt and began to move with resolute, accelerated thrusts.

The ripples of sharply-defined biceps, pecs, and abs flexed and tensed against the strain as he gripped my hips and drove into me, pulling me toward him to meet each driving thrust. I lay back and lifted my pelvis, arching up to further deepen the plunge of that thick bulk of pulsing flesh.

"You are so beautiful, Angel. You steal my breath with your

unadulterated beauty." His words scraped breathlessly past his arousal as he lunged into me, and laying the flat of his hand against my lower belly, he began to massage my clit with the pad of his thumb.

I felt myself building again, the searing energy of a rising orgasm spiraling through my body like a wild, unstoppable tornado as he stroked his cock inside me over and over. Every muscle in my body tensed and clenched as I bucked wildly against him.

"That's it, baby. Come for me and me alone. You are mine, Angel." His eyes were black with desire, his tone frenzied and possessive.

"Yes," I cried out as I raced toward my climax, grinding my hips with brazen abandonment.

"Say it," he demanded.

"Yours, Ethan. All yours," I screamed with agonizing pleasure as the orgasm reached its crescendo, my body quivering and contracting as the scorching ecstasy washed over me. He rocked into me ferociously, reinforcing and prolonging my blissful state until I fell apart helplessly beneath him.

Ethan slowed and slanted down over me, kissing and licking my throat as he soothed my quivering, sensitive body from the ravages of extreme sensation. The remnants of my quaking orgasm subsided as I arched my neck to allow him easier access, my body awakening to a new sensation.

"More," Ethan growled and gripping my hair, claimed my mouth once again.

A primal groan escaped his throat as his tongue tangled with mine. I placed the flat of my hands on his slick-with-sweat muscular back and drew him to me, reinforcing our contact. Lifting my legs, I wrapped them around his waist, linking my feet together to lure him even deeper. He cupped my ass, angling me so his entry rubbed deftly over that hot bundle of nerves inside me, and despite my exhaustion, I felt myself building again. I clenched my sex to intensify the sensation as he ground his hips, pounding into me deep and hard.

"Oh fuck. Oh, Angel…" His voice was husky, dense with untamed lust, making me crazed with desire.

I came violently, shuddering beneath him, my cries weak with insanity. Ethan shifted for greater leverage and with one last driving force, arched his neck and slammed into me, gasping my name. He sucked in a harsh breath, stilled, and erupted, spurting hot and thick inside me, his body shaking and jerking with the violent intensity of his climax.

When his body finally calmed, he opened his eyes to gaze down at me. Fresh tears spilled down his cheeks and face, tumbling gently to splash onto the heated skin of my swollen breasts. "I love you, Angel," he whispered.

I lay in my bed, gazing at the most devastatingly beautiful man I'd ever seen.

My man.

He was beyond rich and dangerously powerful. He commanded an empire and commanded respect. But in reality, none of that really counted, because inside he was fragile and vulnerable—like me. This strong, respected, wealthy man could easily be broken; I'd seen the destruction myself. All you had to do was find his weak spot—me. We were each other's weakness—our Achilles' heels. Yet at the same time, I believed our weakness was the thing that fortified us, made us resilient and impenetrable. Together we were an army and a force to be reckoned with.

The depths of the hold Rebecca had over Ethan, or the degree of damage it was capable of inflicting, I was yet to understand. I'd had a glimpse of her vicious, unrestrained insanity, and it had chilled me to the bone. But I knew that together we would confront it, and together we would win. Although I knew tomorrow would bring us untold complications and burdens anew, at least for now we were safe in each other's arms.

I recalled Ethan's words before he'd drifted off to sleep, taking comfort from their conviction. *I know that I don't want to spend another moment of my life without you, Angel, and I'm willing to do whatever it takes to make that happen.* Yes. Rebecca could wait until tomorrow, because neither she nor anyone else would ever drive us apart again.

My eyes feasted on my man before me, the slight flickering of his eyelids, the gentle rise and fall of his chest while he slept reaffirming his realness. Snuggling into him softly, I took a deep breath and inhaled his heavenly scent, being careful not to wake him in case I broke the spell. If I could pause time and stay in this moment forever, I would. My dreams had encompassed this very scene many times, only to be shattered into millions of particles of ugly truths when reality robbed me of hope and my ability to breathe. And now I was terrified that any moment I would wake, sweating and delirious on the floor of my closet.

The thought made me shudder involuntarily, and Ethan's eyes fluttered open. "What is it, baby?" There was a trace of alarm in his voice.

I gazed into his eyes, unsure whether I should speak of the horrors which roamed unfettered through my tortured mind. But I'd almost lost this man once already by failing to confront my fears—reticence would now become a thing of the past.

"I'm afraid to sleep in case you're not here when I wake," I whispered.

He blinked once on a wince. "I'll be here, baby. From now on, I'll always be here. If I have it my way, you'll never wake up alone again."

The comfort of his words lapped gently around me like warm water, my anxiety instantly quieting. I nodded, relishing in the warmth, feeling loved and secure and cherished, and suddenly so incredibly sleepy.

"I thought I'd lost you forever, Angel." His voice was raw with the memory.

"I'm here."

"I'd rather die than live without you."

"Shh," I put my finger to his lips, "I'm here—I'm not going anywhere."

"I love you, Angel. So, so much."

"I know." I paused. And then the words came so easily, with no hesitation and no fear and no doubt.

"And I love you, Ethan. I… Love … You."

We held each other, sobbing quietly until our heartache eased and faded—our tears and bodies, hearts and minds melding together, bound as one. Together we were indestructible, solid, eternal. Together we would prevail.

I'd had my fill of hell. For the first time in a long time, I could breathe.

CHAPTER TEN

The air was thick with the scent of earth and cold, damp leaves, and when I opened my eyes, I saw that the sky above me was shadowed in gray. Suddenly, I felt the chill seep into my bones and immediately had the urge to fold my arms around myself for comfort.

Shifting, I pushed myself up into a sitting position, becoming immediately aware that I was lying on a carpet of leaves and moss in the middle of a dense wooded area. The sun had only just begun to light the sky, and the early morning mist still hovered in the air around me like a ghostly blanket. I pulled my knees to my chest, hugging them tightly, as an unmistakable awareness tugged at my senses, and suddenly I was certain of two things: All around me was eerily silent—and I was alone.

Terrified, I buried my face into my knees, praying I was mistaken and that when I looked again, I would no longer be in this cold, unfamiliar, wide-open space—alone. But the scent of damp, musty earth and the cold, misty morning didn't vanish as I'd hoped. And neither did the vast lonely space. What I saw when I finally pried my face away from the comfort of my knees and opened my eyes was my shoes. Peeping out from underneath my long, flowing white dress were the toes of a pair of shiny, red shoes, and a fresh wave of anxiety flared within me.

Then through the dense, misty silence came the frenzied, raucous barking of the spotted beasts. Fear closed around my heart with the vise-like grip of icy fingers, each passing second drawing them closer. My *chest ached with the need for breath as I narrowed my eyes and squinted into the gloomy, vaporous space between the throng of claw-like trees. At first they appeared in the distance, a jostling fusion of black and white effigies hurtling toward me. Sat astride one of the animals was a pale-faced woman, her strawberry blond hair billowing out behind her as she rode the beast toward me at a terrifying pace.*

Rebecca.

Without pause, I pushed to my feet and began to run blindly through the trees, away from the impending danger. The ground was uneven, strewn with fallen branches and hidden complications, and as I ran for my life the most ludicrous thought came crashing into my mind: Don't scuff your shoes, don't scuff your shoes.

My legs ached with the speed at which I ran, my lungs burning as I grappled desperately for breath. But I didn't stop, because I knew my life depended on it. All of a sudden there was a clearing, and I ran out on to a path at the side of a pond. Ahead was a bridge, curving gracefully over a narrow body of water, and I realized my surroundings were familiar. The bridge seemed to beckon me, a strong sense of safety emanating from the simple stone arch.

It was then that I heard him.

"I'm here, Angel," Ethan called to me. "I'm over here. Run to me." His voice was warm and alluring, and I knew that if I could only reach his arms, I'd be safe.

The sound of Ethan's disembodied voice led me up on the bridge, but as I searched for him, it began to fade into the distance. I kept running and before I knew it, I was out on the street. A group of people stood huddled together, shoulder to shoulder, pushing and shoving to gain a clearer view of something lying on the ground. The police were there attempting to calm the crowd and keep the people back, away from what seemed to be a crime scene.

Realizing the barking had suddenly ceased, I glanced over my shoulder to see the angry beasts had retreated and were skulking stealthily back into the shadows of the woods. The pale-faced woman cackled raucously as she rode away into the distance, recoiling like a menacing, poisonous vapor. Feeling suddenly compelled to see, I began to force my way through the crush of people.

A policeman reached out to grab my arm. "Go back, you can't come through here."

"But I know her, you must let me through. I have to see," I insisted, pushing his arm away.

Then I noticed Ethan.

He'd fallen to his knees and was sobbing inconsolably. Next to him lay the body of a woman.

"It's best you don't look," said the policeman, "they fucked her up real bad."

Pushing him away, I ran to Ethan who was leaning over the body, his face contorted with anguish. "Ethan, Ethan." I screamed his name to no avail, for no matter how hard I tried, or how loud I screamed, I knew he would never hear me.

Helpless, I watched as he sobbed for the woman on the ground, forever alone in his private, inconsolable grief. Suddenly, he shifted, reaching out to the lifeless, marred face of the woman. His fingers gently parted her lips, withdrawing the balled up piece of paper from inside her mouth. The crinkled, aged paper was immediately familiar—a newspaper cutting reporting the tragic death of a woman.

I looked again at the woman, her long mahogany hair flowing endlessly around her shoulders, her white dress limply covering her lifeless body. And peeping out from beneath the long, flowing fabric—a pair of shiny, red shoes.

Heaving in great gasps of air, I tore myself from the ravages of my fear-filled sleep, my body trembling as I forced away the fragmented images that seemed burned into my vision. Mercifully, the impression slowly began to fade as I reacquainted myself with the familiar sights and shapes of my surroundings. It was then that I reached out into the cold, empty space beside me and entered my nightmare all over again.

I was alone.

"No! No!" The chilling scream which racked my body penetrated the unbearable silence of my apartment. Hauling my comforter with me, I staggered from my bed and bolted for the sanctuary of my closet. Once inside, I tunneled to the back and curled up into a ball, my body besieged with jolting, aching sobs.

Then I heard a voice that wasn't my own, its tone steeped in panic and fear. The voice was calling my name. "Angel, Angel! Where are you? Dammit, where are you, baby?"

He was here.

"Ethan ..." His name scraped past my lips in a desperate plea and suddenly he was there, his glorious, naked frame filling the space in the open closet doorway.

Sinking instantly to his knees, he crawled into the airless space, his hand reaching out to tug me into his arms. "What happened? What are you doing in here?"

"I thought you were gone. I thought it was all a dream," I sobbed.

"I'm here, baby girl. I'm here." He pulled me into his lap and laid my head against his chest, his hand stroking my hair to gently soothe my distress. When my body finally stopped shaking, he reached up tilting my chin to brush away the tear tracks from my sodden face. "Don't be afraid, baby. You don't ever have to be afraid again."

His lips brushed mine with a gentle kiss, and I closed my eyes, relishing the feel of his soft, full mouth, and familiar scent I'd missed so dearly.

"When I woke, you were gone, E. Where were you?" I whispered against his lips.

"I just went to get a glass of water. I was gone for barely a minute."

"I must have sensed it in my sleep. Sensed that I was alone."

"I'm sorry, baby. I didn't realize. Did you dream?"

I nodded as the remnants of my nightmare flitted into my conscious mind. Most of it had faded to distant echoes, floating around like dust motes in a stream of shimmering light, but a tiny fraction remained and the memory made me shudder.

Rebecca's sadistic threats rang in my ears. *I know people who will rape you and leave you for dead. I'm going to make sure they fuck you up so badly, you'll think you're in hell.*

I shuddered again.

"What is it, Angel? What did you dream about?"

There was no way I could reveal to Ethan anything of Rebecca's threats. If I did, I knew he'd be reluctant to go through with his plans to get her out of our lives. He would fear too much for my safety, and I just couldn't risk that. I wanted her gone and gone for good. So no matter whether they were idle threats or sadistic intentions, for now they would remain my secret.

Feigning a smile, I shook my head. "Nothing. I can't even remember it now."

The concern etched in his furrowed brow suggested I hadn't quite convinced him, but he didn't press me. Not about the dream.

"Angel?" He asked cautiously.

"Yes."

"Why are you in the closet?"

Needing to puzzle out a logical, plausible explanation in my own mind before I could answer, I paused for a few beats. Finally, I answered in the only way I could. "It's safe in here."

"Safe? Safe from what?"

I shrugged. "When I'm alone and afraid, I feel too exposed lying in my bed. When I open my eyes in the dark, the space is too vast, and I don't know what lies in the shadows. I can contain my fear in here. I can reach out and know exactly what to expect. The restricted space somehow makes it easier to breathe."

Ethan gazed at me like I'd just grown a second head, and immediately I wondered whether I'd said too much. I must have sounded miniscule, like a child almost—pathetic.

"How long have you felt like that?"

I shrugged again.

"Have you been *sleeping* in here, Angel?" When I didn't answer, he reached out, gripping the comforter that I clung to and yanking it from my body to expose my naked flesh and the fading bruises marring my hips, ribs, and spine—marks left behind from the pressure of lying on a cold, hard floor. "These marks on your body—they're from sleeping in here, aren't they?"

I shivered and pulled the comforter back around me.

"How long?" Then, when I still didn't answer, "How long, Angel?"

"Just since... you know. Since... her."

"You slept in here all that time? It's a fucking closet, you must have been... Christ, you've not been eating, you've barely slept—what the fuck have I done to you?"

I reached out to stroke his face, hating that he was bearing the weight of my weaknesses. "You didn't put me in here, E."

For a second he appeared to consider what I'd said, his brow crumpling as he tried to make sense of it. Then his features seemed to smooth as if he'd reached a conclusion. "No. But I put you *back* in here. That's what you said to me—I couldn't understand it at the time—but that day here, you told me it was my fault you were back in the closet. That's what you meant, isn't it?"

I shook my head as I stared at him, aghast. Not because the assumption he'd arrived at wasn't true, but because I couldn't remember saying it. "It's over now. It doesn't matter anymore."

"If that's true, why are we in here now? You crawled in here because you're inherently alone. That's what you think. Despite the promises I made you last night, your first instinctive thought when you awoke was that you were alone, that I'd let you down. I was supposed to mend you—but instead, I broke you all over again."

"Don't do this, Ethan. You're not responsible for my fucked-upness. That all stems from... a long time ago. I just got lost for a while, reverted back to an old coping habit. We've both made mistakes. You did let me down, yes, but I let you down also. I could have done more to avoid this. I should have been strong enough to hear you out that day. At least we'd have had something to build on. But I was weak and scared and stubborn, and I did what I always do. When you think the horse is going to bolt anyway, just jump before you're thrown, at least that way you control when you hit the ground, and you know exactly when the pain is going to come. That's what I do, E.

"Or at least, that's what I did. Now I've learned that jumping just causes a shitload more unnecessary pain, and what you should do is hold on tight, fight to gain back control, believe in yourself. Because the pain only hits if you let it. This whole thing has proven to be destructive, but it only wins—*she* only wins—if we let her. You shouldering the blame for my... fragility is not going to help us win this battle."

Slowly, he nodded, absorbing my words, knowing they made sense. But his eyes betrayed the guilt that tore him apart inside, and I knew it would take time to soothe that ache completely.

In a bid to ease his conscience and lighten the mood, I quickly added, "Besides, spending a week in here was a piece of cake. It took me three whole years to haul my ass back into bed last time, and that's only because I grew too big for my closet. By the time I was ten, I walked with a stoop..." The look of horror on Ethan's face stopped me in my tracks and had me metaphorically yanking my foot out of my very large mouth.

"Three fucking years? You slept in a closet for three fucking years? Why?"

Until the words seethed with incredulity passed Ethan's lips, I hadn't realized how extraordinary it sounded. The answer was no less surreal. "It was where I hid the pendant."

"What?"

"My mom's diamond pendant," I explained in quiet voice. "I used to believe it somehow magically connected me to her. After she died I used to sleep with my hand clasped around it under my pillow. And then after a while, I started to forget what she looked like, what she sounded like, and I thought it was because the pendant was losing its magic. So I buried it beneath a loose board in the floor of my closet, hoping that in time the magic would rekindle and the memories would return. But I couldn't bear the distance, couldn't sleep without it. So I slept in the closet. After a while, I just got used to it. The tight enclosed space became the comfort I needed, and sleeping in my bed in a wide-open space became an issue."

"Your father didn't do anything about it?"

"My father? I don't think he ever knew. I can't remember him ever coming in to my room."

"What, never?"

I shook my head.

"Your father *never* tucked you into bed?"

"No!" The very idea seemed bizarre.

Ethan closed his eyes, as if the gesture would somehow help him draw strength. When he opened them they were filled with regret and the unspoken words that ran parallel with that emotion hung heavily in the air between us.

"Let's get out of here," he said simply.

Nodding, I clambered off his lap and crawled out of the closet. When we emerged into the dim light of my room, I realized how cozy and inviting it suddenly seemed—a far cry from the bleak, desolate space I'd fled from when I'd awoken, delirious and alone. The morning had barely broken, just the subdued tones of a rising sun filtering through the cream, lightweight drapes to form a hazy pattern across the room.

Ethan tugged at the comforter I still held around me to conceal my nakedness. His expression was inscrutable, but the desire behind his eyes was unmistakable, and I willingly allowed it to fall to floor. He began to circle around me, his gaze skimming gently over the surface of my skin, appraising every curve and hollow of my body, which seemed to react to his look alone. I felt the tiny hairs on my arms rise to stand on end, my nipples taut and jutting, beginning to tingle. Then he started to back away, his focus dipping to rest smoldering hot on the sensitive flesh at the summit of my thighs. The raw hunger in his eyes sent a prickle of awareness straight to my pussy, and I grew instantly damp.

"Come here." His commanding tone was absurdly arousing, and I responded immediately, moving across the room to where he stood at the end of the bed. His tall, naked, muscular frame oozed strength and power, and the urge to reach out and touch him was overwhelming. But I didn't, because I knew better than to try and steer what was about to happen between us.

I knew that the mood in the room had shifted, the atmosphere suddenly ignited by a magical force created by the connection I had with Ethan. A force so powerful and crammed full of energy, you could almost sense the crackling and hissing of electricity in the air. And I knew that Ethan needed to be the one who controlled how this magic affected us, to regulate the level and intensity of pleasure my body was about to endure. He needed it to reassure himself that I was his and his alone, to reaffirm that he was the master of our destiny and our future happiness. He needed it to soothe the ache of guilt that still tormented him relentlessly, to mend the gap, to mend us—to mend me.

And I needed it, too.

He didn't touch me, not with his hands. Like mine, they remained by his sides. Instead, he stepped forward, placing one foot between both of mine so our bodies touched. His breath was warm against my neck, his taut chest pressed against my swollen breasts and the pulsing flesh of his erection straining against my hip. My sex clenched deliciously with the contact I yearned for, and I silently begged him to touch me.

His fingertips grazed gently over mine, then trailed up between my fingers to circle my palm with a featherlight touch. I closed my eyes, losing myself to the intensity of the sensation. Without breaking contact, he moved slowly behind me, the warmth of his skin gliding over mine, my nerve endings tingling from the mere connection. Then

I felt the heat of his solid, bulging cock as it nestled into the curve of my back, and I shivered with longing. He leaned in to graze the top of my head with a gentle kiss, his hands coming to rest lightly on my hips, and slowly he began to turn me very slightly to the left.

"Open your eyes," he instructed.

I did as I was told and immediately my brown eyes locked into his oceans of blue as I gazed at him through the glass of the floor-to-ceiling mirror.

"I want you to see how beautiful you are," he whispered into my ear.

My eyes flickered uncertainly to my face, lingering for just a second before returning to his.

"No. I want you to *see*, Angel. Really see."

Reaching down, he clasped the back of my hands, his fingers threading through mine as he guided them to my face. Slowly, he trailed our entwined fingertips gently over my jaw line to my slightly parted lips.

"See, baby. Look how sensuous your mouth is. How soft and full your lips are. I've pictured these beautiful, succulent lips on mine a million times over the last week. Imagined them trailing gently over my body—enveloping the head of my cock as your tongue laps gently against my oozing tip."

I gasped at the seductive tone of his voice, the licentiousness of his words, and I knew from the way his cock flexed against my ass that they affected him too. Parting my lips a little wider, I flicked my tongue delicately over our fingertips, emulating the action he'd described. Ethan groaned, his eyes darkening with primal lust. Gradually he steered our hands downwards, over the curve of my chin and the dipping hollow of my throat where my pulse pounded wildly against my skin, and then softly through the valley between my breasts.

"See your beautiful tits, Angel." At his command, our touch continued over my heated skin, making a circular motion around my left breast, dipping into the valley and back up to circle the right. "Soft and plump and perfect," he whispered as our rotating fingertips began to narrow the circle, growing closer to my painfully rigid nipples.

My breath was coming in short, sharp gasps, my heart thumping loudly in my chest as we finally skimmed the surface of my nipples, moving around and around the tight puckered skin of my areola. Suddenly my nipple was caught between our fingers, and Ethan squeezed, pinching the jutting flesh sharply. The action sent a brusque, pleasurable pain straight through my nerve endings, the sensation racing directly to my sex. I arched my back, pushing my breast against our hands in a silent plea for more.

"You see? Just watch how you respond to our touch. See how your tits swell and how your nipples become harder." He pinched the hot button of flesh again, and I groaned, closing my eyes and laying my head back against his shoulder. "Open your eyes, Angel."

Obeying his command, I snatched a fortifying breath and focused my hooded eyes on the erotic reflection in front of me, watching as our hands began to tug and stretch at my nipple, before closing entirely over my breasts, squeezing and kneading until my breath was ragged with arousal.

"Move forward." His voice was husky, laden with desire.

I took a cautious step forward, then another and another, until we were just a matter of feet away from the mirror. Ethan continued to control the pressure of our touch on my breasts and nipples, rolling and pinching, as I battled against the need to close my eyes to the pleasure.

"Get down on your knees, Angel."

Without hesitation, I complied, dropping gently to my knees, Ethan never breaking contact and moving with me, until we were both kneeling on the floor in front of the mirror. His hands began to move, directing mine away from my now bereft, aching breasts, down over the flat of my stomach and out toward my hips.

"Now spread your legs," he ordered, using his own knees to force mine apart. Immediately, his lust-filled gaze fell on the pulsing flesh between my legs, his lips parting to allow his tongue to glide hungrily over his lips. "Oh, baby." Steering us slowly to the apex of my thighs, our fingertips stroked gently into the strip of pubic hair leading down to my aching sex. "Jesus fucking Christ, you are so beautiful."

His cock flexed and pulsed against my lower back, eager and untamed, like a caged animal, and the knowledge of how much I affected him sent a rush of heated pleasure rippling through my blood.

Suddenly our fingers flicked over my clit and my hips jolted forward in delectation. I glanced up to Ethan's face, watching as it flooded in pure, raw longing. His eyes dark and hooded, his lips red and hungry, as a low guttural groan grated from somewhere deep within him.

"Now see this, Angel." Our fingers glanced over my sex again. "Look closely at this soft, plump, mound of decadent, mouthwatering flesh." He began to circle the tips of our forefingers around my aching clit. "See how pink and ripe and juicy your pussy is." He pressed his finger against mine, building the pressure against my throbbing nub of flesh. "Now watch your body respond."

Swiftly, he pressed downwards, forcing both our fingers between my soaking folds of flesh, and I groaned loudly, my hips thrusting forward in a demand for more.

"See, baby. See how much you love this," his voice crooned seductively.

My body was suddenly on fire, burning with the heat of desire, but also from the warmth of the sun, which now fully rose was shining in beams of hazy light across the room to focus on us like a spotlight.

Our fingers plunged inside me, gliding through my slick, sticky arousal. "Look at your soaking pussy, baby, see how it drips for me. See how the moisture glistens in the sunlight." His other hand guided mine to my breast to tug at my erect nipple, and together we pushed my body to the edge of decadence. I groaned loudly, bucking against our hands, riding our fingers as they moved inside me.

My body was lost in a storm of almost unbearable hedonistic sensations. The sound of Ethan's low, growling voice uttering sinful, wicked words. The vision of us with our legs splayed wide open, his arms enfolding me possessively while our entwined hands rampaged over my body, caressing and delving and plunging.

"Oh my God, Ethan, what are you doing to me?" The words came out broken and faltering and gasping, as I raced toward climax.

"I'm teaching you to love yourself, Angel."

His words were my undoing and I exploded with pleasure, my vision blurring as I reached the dizzying heights of ecstasy, and my orgasm rippled through my quaking body. The euphoria rumbled on and on, until finally, my body wilted and Ethan enfolded me in his strong, capable embrace, his mouth grazing across my neck and shoulder, nibbling and suckling as he brought me down from my high.

But it wasn't enough. I tilted my face toward him and gazing up into his burning eyes, whispered, "More, E. I need more of you."

A slow, wicked smile curled the edge of his lips. "There she is, my girl. My dirty, dirty girl."

Leaning back on his haunches and taking me by the hips, he gently guided me back until I could feel the crown of his throbbing cock at my saturated entrance. He pushed inside me, the size of his swollen, rigid member stretching me open, and the sensation was utterly delicious. With his hands on my hips to guide me, he slid gently out to the tip, and then repeated the action once, twice, until his entire length was gliding inside me with ease. Then, pushing up onto his knees, he edged us forward until the mirror was in easy reach, and gripping me by the wrists bent me forward to lean with my arms outstretched on the cold, reflective glass. We watched each other closely as he began to move inside me again, each delectable thrust evident in my lust-filled expression.

"Keep watching, baby. I want to look into your eyes when you come for me," he rasped as he withdrew to the tip and slammed back into me again and again. His frantic pace had me gasping, and the feeling of his wonderfully firm balls banging against my ass soon had my body shuddering and jolting as orgasm once again swept me into a state of insanity.

"Angel," Ethan cried out as he joined me in ecstasy, his climax thundering through his rigid body as he spurted hot jets of semen inside me.

We remained in that position until our panting eased and our muscles relaxed, our eyes still locked on each other. Slowly, he withdrew and taking me in his arms, we curled up on the floor.

"You are the most precious, wonderful creature in the entire world, Angel."

Smiling, I reached out to stroke his beautiful, chiseled features, my heart seeming to swell inside me with an unusual transcendental, glowing sensation. "I love you, Ethan Wilde." The words were real and heartfelt and poured out of me with the fluidity of liquid to coat us with a strong, indestructible layer.

Ethan's eyes misted instantly and the look on his face was as if I'd just given him the world. "And I love you, Angel Lawson. More than the oxygen I breathe." Leaning forward, he kissed me gently on the lips, but as he pulled away, I noticed his expression seemed to morph into one of anxiety.

"What is it, E?"

"We have a tough journey ahead, baby. A mountain to climb."

"I know," I nodded. "But we're strong now. Together we can climb anything, achieve anything. I'm sure of it."

"Yes, I think you're right." He kissed the tip of my nose. "And climb we will, but first I need you to eat. You're fading away in front of me and it simply won't do."

"Let me shower first and it's a deal."

His eyes lit up. "Only if I can shower with you."

"Where do I sign?"

CHAPTER ELEVEN

We made it as far as the shower—just. But the moment the warm torrent of water began to run blessedly over our hyper-sensitive skin and the soap lathered into a frenzy of bubbles, we were lost to each other again. It was as if we needed the connection like a drug. As if Ethan burying himself inside me could make us forget the distance we'd endured while we were apart, and as if the very act of indulging in each other's bodies so carnally would bring us the fortification we needed to prepare us for the battle we had yet to face.

Afterward, we dressed casually—him in sexy-as-sin, low-slung jeans and T-shirt, me in a denim skirt and blouse—and then together we raided the refrigerator. We set about making crispy bacon with eggs and toasted bagels, touching and kissing each time we were close enough to do so. Which was often.

I was folding eggs in a bowl when I sensed him close behind me, the heat from his body absorbing into mine like liquid into a sponge. His breath was warm on my neck, his scent filling my nostrils, so familiar and so—Ethan. Suddenly from nowhere his hand found its way up my skirt and tugged my panties aside. Without a word he plunged two fingers inside me, moving them in time with my motion to fold the eggs. I groaned and arched my back, leaning slightly forward to accommodate his thrusts, his fingers working their magic as they slid in and out, massaging and spreading.

"I've missed this so much," he breathed, nibbling my ear.

"What? Finger fucking me while I make eggs?" I croaked against the building desire. I felt him smile against my neck.

"Well, yes. But more precisely, being able to take you whenever and however I want." He picked up the pace, his fingers moving nimbly and with purpose, angled to hit my most sensitive zones.

My skin began to heat and burn in that unique way it does when building toward climax, my muscles clenching and squeezing as I thrust my hips back to meet his skillful fingers. My hands around the bowl and whisk went lax as I gave myself up to his delightful interruption and his need to explore me.

"Being able to enter your tight, wet pussy and make you come anytime I like. Because you're mine," he growled, his thrusts coming harder and faster. "Come for me now, Angelica. Come against my hand," he commanded. "Now."

I closed my eyes and obeyed, coming apart as my orgasm exploded, and I rocked against his hand like a wild and wanton creature, the scorching, ecstatic sensation rolling on and on like a relentless storm. When it was over and my breathing had calmed, I felt his jubilant smile again.

"Good girl," he rasped through his own arousal, and gently removing his fingers placed them provocatively into his mouth and began to suck. He closed his eyes as if to savor the taste and whispered, "So sweet, Angel."

A smile tugged at the corner of my mouth as I gazed at him, mesmerized by the gesture. He responded by slapping my butt. "Now make me my eggs, woman."

"You're insatiable, Mr. Wilde."

"For you, yes, there's no question. I can never have too much of you."

Folding the eggs, I smiled in wonder. "Nor I you, Mr. Wilde."

"Glad to hear it." He opened the cupboard and reached up for the mugs. "Coffee or tea?"

The very instant the question left his lips, he closed his eyes as if in regret. I never drank tea, and the last time I'd reminded him of the fact was after Rebecca had showed up, and I'd accused him of confusing my drink preference with that of the *English Rose*—not.

"I didn't mean… It's just words, Angel. Something you say."

"I know. It's fine. Don't worry." I tried to reassure him, but it was a futile effort.

The problem was all too evident. There was a huge, fat, motherfucking elephant in the room. A sore that would fester and rot the longer we avoided it. It was tainting our reunion, and we both knew it.

How do you solve a problem like Rebecca Staunton?

Of course, her being a problem was where the similarity between her and Maria von Trapp of *The Sound of Music* ended. Who was I kidding? There was no way you could even begin to compare the two.

We gazed at each other knowingly, the huge, fat, motherfucking elephant taking a huge, fat, motherfucking, crap in the middle of the floor between us. Figuratively speaking, of course.

"Let's eat first," Ethan suggested. "I need to see you eat something." Knowing better than to argue, I nodded my agreement.

After ten minutes of pushing the food around my plate and nibbling on the tiny bits my dry-with-nerves palate would allow, I gave up. Ethan didn't look like he was doing much better when he transferred his gaze from his plate to mine and said, "Please try to eat, baby."

Sighing, I put down my fork. "I can't."

He pushed his plate away. "Me neither."

Once again, I saw the dark depths of worry begin to crinkle and pale his beautiful features, and my heart swelled with love, but also fear. "Speak to me, E."

His eyes seemed to widen as if something he'd dreaded forever was finally upon him, and he was unable to procrastinate any longer. Pushing to his feet, he took my hand and led me to the lounge to settle on the sofa.

"I told you last night that I'm willing to do whatever it takes to spend my life with you, Angel. And I meant every word. I'm ready to tell you everything." He paused as I nodded nervously to reassure him I was ready. "What I have to say is going to be hard to hear. By telling you, I risk losing you, because you may never feel the same way about me ever again. But I know that not telling you would be a far greater risk, because then I'm certain of a future without you."

He swallowed hard.

I swallowed hard.

"I need you to promise me two things, Angel."

"Anything, you know that."

He threaded his hands into my hair and pulled me closer, our foreheads touching as he gazed into my eyes. "You have to promise that you'll hear me out until the end, before you judge me. And when you do—please try not to hate me."

Although I was terrified of what I was about to hear, deep down, I knew there was nothing he could say that would change the way I felt about him. I nodded. "I promise you, E. I know I could never hate you." I paused for a beat and added, "And the second thing?"

"If you find that, despite everything, you really do love me, if you decide to stay by my side until all this over… your demons are next. We slay my demons and then we slay yours—together. You have to promise me. No more sleeping in the closet, Angel. Not ever."

"Okay." I nodded, knowing he was right, and that the time had come for me too. "I promise."

Releasing me, he sat back in his seat, inching sideways to create some space between us. Space for me to process what he was about to say and space for the enormity of the secret he was about to reveal. He took a breath and began.

"Almost from the first moment I set foot on British soil, I had a best friend. His name was Alistair Brown. We met on my first day in school and by mid-term break we'd become inseparable, like brothers. He was an only child, putting in a late appearance into his parents' lives.

They'd apparently tried unsuccessfully for kids for years, and when they'd finally given up, nature blessed them with Alistair. Needless to say, they worshipped the ground he walked on, and vice versa. When my folks came back to the States, they became like my second family. Anne had given up her career in law when she fell pregnant with Ali, but his father, Sir Edward Brown, was a senior judge. He was appointed a Lord Justice of Appeal shortly before Alistair's twenty-second birthday."

I frowned, momentarily confused. "Well that all sounds great, and I'd love to hear more about him sometime, E, but what has this got to do with Rebecca?"

"Do you remember I told you something happened? Something which threw me and her together?"

"'An unfortunate incident,' I think is what you said."

"Did I?" He flinched, seemingly offended by his own choice of words, and then blinked several times as if to refocus. "One weekend a group of us had gathered at a friend's house in the country. Alistair was all excited about a girl he'd invited; they'd only dated a couple of times, but for some reason he was convinced she was The One. When they showed up, I recognized her instantly. She was someone I'd hooked up with about a month before, at the end of a drunken night. The girl was Rebecca."

"Oh." Despite myself, the jealousy hit me like a tidal wave. "Well, she must have made something of an impression if you recognized her straight away."

He laughed mirthlessly. "The only thing memorable about her was her unrelenting persistence. I'd made the mistake of taking her back to my place that night, so she knew where I lived. She'd bombarded me with texts and phone calls for weeks, and when I ignored them, she began showing up at my home and my office. Eventually, I resorted to being downright rude to her, and I thought she'd finally got the message—until she showed up with Ali at the country house.

"I was going to tell him straight off, but he seemed to like her so damn much, I couldn't bring myself to burst his bubble. She clearly hadn't let on that she even knew me, let alone that we'd slept together, so I kept quiet. By the end of the first night, I thought that maybe I'd got her all wrong. They looked pretty tight, and she looked like she was into him, so I decided to ride the weekend out, give her the benefit of the doubt.

"On the second night, I went to bed a bit worse for wear. We'd ended the night on a few rounds of poker and far too much bourbon. At some point in the early hours, I awoke to someone in my bed. She was naked and straddling me, her hands were—well, everywhere."

Ethan shifted in his seat, moving to rest his elbows on his legs, as if what he'd said was making him genuinely uncomfortable. The jealousy bubbled away inside me, my nerves practically twitching with anger at the thought of that venomous bitch pawing at my man. I reined it in and let him continue.

"For the minutest fraction of a second, I responded." *Oh shit!* "It was just an instinctive reaction, a red-blooded young man in a bourbon-induced haze. I'm not even sure I realized who it was, but as soon as I did, I pushed her away. When I asked her what the hell she was doing, she turned it around on me, saying that I'd been coming on to her all weekend and that I'd invited her to my room. She said I wanted it as much as she did, and that it was obvious we were meant to be, because fate kept throwing us together. When I told her she was deluded, she swore that would be the story she'd give Ali if I told him otherwise."

"What?" I asked, my face creasing into a befuddled scowl. "The woman's got serious mental health issues."

Ethan made a face, inferring that was a major understatement. "I quickly realized that my concealment of the truth—that I'd waited almost an entire weekend to tell him, that not only did I know his new girlfriend intimately, but she was also a crazy stalker—actually made her story more credible. I even wondered if I *had* inadvertently flirted with her. Anyway, I couldn't see a good outcome, so I kept my mouth shut. I know it was stupid, but I thought we'd just move on from it, that finally she would see I wasn't interested and keep her distance, and maybe the thing with Alistair would just fizzle out.

"After the weekend, I avoided seeing Ali for a few weeks. But then there were a few social events that we were both invited to. To my horror, things had gotten a whole lot worse. He'd fallen for her, and it became swiftly evident the feelings were not mutual. Every opportunity she got, she'd find an excuse to be alone with me. She did crazy things, like plant her panties in my pocket and then sit with her skirt hitched up or giggle coyly when he entered the room, going silent when she glanced up at him, all guilty as if we'd been carrying on."

My stomach was turning in on itself by now, anger and hatred for this woman multiplying by the second. "Fuck, Ethan, why didn't you just tell him."

"I did." He ran his hands over his face and into his hair, like the memory alone made him sick. "It was a New Year's party. The bitch had hounded me all night with flirtatious looks and suggestive comments. She made sure to sit next to me at dinner, touching me up under the table—the whole thing going right over Ali's head. When she followed me to the bathroom and shoved my hand between her legs, it was the final straw.

"I'd gone over and over it in my head, worrying about what I'd say, about how Alistair would take it when I told him. I was afraid that he'd question me, my loyalty—question our friendship. But nothing prepared me for the way he reacted. He didn't believe a word I said. He accused me of being jealous. Said that she'd told him I'd made some inappropriate comments to her, that I'd been making passes at her at every given opportunity and wouldn't leave her alone. We had a huge fight and they left.

"An hour or so later, I went after him to try and sort things out. I thought, if I could just get to talk to him alone, I'd make him understand. When I got to Ali's apartment, I knocked, but there was no answer, so I let myself in. He had keys to my place, I had keys to his—it was the way things were between us.

"I could hear some strange noises coming from the living room, but couldn't figure what it was. I'd had a lot to drink, and after the fight, my head was all over the place. The apartment was in virtual darkness, so I just stumbled through the hallway and pushed open the door."

My mind was reeling as I listened, my blood pumping with fury at what that bitch had done and Alistair not believing him. But despite my agitation, what Ethan said next soon had my blood running ice cold.

"They were on the floor." His voice was broken and strangely distant as he stared unseeing at the space in front of him, the painful memory clearly arduous to relive. He swallowed hard. "Alistair had her arms pinned above her head with one hand… his other was over her mouth. I froze—thought I'd walked in on a private moment, at first. Then I realized she was fighting him… that he was holding her down. That's when she saw me. Her eyes wide, staring at me. Suddenly, she seemed to struggle more, tried to scream through the fingers clamped over her mouth, but he didn't stop, he just went harder."

"Oh my God," I whispered, struggling to process the horror of what he was saying. "Ethan, are you telling me he was raping her?"

His gaze didn't leave the floor, and his answer came in a barely perceptible, single nod. I felt overwhelmingly confused. A strange sense of sympathy for this woman I'd found so easy to hate washed over me. Yes, she was a vile, evil person; there was no doubt of that. But what horrors had conjured the devil inside her?

"What happened?"

Ethan's eyes fluttered up to look at me, his gaze penetrating mine in what looked like a silent plea for my understanding, and my heart thundered into my mouth.

"What happened, Ethan?" I repeated.

He swallowed hard, then whispered, "I ran."

I stared at him dumbstruck, certain that my countenance was dripping in the horror I could feel clawing its way under my skin.

Ethan's responding expression implied that I'd reacted in the exact way he'd feared I would. He'd trusted me enough to tell me, and I'd promised to hear him out before I judged him. And that's what I would do.

I took a breath to compose myself and uttered the question that was waiting patiently on my lips. "Why?"

"I don't know why. I've asked myself that same question every day since. Why didn't I do something, why didn't I stop it? I've pictured myself in that same scenario a million times, asking myself what I'd do if—God forbid—I was dropped in that situation again, and every time the answer's the same... the right thing.

"I could tell you it was because I hated her, or because I thought she had it coming for being a poisonous, despicable bitch, but neither would be true. I'm not an animal, nobody deserves that. But something held me back that night, something told me not to interfere. I can't explain what it was, it's like my logical mind can't quite grasp hold of it, like it won't properly manifest itself. I know it sounds like an excuse, and I can battle with my conscious and regret my decision every day of my life, but it won't change that I made it. I have to live with that."

Remorse was etched into his features; it was plain as day to see. The strain in his voice left me in no doubt how these events had haunted him, and how difficult it must have been to confess them to me. He hadn't been obliged to tell me, he could have lied. Ethan knew without anyone having to tell him, that his attempts to justify his actions were flimsy. But who knows how one will react to unexpected, horrific situations. It was easy to say what someone should have done. Given the chance, most of us would do things very differently a second time around. I, of all people, knew that.

The pieces of this bizarre enigma were beginning to fall into place. The stark reality of why Rebecca had such a hold on Ethan, suddenly coming to life in my mind.

"You said that she saw you."

"Yes."

"Which is why you feel obligated to her. She's held it against you. It's why she has such a hold over you." It wasn't a question, more of deduction. A way of audibly slotting in the pieces of the puzzle as they manifested in my mind. I had no doubt that Ethan failing to react that night could be considered a crime, if not in the eyes of the law, then surely in her estimation.

"In part, yes," Ethan replied.

"In part? Are you saying there's more?"

He nodded. "I'm afraid so."

God, how much worse could this get?

I took a bracing breath. "Go on."

Standing, he moved to gaze out of the glass doors leading to the terrace. The sunlight emphasized the perfect lines of his chiseled features. His complexion was pale and sleep deprived, the dark circles under his eyes reflecting the weight of this interminable nightmare. He closed his eyes for a second, as if drawing strength from the light, and then went on.

"After I left Alistair's, I couldn't face going home. I wanted some normality, needed something to center me, something to oust the image of them from my mind. So I went back to the party, got piss-ass drunk, and crashed. When I woke the next morning, I was convinced I'd dreamed the whole thing. Until I arrived home and found Rebecca on my doorstep.

"She was a mess—shaken, bruised. She told me that when they'd left the party they'd had this huge fight about me. Apparently, he'd quizzed her about what I'd accused her of and she'd fallen apart under the pressure. She'd admitted to having feelings for me, told him the only reason she'd gotten with him was to get close to me. When she'd tried to leave, he'd gone ballistic and forced himself on her."

"Oh God," I muttered. "So not only has she got you for failing to protect her, she's got you as the cause of the fight and the trigger for the rape?"

He nodded, but something in his eyes told me he wasn't done yet.

"Go on," I urged.

"Well, of course she wanted to go to the police. Asked me if I would support her—tell them I'd witnessed it. She said I owed her. And I know that I did, but he was my best friend. I knew him better than anyone, and I just couldn't shake this feeling that somehow it was just one mammoth... misunderstanding. The Alistair Brown I knew just wouldn't do something like that. I know it sounds cheap considering I saw it with my own eyes, but I needed to hear it from him. I needed him to admit it to me before I could justify betraying him."

I nodded to show that I understood.

"I managed to persuade her to wait until I'd talked to him. Said that I wanted to give him a piece of my mind before the police picked him up, and that as soon as I'd done that, I'd go with her to report it. I just needed time to sort through the fucking mess and hoped that once she'd calmed down, maybe she'd have a rethink.

"When I went round to his place he wasn't there. The place looked like there'd been a struggle; there was a drop of blood on the rug, some torn clothing. I searched everywhere I could think of to find him. It was only when I tried to call him as a last resort, that I found several voicemails on my cell. They'd been left reasonably close together, a couple of hours after... after I'd seen them. By which time I would have been virtually comatose, lying on someone's sofa in a drunken fucking stupor. He'd called for my help. He'd needed me, and I hadn't answered. In the messages, he sounded distraught, his words barely coherent. The earlier ones were him begging me to answer my phone, saying over and over that he was sorry. And then later, he said that he'd done something really stupid and pleaded with me to forgive him.

"It was as much of a confession as I was ever going to get. I never saw him again. They found him face down in the Thames a couple of days later. They reckoned he jumped from the Albert Bridge, and from the state of the body, probably before the sun had even risen on the New Year."

I stifled the gasp of horror from escaping my lips with the pressure of my hand clamped firmly over my mouth. But my eyes betrayed the surge of emotions I was feeling, when a solitary tear spilled from my eye and onto my cheek. My poor Ethan. My poor, poor Ethan.

"I pleaded with Rebecca not to go through with reporting what had happened. Going to the police would have served no other purpose than to punish those who were innocent. The scandal would have torn his parents apart, destroyed his father's career. They'd suffered enough—they'd lost their only son to suicide and would never understand why. And Alistair, unable to live with what he'd done, had paid penance in death.

"Did she agree?" I asked, surprised by the sound of my own voice.

"Eventually. But she had conditions."

Why did that not surprise me?

"She agreed to allow Alistair to take his secret to the grave. To spare me the humiliation of explaining why I'd stood by and allowed my best friend to rape his girlfriend. And to protect Ali's parents from the scandal and devastating revelation that their son was a monster. All on one condition." He turned to face me. "That we became a couple. That I accepted her as my girlfriend, and that I'd stay with her no matter what. I told her that I didn't love her, that it couldn't possibly work. She said she didn't care as long as outwardly it looked as though I did. And that one day, who knows, maybe I would grow to love her. So we're bound by a secret, by betrayal, by lies—but definitely not by love.

"I thought at the time it was a small price to pay. After all, if I'd done something that night, things could have turned out very differently. Rebecca would have felt rescued, hopefully less traumatized. Alistair... Alistair would still be alive. I owed them both.

"Like I said, it was okay at first—convenient. I thought she'd tire of it eventually. I even screwed around and made sure she found out, hoping she'd finally get the message and give it up. But she didn't. She didn't seem to mind my sleeping around, accepted it as long as no one really got past one date. If they did, she'd make sure to sabotage any kind of relationship. Rebecca can be very cunning, sly, nasty—used to getting what she wants by any means necessary. Mercifully, she didn't even seem to mind that I wouldn't sleep with her, unless I was very drunk—God, you'd have to be. Fortunately for me, she wasn't highly sexed, but I imagine that had something to do with what had happened. She wasn't exactly frigid, but she could definitely take it or leave it. I guess that's why it didn't bother her that I went elsewhere. Sort of expected that I would."

I tried to ignore the way my insides burned with jealousy. Of course he had a past, we all did.

"Weeks turned into months, turned into years. The rest you know. I've tried to reason with her time and again. She knows I hate her, and she still keeps coming back for more, tightening the fucking noose around my neck every time she does. But recent events have taught me a valuable lesson. I feel like I've just opened my eyes after a long, deep sleep. I've spent the last seven years treating her like a constant, niggling headache that won't lift, but living in the hope that one day I'll wake up and it will have gone. But it won't—she won't. Because she's not a damned headache, she's a fucking cancer, and if I don't cut her out, she's going to kill me. I know that because I know I won't—can't survive without you. I wouldn't even want to. Without you, I'm nothing. When I thought I'd lost you, it took every scrap of strength I had just to take a breath. Nothing matters if I'm not with you, Angel.

"So I'm ready to do whatever is necessary to make this go away—to make her go away. The crazy thing is, telling you all this has made me see things much clearer. I've feared what she's capable of doing for so long that the fundamental reasons for doing so became distorted, and I just feared her, period. Somehow, somewhere along the line, I attributed her with more power than she has. And she's thrived on that. Guilt—that's all there is to this. Guilt for what happened to her, for what happened to Alistair, for how it would affect his parents if they discovered the truth. But I've paid my dues. I have to live my life now."

His words resounded in my head, thoughts of slaying our demons together, demons that were all bound by guilt in some form or other, and I knew he was right. He had paid his dues; we both had. I jumped to my feet and moved to his side, feeling the need to spur his resoluteness. "What will you do?"

"I have to go to London."

"London? Why?"

"I have to go back to where this all started. It's the only way I can end it. I'm going give Alistair's parents their answers. I can't protect them anymore. If I don't tell them, she sure as hell will. Then I'll go to the police, tell them what I know."

"What will happen to you?"

"I don't know. But whatever it is, it has to better than the hell we're in now. At least then she's got nothing on me. The only thing I can't control is how she'll react—and *that,* I realize, is my biggest fear. The fucker is, if I'd dealt with this before I met you, there would be no way for her to harm me. But what's been terrifying me from the second I found you is how she might take her revenge on me through you. I couldn't bear it if she did anything to harm you. That's why I had to pretend you didn't matter to me. I couldn't afford to give her the ammunition."

Fuck, how everything becomes clear when you're in the know. I thought of the countless times Ethan had voiced concerns over my safety, and that I'd shrugged them off. How distant and uncommunicative he'd been when he was in London. How, when he'd returned, he'd seemed so angry with the city, wanting to cut all ties and describing it as a love affair that was over. How I'd doubted his feelings for me for not speaking up and giving the bitch her marching orders that night at his apartment. How he'd jumped when she'd called him to heel. It was all about protecting me.

"If I'd known…"

"You didn't. And that was my fault too." He paused. "The thing is, after last night, I think we can safely assume she no longer believes we don't mean anything to each other."

"What do you think she's capable of?"

"I honestly don't know. But the break-in, Ponyo, writing you that check—they're just scratching the surface."

"Why do I suddenly feel that feeding that check to her wasn't such a good idea now?"

"That's why you can't be alone, not even for a single second. You have to promise me, Angel. We can't afford to take any risks with your safety. You've seen how manipulative and twisted she can be. Last night, she practically raced down that corridor like a rabid dog frothing at the mouth. It was only when she saw me that she reined it in. She's sly, Angel. She's got a sick, warped mind."

A chill ran through me as fragments of my nightmare ricocheted around my head like broken glass—the repulsive aftermath of her malevolent, violent threats toward me. Yes, I'd seen and heard more than enough evidence of Rebecca's depravity.

"I promise." I paused. "When will you go to London?"

"I made a call this morning." He smiled apologetically. "When I was… getting a glass of water." I nodded, understanding that he couldn't have exactly been honest with me at the time. Not without knowing about all of this first. "The earliest Alistair's parents can see me is Wednesday. I tried for sooner, but I didn't want to be too pushy. I didn't want to alarm them. His mom's so frail these days, she never recovered from losing Ali. She's been dying slowly herself, ever since. I'm afraid of what this news might do to her." Suddenly, panic flashed through his eyes, an element of doubt. "Do you think I'm selfish for doing this?"

"God no. You can't keep this secret any longer, you've suffered enough. I can understand why you made the choices you did at the time, why you felt you had to protect them. But enough is enough. None of what happened was your fault."

"Really? Is that what you really think, Angel? I was so afraid you'd hate me when you found out what I did."

"You didn't rape her. And you didn't drive Alistair to it either. You need to stop absorbing his guilt. Rebecca knew what she was doing when she chose to play with Alistair's feelings the way she did. She has to take responsibility for her own manipulative actions. I'm not saying she deserved it, but what she did—using him to get to you was despicable. Behavior like that isn't normal. They're not the actions of a sane person. And everything I've learned about her since, everything I've seen or heard just corroborates that fact. She's sick, Ethan. And apart from all that—there is absolutely nothing you could do that would make me hate you."

The relief on his face was almost palpable, and for the first time since he began this horror story, the lines on his worry-stricken face began to smooth. I held out my hand and he took it eagerly, pulling me into an embrace so tight, I almost had to gasp for breath.

"Please tell me you can see why I didn't tell you all this in the beginning. In retrospect, I know it would have been the most sensible thing to do, but you were so angry and I was desperate to protect you."

"I know, E. I know. Of course, I understand. But you should have trusted me. Trusted that we could have gotten through it together, just as we will now."

"I wasn't sure we were strong enough to endure it then. I knew that I loved you from the beginning, when I realized you were the reason I got up every morning, my reason for breathing. I knew that you were the only person I would ever love. But you weren't there yet. You were so vulnerable and fragile, and you had a right to be, you'd been let down at every turn. You were resisting your feelings and I got that. I just needed to be patient and hope that one day you'd catch up. But I knew that until you did, one wrong move would have you running in the wrong direction. And it did. When you told me you didn't love me... I died a million times inside."

The impact of his words was like a cold, steel blade, cutting and slicing into my heart—the searing pain of twisting guilt.

"No, Ethan, no. They were just words I used to protect myself—I didn't mean them." I glimpsed his pain right then, as if it were a physical, tangible thing. His eyes were brimming with it—suffering I'd caused on top of all this stinking bullshit that he'd been drowning in, alone, for Christ knows how long.

My hands fisted into his hair, as though the tighter I held him, the more emphasis and value my words would have. "Ethan, you must know that I've loved you in this. I loved you the second I stumbled into your arms outside my father's office. I felt myself begin to mend in that very second, like I'd been holding my breath my entire life and suddenly I could breathe. I didn't say the words until last night, because I was weak, afraid of them—but I thought you knew deep down. I'm so sorry, Ethan. I thought you knew."

As I searched his eyes, I saw the love and passion that burned inside me—the only thing that could fuel my heart—staring straight back. His actions mirrored mine as his hands pushed into my hair to grasp the back of my head in his hands.

"I know now."

He kissed me with a hunger that was essential to us both, our lips melding and our teeth clashing in our race to slake our hunger. It was a passion fueled by the desperation to erase any lingering doubts and to avow our love and devotion to a level that was sacred and untouchable.

Suddenly he was pushing up my skirt, his hands skimming the flesh of my thighs with a brutal urgency. As if with a mind of their own, my fingers had found the fly and button of his jeans and dragged the thick denim fabric down over his hips, his bulging, frenzied cock springing ardently free.

Within a second we were on the floor, Ethan's fingers closing around the delicate lace of my panties and tearing them from my bucking, soaking sex. Then he was over me and pushing inside me, stretching me and spreading me, filling me so completely that the noise which ruptured from my body was a shrill and sated whimper.

"Yes, Ethan. Fuck me. Fill me. Own me." My words were wild and feral, and Ethan's response was equally so.

He moved inside me as if his life depended on it, pounding and thrusting until I had no choice but to reach out with one hand and grip the leg of the coffee table to prevent from moving across the floor.

"Yes, harder. Fuck me harder." The fingers of my other hand dug into the flesh of his butt cheek as I urged him deeper into me, thrusting my hips shamelessly to meet each driving plunge.

My orgasm ripped through me with such burning pleasure that my body seemed to sing. Each muscle and nerve ending jangling with intense, decadent sensation.

"Mine," Ethan hissed through clenched teeth as he exploded hotly and thickly inside me.

He collapsed by my side, his fingers stroking my cheek gently. "Promise me you'll never leave me again, Angel."

"I promise. With every remaining beat of my heart, I promise. I love you, Ethan. I love you."

"Thank God," he breathed, closing his eyes as if to savor and cherish my words and my pledge. "Thank fucking God."

CHAPTER TWELVE

"**I** could come with you," I suggested thoughtfully as I lay enfolded in Ethan's arms on the sofa.

We'd lain for hours, deep in our own thoughts as we contemplated how to win the war that was Rebecca Staunton. Ethan frowned at me questioningly, clearly on a different page of the plan in his own mind and having no clue as to what I was referring to.

"To London," I clarified.

His face fell. "No. You can't."

"Why not?"

He paused for a few beats as if mindfully editing his words in to some sort of appropriateness. "Because I have to take her, Angel."

The horror in my eyes must have been unmistakable, because he sat bolt upright and took me by the shoulders. "It's the only way. When I drop this bombshell, I want her out of the States and at least the distance of an ocean away from you. Fuck, I want her as far away as possible from you."

"How can you do that? If she knows what you have planned, there's no way she'll go with you."

"Exactly. That's why I won't tell her. I won't tell her until I've spoken to Ali's parents."

"But she'll know we're together now. So how's that gonna work? She'll know something's up, Ethan. What are you going say, 'Hey, me and Angel are a couple, but do you fancy a day trip to London?' We both know she isn't dumb enough to fall for that."

"That's why I'm going to have to convince her that we're not together. And that—for a reason yet to be determined—I've decided to make it work with her, and I want us to move back to London."

"What?" I hissed in disbelief. I shrugged out of his grasp and pushed to my feet, clutching at my throat as bile bubbled up from my gut like rancid poison threatening to make me gag. "You can't be serious, Ethan. I can't go down that road again. You pretending I don't mean anything to you while you soothe and coddle her psychotic befuddlement. I don't want the venomous bitch anywhere near you. Fuck knows what she's capable of. No… just, no. We'll have to think of something else."

"Wait, Angel," he replied, getting to his feet to join me in my frantic pacing. "Before you throw this out altogether, just hear me out. I have to see the Browns in person, that's a given, so I have to go to London. We can't risk leaving her here, even if I did take you with me. She could do untold damage—I have to think of my family and Wilde Industries as well. Besides, when she finds out what I've done, there's no way we'll get her on a plane. She'll disappear off the radar and we'll be looking over our shoulders forevermore.

"I can't risk telling her before we leave for the same reasons. Even if I did manage to get her to come with me, Christ, it would be like carrying a ticking bomb on board. She's too unpredictable. It's way too risky. The only way she'll go with me willingly is if she thinks she's won."

I halted and glared at him. "Won? Won what? Won you over? Won the battle with me, with you as her prize? And what will she expect in her triumph? What exactly does pretending you want to make it work with her entail?" My lip trembled as torturous images of the two of them together raced around my mind, as they had a million times before.

Ethan winced, his expression torn between hurt and confusion. "What kind of fucking question is that? Do you really believe I could go near her in that way? Do you believe I could ever touch any other woman, who wasn't you, in that way?"

Damn! I closed my eyes in regret of my outburst, but nonetheless fearful about her expectations.

"No. I don't. But she'll be expecting more than the display of hatred she's come to expect from you so far, if you're to be believed."

He seemed to process this remark, as if the thought hadn't actually yet occurred to him. Letting it roll around his thoughts until the reality of it sank in. The only sign that it had was a single nod of his head.

"Let me just get her on the fucking plane. I'll deal with shit like that when I have to. But you can rest assured, you have nothing to worry about."

"How can you say that, E? I will worry for every second you spend with her. For your sanity, for your safety, for every devious, bullshit artifice she has up her sleeve. We've already deduced that she's a sick individual; the only thing we don't know is *how* sick."

Ethan nodded. "I know. But it's our only option. We have one chance to get this right. We have to be positive about the outcome. We can't ponder the what ifs and the alternative endings, or we'll talk ourselves out of it." He held out his hand to me and I took it, grateful to be pulled into the comfort of his embrace. "You have to trust that I'll handle this right, baby. This should be the best time of our lives. We've fallen in love and should be overflowing with happy events that will one day become memories to share with our grandchildren."

What he said warmed my heart and for the first time in forever, ignited me with hope and a thrill of excitement for the future. He pulled me in tighter and kissed the top of my head before continuing.

"But she's diluting that happiness—ruining our future memories."

This time his words had the opposite effect. He was right. He'd always been right. There was only one way to deal this impediment.

I tilted my chin just enough to look up at his face and nodded slowly. "Let's do it, then. Let's cut this fucking cancer out, once and for all."

We spent the next few hours devising a plan. Well, trying to, anyway. But every strategy we came up with was flawed in the same way. Whatever bullshit story Ethan hit her with, as to why he suddenly wanted to fly off into the sunset with her, just didn't seem credible. We couldn't underestimate her ability to spot a ruse when she saw one; after all, she was the motherfucking master.

Suddenly, the answer seemed to hit me between the eyes.

"It has to come from me," I blurted, almost before the idea had fully materialized.

"What?"

"She has to believe that *I* no longer want *you*. And she needs to hear it from me."

"No fucking way, Angelica. There is no way you're going anywhere near her."

"Hear me out, Ethan. I've been hearing you out all goddamn day. The least you can do is listen to the idea. Just be open-minded for one minute, and if you don't like it, then… then we'll just have to shoot ourselves, because frankly we're out of options."

"I don't like it."

"You haven't heard it."

"I still don't like it." He folded his arms, his jaw muscles beginning to bunch again.

I mirrored his actions, folding my arms, my brows arching obstinately.

He rolled his eyes. "I'll listen, but I won't like it."

"Don't interrupt until I'm done."

He sighed. "Yes, miss."

From where it came, I had no idea, but suddenly this plan was taking shape in my mind, rolling off my tongue like I was some sort of expert conspirator. Perhaps I was worried that if I didn't get it out quick enough, Ethan would just dismiss the idea out of hand.

So, I launched into my plan.

I would go to her tomorrow and explain that I'd spent the last couple of days trying to convince Ethan to commit to me. I'd say that he had explained how they were connected by some tragedy in their pasts, one which he wouldn't reveal to me, but that because of it, they'd formed an unbreakable bond. I would pretend that Ethan had made his intentions very clear, that he'd refused, point-blank, to end their relationship. And that although he had feelings for me, they would never compare to the connection he had with her, and therefore, all he could offer me was a casual affair.

I'd tell her that I wasn't the sharing kind and had said as much to Ethan. His response had been staunch. If I was going to force him to choose, it would be the same outcome every time—her. So, I'd decided to leave town, to move on with my life. I'd tell her I was angry, felt short-changed. I'd say that she was welcome to him. But that I'd changed my mind about the money she'd offered—hence, the reason for the visit. She'd expected me to be a gold-digging whore, it wouldn't be hard to convince her she was right.

Then Ethan would arrange to take her out to dinner and give her a similar rendition of the same story. That I was a fling who wanted more than he was able to offer. Except, he would add how he's now realized no other woman would ever understand him the way she did. And that he was finished with New York and wanted to fly back to London, as soon as possible.

Hopefully, she would then believe that, at best there was hope for them as a couple. At worst, that things were back to how they once were before I came along to muddy the waters. That I was no longer a threat and Ethan was happily sticking to his side of the bargain.

Ethan was staring at me, mesmerized, a single raised eyebrow and pursed lips creating an expression which implied he thought I'd gone completely mad. I think.

"At least then she won't be expecting you to throw your arms around her, or worse…" I couldn't bring myself to finish the sentence. He blinked, narrowing his eyes, and I knew I needed to give him one last little shove. "And of course, there's the added bonus that when you reveal you've confessed all to Alistair's parents and been to the police, she'll still believe I ran off with your money to—who-knows-where—but miles away from here."

Suddenly, his face relaxed, his focus straying from my face as if he was actually contemplating the plausibility of what I'd said. I waited a few minutes for him to process, using the time to concoct a slightly different version of the plan in my head. Of course, I was all too aware that the idea worked well in theory, but I had the threat—her "Plan B" to consider. However, I wasn't about to let that slip to Ethan, or there would be no way he'd agree to it.

"Well?" I asked, resolving to think about it later.

"I'll admit it sounds like a workable platform." Oh, my hopes were raised. Then he shook his head. "But although I agree it's the most convincing approach to the problem, I would be crazy to let you do it. It would be like allowing you to walk into the lion's den with a bomb strapped to you just for good measure. It's not even as though I could send one of the security team with you; she'd rumble us in seconds."

The idea that he thought I was no match for her suddenly irked me. "Oh for Christ's sake, E, what do you think she's going to do to me? She'll be alone and she won't even know to expect me. I can handle her. She might have a badass attitude, but she's almost a foot smaller than me."

"Don't let her slight form deceive you, Angel. You can fit a lot of poison into a small package. Look at Jia, would you underestimate her?"

"Don't let *my* fragile soul deceive *you*. I may have some… imperfections on the inside, but there's nothing wrong with the outside. I'm tougher than I look," I spat angrily, his words grating like sand paper. Then I thought again about what he'd said. "Wait a minute—that could actually work."

"What could?"

"Jia. If it makes you feel better, I could take *her* with me." I smiled triumphantly. "Problem solved. It's perfect."

Ethan looked slightly panicked. "Oh, fuck, baby. I don't know. That's a lethal combination—like throwing a lit cigarette into a room full of highly flammable liquid. I thought you wanted to convince her, not antagonize her. Plus it would mean telling Jia everything, and she's not my biggest fan as it is."

"Jia is the last person who will judge you. She hates the bitch almost as much as I do. And actually, it was Jia who helped me to see this situation more clearly last night. Urged me to see what was going on with you, even before you begged me. In fact, she couldn't have been more flattering toward you. You requesting her help would even things up a little, get you back in her good books. And she makes a far better friend than an enemy. If I tell her to behave herself, she will." I paused for a second, feeling like I was almost there. Just the slightest tweak. One more shove in the right direction.

"Think about it, E. Think about the way her mind works. She is content so long as she has you in her life. She doesn't care that you don't love her, or that you sleep with other people. And although the concept seems totally off the wall to us, on her planet it makes perfect sense. She believes that one day she'll be enough for you—that all she has to do is wait. In her eyes, I'm the kind of person who would give you up and walk away quietly in exchange for a big fat check. We're just telling her what she wants to hear, what she believes is real already. All we're doing is reinforcing her delusion."

Ethan shoved his hands into his hair, letting one drop to rub at the tension in the back of his neck. His jaw muscles worked furiously as he paced up and down, up and down.

Finally, he halted. "What if—"

"I thought we weren't pondering the what ifs and the alternative endings. Diluted happiness, remember?"

He nodded slowly. "I'll never forgive myself if anything happens to you."

"Ditto. But we're doing this together; it's what we agreed. Your demons—then mine. And besides, nothing bad is going to happen. Trust me."

"I do trust you. More than anyone I know."

I smiled. "So, are we gonna shake on this?"

"Shake?" he asked with a crooked smile. "I don't think so, you gorgeous woman. Come here. I can think of far better ways to seal the deal."

I stepped into his embrace, his arms squeezing me to him so tightly it forced a tiny squeal to escape my lips. A warm, familiar fluttering stirred deep down inside me as he peered down through long, thick lashes, his eyes as blue as the ocean, reaching right into my heart.

"You're right, you know," he said wistfully, as he studied my face. "You are an incredibly strong person. I don't know how you manage such tenacity. Anybody who dared to underestimate you would be a damned fool. It's you who's given me the strength and determination to finally face this nightmare."

"Nonsense. You're the formidable Mr. Wilde, COO, approaching CEO of Wilde Industries. How could I possibly inspire *you*?"

"You have no idea, Angel. Don't be fooled by my title. It takes a different kind of strength and grit to overcome the kind of battles you've faced. Something which runs far deeper than boardroom capabilities or pulling off superlative commercial deals and accruing lucrative acquisitions. Something which far exceeds knowing when to buy and when to sell or when to build. No—you're a gift. A gift to me from Heaven." Barely grazing my lips, he kissed me. I tugged him closer, sinking my hands into the rear pockets of his jeans to cup his ass.

"But without you, I would be completely unaware of that, E. It's because of you that I've learned to believe in myself. So it seems we both came along just at the right moment—just in time to save each other."

My words were disrupted by a sudden quivering sensation against my pelvis. "You're vibrating," I said, releasing him reluctantly.

His expression seemed to tighten again as he reached inside his jeans pocket to retrieve his cell. Glancing at the display, he sighed, the tension in his bunching jaw reaching his eyes as his gaze found mine.

My chest contracted. "Is it her?"

He nodded. "Again."

"How many times?"

"There are several texts, a half dozen missed calls, and a couple of voice messages."

"Have you listened?"

"No."

"You can't keep ignoring her. We need to actuate this plan soon, or it won't be believable." My belly fluttered with nerves as I spoke the words. I nodded toward his cell. "Let's listen together."

The texts were pretty much what we expected, basic, brief commands: Where are you?; Answer your phone; Call me, Ethan. The voice messages, however, were terser—threatening even, her voice whiney and affected. God, how I hated her voice.

Ethan, darling, you know how I despi-i-ise insolence. You'd better call me—or else. Progressing to: *I'm getting a tad irate. I do hope your elusiveness isn't anything to do with your little friend. It had BETTER not.* And finally: *You have two hours to make contact. DO NOT disappoint me.*

The latter had been left a few minutes ago. I shuddered, my flesh crawling at the sound of her voice and her unmitigated effrontery. I replayed her words in my head, hating the way she spoke to Ethan—hating her.

"I can picture her now," Ethan said, "wearing out the soles of her Jimmy Choos as she paces the carpet, waiting for me to jump to her command. She hates it when she's not in control."

"Then I think you should call her—keep her sweet. It's important she thinks she is in control. The last thing we need is her coming here to hunt you down." I glanced at the door nervously.

"I'm surprised she hasn't done exactly that. But at least we know she hasn't left the hotel since last night. Jackson would have let me know if she'd called for him to take her anywhere. And the hotel security have been put on alert. They'll inform me if she leaves. I think you're right though. I should call."

"Wait a minute. Hotel? Last night, she went to a hotel?"

"Yes, Jackson took her. But not just last night—she's been there ever since she arrived in Manhattan."

Oh!

That absolute gem of knowledge instantly erased so many torturous images that I'd concocted in my mind over the last week. I'd pictured her roaming around Ethan's apartment—somewhere I'd come to think of as home, until she turned up—wearing nothing but Ethan's shirts—my shirts. In my mind her vileness had desecrated every room, leaving her scent—her mark. Suddenly, like in a cartoon, the image in my mind burst into flames, gradually burning out to leave nothing but a puff of smoke. The comical illusion made me smile.

"You didn't think she was at the apartment?" Ethan looked stricken by the idea.

I shrugged. "She had Jackson take her things to 'her room,' I distinctly remember."

"She doesn't *have* a room. She'd never set foot in the place until that night. And *I* had Jackson remove her things and check her into one of our hotels the moment you left. It's one of Manhattan's best, over on Park. I made certain she was given one of the best suites so she didn't complain for long. That whole luggage thing was purely a performance for your benefit—she was pissing on her territory. Except it wasn't hers to piss on," he added quickly, shaking his head. "God knows the images you've conjured."

"You're doing a fine job of dispelling them one by one," I assured him. "Although, I did have this wild one of you taking her back to the apartment last night and then sneaking out again to come here. I pictured her waking this morning and calling out your name in that insufferable, pretentious tone of hers. *Ethan, dar-r-rling!*" I mimicked. "I've been trying to think of places you could tell her you've been. I must admit though, I am so incredibly relieved to know she's not there, and it's an even bigger bonus that she has no idea you're not."

Ethan smiled. "Still, it's probably safer to tell her I'm with Damon. I'll say I had a business crisis and had my phone on silent. When I take her to dinner, I'll tell her I was putting things in place to leave for London."

"Good idea," I nodded. "So how exactly did you leave it with her last night?"

"She fled to the bathroom to compose herself after you left. She would have been furious about the whole check-eating thing, but I think she was more focused on how much of the debacle I'd witnessed. Rebecca doesn't *do* humiliation, and you gave her a huge slice of it." He paused. "That's what concerns me about this plan of yours. She won't forget that in a hurry."

"Stop worrying, E, we've agreed now. What happened then?"

"I had a few choice words with your father—the fucker—about what I'd do to him if he ever laid so much as a finger on you again. Then I gave him a few ideas about where he could stick his donation. He just sneered and stormed off, muttered something under his breath like, 'like father, like son.' Not quite sure what he meant by that."

I winced, feeling another layer of dread settle in the pit of my stomach. We would have to wait for another day to set about slaying that particular demon. For now it wasn't something I even wanted to think about. "What then?" I steered the conversation back to the here and now.

"I had Jackson take Rebecca back to the hotel, grabbed a cab, and came here."

"A cab?"

"Don't look so surprised. I'm not opposed to public service transport."

"I just can't picture it."

"I wasn't bothered how I got here as long as I did. I was too busy having haunted visions of my own, about you here with the good ol' Dr. Foster."

Of course, I hadn't thought of that. God, how we'd inadvertently tortured each other's minds. Taking his hand, I laced my fingers through his. Then retrieving his cell from the coffee table, I placed it in his hand and closed his fingers over it.

"Call her," I urged as he glanced down at the object like it were something odious. "Why don't you go out onto the terrace to do it? I'll call Jia from inside—ask her to come over. It's time we got this mission underway."

Grateful, I think, for the suggestion of making the call privately, he took a deep breath and nodded. It would be a grueling task to feign charm and amiability toward her, as it was, without having to consider my feelings. Swiftly, he kissed me on the forehead and began to make his way out to the terrace, closing the doors firmly behind him.

I felt sick as I watched him go, my stomach twisting into a tight, painful knot. Turning on my heel, I headed to the bedroom to find my cell.

Less than two hours later, Jia was sitting open-mouthed at my breakfast bar. In one hand, she held a glass of wine and in the other, a slice of suspended pizza—which she'd insisted on picking up on the way over. She ate junk food constantly; her metabolism was like that of a freight train.

We'd given her a condensed version of the story, so much as we could manage without omitting any crucial factors. Throughout, she remained silent and virtually expressionless, her eyes only flickering fleetingly at the point in the story where Ethan had walked in on the incident at Alistair's apartment, and again when Alistair's body had been found, but she didn't comment until the story ended. And more importantly— as I'd anticipated—she didn't judge. Well, not Ethan, anyway.

"Wow. That is super fucked-up. I mean, you couldn't even write that shit. What planet did you say she came from again?" It was a rhetorical question, and she didn't wait for an answer. "So, I'm guessing you want some kinda help kicking Bo Peep's prissy little ass outa here, right?"

I nodded. The only thing I'd told her when I called was that we needed her help. Without question—apart from the toppings we preferred on our pizza—she'd dropped everything and rushed right on over.

Mercifully, the conversation between Ethan and Rebecca had remained brief too. After apologizing for taking so long to call her back, he explained he'd been tied up in a crisis meeting with Damon, but would expound all at the dinner he planned to spoil her with tomorrow evening. He told her he thought she'd be pleased about a decision he'd arrived at and that he had some exciting plans for the future. Suggesting she buy a new dress for the event, he ended the call saying he would send Jackson to collect her at seven. The bitch, it appeared, had been satisfactorily appeased.

Together, we told Jia the plan, her eyes lighting up with the suggestion she accompany me to see Rebecca at the hotel.

"It's purely precautionary, Jia," Ethan warned. "I don't want Angel going there alone, but it would help if you—"

"Stayed in my cage?" Jia cut in.

"Something like that." He nodded. I shot him a look and he swiftly added, "We would be really grateful, of course."

"Of course," she repeated, smiling sweetly. "And I can do that. The cage thing, I mean. Unless the fucker flicks her crazy switch—then I'll kill the bitch." Her smile grew wider as she beamed across at us, and I couldn't help but giggle.

Ethan looked as nervous as ever.

"Chill the fuck out, Wilde. We can *so* do this." Turning to me, she raised her glass. "Here's to you and me, bitch. You can be my wingman, anytime."

"Bullshit! You can be mine," I giggled, my Maverick standing up to her Iceman.

Ethan scowled. "Is now really the time for insouciance, ladies?"

"Insi-what?" Jia looked bemused.

"Flippancy, Jia," he clarified. "It's not an episode of *Cagney and Lacey.* You need to take this seriously."

Knowing he was right, I reined it in swiftly, shooting Jia a warning look which advised her to do the same. Collecting herself, she sucked in her cheeks to refrain from releasing the bubble of laughter I knew was building inside her. After a moment, she cleared her throat, adopting a more somber look.

"I've got this, Wilde, you don't need to worry. I can do serious." Grabbing her purse, she pushed to her feet. "I'll bring breakfast and be here by eight." She made a move to leave, heading off toward the door.

"Jia," Ethan called after her. "I am worried—but not about you. Angel trusts you. And that means I do too. Thank you."

Jia stared at him blankly for a few seconds before the edge of her lip curled into a smile. She nodded and opened the door. "It was *Top Gun,* by the way," she called over her shoulder.

Then she was gone.

"Oh. Do you have a copy?" Ethan asked later, when I explained what Jia had meant by her parting shot about *Top Gun* and the wingman reference.

"No actually. It's one of Jia's favorites."

"Let's watch one of your movies, then. It will be a good distraction, take our minds off the hideous task ahead."

"Really, one of mine? You wouldn't prefer to watch the news channel, or the game, or a documentary?"

"God no. As usual you made a persuasive point when you highlighted the advantages of animation. The world *is* full of grim reality without watching it for entertainment."

I scrambled off his lap where I'd sat comfortably for the last hour since Jia left and opened the cupboard to view the array of DVDs.

"What would you like?" I asked eagerly before he could change his mind. Escaping to the world of animation sounded like an amazing idea.

"Oh, I don't mind. You choose. Anything but the one with Cruella de Vil. I've had enough of *her* to last a lifetime."

"You've had enough of Cruella de Vil?" I turned to look at him quizzically.

"It's Jackson's nickname for *her*. He isn't aware that I know, of course, but it's very fitting, don't you think? Especially as the name appears to be a play on the words, cruel and devil."

"Ah, yes, I hadn't realized. How very appropriate."

An involuntary shiver slithered down my spine as I thought of the film which featured the aforementioned antagonist. It was the only Disney film I hated, but ironically, not because of the Rebecca-like character. It was because of the dogs. Well, not dogs per se—I love dogs. Just not Dalmatians.

"I haven't got that one, oddly enough. I have a strange aversion to Dalmatians."

"Oh? Strange how?"

"Well, strange because I can't really explain why. They appear in my dreams a lot—the bad ones. Always large and sinister and vicious." I shrugged. "Stupid really."

The dream I'd had the night before came flitting unbidden into my mind. The one in which *Cruella* had ridden a Dalmatian like a horse, driving the pack of hungry beasts through the woods as she gave chase. Then I realized how absurd it was that we should have this conversation only the following day. I trembled again.

"You're shivering. Come here." Ethan's voice was soft and warm, immediately chasing away the dreadful memory. Willingly, I settled onto the sofa beside him again, his arms folding around me protectively.

"Do you think Jia might consider staying with you for a few days? Just until this nightmare is over?"

"No! I don't want her to. Why would you ask?" I paused to examine his expression. "Is this about the closet again?"

"I don't want you to be alone."

"Ethan, being in the company of others doesn't mean you're not alone. You could invite the whole of Manhattan to share my bed—it wouldn't make the slightest difference. It's you that I need."

"But I won't be here, baby, at least not for a few days. I have a really important meeting tomorrow that I just can't get out of. I'll need to leave here by 7:00 a.m. if I'm to get home and change, and we can't risk me coming back here tomorrow night. And then there's London. Realistically, this could be the last night we spend together for a while."

The thought made my stomach churn with anxiety. Of course, it had been lurking at the edge of my conscious mind all day, waiting for me to acknowledge it. "And you're worried I'll head back to the closet?" I touched his face tenderly.

"I'm terrified you will."

"E, I won't lie to you. I'm dreading being apart from you again. Especially, given the circumstances—London, with her, the pretense, and you having to face Alistair's parents and the police. But as long as you are in my life and I know you're coming back to me, I know I'm not alone. It's only life without you that I can't face. I can't promise that I won't have nightmares—they've been a part of my makeup for as long as I can remember—but I can promise I won't camp out in the closet. You're back in my life now, and I'm no longer afraid."

"I never want you to feel that lost and alone ever again, baby."

Suddenly, I thought of something and pushing to my feet, I ran into the kitchen to search through the drawer.

"Angel, what... what are you doing?"

I rummaged until I found what I was looking for, my fingers closing over the object, creating an instant feeling of comfort and familiarity. Feeling pleased with myself, I strode victoriously back in to the lounge and held out my hand for his. When he acceded, I placed it in his palm, closing his fingers around it. Then I watched as his expression changed. At first, his brow furrowed in puzzlement, and then I saw that with touch alone, he'd identified the thing in his hand, and his lips curled up into a heart melting smile.

Closing his eyes, he whispered, "Thank you."

Pulling me into his lap, he raised his hand to kiss the object zealously, the way you might kiss a dice for luck. The key ring glimmered, the warm glow of the red catching in the light from the lamp. But it was more than just a key ring. It was a symbol—or one half of a symbol. When united with its other half it would form the unmistakable image of a red gemstone heart surrounded by diamond-encrusted angel wings. I'd given it to Ethan as a gift, attaching it to the key to my apartment and explaining that as long as we were together, I would be whole—just like the two halves. It had been my way of conveying to him how much he completed me, and how much he'd mended my brokenness by putting back the pieces of my damaged soul. Then, it had been the only way I knew how to tell him I loved him.

Ethan had returned the key to my apartment when I'd refused to listen to the only explanation he would give me about who Rebecca was and why she was in his life. At the time, he couldn't bear to tell me the truth, and so I'd rejected him, ordering him out of my life. The key had remained attached to the partial symbol, and its return had broken me all over again.

Now I was giving it back to its rightful owner, this time to reassure him of how strong I was when we were together—mended and complete. But I no longer needed it as a means to speak those three little words I was once scared to utter.

Because I was no longer afraid.

"I love you, Ethan Wilde."

A beaming smile stretched across his face, his eyes glowing as he seemed to burst with pride.

I gazed into his eyes, wishing I could read into his mind. What thought was filtering through it to create such a self-satisfied grin? "You look as if I've just given you the world," I muttered.

"That's because you have. You've given me you."

CHAPTER THIRTEEN

Ordinarily, I wasn't one to bite my nails, but right now, I was doing a damn fine impression of someone who did. As I paced the terrace waiting anxiously for Jia's arrival, I inhaled great gulps of air attempting to steady my nerves and calm the queasiness. My stomach roiled as if I were in the midst of a turbulent sea.

Ethan had left at seven with an encumbered weariness I was frankly worried about. We'd luxuriated in sweat-soaked sex until we'd fallen asleep in the early hours, waking a couple of hours later, at around 4:00 a.m., only to start all over again. After finally grabbing the bare minimum of sleep, I'd awoken to the sound of the shower. It had taken a matter of seconds picturing him naked in a steamy room with the hot spray of the water pounding against his wonderfully firm body to realize I was horny again.

What the fuck?

I'd closed my hand over my tender sex, hoping the pressure would alleviate my unreasonable, insatiable appetite, but to no avail. I was wet and throbbing, and my sensitive, inflamed flesh just served as a reminder as to why I was sensitive, and therefore only succeeded in exacerbating the sensation. So, powerless to resist him, I'd wandered quietly into the bathroom to gaze longingly at his nakedness through the glass shower wall.

He'd had his back to me, his hands running gently through his hair as he rinsed out shampoo. The soap suds were trailing gently down his immaculate form, caressing his skin in a way which made me feel irrationally envious.

Sensing my presence, he'd turned, his eyes lighting up with something unnamable as my eyes flickered voyeuristically over his body. My breath had caught as my hooded gaze settled on his cock, the rush of blood causing it to swell and twitch under my scrutiny. I'd bitten down into my lower lip, trying, albeit half heartedly, to curb my hunger. It was futile. The apex of my thighs was now slick with moisture, my breasts, full and heavy and beginning to ache. Then, without realizing, my hand had suddenly drifted up to my nipple to ease the jutting tension.

"Oh hell, woman," Ethan had growled through clenched teeth. "You're going to fucking kill me. Come here." The series of all-consuming orgasms which followed would remain ingrained in my memory forever.

No amount of Ethan Wilde would ever be too much for me. I needed him like I needed my next breath, like a drug. We gave ourselves to each other unreservedly and without restraint. It was as if basking in the hedonistic bliss we took from each other's bodies was a constant reminder of what was crucial to our existence. The reason we bothered to breathe our next breath in the first place. Sex seemed to fuel us, to incite us, and give us strength and power—a catalyst to drive us forward and give us the courage to fight. It seemed to bind us together, melding our hearts and souls, until we no longer knew where he ended and I began. To us, sex was fundamentally essential.

After leaving himself barely ten minutes to dress, we'd finally tore ourselves away from each other with as little drama as we could muster—no prolonged goodbyes. We parted with intentional poise, cool and relaxed, as if we would see each in a couple of hours, when of course, the reality was we had no idea when the next time would be. By remaining detached from this facet of truth, we hoped to preserve our mindset and reserve our energy for the drama the day was sure to bring. We both did a pretty good job, considering. But behind the feigned nonchalance, the strain and the weariness had been evident in Ethan's eyes.

Jia arrived, as promised, at eight with coffee and pastries, which she subsequently forced me to eat.

"What use are you to me, bitch, if the shit goes down and you're out of fuel. I'll have to bust her ass on my own. Just eat the goddamn pastry, will you."

I did as I was told, and actually found that she was right. A sugar rush was exactly what I needed.

We spent some time talking about how we would approach the task ahead, Jia wanting to plan for every possible outcome, inventing all sorts of what-if scenarios. It wasn't the way I liked to do things, you could be over prepared, and besides, nothing ever went the way you envisioned it would. I preferred to be more impromptu, to do things off the cuff.

"Look, Jia, can we just go," I said, feeling frustrated with the talk and no action. "I just want to get this over with."

She held up her hands in surrender. "Okay, honey, this is your party. If you want to go, we go."

Just as we were about to leave, my cell rang, and my heart lifted the instant I saw Ethan's name lighting the display. It had only been a few hours, but I missed him like crazy.

"Hey, baby," I greeted him warmly. Jia rolled her eyes.

"Angel, thank God. Tell me you haven't left yet?" The anxiety in his voice crackled with electric intensity down the phone line.

"Not yet, why? What's up?"

"I'm not sure this is a good idea anymore. I don't want you to go. The thought of you and her together scares the shit out of me. I can't function. I'm in the middle of closing a huge deal and my head is all over the place. I can't deal with this right now."

"I know this isn't the best timing, E, but what choice do we have? I can handle this. I'll be fine. Please, try and focus on the meeting. When I have news, I'll call you."

Jia hitched a brow questioningly.

"No, Angel, wait. There has to be another way to deal with this without getting you involved. Just leave it to me. I promise I will sort this."

"I'm already involved. Don't you think the thought of *you* and her scares the shit out of *me*? My stomach is eating itself from the inside out with the thought of you and her having dinner tonight. You having to pretend that I mean nothing, telling her what she longs to hear. But I'll have to endure it. We get one shot at this."

"Angel, just listen. I'm not convinced we've covered all of our options. Something just doesn't feel right. Please, I'm begging you, just wait a couple more hours, think about what I've said. There has to be a more viable route to dealing with this."

I knew there was no way he was going to shift on this. Part of me was wishing I hadn't shared my idea of going to see her with him. That way he wouldn't be worried, and I wouldn't be worried about him worrying.

"Angel?" he prompted when I didn't answer.

"Okay," I acceded, reluctantly. "I'll wait a couple of hours. Jia's here. We'll put our heads together, see if we can figure something out."

Ethan exhaled, audibly relieved. "Good. Thank you. Listen, I have to go, they're waiting for me. I'll call you later so you can tell me your plan B."

Plan B.

The words were like ice-cold fingers closing viciously around my throat, a sharp foreboding reminder of just how sinister and twisted Rebecca Staunton actually was.

"Yes. Plan B." I paused for a beat and then added, "I love you, Ethan."

"I love you too." He hung up.

Jia glared at me. "You have got to be kidding, bitch. I thought you were hell-bent on showing her how big your balls are?"

I shoved my cell into my pocket and strode toward the door. "I still am. Let's go."

The hotel was in the Upper East Side on Park Avenue. Ethan hadn't been kidding when he'd said it was one of the best in Manhattan. In fact, he couldn't have understated it more. The hotel was a paragon of timeless luxury and sophistication. After strolling casually through the gleaming hotel foyer, doing our best to look like we knew exactly where we were going, and not at all mesmerized by our surroundings, we took the elevator to the 42nd floor and exited cautiously.

Part of the reason I hadn't wanted to plan too much for this conversation was because I hadn't divulged to Jia anything of Rebecca's vile and evil threat—or Plan B, as she'd termed it. I'd considered telling her, for all of thirty seconds, but in the end decided against it. The phrase *red rag to a bull* had swiftly sprung to mind, and I needed Jia to be as calm and compliant as possible.

The truth was I had no clue how this conversation was going to pan out. Anything was possible and nothing could surprise me. I'd found myself feeling torn between being afraid of Rebecca and what she was capable of, and being angry enough at the turmoil and heartbreak she'd caused to want to rip her pointed little face from her scrawny little neck. But fear and anger were two emotions I was absolutely certain I couldn't afford to embrace. It would be suicide to reveal my true feelings to someone as calculated as her. No, I needed to remain calm, make it seem like I was playing into her hands, appeal to her amenable side. If she had one.

When the elevator slid open, we exited, and following Ethan's instructions, made a left turn toward the Premium Deluxe Suite.

"Remember—polite, persuasive, smile," I prompted Jia.

"I've got it," she said, flashing a set of perfect teeth.

We moved slowly, but confidently down the wide hallway, my heart hammering wildly in my chest. Suddenly there was the sound of a door opening at the end of the corridor and a sharply dressed man stepped into view, filling the space in the doorway. His head was lowered, his attention focused on the buttons of his fine suit jacket, which he fastened with precision. The man was instantly familiar. Everything about him, from his clothes, to his stance, to his stubbly chin and buzz cut—Jackson. The sight of him sent me scurrying into an instant panic.

What the fuck was he doing here?

Jia spotted him at the same time and shot me a *what now* look. I dove into the open doorway of another room, pulling her with me and paying no heed to who might be inside, just desperate to be out of sight. My heart hammered as I leaned up against the wall just inside the open door, trying to compute what I'd just seen and what the hell I was going to do. No amount of planning could have prepared for this.

"Excuse me, can I help you?" The housekeeper was suddenly beside us, appearing from somewhere inside the suite. Jia acted quickly, pulling a couple of twenty dollar bills from her jeans pocket, and ushering the woman back into the suite, speaking quietly to her.

Then I heard a voice.

The unmistakable, snooty, supercilious tones of Rebecca Staunton drifted down the hallway toward me like a poisonous fog, and I felt my throat constrict with bitterness.

"Stop right there, you forgot something," she ordered.

A movement in my peripheral vision caught my eye, and my gaze flickered to the housekeeping cart parked just outside the door. The cart was a large metal cabinet on wheels, and the side facing me was open, revealing plush, freshly laundered towels and luxury linen. The front of the cart facing the doorway where Jackson stood had a shiny chrome finish, and to my utter amazement created an almost perfect mirror.

Keeping perfectly still, I watched as Rebecca drew up behind Jackson and slid a tie around his neck.

"You really ought to take more care, Jackson, dear," she purred in her pretentious accent, moving around to his front to do up his tie.

"How would it look if you were to be observed leaving my room with only half the clothes you arrived in? You need to slow down, you eager little man."

What the fuck?

"I have to get back to work," Jackson replied impatiently.

"Yes, you do. And I need to go and have a bath. I need to rid my skin of this vulgar scent you insist on leaving behind. Eww."

Holy fucking Christ—he's sleeping with her.

My mind felt like it had suddenly been hurled into a brick wall, my thoughts scattering into a million pieces and leaving me drowning in a wave of confusion. Almost retching with repulsion, I watched as she reached up on tiptoes, planting a kiss firmly on his lips. As she did, the pink, silk robe she wore slipped off her bare shoulder, the weight of it causing it to gape at the front. A fleeting glimpse revealed nothing but a pair of panties underneath. And then she slammed the door shut.

Jackson began his approach toward me, his reflection in the cart drawing nearer as I pressed my body against the wall and held my breath. As he drew level with the doorway, I caught a glimpse of his expression. His usually handsome face was twisted into something that could only be described as revulsion, his sleeved arm rising to his face to swipe at his lips. It reminded me of a small boy's reaction to the sloppy, unwanted kiss left by his aged aunt.

My God, he hated her as much as I did. As much as Ethan did.

What in the hell was going on?

The second I heard the elevator door slide closed, signaling its departure, I stepped out into the hallway, and ran full pelt down the corridor in pursuit, pressing the call button for the one adjacent to the one on its decent. Rebecca would have to wait, I needed answers.

The elevator car arrived in a matter of seconds—though it seemed like hours—and I entered quickly, Jia appearing at my side as I reached out and pressed the button for the foyer.

"What the fuck, Angel? What's going on?"

"I have no idea, but I intend to find out."

She nodded as we began our descent.

"I need to speak with Jackson alone, Jia. Go home and I'll call you when I'm done."

"Are you kidding? Wilde will have my balls served on a fucking platter. I promised him I'd stay with you."

"Jia, you don't *have* balls, and I can handle this. Please, I don't have time to argue."

The elevator came to a halt and we stepped out into the foyer, our eyes scanning around for Jackson. But he was nowhere to be seen. Turning, I glanced up at the floor counter above the elevator next to mine and instantly realized my mistake. Of course, the car. He'd continued on to the basement garage. Stepping quickly back inside, and shouting out a promise that I would call to a dumbfounded Jia, I made my way to the basement.

I spotted him instantly, making his way across the deserted parking lot to the Cadillac Escalade. Following swiftly but stealthily, I made up the space between us, and by the time he reached the vehicle, I was only a matter of feet behind him. He spun around defensively, suddenly alerted to my presence by my not-entirely-silent footsteps. I watched as his expression morphed from nauseated shock to one of feigned, pleasant surprise.

"Angel. What are you doing here?"

"I could ask you the same thing," I snapped. He opened his mouth to speak, but I was quicker. "Save it." He clamped it shut in a tight, straight line. "You're fucking screwing her."

It was a statement, not a question.

For a couple of beats, he said nothing, eyes narrowing, jaw muscles working furiously. "You'd better get in."

We sat in the same booth of the same coffee shop we'd sat in the night of the break-in at my apartment. After Ponyo.

"Thanks, Annie." Jackson smiled at the waitress, a small portly woman in her early sixties, as she filled our mugs with coffee. She responded with a weary squeeze to his arm and wandered away.

"You a regular here or something?" My tone was churlish as I glanced around at the worn, outdated décor and furniture, all of which looked like it could have benefited from a decent clean. Funny how I hadn't really noticed it the first time I'd been here.

Jackson shrugged. "This place is the nearest thing to what—back in London—I would call a 'greasy spoon.'"

"A greasy what?"

"A cafe… a diner, or coffee shop to you. Listen, it doesn't matter, I just feel comfortable here, that's all."

I didn't say anything, just glared across the table at him.

"What did you see?" he asked, tipping a mammoth amount of sugar into his coffee.

"Enough."

"I know it sounds cliché, but it's not what you think."

I laughed mirthlessly. "It *sounds* like bullshit, Jackson. He thinks of you as family, you know." I meant Ethan, of course, but I knew there was no need to elaborate.

"Don't you think I know that?" The words hissed from him furiously, but somehow the anger seemed to be aimed inwardly. Like he was mad at himself because of how true the statement was, rather than at me for drawing attention to it. "What I do is as much for him as it is for me."

Confusion hit me anew, and then irritation—because nothing made any damn sense. "What the fuck are you talking about?"

He held up a hand to halt me. "Just let me think for a minute."

Averting his gaze, he turned to stare out through the window, his fingers kneading the tension from his forehead. I could almost hear his mind working furiously through his options, the cogs and wheels turning wearily, as if he were trying to determine exactly how much of the truth he could tell me. Finally, his gaze returned to mine, and with it, a look of staunch resoluteness. Whatever decision he'd arrived at, he was sticking with it.

"I am about to put everything I am, everything I have—including my freedom—in your hands." He paused, allowing me to grasp the magnitude of his words. "Aside from my grandmother and the boss, I've never trusted another living soul. But I'm about to." The furrow in his brow deepened as he shook his head. "And strangely, I feel okay with that."

Unable to find words through fear of what I was about to hear, I simply nodded.

"I feel okay with it, because despite not having a fucking clue what the deal between her and Mr. Wilde is, I know he loves you—and I know he would trust you with his life. So I trust you too."

I nodded again.

"She's blackmailing me." A look of utter relief swept over his face, as if finally having the words out there was a physical release.

However, his words didn't surprise me. After what I'd learned recently of Rebecca's sly and conniving capabilities, nothing would surprise me. After all, hadn't she been blackmailing Ethan for years? Forcing him into a "relationship" by holding his guilt-ridden conscience against him, like a knife to his throat, threatening to divulge injurious information about those he'd cared deeply for and would go to great lengths to protect.

But what dirt could she possibly have on Jackson? And what could he offer her in return for her silence?

"Blackmailing you how?"

"There was an incident a few years back. I got involved in something… shady. Mr. Wilde stood by me. If it hadn't been for him—"

"He saved you." The words were out before they'd fully entered my brain, because they weren't my words, they were a recollection. A fragment of a prior conversation that I'd shelved, because I hadn't understood it at the time.

Jackson narrowed his eyes, as if to question my choice of words.

"That's what you said," I explained. "Last time we were here, in fact. You said 'he saved you.' Is that what we're talking about?"

He nodded, his frown smoothing out as confusion lifted and he recalled the conversation. I waited for him to continue, but he suddenly seemed to dry up.

"Jackson, you're going to have to give me more than that—"

"I killed a man."

The blurted confession sat like a boulder, cumbersome and heavy between us, Jackson waiting for me to react—me not knowing how to.

I nodded once. "Tell me."

He took a gulp of coffee and a deep breath to ready himself.

"I worked security at a high-end club in London, one of Mr. Wilde's. It paid well enough for that kind of work, but my grandmother fell ill and needed round-the-clock care—the kind I couldn't afford. She'd given up her life to bring me up single-handedly, and I wasn't about to let her down when she needed me. So I started fighting to make up the shortfall—organized fights, but illegal. There's a lot of money to be earned if you win. And I always won."

Another piece of the jigsaw slotted into place. What Jackson said echoed yet another prior conversation, one I'd had with Ethan. In that same conversation, I recalled he'd spoken of a time when Jackson had made an impression on him, because he'd intervened in a tricky situation, proving himself by going the extra mile—or words to that effect. I remember wondering about it at the time, but hadn't wanted to pry.

"Mr. Wilde saw something in me," Jackson continued. "I don't know, dedication, determination—something. He took me into his trust, more so than the rest of his team, and we formed a mutual respect for each other. Before long, I was heading his personal security team.

"One night, Mr. Wilde was entertaining at one of his clubs in the city. He'd just closed a major business deal and was treating his clients to a night on the champagne. I had my best team in there, and to this day, I don't know how it happened.

"I'd had a report of something going down outside, a scuffle in the alleyway, so I sent out a few of the guys to check it out. A few minutes later, I spotted Mr. Wilde heading through the club toward the offices. He was with another guy. He shot me a look, only a glance, but there was something about it that put me on edge, and the guy who was with him was walking close—too fucking close.

"I watched them move out of sight and then followed. By the time I caught up, they were in the manager's office. I could only hear snippets of the conversation, mainly mumbling through the door, but the guy sounded... off. I pushed the door open quietly. Mr. Wilde was at the safe; the guy was behind him with a gun to his head."

Oh my God, Ethan. Why hadn't he told me?

"I moved inside and the guy swung around, pointing the gun at me. Before I knew what I'd done, I'd wrestled him to the ground, grabbing his gun, and I thought I had the situation under control. Everything moved so fast after that. I threw the fucker down in a chair; he was winded, breathless from the struggle. Mr. Wilde reached over the desk for the phone to call the police, and I turned my back to go and secure the door. The guy pulled a knife from somewhere and lunged at Mr. Wilde, catching him on his shoulder—it was only a surface wound, but we didn't know that at the time."

Shit, the scar on his shoulder blade.

I gasped, the horror of what might have happened showing plainly on my face.

"Do you want me to go on?" Jackson asked with concern.

I nodded.

"I lost it." He shook his head as if the memory was still hard to believe. "I launched myself at him, throwing a punch—one single punch and he was down. At first we thought he was just out cold, that the fucker would get to his feet and make a run for it. But he didn't get up. I quickly realized he wasn't breathing, there was no pulse. I can't even remember where the blow landed, if it caught him in the throat or… All I know is one punch and he was dead.

"We both knew how it looked—billionaire businessman, safe full of money, an armed robber and a loyal henchman who liked to fight for a living." He paused. "It was then that Mr. Wilde had this idea. It was then that he saved me."

"What idea? What did he do?" I asked quietly.

"We figured that the scuffle in the alley was a diversion tactic, created to get my men out of the club, in order to render us unmanned and vulnerable to attack. When we checked CCTV later, a gang of six men had entered the alleyway, and the first thing they'd done was take out the camera, smashed it with a brick. My men had entered the alley a few minutes later. Of course, there was no footage of this, but the guys were able to tell us what happened. There'd been an exchange, some pushing and shoving, a few fists thrown and some choice words, but after a while, the gang took off and my men moved back inside. There was no clear indication by what the guys said as to what started the scuffle, so we used it to our advantage. We waited until the club was empty and moved the body to the alley. None of my security team had searched the area, so they couldn't swear the body wasn't there when they left. As the CCTV had been taken out, there was no video evidence of the altercation, so it was assumed that the guy had been chased into the alley by the gang—hence the reason for the scuffle— beaten up and left for dead. His accomplices had unwittingly become the 'persons of interest.'

"The body was found the next day. The guy was a well known crook, so he was identified pretty much right away. He had quite an impressive record, by all accounts, been in and out of prison since being a juvenile, mostly for assault and armed robbery. After the police interviewed my guys and saw evidence of the gang smashing up the camera, it was all they needed to put two and two together and come up with dirt-bag-who'd-got-his-just-deserts. They said it was likely to have been a revenge killing. That he'd probably double-crossed one of his associates, and that people like that often became a victim of their own crimes. I suppose they were right in a way. If his life hadn't ended that night, he'd have taken someone else's without so much as a sleepless night to follow—Mr. Wilde's, maybe even mine as well, purely because of greed. The police didn't get anywhere with the case; there wasn't enough evidence to identify any of the gang. So don't worry, no-one was convicted of a crime they didn't commit.

"There was nothing to connect me or Mr. Wilde to the scene. By smashing the camera, the gang had implicated themselves, but they'd also made it easy for us to leave the body there without it showing up on film. The only other CCTV footage was of what happened in the office. Mr. Wilde removed the disk and gave it to me—told me to destroy it."

For a few minutes we both stared down into half empty cups of coffee, me trying to process what Jackson had told me and him, I suspect, savoring the relief he felt for finally getting it all off his chest.

"I'm not an animal, Angel," Jackson said suddenly. "Or a murderer, it was an—"

"An accident, I know." I finished his sentence.

"I would have done time for it. It would have been manslaughter, but I'd have done time, nonetheless. If it hadn't been for Mr. Wilde…"

"I know. It's okay, Jackson, I get it."

And I did.

Although the story was disturbing, and what they'd done illicit, clandestine, at best, it would have been a bigger crime to allow a good man to go to prison for protecting himself and his boss against a well known criminal—for ultimately doing his job. Yes, I totally got it.

And I also now got the connection between Ethan and Jackson. The way they communicated without words. The way the "extra mile" thing was clearly true for them both. They'd built an impenetrable union, had come to rely on each other, which is why I didn't get what remained of this puzzle—the reason we were here in the first place.

"Jackson, what the hell has all this got to do with *her*?"

Dread crumpled his forehead once again, as if he'd just reached the summit of a mountain after an exhausting climb, only to be told he had to climb it again. He took a breath, resigning himself to the grueling task.

"She used to quiz me about his comings and goings all the time. Where he went, how long he stayed, who he was with. He knew; I told him, and he instructed me to tell her the truth—mostly. If he'd been out with a woman, he wanted her to know. I didn't really get why she was so hung up it; it's not like they were in a relationship. Well, not a conventional one, anyway. Like I said before, I don't get what the deal is between them."

Of course, I knew exactly what the deal was, and why Ethan wanted her to know about his flings, but it wasn't my place to tell Jackson.

"The day after the... incident at the club, she turned up at my apartment asking questions. Wanting to know where he'd been, who he'd been with, why he hadn't been answering her calls all night. Somehow she knew he hadn't got back to his place until early that morning—I'm sure she used to have someone stake out his place. I wasn't handling the whole thing too well, felt totally out of my depth—killing someone does that to you." He grimaced, like his words had left a bitter taste in his mouth.

"I'd had a few glasses of bourbon to mellow me out. She was all upset and tearful, playing the victim role real well, so I offered her a glass. Before I knew it, the bottle was empty, and I'd fallen asleep. When I woke up she was gone—but so was the disk with the CCTV footage. I hadn't gotten around to destroying it like Mr. Wilde had instructed." He shook his head in regret.

Shit!

I took a sip of my now cold coffee, trying to let the enormity of what he'd said sink in. Not only did she know about him killing a man—accident or not—but she had video imagery of him doing it. On top of that, the footage showed him trying to cover it up by moving the body.

Wait a minute. The footage showed *them*, both Jackson *and* Ethan moving the body. Ethan was just as involved in that cover-up as Jackson was, and that bitch had the evidence to prove it. She had him well and truly by the balls—far more than he was even aware. And that made what he was about to do in London even more dangerous.

"Jackson, does Ethan even know she has the disk?"

"No. It's part of the deal."

My mind was reeling. "Part of what fucking deal, Jackson? I understand what she's got on you, and it certainly explains why you jump when she tells you to, but what else? What do you have that you can give her in return for her silence? What is she blackmailing you for?"

He cut his gaze to the window, his face coloring slightly.

"Are you paying her? Is this about money?"

"Fuck no, she doesn't need money. She comes from a very long line of blue-blooded assholes. People that give social class and wealth a whole new meaning."

"What then? Jackson!"

"Sex," he said quietly, turning to look at me.

I half laughed, shaking my head. "What—that's it? She'll agree to keep quiet as long as you continue to fuck her? What are you, some kind of stud muffin?"

The implication made him grimace. "She has... an acquired taste."

"*An acquired taste*?" I shook my head in disbelief at what I was hearing.

As I asked the question, something shifted in my thoughts, like I'd glimpsed something that had been nagging at me from the moment I'd seen Jackson in the corridor, when I'd realized what was going on between him and Rebecca. But in my state of panic and confusion, I hadn't been able to pin it down, hadn't been able to nail exactly what it was that was bothering me. And suddenly, it was there. The most surreal thing in this maze of utter absurdity.

This woman didn't even like sex. What was it Ethan had said?

Fortunately for me, she wasn't highly sexed, but I imagine that had something to do with what had happened. She wasn't exactly frigid, but she could definitely take it or leave it.

I shook my head again, trying my best to wrap my brain around it. "What do you mean, Jackson?"

"I mean you can't just take a guy home and have the kind of sex she likes to have, without a shit load of questions. That's what confuses me about hers and Mr. Wilde's relationship. They can't have been intimate. If he was into that sort of stuff, trust me, you'd know exactly what I was talking about. I imagine it takes a certain kind of guy to get off on that shit."

"And you're that kind of guy?" I asked, still unsure what "shit" we were talking about.

"Jesus, no. But then it wouldn't be blackmail if I was doing something I wanted to do. This isn't something I have a choice in, remember."

I nodded. "So, this acquired taste?"

He looked down into his empty cup. "She likes it... she likes it rough."

"How rough?"

"Very."

"How rough, Jackson?"

"Do you really need to know the details?"

"Yes!" I snapped rather too loudly. "I know this can't be easy for you, I do, I get it. But it's important that I know. I can't tell you why, but... I need to know," I paused, before asking my question again. "*How* rough?"

Jackson rolled his eyes and slid a finger down the collar of his dress shirt like it was suddenly too tight. Clearing his throat, he fixed me in a staunch gaze. "I hope you've got a strong stomach."

Oh. Swallowing hard, I nodded once for him to go ahead.

"Female submissive sexual fantasies. That's what she's into. Domination, extreme bondage, consensual erotic torture, role play, humiliation—you name it. So, in answer to your question—*fucking* rough, Angelica. Believe it or not, she keeps me around for the mild stuff, just a bit of your everyday kink—restraint, minor-league punishment, the role playing. The real hardcore stuff—the bondage dungeon entertainment, she reserves for the clubs. She needs someone like me to ferry her around and deliver her safely to these places. And they are not for the faint hearted, I can assure you. Occasionally, she expects me to escort her inside; I think she does it just so she can see me squirm. Seriously, at these establishments—anything goes. There are rooms for non-participants just for viewing, private rooms, rooms used for group sex, torture chambers, rooms where women are restrained and overwhelmed by three, four men at a time with more watching—a favorite of hers, apparently. A preoccupation like hers isn't something you want broadcasted, especially when you come from aristocracy. What she gets from me is discretion. I keep her secret—she keeps mine. That's the deal."

For a few minutes I couldn't even speak. I don't quite know what I'd been expecting to hear. But it wasn't this. My brain was in some sort of tumultuous conflict, a disorderly riot where scraps of opposing data struggled to connect and make any sense. Everything was a contradiction. Everything I'd learned about her and what she was capable of was logically incongruous. This snooty, silver-spooned, prissy, frigidly formal, supercilious bitch that I'd learned to hate, liked to be tied up, dominated, humiliated, and fucked in every orifice of her body by multiple men while people looked on.

Didn't sound much like someone who was wary of sex to me—a take it or leave it kinda girl. And it definitely didn't sound like a rape victim.

"Are you going to say something?" Jackson asked after a few minutes had passed.

My eyes blinked as I gazed at him without really looking at him. My mind was too busy processing to focus. "What kind of role play?"

"What?"

"You said you took part in role play. What did it involve?"

Jackson looked uncomfortable again, the corners of his mouth turning down, his shoulders shrugging in a gesture of indifference. "It took various forms. But ultimately, it was the same fantasy—she liked to take on the role of a victim. Pretend she was being taken by force."

Clunk! The missing piece slotted firmly into place.

Jackson was still talking, his voice sounding tinny and distant. I could just make out what he was saying, something about how the term "taking her by force" was so ludicrous as to be amusing, because if she didn't have his balls in a vise, he wouldn't touch her with someone else's, let alone force her.

Like an epiphany, the truth of this whole sordid affair hit me with the clarity of crystal clear waters. Ethan was preparing to make the biggest mistake of his life. He was about to inform Alistair's parents that their son was a rapist. About to confess to witnessing a crime that he'd done nothing to prevent. Ethan hadn't witnessed a rape that night—he just thought he had. What he'd seen was a couple partaking in role play. They'd been acting out a fantasy.

From the second I'd heard the rape story cross his lips, it hadn't felt right. At first I'd felt ashamed for not feeling bad for her, wondering if my hatred for her was so intense that I was unable to see past it long enough to pity her. I mean anyone who goes through the ordeal of a rape is worthy of sympathy, right? But something just didn't fit. Something in my gut was telling me that Rebecca Staunton had never been a victim of anything in her entire life. Oh, she'd worn the mask of a victim well, that's got to be said, because she'd had Ethan fooled. But now her mask had slipped and I'd glimpsed what lay beneath. And finally, my gut instinct was beginning to make sense.

But there were so many unanswered questions. If I was right, it still wouldn't explain the messages Ethan had received from Alistair, confessing to the rape. Nor would it explain why he'd killed himself. And this was exactly the reason why I couldn't tell Ethan about my theory—not yet. But I was in no doubt that I had to stop him going to London, and stop him talking to Alistair's parents. Because if he crossed Rebecca now, the backlash would be far greater than ruining a man's reputation or breaking the hearts of already grieving parents. While she was in possession of that disk, she held all the cards. She was no longer a cancer—but a weapon of mass destruction.

I needed to act, and I needed to do it quickly.

My gaze fixed on Jackson's expectant face. "I need to get into her suite at the hotel. You have to help me."

His brow knitted in puzzlement. "Why would you want to do that? What's going on, Angel? What are you not telling me?"

"There isn't time. Look, Jackson, earlier you said you were laying everything on the line, putting your trust in me. Well, it's *now* that I need your trust. This… whole thing has never been about you, it's about Ethan. You said you didn't understand the deal between them. Well, it's not so different to yours—blackmail. Albeit, under very different circumstances. Rebecca never had any intention of using that disk against you. It's her insurance policy—her ace card for if Ethan steps out of line. I'm afraid you were just the added bonus— another puppet whose strings she could pull. The problem is Ethan doesn't know that disk still exists, let alone that she has it." I paused for a second, allowing him to fully absorb the grim reality of what I was saying.

"Jackson, Ethan is my entire life now. Without him my world stops turning. Tomorrow, he's planning to board a flight to London. He plans to take steps to remove Rebecca from his life—permanently. If he goes through with it, she will use that disk, and his world, your world, and my world—stops turning."

Jackson's face paled, his eyes widening with the sudden realization of what was at stake.

"Jackson, I need to find that disk." I nodded for emphasis, like the action would drum my words in quicker. "I *need* to get into that suite."

"Oh Jesus." He rubbed his hands over his buzzed head. "If I let you do this and something happens to you, Mr. Wilde will have me killed. You do know that, right?"

"There is no time for this, Jackson. I'll do this with or without you—but remember this is your ass on the line as well. So, are you going to help?"

"Of course, I'll help. But what makes you think she's got the disk here? It could be in London."

I shook my head. "That disk is vital evidence, her insurance policy, remember? As far as she's concerned, she's here to stay. She's not going to have left it behind. She'll want it here where she can lay her hands on it quickly."

Jackson shrugged acquiescently. "Okay. What have you got in mind?"

CHAPTER FOURTEEN

Jackson pulled into a space in the hotel parking lot, the same space he'd occupied earlier. I reached for my cell to silence the ringer, automatically switching it to *vibrate only*. As I was about to return it to my pocket, it began to *buzz* in my hand—it was Ethan. I took a deep breath in the hope it would steady the tremor that was certain to be evident in my voice and answered.

"Hey."

"Hey. So, did Maverick and Iceman come up with a plan?"

Despite my nerves, I smiled at the *Top Gun* reference. "Not exactly." Grimacing, I closed my eyes, hating that I was lying to him, but knowing I couldn't possibly tell him what I was about to do. Jesus Christ, he'd have a heart attack. "But you're right, us going to see her probably isn't the smartest move to make. I'm afraid it's all down to you and your charm now."

"It's the right decision, baby." He sounded beyond relieved. "The thought of having to sweet talk her makes me sick, but if that's what I have to do, then it's a small price to pay to get her out of our lives. I need you to know the reason I changed my mind wasn't because I didn't have faith in you, Angel. It's her I don't trust. She's inclined to act erratically. You going to see her could well have been like handing her a stick to beat the shit out of us with."

"I know. It's okay, you don't have to explain."

A voice sounded in the background and Ethan muttered a reply.

"I have to go, baby. I'll call you on the way to pick her up tonight." He paused. "What will you do today? I'd rather you weren't alone."

"Don't worry, I'm going to hang out with Jia," I lied again. "You just concentrate on business for now and we'll speak later."

The voice in the background yelled his name again, more urgent this time.

"I'm coming, Damon," Ethan muttered impatiently, and then to me, "Okay, speak later then, baby."

"I love you, E."

"I love you, too."

He hung up and for a few seconds, I just stared at the phone, feeling miserable about my own ability to lie. I just hoped it was going to be worth it.

"Are you sure you want to do this?" Jackson asked for the millionth time.

"Got any better ideas?" I snapped, shooting him an infuriated look. My nerves were already in tatters without Jackson having a last minute wobble.

"I could do a sweep of the suite later, when she's at dinner with Mr. Wilde."

Though it wasn't his fault, I glared at him. The thought of Ethan sharing breathing space, let alone dinner, with that woman made my stomach roil. "I'm hoping it won't come to that. I don't want that deranged bitch anywhere near him. But the only way I'm going to put a stop to it, is if I find that disk. So it's all a little time sensitive, Jackson. I need to get in there now. So we do it like we said." I glanced at my watch. The time was just approaching midday. It was time to get moving. "Come on, let's get this over with."

Jackson had arranged to collect Rebecca from her suite at twelve o'clock. On leaving, he would tamper with the door lock, allowing me to gain access to the suite unimpeded. From there, he would accompany her to the shops, where she would do as Ethan had insisted, and buy a dress for dinner. In the meantime, I would do a painstaking search of her suite and hope beyond hope that I came up with something to lead us out of this nightmare. I knew the odds of finding the disk underneath her rancid panties were low, but if we were ever going to have a chance of finding it, her suite was the best place to start.

As we entered the elevator, my cell began to vibrate again. I glanced at the caller display and answered. "Jia."

"Don't Jia *me*, bitch. You said you'd call. Where the fuck are you? What the fuck am I supposed to tell Wilde when he asks why I let you take off like that? He was adamant that you weren't to fly solo. If all this goes to shit, he will blame me, you know this, right?"

"Jia, everything is cool, don't worry. I haven't got time to do this right now. I will call you back and explain soon, I promise."

"No, Angel. Don't you fucking dare hang up—"

I hung up.

She called right back, as I expected she would, but the elevator had come to a halt on the 41st floor, so I slid my cell back in my pocket and exited. Turning, I met Jackson's gaze as he popped a piece of gum into his mouth and began to chew nervously. We exchanged a brief nod before the door slid closed to continue its journey up to the next floor. I would use the stairs for the final stint, and wait inside the stairwell until Jackson and Rebecca left. Then I would make my way down the hallway to her suite.

Ten excruciating minutes passed as I waited. I'd never done anything like this before, I'd never even gotten a ticket, and here I was, about to break into someone's hotel room and search through their belongings. I felt sick.

Suddenly, I heard a cough and the sound of voices, distant and distorted, but drawing nearer. Jackson's voice, pointed and clear, followed by her putrescent, bleating tones, fussing and condescending. I shuddered and held my breath until I heard the sound of the elevator arrive. They boarded, the door closed, and all was silent. I let out my breath.

Pushing open the door from the stairwell to the corridor, I paused to take a cautious look around. There was nobody in sight, so I scurried down the hall toward Rebecca's suite. The door, as promised, had been rigged so that it would close without locking, and as I pushed it open, I could see exactly how it had been meddled with. Gum—clever. Jackson had forced his gum into the latch receiver preventing it from locking. Screwing my face up in disgust, I dug my finger in to remove it. I did not want anyone noticing the door had been left on the latch and reporting it to housekeeping, or worse, coming to investigate.

The suite was dripping in luxury, solid wood floors and handcrafted furnishings draped in pale, textured, natural silks. The space was light and airy with buff-toned wall coverings and large bay windows. The entrance opened up into a spacious living area with a solid wood door separating it from the bedroom.

I moved quickly and quietly through the suite, checking the rooms to reassure myself that I was alone. The place really was amazing, and I found myself cursing with a venom that frankly surprised me at the thought she'd been living in the lap of luxury, courtesy of my boyfriend, when I'd pretty much been holed up in a closet for the past couple of weeks. This woman had brought out a side of me I hadn't known existed and wasn't even sure I liked. Hating someone was fucking exhausting.

My cell *buzzed* again, the vibration against my body making me jump out of my skin. A quick glance at the text told me Jia was pissed. I returned the phone to my blazer and headed over to the desk in the corner of the room to begin a search of the drawers. Hotel stationery and info on the services and amenities; room service, the spa, the restaurant, the fitness center, yada-yada. I searched everything with a cupboard or a drawer or a shelf, turning up nothing remotely personal, then moved into the bedroom and started in on the bedside drawers.

Both of them were filled with obscenely expensive looking lingerie in every damn color of the rainbow. Everything was satin and lace, organized into neat piles of matching items, which was fortunate, because it meant I didn't need to rummage to see there was nothing of interest. There was no way on this planet I was going to stick my hand in her panty drawer.

Aside from the bedside drawers and the mattress, which I checked thoroughly, there was literally nothing else to search. Other than an array of magazines, you couldn't even tell there was anyone staying here. The bathroom was slightly more personalized, the drawers filled with luxury cosmetics and pampering items, but again, everything was impeccably organized and uncluttered. In fact, the whole place was borderline OCD neat.

I moved back into the bedroom, ignoring the buzz of another incoming text from Jia, and opened the door to the large walk-in closet, flicking on the light. The rails and shelves were lined with luxury designer dresses, suits, purses, and shoes, most of which still had price tags attached, and all of which were ludicrously expensive and probably purchased with Ethan's money.

In the corner was a large, black leather trunk, partially draped in a black satin sheet. It looked like an incredibly expensive piece of luggage and was no doubt filled with even more expensive items of clothing. Folding back the sheet, I tried the locks, but as expected the latches were secure. I would have to try and pick them—Christ, I didn't have time for this.

My skin began to itch with irritation. With every second that ticked by, I was getting more and more frustrated. I mean, who the hell paid so much attention to detail that they left their damned luggage securely locked. Who the fuck had time to be so obsessively meticulous? To top it all off, I'd turned up absolutely nothing in this seemingly hopeless search, and my temperature was swiftly rising to beyond panic level.

My cell *buzzed* AGAIN, and suddenly I wanted to sling it across the room in temper. "Not now, Jia!" I snapped, ignoring the call and shoving my hands into my hair. Why in the hell had I thought this woman was stupid enough to leave anything incriminating lying around in a hotel room?

Just then, I heard a click—the sound of a key card in the door—and my heart stopped dead. The sound of someone coughing and then heels *click-clacking* over the wood floor. Shit!

"I'm just trying to help, Rebecca," Jackson said in overly loud sing-song voice

"Do-o-o stop fussing, Jackson, dear." *Her* voice. "I am quite capable. And don't bring your germy cough in here. Wait there!" she snapped as if speaking to a dog.

Frantically, I scanned around for somewhere to hide and then remembered the door and the light. Flicking it off quickly, I pulled the door to just as I'd found it. Then moving swiftly and quietly, I tunneled underneath the array of floor-length dresses with the enormous price tags, and stood upright with my back flush against the rear of the closet. I just had to hope and pray she wasn't planning on rifling through her previous purchases to see if she had something suitable for the evening.

"Ethan told me to shop and that's exactly what I'm going to do. But I won't get far without the old plastic, will I?" Her voice was getting closer, she was headed my way.

My cell began to *buzz*. Panicking, I reached into my pocket and rejected the call. As I stared at the screen, only inches from my face, I noticed the missed messages from Jackson. He'd been trying to warn me of their impending return, and I'd assumed it was Jia on the warpath.

Suddenly the closet door flung open and the light switched on. I could smell her first, that sweet, sickly, potent whiff penetrating my nostrils, and then she was there in front of me. She was humming happily, her stupid, strawberry blond head bobbing along to her tuneless melody.

My entire body froze, stiff and barely breathing, my hand immobile in front of my face, still clutching my cell. I watched wide-eyed, peeking through the gap of the dangling dresses, praying she wouldn't turn around. She sank to her knees and placed the flat of her hand against a panel just off to the right of a set of drawers and pushed. The paneled cover sprang open to reveal a hidden cupboard behind, and encased inside, a safe.

A safe? Of course—a fucking safe.

She raised her hand, her finger hovering over the digital keypad, and my brain sprang into life. Silently, I tapped the screen on my cell and suddenly I was recording, my hand moving deftly between the suspended garments for a closer, clearer view. Slowly, she inputted the code, pausing briefly between each digit of the combination so that the system could process the entered numbers. Finally, she pushed the "Enter" key and the LED light switched to green. Then, turning the bar downwards, she yanked open the safe.

Silently, I withdrew my hand, retreating back out of sight. Rebecca leaned forward and began rummaging through the contents of the safe before eventually laying her hands on the item she'd returned for.

"There you are," she triumphed, pressing a credit card to her lips, as though it were a long-lost precious stone. "My trusty plastic friend. Thank you, Ethan, darling."

Anger bubbled inside me as she popped her "plastic friend" into her purse, closed the safe, and the panel behind it, and pushed to her feet. The light went out, and as I listened to her retreating footsteps, I took a long, deep, replenishing breath.

"Everything okay?" I heard Jackson ask, the slightest trace of surprise in his tone.

"Everything is purrfect, Jackson dahling. Come. I want to shop."

The main door slammed and once again there was silence.

For a minute or two, I remained where I was, my heartbeat finding its rhythm, my eyes closed to prevent the room from spinning with the surge of adrenaline rushing through my body. Suddenly, I felt quite giddy and to my horror, I began to giggle. It was a nervous titter at first as I tried to repress the sudden absurd urge—I mean this situation wasn't in the least bit funny and to laugh would be totally inappropriate, right? I slithered out of my hiding place as the giggle turned into hysterical shoulder-shaking laughter, my tongue pressed against the root of my upper teeth in an attempt to do it silently. Doubling over, I held on to my aching sides until the giddiness finally subsided.

"God Almighty, this is so fucked up," I said out loud to myself as I worked my fingers into my jaw muscles to relieve the tension.

My cell *buzzed* with an incoming message, jolting me instantly back to reality. It was Jackson and for one horrendous moment, I was terrified he was trying to forewarn me again. I opened the text: Christ, I'm sorry. Tried to warn you. You okay?

Flicking on the light, I replied quickly: Yeah, don't worry, I'm good. Making progress. Keep me updated of her movements.

Pressing send, I settled myself on the floor in front of the secret panel and laying my fingertips against it as she had, pushed the panel inwards. It sprang open as it had earlier to reveal the safe. I breathed in deeply, and with everything crossed, began to play back the recording.

There were six digits to the combination, and I could make out five of them with no trouble at all. Not because the recorded footage on my cell phone had been clear enough for me to see the numbers, but simply because of where specifically she'd positioned her finger on the keypad. Fortunately, she'd pressed each digit slowly and precisely with a pause in between. For instance, I could clearly make out that her finger had pushed on the middle key of the top row for the first number in the sequence—which had to be number 2. Next, she'd pushed the first key of the third row down—number 7. The last three digits were also easily identifiable—1, 3 and 5. But the middle number of the combination wasn't quite as simple. When she'd pressed the third digit, she'd shifted her weight, slightly altering her position, and for that brief second the bottom right quarter of the keypad had been partly obscured. I watched the recording back several times, trying to use a sort of elimination process to figure out the missing number.

What stood out were her fingernails, impeccably manicured and incredibly long. On observation, the tip of her nail could clearly be seen overhanging the keys on pushing them. And as the edges of keys

5 and 8 were just about visible, but with no evidence of a jutting nail, I felt I could safely exclude them. Which left only 6 and 9.

I didn't believe for a second that the combination would have any meaningful significance—a memorable date or anything like that. She wasn't that stupid. No, it would be random, but perhaps a memorable pattern. I went through the sequence several times, my finger hovering over the keys without actually touching. The first few times I slotted the number 6 into the middle of the sequence and then swapped it out for the number 9.

9. It had to be 9. I had little doubt. It would spell out a dainty, memorable pattern—2, 7, 9, 1, 3, 5. I wasn't certain, but I was guessing I'd get more than one attempt before the system froze me out. I'd try it with the 9 first, and if I was wrong, hope that I got another shot at it.

Flexing my fingers, I adjusted my position for better comfort, repeating the sequence in my head, over and over like a mantra—*2, 7, 9, 1, 3, 5—2, 7, 9, 1, 3, 5.*

Then slowly and with great precision, I did it for real. My heart boomed madly as I made my way through the sequence, pausing carefully between each number, and finally, after hitting the 5, I pushed the "Enter" key. The LED turned green, and my scalp began to prickle, a tiny squeal bursting unbidden from my lips. I turned the lever down and pulled open the door of the safe.

"So, let's see what you've got, bitch," I mumbled under my breath.

Inside there was a large compartment with a shallow shelf at the top. A stack of $100 bills was the first thing to catch my eye, at least three thousand, at a guess. Then a selection of credit cards, a couple in her name, the rest in Ethan's—*growl*. On the shelf was what looked like a black leather jewelry pouch, but apart from that, all that remained were three brown envelopes. Rebecca's passport and driver's license were in one—eww—her sneering pointy features gaping back at me, like butter wouldn't melt, made me sick. And in the second were promo details for a New York PI.

The info was printed on a shoddy piece of paper, the ink faded and blurred as if reproduced from a low quality copier. Among other things, it boasted confidentiality, discretion, and competitive rates for a selection of highly-skilled services, such as infidelity investigations, missing persons investigations, background investigations, surveillance services, and so forth. There was no office address, just a cell phone number and an email address. There were no background references or training and qualification credentials, just a brief note stating that he was a retired cop.

I squinted at the photograph in the top left-hand corner. The man had his arms folded; the knuckles of one hand supporting his chin in a creased-brow-thinking-pose. He looked like he was doing a bad impression of Columbo—all he needed was a raincoat and an unlit cigar in his hand. I could picture him scratching his head, *Oh, just one more thing...*

But this guy was no fiendishly clever homicide detective. Nor was he a highly-skilled, highly-trained professional from one of the many leading New York private investigators which Rebecca could have chosen from. No, he was a lowlife private eye, a crook, an ex-cop who'd probably been pushed off the force because he was bent, and now provided a underhanded, surreptitious, shady service for anyone who was equally underhanded and shady, and all from the penurious, insufficient surroundings of his car—probably.

His name was Tim Tillman; he even sounded like a prick. Tim had, of course, been Tom when he'd originally introduced himself to me. I'd known it the second I saw his ugly mug on this cheap piece of promo. He was the man who'd approached me at Damon's party. He was also the man who'd broken into my apartment—the man who'd killed Ponyo.

I'd asked myself the same question time and again. *What kind of asshole does something like that?* Well, here was my answer. This kind of asshole; Tim fucking Tillman.

"Got you, you fucker," I mumbled with venom.

Pushing the details into the envelope, I placed them back inside the safe, my fingers shaking with fury at finally discovering the bastard's identity. I would deal with Tim Tillman later. Then with fingers crossed in the vain hope that I would find what I was looking for, I reached for the last envelope and took a peek inside.

"Damn," I cursed. Nothing but bank papers. No disk.

Panic started to bubble in the pit of my stomach once again as I checked the safe for a second time, to make sure I hadn't missed anything. There had to be more than this. I had to leave here with something sufficiently vital enough to at least lead me to the whereabouts of that disk. Because without it, we were all screwed.

What if Jackson was right? The thought crept darkly into my mind. *What if she* had *left it in London?*

Dismissing it almost as quickly as I'd summoned it, I shook my head. For some reason, I just couldn't envision it. She was a cunning bitch and fastidious to a fault in everything she attended to—even organizing her panty drawer for Christ's sake. No, she would keep it somewhere close. It had to be somewhere close.

"Think, Angel. Think," I whispered, massaging my temples as if urging my brain to work faster.

My eyes fell on the jewelry pouch, the only thing I hadn't searched. I didn't need yet further testimony as to how much of Ethan's money she'd spent; the colossal amount of designer dresses hanging in this very closet was proof enough of that. Reluctantly, I grabbed it from the shelf, untying the bow of the satin ribbon which bound it, and carefully unraveled the rolled up pouch. It was surprisingly lacking, considering. I'd expected it to be bursting at the seams with diamonds and an array of other priceless gems. There was a beautiful emerald necklace with matching earrings—probably worth a fortune—and a pretty pearl necklace, but the remainder were just regular, run-of-the-mill stuff: a crucifix on a chain which looked quite old, a couple of cocktail rings, and a silver box chain with two keys attached.

Removing the chain from the pouch, I held it aloft to examine it, my brow furrowing in confusion. Rebecca Staunton did not look like the kind of girl who wore keys on a chain around her scrawny little neck. The smaller of the keys looked like a regular key, one that might fit the locks on a large suitcase, or a… a trunk.

Scrambling to my feet, I tugged back the satin sheet covering the leather trunk. With key in hand, I push it into the central lock and with one turn the lock sprang open. Repeating the action with the two remaining locks, and silently thanking God there was only one key required, I cautiously gripped the lid of the trunk with both hands and hauled it open.

The contents shouldn't have shocked me, given what I'd learned earlier that day, but so help me, they did. The kind of paraphernalia which came into view was usually reserved—or so I thought—for hard-core, under-the-counter porn DVDs, all of which usually had titles that implied violence. Everything from handcuffs and various other restraints, to ball gags, nipple clamps, butt plugs, and dildos of all sizes and ominous shapes filled the top layer of the chest. Underneath them were items of rubber clothing, latex crotchless panties, and bras with open cups. There were whips and floggers and other strange items I assumed were used to inflict pain. Sickeningly, there was also a selection of medical-like instruments. Among things I couldn't even begin to wonder of their purpose was a vaginal speculum, and beyond my wildest imaginings what looked like an anal proctoscope.

Although I wasn't completely averse to a bit of kink—I mean a blindfold, a vibrating toy, and even some mild restraint could be hot—this took it to a whole new level. The majority of the contents had me screwing my face up in absolute abhorrence, but the most appalling and frankly frightening looking item was a black leather hangman's mask.

What the fuck? No wonder she kept the trunk locked and the key in safe. You do not want your housekeeper finding that shit!

Slamming the lid closed, my skin crawling with loathing for the owner of the items inside, I took a deep breath to try and steady my trembling hands. I fumbled to re-lock the trunk, half wishing I'd never found the damn key and was about to return it to the pouch when I began to wonder what the other key on the chain was used to hide.

I held it closer to inspect it, trying to hazard a guess as to what it was for. It was a peculiar looking key, relatively small with teeth on both sides and a number engraved on the rim of the oval shaped head—2009. A date? Why would you engrave a date on a key?

Then something struck me.

Quickly, I reached for the envelope, the one with the bank stuff, and pulled out the contents. I began to leaf through them, just regular account info from some bank in London, and then something caught my eye. It was a document for a bank here in New York over on 8ᵗʰ Avenue, between West 52ⁿᵈ and 51ˢᵗ Street. A rental agreement.

"Well, hello there."

My focus oscillated between the key in one hand and back to the document in the other, my heart thumping madly. And suddenly, I knew exactly what the key was for. Safe-deposit box number 2009. For all intents and purposes, it looked like a pointless bit of forgotten metal left among other pointless bits of forgotten metal. But then it was supposed to.

"You freaking beauty," I whispered to the key as I held it suspended from its chain, watching it swing back and forth. In that moment, I felt a fresh wave of optimism. There had to be something very valuable inside that box, or something she couldn't afford for anybody else to find—or both. The thing of value may only be of some use to her, but the only way I was going to find out was if I took a look. I was pretty sure that if that disk was in New York that's where I was going to find it.

Quickly, I dug out my cell and snapped a quick photo of the image on her driver's license, and another close-up of her signature, before carefully placing everything back where I'd found it. The odds were she'd put the credit card back inside the safe the second she returned, and I didn't want to risk her noticing anything was missing or out of place. Then, locking up the safe, I backed slowly through the suite of rooms, checking every surface I'd touched, every drawer and door I'd opened, making sure not to leave any evidence of my presence behind.

Inhaling a much needed, replenishing breath, I boarded the elevator, my insides twisting and turning with bordering on excitement. The screen on my cell spoke of countless missed calls and abusive text messages from Jia. Grimacing, I dialed her number.

"Finally!" She sounded furious as she answered.

"You can yell at me later, I promise," I interjected swiftly. "But right now—we're going shopping."

CHAPTER FIFTEEN

J ust under three hours later, I stood gazing at my reflection in my bedroom mirror. But the image which gazed back was one I barely recognized. Jia had said I needed something *twee*—a British word, apparently, which meant affectedly dainty and sickeningly prim—so with that in mind, I'd purchased a navy-blue calf-length sheath dress with a large ivory bow slap-bang in the middle of the neckline. It was definitely twee. The wig though, had been the star purchase. It was a dead ringer for Rebecca's strawberry blond, immaculately shaped bob cut; it actually even swished when I moved, just like hers did. I despised the look.

"Fucking brilliant," Jia exclaimed. "That is some transformation. You don't look anything like *you*."

"I don't look anything like *her* either." I frowned, my eyes flicking between the image I'd snapped on my cell and the look-alike creation in the mirror.

"Well, no." Jia crumpled her brow and snatched the cell from my fingers. "You're a million times more attractive—but then who isn't? She looks like a fucking goat. It's a closer likeness than it was a half hour ago, at least."

I grabbed it back to take another look. "It's the eyes. Hers are an evil, sickly blue, all pale and wishy-washy. Mine are a deep shade of chocolate, almost dark as bullets. It's a dead giveaway."

"What about whore-goggles, you must have a pair around here

somewhere."

"No. Wearing sunglasses will just draw more attention to me, especially if they ask me to remove them. Complete fail."

"Wait a minute," Jia stuck her arm in her oversized purse, presenting me with a pair of dark framed, rectangular eyeglasses. "Here, try these." She shrugged when I eyed her questioningly, muttering, "Improvise."

I tried them on. "I'm not sure."

"Do they detract from your eye color?"

"Yes, I suppose."

"Then they work. This time tomorrow you'll be good to go."

We spent the remainder of the day talking through our plan and drinking wine. Jackson had called for an update the moment he'd left Rebecca back at the hotel to prepare for her dinner date with Ethan. I reported that I'd found something in her room worth investigating further, but didn't yet know how useful it would be so needed more time to figure it all out. After a few minutes of intense persuasion, he agreed to get Rebecca out of the suite again tomorrow, so that I could once again access her rooms. We agreed he would tamper with the lock again when leaving, and keep me regularly informed of their movements. Several times, he'd asked me what I expected to find tomorrow that I couldn't find today, but at this stage, I didn't want to divulge my findings or my plans to anyone, in case they tried to stop me.

I hadn't even disclosed the truth to Jia about what I'd discovered after following Jackson from Rebecca's suite—about how Rebecca was blackmailing him for sex in exchange for keeping his dark secret. Jackson had divulged that information to me in confidence, and I wasn't about to break it. Fortunately, Jia had been sidetracked by the housekeeper at the time of their exchange so had missed it entirely.

Somehow, I managed to convince her that I'd changed my mind about confronting Rebecca, and instead, I'd talked Jackson into getting me into her suite. For some reason, I'd had a feeling it might be worth a nosey around. Luckily, she'd been too excited about the shopping trip and the idea of aiding and abetting in identity theft to ask too many questions. After cutting me some slack for not letting her in on the room search, she finally accepted that my curiosity in the safe-deposit was to see if I could dig up some dirt on her.

Deciding it would be more likely to give the impression of a general robbery, I'd planned to empty the contents of the safe entirely. Stealing just the key, the ID, and the rental agreement would raise too many eyebrows, and she would be on to me right away. To further avoid suspicion, I would rifle through the rest of the suite, leaving drawers opened and contents scattered—if nothing else it would drive her obsessive compulsive side completely crazy.

From there, I'd head to the bank armed with the rental agreement, the key, and Rebecca's ID, and posing as her, would attempt to gain unlawful access to the safe deposit box. What happened after that was anyone's guess. Victory, defeat, a prison cell—who knew?

After Jia left for home at around six, I practiced forging Rebecca's signature and worked on my British accent, but as the time drew closer to seven o'clock, the more anxious I became. I hadn't heard from Ethan since midday when he'd promised to call on the way to meet Rebecca for dinner. The evening was certain to have me scratching my own eyes out, knowing Ethan was with her and feigning compliance. But the idea of lying to him about what I'd been doing all day, and even more, what my plans were for the following day made my anxiety levels climb ten-fold.

Finally, at ten minutes to seven, the screen on my cell illuminated with Ethan's name.

"Christ, I'm sorry it's so late, baby," he said when I answered, "Damon and I have been stuck trying to put this damn Valiente deal to bed the whole fucking day. They're quarrelling over a few measly million and refuse to budge an inch. In the end, I left Damon to reschedule another meeting. I refuse to allow them to waste any more of my fucking time today. I'm sorry, I'm ranting. It's the nerves."

I marveled at the loose way the Wildes spoke of millions as if it were spare change—something I'd probably never get used to. "You have every right to be nervous. It's probably best that you finalize the deal on a day when your head's in the game, anyway."

"Yes, you're probably right. How are you feeling?"

"Honestly? Sick—very sick. What if she doesn't buy it, E?"

"She'll buy it, baby, don't worry. Jackson has reliably informed me that she's been strutting around Manhattan spending my money and grinning like the cat with the cream the entire day. You have to remember that the conversation I had with her yesterday hinted at the possibility of a future for us. It would have stirred up more hope than I've ever offered her before, and I'm confident she'll cling to that."

I didn't know whether that made me feel better or worse.

"Okay, so what if she buys it so much that she expects you to stay the night? To... consummate the new arrangement. I don't think *that's* a deal you'll have any trouble putting to bed." I was finding it impossible to keep the bitterness out of my voice and quickly had to remind myself why Ethan had arranged to meet with her, that he was doing it so we could be together. "I'm sorry, E, you didn't deserve that."

He sighed heavily, the sound steeped in frustration reverberating down the line. "It's okay. We're both wired to the max. But you really don't have anything to worry about. I wouldn't go there even if my life depended on it. And I don't think I'll need to be fending her off anyway. She's never pushed that side of the relationship. I think she's a bit a prude if truth be told."

Holy mother of fuck, how wrong he was! My stomach roiled as images of bondage, torture implements, and crotchless panties swarmed through my mind, and I had to fight to control the urge to gag.

"Besides," Ethan continued oblivious, "when I tell her we're flying back to London tomorrow she'll be desperate to go back to her suite and pack."

Oh shit. I hadn't considered that. If Ethan told her they were off for a new life in London, the first thing she would do was head to the bank to empty her safe-deposit box.

"I've been thinking about that," I said swiftly. "Maybe it's better to hold off on telling her about London for the time being. We don't want her becoming suspicious. You could just spring it on her as a last minute surprise tomorrow evening, that way it doesn't give her time to question your motives." With breath held and fingers crossed, I stood stock-still as he seemed to consider it.

"I'm not sure. Rebecca hates surprises, and besides, the flight's booked for ten tomorrow night, so I can't leave it too late."

"You've booked flight seats? I assumed you'd travel on the company jet?"

"You have got to be kidding. I don't want to be alone with her for even one second; the more people that are around the better. And I thought an evening flight would give me the excuse to sleep for the entire journey. It will get me into London in good time to meet with Ali's parents on Wednesday."

Of course, I hadn't considered the time difference.

"But you may be right," he continued. "The less she knows the better. I'll just tell her I'm coming by the hotel tomorrow evening with a surprise. I'll get housekeeping to pack her things; we can be out of there in an hour."

"Yes, that's a brilliant idea," I agreed, breathing my relief.

"I have to go, baby. I'm outside the hotel."

My heart faltered, seeming to miss a beat, and then suddenly it was racing erratically as panic welled inside.

"Will you… call me later?" I stammered, doing my best to mask my anxiety.

"Of course. Try not to worry."

"I'm fine, E," I lied. "Good luck. I love you."

I could almost feel his smile seeping through the air waves. "I'll never get tired of hearing you say that."

"Good, because from now on you're going to hear it a lot."

"That works for me. Speak later, Cinders."

"Yeah, later. Take care."

For the next ten minutes, I paced my apartment while counting back from a hundred, trying desperately to stave off a looming panic attack. Images of Ethan collecting Rebecca from her suite, kissing her hand and telling her how exquisite she looked blazed like an uncontrollable fire through my heart and mind. Although I knew those gestures were not only fake, but vital to the plan if Ethan was to be believed, it didn't prevent them from being agonizingly torturous to bear.

When I could no longer endure the pain, I changed quickly and headed down to the gym in hope of seeking an alternative agony to occupy my mind. Unsure of where I actually found the energy, I managed to pound the treadmill for almost forty-five minutes. I ran until my body was drenched in sweat, and all I could focus on was the burning pain in my lungs and legs. Unsatisfied, I continued the onslaught to my body with a further twenty minutes on the cross-trainer and another ten on the weight machines.

Finally exhausted, I was about to return to my apartment with ideas of a steaming hot bath and another glass of wine, when I remembered Jia and I had drunk the last of it earlier. I reached into the pocket of my hoodie and pulled out the emergency twenty dollar bill I always kept in there, smiling gratefully. Then heading out of my building, jogged the short stretch to the convenience store.

After making my purchase, I stepped out onto the sidewalk and came face to face with Jean-Paul. My instinctive reaction was to back away from him; I didn't have the physical or mental energy for a confrontation. My response seemed to surprise him and his brow furrowed in a noticeable wince.

"Am I so repelling to you that you can't even say, hi?"

"I thought we were way past polite gestures and small talk, Jean-Paul. Or are you forgetting our last encounter?"

He laughed mirthlessly. "No, that isn't something I'll get over in a hurry, Angel. I'll bet you and your boyfriend are still laughing about it now, though."

"What are you talking about? Why would either of us find anything about that evening amusing?"

Confusion crumpled his brow. "You don't know, do you?"

"Know what?"

"How your boyfriend deals with your unwanted admirers."

"Ethan wasn't even there. What are you getting at?"

"No, but his monkey was." He paused and took a step toward me. "And he took great delight in taking instruction, then relaying the results back to the big-I-am billionaire."

By now I was getting pissed. "What *are* you talking about?"

Suddenly, he raised a hand and pointed two fingers toward my head mimicking a pointed gun. "You're boyfriend ordered me to stay the fuck away from you while monkey-boy held a gun to my head. He said if I so much as breathed the same air as you again, the next time he would pull the trigger. They were both satisfied I'd got the message when I pissed down my leg and saturated my shoes."

For a second, I was speechless, unable to process what he'd told me into anything that made sense. I cleared my throat. "No. I didn't know about that, Jean-Paul. And I'm not excusing it, but you can't deny that you played a part in it yourself. The way you behaved toward me was gratuitous. Like I said, I'm not excusing that kind of conduct, but it might help to know that, at the time, Ethan had reason to believe my safety was seriously under threat and he was uncertain of the source. When you admitted to making anonymous calls, and it became obvious you were following me, you made yourself a suspect. We know you weren't involved now; we got it wrong, and I apologize for that, but you fucked up too."

A few moments passed, as he seemed to gauge my sincerity. Then his displeasure appeared to wane, his stance relaxing a little as he backed off from my space.

"Yeah… I fucked up. I fell in love with the wrong girl and made an ass of trying to get her to love me back. I can see that now. I was a complete prick—and for that I apologize too." He took another step away from me, this time making to go around me, but halting when he was level. "I won't bother you again. I hope he makes you happy, Angel. I mean that."

I nodded. "Thank you. And I know you'll find the right person, Jean-Paul. Someone who deserves you."

Smiling tentatively, he moved to walk away, stopping after only a few steps and turning. "Angel?" he called. "Did you find out who it was? Threatening you, I mean."

"Yes."

"And was it sorted out?"

"It will be," I replied resolutely.

"Good. I'm glad. At least I'll not be the only person walking around Manhattan with their shoes drenched in piss." With that he turned and walked away.

As I lay back in a steaming hot bath, sipping a glass of wine, my mind worked over what Jean-Paul had said. Whether or not Ethan's methods of protecting me were morally right or wrong, there was no disputing the lengths he would go to, to do it. Prior to Rebecca joining the mix, I might have been annoyed by how Ethan had chosen to handle the situation with Jean-Paul, furious even, but Jean-Paul's behavior had been questionable, and given the circumstances, I could now understand why Ethan had responded the way he had. Under the same pressure, I would do the same for him. My plans to illegally gain access to a bank vault in order to protect him were proof of that.

With a fresh awareness of my current predicament, I felt the fluttering of panic begin to surface once again, my lungs constricting, my heartbeat fitful. Before I'd even realized what I was doing, I'd filled my lungs and was immersing myself under the water, allowing my mind to drift. Holding my breath, I focused on the blissful silence, until my heart rate slowed and my mind entered that celestial place. A place that had, so often in my life, been the only place to find peace. And—although not in physical sense, but spiritually, emotionally—

the only place I could breathe.

When my lungs could take no more, I resurfaced and took a long, deep, restoring breath. Suddenly exhausted, I climbed out of the bath and after patting my skin dry, wandered into the bedroom to dress for bed. In my bottom drawer was the dress shirt Ethan had worn to my father's charity event, the night we'd reunited. It was folded neatly, where I'd purposefully placed it, button-less, unwashed, and reeking of his heavenly scent. I held it to my nose and inhaled. The effect on my senses was intoxicating, a pleasant, soothing head buzz which left me barely able to think.

Pulling it on, I lay down on my bed, relishing the sensation of the cool, fine fabric against my soft, heated skin. The heady combination of Ethan's scent and the sensation of my taut nipples brushing softly against the material as my chest rose and fell were hypnotic and before I realized I'd drifted off to sleep.

Shimmering moonbeams casting shafts of light across the sky were the only thing to illuminate the darkness. As I lay watching, the twinkling images danced out from the shadows, like fairies with sparkling wings. The images were a mirage—an optical illusion created by the light-reflecting rays of the moon and the glimmering, glistening diamonds which hung from the tip of my finger, swaying in the cool night breeze.

The twirling shapes filled me with happiness, seeming to warm my heart like a flood of treasured memories. Suddenly, the images became dull and formless, and as I focused on the diamonds, they too had morphed into some other configuration—that of a key on the end of a chain.

Suddenly, I remembered why I was there in that darkened, unfamiliar place, and I cursed myself for having been so easily distracted. Grasping the key in the palm of one hand, I began to look around in search of the hidden box I knew I was there to find.

Ahead, in the distance, I could see the shapes of the two spotted beasts digging in the musty earth and was momentarily paralyzed with fear. I was afraid to approach the creatures, but if I failed to act, they would be sure to discover the box and the contents within. I glanced around my feet at the crisp, fallen, autumn leaves, my gaze falling on a rock the size of my fist. Stooping to retrieve it, I held it firm and then launched it into the air toward the patch of earth where the beasts were digging frantically. As the rock fell, the startled beasts scattered and bolted, disappearing in the dense array of shadows and undergrowth.

I ran over to the patch of earth, falling to my knees, and continued to dig the hole the dogs had started, scraping at the cold, damp soil with my fingers until they hit the surface of a small box. As I brushed the earth away to uncover it, I realized I didn't need the key after all, because the box which lay buried was a simple shoe box, bound by a red velvet ribbon.

Tentatively, I loosened the bow and slid my fingertips underneath the rim of the lid, my heart pounding rhythmically with nervous anticipation. I flipped the lid and instantly withdrew, falling back on my haunches, as a sharp gasp of surprise burst from my lips. Staring back at me was a black rubber hangman's mask. The sight made my skin prickle with abhorrence, an unearthly shudder passing without warning through my body. But just as I was about to replace the lid, something beneath the mask caught my eye. Curiosity prevailed, and cautiously, I moved toward the mask, flipping it free of the box with a twist of my hand.

The color of startling crimson gleamed in the moonlight—a pair of shiny red shoes. Gasping in horror, I slammed the lid firmly back in place, but now the surface was coated in shiny chrome, creating an almost perfect mirror. The reflection gazing back at me was one I recognized—but it wasn't my own.

"No!" The word filled the deathly silence as my hands fisted into my hair, desperately yanking the strawberry blond wig from my head, but it wouldn't budge. Instead, my fingers were painfully tearing handfuls of hair from my burning scalp. And then I felt something cold and hard

digging fiercely into my temple. Focusing on my reflection it became horrifyingly clear what it was. The ostentatious tones of a British accented voice spoke to me.

"Is this what you're looking for?" she whispered as she drilled the barrel of the gun into the side of my head.

Clambering to my feet, I began to run, blindly at first, until suddenly I was falling into the light, and all around me was the soothing comfort of heated water. I held my breath and slowly my heart began to calm, the warmth and the silence filling me with a tranquil, inner peace. Suddenly, my senses were alerted to a familiar scent, and the musky male smell of Ethan permeated my core. My body began to tingle as the sensation of a soft whispery touch made its way up my inner thigh. My flesh quivered and quaked, as all at once I was immersed in a warm, sensual haze of arousal and...

My eyes flew open, my sleep-filled mind reeling from the vividness of my dream. I closed them again, not wanting to wake from where I was sure the dream was about to take me. The throbbing ache between my legs was proof enough of that.

Suddenly, my skin began to prickle with awareness, alerting my senses to a presence in the room. I lifted my head from the pillow, my eyes quickly adjusting in the dim light, illuminated only from the candlelight still glowing from the bathroom. When my eyes focused on the familiar figure at the end of my bed, I froze. My pulse rate quickened, my blood pumping frantically to my heart as my breathing grew fitful and a light sheen of sweat sprang to layer my sensitive skin. But it wasn't because I felt even a fragment of fear—it was because I was impossibly aroused.

Ethan stood with his legs slightly astride at the foot of my bed, gazing down intently at my part-naked body. His hands were thrust deep into his suit pants' pockets, his tie pulled lose, and the top two buttons of his shirt undone. His head was cocked to one side, his sexy mussed-up hair flopping lazily into one eye. As our eyes locked on to one another's, his lips parted and a soft moan escaped, revealing his unmistakable desire.

"How long have you been watching me?" I whispered through the dim light.

He drew in his bottom lip, scraping it past his upper teeth in a slow, erotic gesture. "Long enough to discern that you're a dirty, dirty girl even when you're asleep, Cinderella."

My breath caught with a coquettish gasp of surprise at being caught visually aroused while sleeping. I opened my mouth to speak again, but Ethan closed a finger to his lips to silence me. His heavy-hooded gaze traveled a leisurely path down my body, his focus so intense I could almost feel the soft whispery touch of those long, dark lashes fluttering against my skin. I glanced down at my own figure lying there on the bed, wanting to glimpse the image which seemed to captivate him so completely.

My legs were spread ever so slightly, my sex naked and exposed and wet. Ethan's button-less shirt had fallen open as I'd slept, and the peaks of my nipples were now hard, rigid nodules of puckered flesh. My skin seemed to glow with flushed arousal, pink and lush and ready.

A vitally important conversation waited patiently in the backdrop of both of our minds, I'm sure. My need to know what had happened between him and Rebecca was burning earnestly inside me, as strong as I was certain his need was to reveal it.

But right then—our need for each other was far greater.

Ethan reached out and placed a finger on the inside of my left ankle and with a gentle pressure, pushed it aside to part my legs. Repeating the action with the other, he widened the gap until my legs could stretch no further. As his eyes wandered, feasting over every exposed inch of my body, his arousal became amorously vivid in his darkening gaze. With measured movements, his hands moved to release the knot of his tie, sliding it seductively around his neck and discarding it. Then, after shrugging out of his jacket, he moved on to his shirt and then his pants, until he stood naked before me.

My eyes slid possessively over his magnificent form, from the sinful look on his beautiful face, down and over the flexing power of his strong arms and shoulders, and further to his taut abdomen which rippled all the way to his eagerly pulsing cock.

He shifted, climbing onto the foot of the bed and moving with virile grace toward me, until he was kneeling between my legs. Reaching out, he fingered the lapels of the shirt, folding it back to further expose my shoulders and collar bone. Then, pressing the palm of his hand to the pulse in the hollow of my neck, he slowly trailed a path down through the valley of my heaving breasts, and across the flat of my stomach. His touch was hot against my skin, eager and covetous, as if the pressure of his hand could brand me as his. His search continued, up and over the hard mound of my pussy until he reached his destination and the soft pink folds of my wetness.

Expertly guiding his fingers, he began to stroke languid circles around my slick opening and then slowly, with a gently measured ease, sank two magical fingers deep inside me. I gasped as he slid them in and out, gliding effortlessly through the slippery silkiness of my arousal, my body arching to meet him greedily. Suddenly, he withdrew, his exit leaving me needy and desperate, but then in an insanely erotic gesture, brought his fingers to just beneath his nose and inhaled my scent, before plunging them into his mouth and sucking my juices hungrily from his fingers.

I gasped my pleasure as he rolled his eyes and groaned. "You taste sinfully sweet, Angel." He moved so he was above me, his hand fisting into my hair to grip me tightly. "I need to smell you and taste you like I need sustenance to survive." Dipping toward me, he crushed his mouth against mine, his tongue pushing inside with the urgency of a starving man.

Then I felt the pulsing head of his cock at my entrance, and pulling back from the kiss so our eyes could meet, he spoke again. His words were precise and unwavering, with no doubt as to their sincerity. "And the need to be inside you is as vital to me as my next breath." He sank into me, pushing every thick hard inch inside, opening and stretching me until my body quivered with the overwhelming sensation of fullness.

Every cell in my anatomy seemed to respond, my mind and body engulfed in a throng of tumultuous emotions. I grasped him to me, tunneling my fingers into his hair as I pulled him down toward my mouth. "Then take me, Ethan," I gasped through my desire. "Take every bit of me, because I am yours."

We moved together, making slow, passionate love, the air around us crackling with the intensity of our deep, profound connection to each other. It controlled us now, dominated our every move, our every breath, controlling the things we said, the way we thought.

As I buried my tongue inside his mouth, swirling and lapping, I arched by back, rocking into the rhythmic movement. The folds of my lush, velvet sex clamped over his thick, hard column, every ridge of his solid flesh pushing me further toward ecstasy as he stroked in and out at a gradually mounting pace. Our mutual pursuit of hedonic pleasure grew like burning ribbons of flames, hot and demanding and relentless. My body shook with the earth-shattering tremors of my orgasm as it ripped through me, my sex clenching around him, drawing him deeper and milking him until he shook with his own release.

Ethan rolled to the side and folded his arms around me in a shielding embrace. I could feel the pounding of his heart slow to a steady beat against my back, his warm breath against my neck as it evened out, and I couldn't think of a single solitary place on Earth I would rather be. My lids were growing heavier by the second as I tried to fight the sleep slowly encompassing my body and mind.

From somewhere, I found the energy to mumble the words which lay heavily on my mind. "Did she buy it, E?"

The sense of calm which enveloped us when he answered was akin to closing the door on a riotous storm; the turmoil wouldn't go away, but we were safe from its clutches for now. "She bought it, baby."

CHAPTER SIXTEEN

The next morning, I woke up alone in my bed wondering if my nighttime encounter with Ethan had all been a dream—a very hot, sexy, wonderful dream. But the combined hedonistic scent of Ethan and sex on my skin, as well as the note left on his pillow, convinced me otherwise. I reached out and grabbed it, rolling onto my back to read.

To my beautiful Cinderella.

Just a quick note to reassure you that you're not losing your mind. Last night, I did indeed pay you a cheeky visit. It was reckless of me, putting you at risk like that. I should have known better, and for that I apologize. Although if I said I regretted it, I'd be lying. My intention wasn't actually to stay. I just wanted to kiss you goodnight and reassure you that all had gone well with the evening.

But then I saw you lying there in my shirt, fast asleep, but aroused by a naughty dream, and you were the sexiest, most beautiful thing I'd ever laid eyes on. Your breasts were swollen and firm and your pussy glistened with moisture in the candlelight. I was so impossibly turned on, I was afraid my dick might actually explode just by watching you.

I couldn't bear to go to sleep without you in my arms. I needed to see you, to smell you, to taste you—to fuck you. Also, I couldn't bear to say goodbye again, so I snuck out before dawn.

Please forgive me.

I haven't told Damon about my trip to London yet, and there are things I need to discuss with him before I leave, so I will no doubt be in the thick of it this morning. However, I will endeavor to call you as soon as I possibly can.
Don't be mad, but I would rather you didn't leave your apartment today, just until she's safely out of the way. As soon as we're gone tonight, Jackson will be in touch. I want him to shadow you constantly, at least until my return.
I don't think it's a good idea to see you before I leave, it will be too risky—last night was too risky, but damn, it was worth it.

I can still taste you.

The next time I hold you in my arms I want to do it without the threat of her lurking in the shadows of our minds—when she's finally gone from our lives for good. I can't wait.

Until then, know that I love you with every beat of my heart.

Yours, E xx

After reading it over at least a dozen times, I clasped the note to my chest, my mind swimming with a torrent of mixed emotions. Although I understood why, I couldn't help the pang of disappointment that I hadn't awoken to Ethan's sinfully handsome face. And then there was the crushing anxiety that came with the uncertainty of when the next time would be. His words had also aroused me. There was something about the voyeuristic way he'd observed me while I slept, caught in the middle of a horny dream, which although made me feel strangely coy, was also wildly erotic.

The worst thing, of course, was that he'd specifically requested that I stay safely indoors, and I hated knowing that I would pay no heed to his wishes. I tried to console myself by keeping in mind that my insubordination was requisite if we stood any real chance of getting rid of Rebecca for good. If the day turned out as I hoped it would, maybe Ethan would forgive me. Shoving it to the back of my mind, I focused on the closing line of the letter—the words that made me feel warm inside, whole and cherished. The words that made everything I was planning to do that day worth every daunting second.

With that in mind, I jumped out of bed and got to work.

Jia arrived mid-morning to help me perfect my "Bo Peep" look, and by the time noon arrived, we were tucked inside a coffee house down the street from the hotel, waiting nervously. When Jackson gave me the all clear, I casually made my way to the hotel, through the lobby, and up to Rebecca's suite, while Jia kept lookout across the street in case there was a repeat performance of yesterday.

Like a true professional, calm and collected and with painstaking precision, I entered the suite and worked my way through the rooms, turning out drawers and filling my overly large purse with the contents of the safe. Everything was just as I'd found it the day before, so it ran like clockwork, just as I'd planned step-by-step in my mind, no hiccups, no surprises—pure fucking genius.

As I emerged from the hotel, I signaled to Jia that all was well and she responded with a beaming smile. We flagged down a passing cab and climbed into opposite sides of the car, Jia's grin of incredulity almost splitting her face in two.

"You badass little bitch," she whispered as the cab pulled out into traffic.

Not wanting to draw any unwanted attention, I motioned to the driver and placed my finger on my lips to silence her. Then I settled into my seat, closing my eyes against the sudden surge of nausea which assailed my body. The enormity of what I was about to do was finally playing havoc with my nervous system.

I was about to carry out a fraudulent act. I'd stolen somebody's identity and was about to attempt to gain unlawful entry into a bank vault in order to steal their belongings. I would be guilty of fraud, theft, and impersonating someone in order to deceive others. To say I was terrified would be a mammoth misinterpretation of the truth.

Retrieving my cell from my purse, I began to type out a text message to Ethan. Two calls had come in from him over the last hour, but I'd allowed both of them to go to voicemail. Although it had pained me more than words could say, I'd decided that ignoring him sat slightly easier with me than lying to him about where I was. But I couldn't stave off his calls any longer. I had to throw him something or he would be frantic with worry.

I'd been hoping to avoid telling him the truth and what I was up to until I was certain of a definitive outcome, but time was ticking and I couldn't withhold what I knew from Ethan any longer. Whatever lay hidden in that box—disk or no disk—there was at least one course of action that wouldn't alter. I had to stop Ethan getting on that plane.

Anxiety swelled inside my chest like a steadily inflating balloon, and as I toyed with the wording on the message, deleting and re-writing, it suddenly dawned on me how difficult it was going to be to tell Ethan what I knew. What would I say? Where would I start? How much time would I have before Rebecca realized I was on to her?

It wasn't until the cab drew to a halt just around the corner from the bank that I finally finished the message, deciding to keep it as brief as possible: Plans have changed. Meet me in one hour at your apartment. I'll explain everything then. Please trust me, E x. Feeling as if I might actually throw up, I pressed send and climbed nervously out of the cab.

"Mother of fuck, what the hell am I doing?" I muttered as I walked down the street with tiny mincing steps. The hem of the dress was so narrow it was difficult to do anything but.

"Breathe," Jia instructed. "You'll be fine. Look, you even walk like her, all prim and prudish and tight-assed. If you ask me, she needs to worry less about propriety and decorum and go get herself a good ass-fuck—she might actually loosen up a little."

Oh, the irony!

The statement was so ludicrously contrary to the truth it was comical, and I almost choked in my attempt to stifle my nervous laugh. From what I could gather, it was Rebecca's predilection for being fucked in the ass—as well as various other unmentionable things—that had resulted in her being fucked in the head. Wearing dresses with restrictive movement was probably the *only* time she kept her legs shut.

"You okay?" Jia asked as I coughed and spluttered.

"Sure, just nerves," I patted my chest. "In retrospect, I'm thinking it may have been better if you'd taken this role—the whole imposter thing. You'd be far more convincing than me."

Jia screwed up her face as if I'd just spoken to her in a foreign language she didn't understand. "I don't know whether you've noticed, bitch, but last time I checked in the mirror I was definitely Chinese. So for some reason, *I'm* thinking that probably wouldn't work."

"Oh yeah. Good point," I muttered as I minced and swished around the corner of West 52nd Street and onto 8th Avenue.

Jia snatched a sideways glance at me and chuckled. "Besides I wouldn't be seen dead looking like that."

I responded with a scorn-oozing smile. In fairness, the look itself could probably be quite tasteful on the right person; it was the association to Rebecca which elicited the urge to gag.

Suddenly the bank was in sight, and it was at this stage in the plan where we'd arranged to go our separate ways. Jia smiled and winked at me. "Break a leg, bitch."

Nodding, I took a deep breath and headed off to commit my crime.

Once inside the bank, I reached into my purse and donned the glasses. The correctional lenses were negligible in strength. Jia only needed them for the computer at work, but they did make my vision slightly wonky and I found myself squinting to compensate.

The bank was relatively quiet; it was only an hour before closing, so there wasn't much in the way of queues. Taking stock of the situation quickly, I surveyed my surroundings through my skewed vision, assessing how many staff were working the counters—their age, gender, and so forth—carefully selecting which line to join. Finally, I decided on the cute Hispanic guy at counter three, deducing that he'd be the most susceptible to persuasion. Nervously, I joined the queue as the man in front took his turn, silently praying that I wouldn't be required to show the ID.

Within seconds, I was moving forward toward the desk, Mr. Cute Hispanic guy smiling widely in welcome, my heart pounding so wildly in my chest I was sure the bow on my dress would be quivering from the vibration.

"Good afternoon, ma'am, what can I help you with today?"

Clearing my throat, I lay the rental agreement on the counter. "Oh, good afternoon," I said, assuming my best British accent. "I wish to gain access to my safe-deposit box."

"Certainly, ma'am," he scanned his gaze over the agreement and then turned to his keyboard. A minute or so passed as he tapped information into the computer and waited for it to process. Finally, he looked at me. "Can you confirm that you are the renter, Rebecca Jane Staunton?"

"Yes, I am," I said clearly and without hesitation.

He pressed a key and the printer sprang into life. Seconds later, what looked like a pro-forma document flopped on to the desk. "If you could just sign the admission documentation?"

I nodded and he slid the document across the desk toward me. Using the complimentary pen, I signed Rebecca's name across the page in the spidery scrawl that was as ostentatious as the woman herself. Mr. Cute Hispanic began to compare it with the one on record. I held my breath and waited.

"Do you have ID with you today, ma'am?"

Oh my God, he suspects me. He knows I'm not me—her.

My pulse began to quicken, my knees trembling beneath the stupid dress. "Yes, of course," I reached into my purse, my mind working furiously through my options. I'd virtually decided that I should just tell him I'd changed my mind and get the hell out there, when instead I found myself handing over the driver's license. He held out his hand to take it, and just as his fingers grazed the edge, there was a pull on my elbow and the card slipped from my grasp, tumbling to the floor.

"Oh my God, Rebecca, it *is* you." I turned to face the person whose grip still held firmly on to my arm. Jia gazed up at me, a smile as broad as I'd ever seen on her face stretching from ear to ear. "I haven't seen you in like *ages*, how *are* you?" she gushed with exaggerated enthusiasm.

In my peripheral vision, I could just make out Mr. Cute scooping the ID card off the floor. "You *look* freaking amazing. Doesn't she look amazing?" Jia directed the question right at him. His face flushed a bright shade of crimson as he smiled awkwardly, glanced hastily at the card and handed it back.

"Thank you, Miss Staunton." He motioned to a set of glass double doors just off to the right. "If you wait just over there a banker will come and escort you to the safe-deposit vault."

I stared at him in disbelief.

"What are you waiting for, bitch?" Jia mumbled under her breath.

"Thank you, you've been very helpful." I smiled at Mr. Cute, gathered my purse, and moved off in the direction he'd pointed me in.

Making a fake show of politeness, I turned to Jia and kissed the air on either side of her cheeks, muttering, "Thank you," quietly into her ear.

An inane grin was firmly plastered in place as she grated through clenched teeth. "I know right, I am *so* fucking awesome." As I joined the banker who'd emerged from the double doors, I heard Jia call out to me. "It was great to see you, honey. We'll do lunch. Call me."

On my lips there was a paltry smile, but inside I was laughing almost hysterically as I minced away, swishing my hair demurely.

The banker led me down a corridor and through an entryway which led into a wide space with several doors leading off. In the middle was a huge, steel security door, which I guessed led into the safe-deposit vault. The banker approached and very discreetly entered a code into the security entry-panel. It *bleeped,* and using both hands she turned the wheel and pulled open the heavy door.

"Do you have your key, Miss Staunton?"

"Yes, of course." I handed her the key and we entered inside.

The vault was a long narrow room with chrome-fronted boxes running floor to ceiling around the entire perimeter. The boxes varied in size, larger ones on the lower rows, growing gradually smaller the higher they went. Each one had two locks and a number. The banker glanced at the key and made her way slowly down the left side of the room as she searched for box 2009.

"Ah, here we are," she halted at one of the medium sized boxes and inserted my key into one of the locks. Then she reached into her pocket and retrieved a guard key, inserting it into the second lock. The panel flipped open and the banker slid out the box.

"Follow me, I'll show you to a room so that you can get some privacy." Leading me to one of the rooms adjacent to the vault, she laid the box on a table and pointed to a button on the wall. "If you press the button when you're done, Miss Staunton, someone will come and get you." I thanked her and she left the room, closing the door firmly behind her.

Forever seemed to pass as I stared at the box, my heart thumping madly as it had before, my mouth sandpaper-dry with nervous anticipation. The contents of this box would decide the future for all us—me, Ethan, Jackson, even Rebecca. I knew it could be a dead end, a box full of empty hopelessness and a life trapped in Rebecca Staunton's sick, sadistic world with no way out. Or it may contain the solution to this nightmare we were in and the answer to our prayers. Either way, this small, rectangular metal box would determine our destiny. My trembling fingers hovered over the box as I swallowed hard and lifted the lid.

Despite the limitations of the dress, I raced into Ethan's building, through the impressive foyer and to the bank of elevators. Mercifully, the door slid open the moment I pressed the call button, so I boarded quickly and returned my attention to the text message I'd received while climbing out of the cab.

The message was from Jackson and read: She's headed for Mr. Wilde's apartment. Unable to delay her. ETA 10 minutes. She's pissed—what the hell did you do?

Fuck! Fuck, fuck, fuck! I cursed as the elevator ascended at what seemed like a painfully slow pace. Of course, I'd known I was on borrowed time from the moment I'd received Jackson's text thirty minutes earlier, informing me of their imminent return to the hotel. But the bitch certainly wasn't one to let the grass grow under her feet. More than likely, she'd have headed straight for the safe the second she lay eyes on her ransacked suite, and of course, discovered it empty. But as I'd predicted, rather than inform the police, she was headed for Ethan. The shit-storm was gathering at an alarming pace.

The hope of sitting down with Ethan before he had to face her—to explain what I'd discovered and give him time to absorb what was sure to be a shocking revelation—was obliterated. The enigma that was Rebecca Staunton had been baffling from the get-go. But even Ethan had no idea of the depths of her depravity, or the lengths she'd gone to claim him.

When I'd left the bank with the contents of the box safely stored inside my purse, my mind had been spinning in confounded bewilderment. I'd studied them carefully, attempting to gain some understanding of how the mind of the person who'd placed them there actually functioned. In the end, I concluded that I'd never really know—and in truth—I wasn't even sure I wanted to. A glimpse into the mind of one so unhinged was almost too much, but to try and empathize with what you find there would be far too disturbing. For me, it was like that of a horror movie—I was intrigued enough to read the blurb, but it would never arouse enough curiosity to watch.

Despite the disquiet that had settled into my bones like a cold, damp intruder, I couldn't help but notice a trace of sanguinity. It was enough for me to at least begin to hope. To hope that by the time the day finally ended, Ethan's demons would indeed be laid to rest, and Rebecca would be gone from our lives.

As the elevator finally drew to a halt, my nerves jangled like a cacophony of bells. I hadn't set foot in Ethan's apartment since the night Rebecca arrived, and although it felt right that I hadn't returned until now—in time for her departure—I was afraid the place would feel defiled. That she would leave behind the residue of her evil, and although her physical presence will have departed, her ghost could well remain.

With no time to spare for further misgivings, I exited the elevator and pushed through the foyer doors to find Ethan pacing frantically in the vast, familiar space of the open-plan living area. One hand was thrust into his hair, the other kneading the knotted tension from the back of his neck. His fitted, black dress shirt was open at the neck, his tie dispensed with, and even in his state of heightened anxiety, he was breathtaking.

I stopped in my tracks, the air from my lungs momentarily stolen by his presence alone. Sensing me, Ethan froze and jerking his head in my direction, locked onto my gaze. For a second he just stared, a blend of horror and confusion marring his perfect features as his eyes raked over me, and suddenly I realized why. I was still wearing the dress and stupid freaking wig. My hand reached up and tore it from my head, allowing the long tendrils of my hair to fall and cascade over my shoulders. Shifting, I began to make my way across the room, watching as recognition and relief began to smooth the creases in his brow.

Abruptly, he pivoted and stalked urgently toward me, as if desperate to bridge the remaining gap, his head shaking with a thousand questions he seemed unable to ask. He thrust his hands into my hair, cradling my head as he brought my lips to within inches of his.

"What the f..." The words faded as he crushed his mouth over mine, hard and fast and urgent, his tongue delving into my mouth in a desperate search for mine. I kissed him back, my hands knotting into his hair as I pulled him in deeper, devouring him. For a second, nothing else mattered apart from we were here, together, alive and safe. Questions and uncertainties hung obnoxiously pungent in the air, waiting for the impact they would have on our union.

Then, as if time and reality had just tapped me impatiently on the shoulder, I tore my mouth from his, and still gripping him firmly by the hair, I held him in place. "Listen, Ethan," I whispered urgently. "You have to listen to me. Rebecca is on her way here, we have only minutes to spare."

Panic and alarm spread rapidly over his features, setting into his deep blue, penetrating eyes as he pulled away. "Then you have to hide quickly—"

"No!" I cut him off. "*You* have to listen. I know about the man Jackson killed in the club. I know about the cover-up." He took a step back, his face paling with shock and shame and incredulity. I followed, closing the gap and gripping the tops of his arms. "But so does *she,* Ethan. Jackson didn't destroy the footage in time. She's had the disk all this time and she's been blackmailing him."

Ethan ran a palm over his face, as if the action would wake him from this seemingly ludicrous dream. "What...? How do you know all this?"

I shook my head. "There's no time." From the foyer came the sound of the elevator and voices. "Please trust me on what's about to happen. There are some things you'll hear that I wanted to explain while we were alone." Suddenly, blood pounded in my ears and everything seemed to slow. Ethan blinked, dragging his gaze from mine to focus on the foyer doors opening up into the living space. "I'm so sorry I didn't get the chance, E," I muttered, moving to scoop up my purse from the floor.

Rebecca Staunton minced into the room, her features pinched and fraught with distress. "Ethan, dahling. You have to do something. My wretched hotel suite..." her line of sight shifted, suddenly finding me in her peripheral vision as I moved toward the kitchen island "... has been broken into..." Her words faded out, her gaze narrowing suspiciously as it rested with venom on me.

For a transient moment, I waited as Jackson entered the room behind her, his expression almost as terrified and wildly confused as Ethan's. And then I fixed her with a steely glare. Although, on the inside I was trembling like a leaf on a breeze, my exterior was a perfect guise of calm, confident composure.

"Yes, that's probably got something to do with me," I said moving slowly toward her. I noticed Ethan's shocked expression snap toward me, but I didn't respond. "Sorry about the mess. I was never that big on orderliness."

As comprehension suddenly dawned, her eyes widened, her face coloring crimson red as blood boiled beneath the surface of her skin. "You!" she spat. "Call the police, Ethan. You heard her, she just confessed to breaking into my suite."

"The police?" My voice dripped with derision as I drew level with her. "Not your usual style, Rebecca. I thought, at least, my actions might provoke you into putting 'Plan B' into action. What was it you threatened me with? Ah, yes. You said you knew people who would rape me and leave me for dead."

"What?" Ethan hissed without a second's delay. Rebecca's gaze flickered nervously toward him. "You said fucking what?"

"Don't listen to her, she's obviously psychotic. I mean, for heaven's sake, what kind of person breaks into somebody's place?" Rebecca spoke with an edge of desperation in her voice, just as I'd anticipated.

Last night was the first time Ethan had ever given her hope that they might have a future together. She wouldn't want anything changing his mind, and I was certain she'd be prepared to say anything to keep that hope alive.

While her focus was momentarily diverted to Ethan, I moved quickly to Jackson in the doorway, thrusting my hand into my purse as I went. Retrieving a disk, I pressed it discreetly into his hands and nodded in the direction of Ethan's office, whispering, "Make sure it's the one."

With wide-eyed surprise, he nodded once and subtly backed into the corridor, disappearing out of sight.

There had been several disks in the safe deposit box. The one I'd given Jackson had the words *The Wilde Manhattan* scrawled over the surface in permanent ink. If my guess was correct, it was the name of Ethan's club in London, the one where the incident had taken place.

Pivoting, I turned to face Rebecca once again.

"Yes, Rebecca, what kind of person indeed?" I answered her rhetorical question. "Someone like Tim Tillman, I expect. He was the low-life private investigator *you* hired to break into *my* apartment, right? Tell me, was he from the same badass crew you had in mind for my rape?"

Looking vaguely appalled, she rolled her eyes as if what I was implying was way too farfetched to be true. Ethan stood with his mouth slightly open; his mind seemingly working furiously to try and figure out what the hell was going on.

"Did you threaten Angel… with *rape*?" His voice was so heavily laden with incredulity that the words scraped hoarsely past his throat.

Ignoring him, she turned back to me, her chin jutting obstinately. "What the hell do you think you're doing here, anyway? I thought you'd have got the message by now. Ethan said he'd explained how things are between us. He'll never give me up. He can't live without me." She held out her hand and glanced down at the diamond solitaire on her finger, adding, "We're getting married. Remember?"

Of course, I knew she was deluded, only inflating the utter nonsense which Ethan and I had agreed to tell her. But the words hit me like a punch in the gut, nonetheless.

"Answer my fucking question, goddamn it!" Ethan's voice tore through the momentary silence, anger practically seeping from his pores.

Rebecca almost jumped out of her skin, her eyes widening in alarm. "Calm down, Ethan dahling. It was an empty threat, designed to get her off *your* back." A quick evil glance in my direction inferred there was nothing remotely empty about it.

"I knew you were capable of some seriously sick shit," Ethan spat the words with venom, "but rape? After what happened to you and you threaten her with *rape*?"

From the edge of my vision, I spotted Jackson silently reentering the room. Our eyes locked across the space as he took his stance, his feet shoulder-width apart, his hands clasped in front of his body as professional as ever. But his ruggedly handsome features held something I hadn't seen before, his soft brown eyes dazzling with awakened resolve. I knew my gaze was filled with a burning question. A question Jackson answered with a single nod, fueling me with fresh conviction.

"Oh, she's capable of some sick shit, alright." Glancing at Ethan, I prayed that the sorrow which filled my heart was easily visible in my eyes. Sorrow for what I was about to reveal.

"You don't know anything about me!" she snapped furiously.

"Well, actually, that's not true. There's quite a lot I know about you." I waited a beat as suspicion burned in her eyes. "For instance, I know that Alistair Brown didn't rape you."

With eyes as wide as saucers, she nodded her head frantically. "Yes, he did. Ethan will testify to that."

Ethan's eyes bore into my mine questioningly. I turned back to Rebecca. "Ethan can only testify to what he *thought* he saw. But what he actually saw was two people engaging in consensual sex." Ethan was frowning in confusion now. "Not of the regular, plain, old vanilla variety, I grant you—but definitely consensual."

"You don't know what you're talking about," Rebecca spat nervously, then craftily trying to deviate from the subject added, "Why is it you're here again?"

Ethan's expression was peppered with doubt and bewilderment. More than anything, I'd wanted to reveal this part of the truth in private, but there was no chance of that now. Needing, at the very least, to address him directly, I turned to face him.

"Do you remember saying that you couldn't shake the feeling that what you saw that night was just a big misunderstanding? That deep down you knew Alistair wasn't capable of rape?"

"What have you been saying, Ethan?" Rebecca hissed accusingly.

Ignoring her, his eyes narrowed at me as he nodded in affirmation.

"You were right to doubt what you saw, E. You did misinterpret the situation—but you were supposed to. You see, our little drama queen here likes to play rough. Although, being a humble, unresisting submissive really isn't her thing. Rebecca Staunton isn't inclined to yield willingly and would never submit to the orders of others. She's a control freak. Obedience wouldn't fit with the overbearing, dominant character she likes to portray. Submissive sex would make her feel weak and feeble. So, to get her kicks, she has to pretend to be uncooperative, she has to at least appear to be putting up a fight. What you saw that night, Ethan, was fantasy role play—Rebecca getting her kicks. You saw Alistair restraining her; you saw her struggling against his strength as he took her by force. But it wasn't real. He did it because she asked him to."

Ethan's eyes flickered as if waking from a daydream, and for a second, I worried that he hadn't even been listening. Suddenly they darted across the room to where Rebecca stood, fixing her in a condemnatory stare.

At the very least, I'd expected her to defend herself, deny everything in the hope he'd think I was crazy. But instead, she rolled her eyes like she didn't understand what the fuss was about, an evil, impenitent smirk curling the edge of her lip. "I never *said* he raped me, you just assumed," she said to Ethan, shrugging casually. "I saw it in your eyes when you walked in, the horror of what you thought you'd stumbled across. I was so aroused by it—you observing whilst I was being taken against my will—that it made me struggle even more. I thought you would see how much he wanted me, the lengths he would go to have me, and that it would make you desire me yourself."

Ethan gaped wordlessly, stunned into silence by not only her willingness to admit the truth, but how sickeningly excited she seemed by it.

"When I realized you actually thought he'd raped me, I saw an opportunity to get him out of the way. The only reason I got with him in the first place was to get closer to you. But then the whole thing backfired when the idiot began to fall for me, and you were too afraid of hurting him to admit your feelings for me."

"I didn't *have* feelings for you," Ethan gasped in horror.

"Of course you did. The only thing standing in our way was Alistair. That's why he had to go."

"What do you mean, he had to go?" Ethan's voice was filled with palpable terror.

"Well, like I said, I saw an opportunity. I told him you'd walked in on us and that it was obvious you thought he was raping me—God the look on his face. Then I told him the truth, that everything you'd accused me of earlier in the night was also true." Suddenly her expression altered, her tone becoming menacingly hostile. "The bloody idiot was more distressed about calling you a liar than he was to realize our relationship was a sham. Instead of trying to win me over, he was straight on the phone to you, bleating his apologies and begging you to answer. Then I realized that the second you knew what had really happened, there would be no chance of you and me getting together. So I told him I was going to the police to report the rape, and that as you'd walked in on it and witnessed it all, you'd be bound to back me. He begged and pleaded with me not to; you should have seen him, it was pathetic. Whining about how it would kill his mother and ruin his father—like I cared.

"So I gave him an ultimatum. Said I'd keep quiet about him raping me if he promised to drop off the face of the Earth." She began to laugh suddenly, an evil cackle. "I was actually joking when I said he'd be better off topping himself. I didn't think the sad little moron would actually go and do it. I mean, how weak?"

Ethan turned gray, his expression shrouded in the shadows of utter consternation.

Rebecca seemed to see it suddenly and in response, took a fearful step back. "I don't see what all the fuss is about. It solved the problem, didn't it? We wouldn't be together now if he hadn't…"

Ethan flew across the room with the speed of a crazed animal before I'd even realized he'd moved, his hands wrapping around Rebecca's throat as she choked on the remainder of her words. Jackson was behind him in seconds, pulling him away with all the strength he could muster. They tumbled into a heap on the floor, Ethan having no choice but to release his grip as Rebecca scrambled to get away from him. As he fought to get to his feet again, Jackson clamped his powerful arms around him, Ethan seething and straining against him.

Swiftly, I moved across the room toward him, taking his face in my hands, desperate for him to regain focus. In a way, I felt responsible for his pain, or certainly responsible for the way he'd been exposed to it. "Look at me, Ethan." My lips were so close to his when I whispered my plea that I could feel the breath heaving out of him. "*Look* at me."

For seconds, I was afraid he couldn't hear me through the anger and hatred oozing from his pores, but gradually, he tore his blazing glare away from Rebecca and focused uncertainly on my face.

"*Don't* do this, E. Don't give her something else to hold against you. *She* doesn't matter." His breath faltered as he struggled to gain control. I kissed him gently on the lips, desperate to center him, but at a loss as to how. "You... and... me. That's all that matters. Yes?" His breathing began to calm, his thumping pulse decelerating, until he finally nodded in acknowledgment. "Do you trust me?"

"Yes," he whispered.

I nodded over his shoulder for Jackson to release him, and with my hands still cupping his face, leaned my forehead up against his, our gazes locking in solidarity. "Then let's cut this noxious, rotting cancer out once and for all."

A calm, steely silence descended on the room, Jackson regaining his stance, Ethan his composure.

Rebecca cleared her throat and began to smooth down her crumpled dress. "Well. I think you need some time to calm down after that little tantrum, Ethan, dear. Jackson, bring the car around. I'd like to go back to my hotel for a while."

We all stared at her in united disbelief, unsure as to whether Rebecca Staunton would ever realize that this game was well and truly over.

"Jackson doesn't take orders from you, Rebecca," I said calmly.

In an instant, her smug smile reappeared to crimp the edge of her lip, her eyes flickering toward Jackson before returning to fix me in an arrogant glare. "I think you'll find if I tell Jackson to *jump*, the only question he'll ask is, 'how high?'"

"Really?" My narrowed gaze never strayed from hers as I addressed Jackson. "Do you feel like jumping, Jackson?"

"No, ma'am." Jackson's response was instant as he shifted his position to stand firmly by my side.

"I didn't think so."

Rebecca's face fell, anger returning to color her cheeks. "Betray me at your own risk, Jackson."

Jackson ignored her warning, a hint of a smile ghosting his lips.

"Fine!" A shadow of unease shrouded her pointed features. "Well, we'll see about that. I think we're all rather tired. It's been quite a taxing afternoon. Perhaps it's best we all get some rest, give ourselves some time to remember where our loyalties lie. In the meantime..." she looked at me "...if you'd kindly give me back the things you've stolen from my safe."

"Was there something in particular you're eager to have returned, Rebecca?"

As if dismayed by the question, she rolled her eyes. "Well, yah. I'd like *everything* returned to me, as it's *my* property."

"What, even the credit cards in Ethan's name?"

"Oh, I see, if this is about money, you can keep it. Just hand over my passport and my jewelry pouch and I'll get out of here. This is all becoming rather tiresome now."

"Of course." I reached into my purse to retrieve both items, tossing them to her. Her scrawny arms reached out like limp noodles to catch them. "Because you'll need your passport..." I stole an exaggerated look at my watch "...very soon. In fact, we need to hurry this along; I do believe your flight for London leaves at ten."

"I'm not going anywhere, you stupid bitch," she spat, turning her attention to the jewelry pouch. She yanked on the ribbon, unraveling it, her eyes frantically scouring the contents.

"Is this what you're looking for?" I held the silver box-chain aloft, the keys dangling in the air, swinging back and forth.

Her eyes were manic, bulging from their sockets as they zoomed in wildly. "Give that to me!"

"Sure. Catch." I flung the keys across the room and watched as they hit the floor, skimming the polished ebony surface, before sliding to a halt underneath the table.

Clumsily, she dropped to her knees, scrambling on all fours to reach them. Both Ethan and Jackson remained frozen to the spot, surveying the scene playing out in front of them, confusion prominent in both their expressions. I decided to enlighten them.

"Rebecca is worried because the key she is searching for is the key to her safe-deposit box at the bank." The blood drained from Rebecca's face as her fingers closed over the metal, clutching the key possessively to her chest as she stood. Then I delivered the blow I'd been waiting for. "But she needn't bother, because the safe in her suite wasn't the only one I emptied today."

Rebecca began to laugh with a forced confidence. "Now you're just being silly. There is no way you could have gained entry to that box. You need my signature, my photo ID."

Ethan's gaze flitted to the wig I'd abandoned when I arrived. As realization of what I'd done dawned, he fixed me with a stare which seemed to hover undecided between awe and fury. I couldn't tell which.

Determined to stay focused, I looked away. "You seem to have a habit of underestimating me, Rebecca."

Something in her demeanor suddenly shifted, the mask of pure evil momentarily slipping to expose the slightest fraction of vulnerability. She knew I was telling the truth. She blinked and the mask slid back in place. "I take it you have the disk?" she asked flatly.

Jackson patted his chest, a sure indication that it was safely inside his jacket pocket.

"She's referring to the CCTV footage from *The Wilde Manhattan,*" I explained to Ethan, who shoved a hand into his hair looking utterly confounded. "Her insurance policy for if you ever found out the truth about Alistair. She's been blackmailing Jackson with it, but of course, her intention was to use it against you."

Innocence slithered onto her features like a shockingly poor disguise, the result only making her look tragically foolish. "I would never have used it against you, Ethan. Look, she's just trying to turn you against me. Let Jackson have his disk. It was just a silly joke, anyway. Let's just forget everything that's happened today. You and me, we're strong. You said yourself, yesterday, how much you want—"

"You're sick," Ethan hissed at her. "You actually believe the shit that rolls off your tongue, don't you? You actually believe that we could be together. I *hate* you, Rebecca. You are poison."

"You're just upset. You don't mean what you're saying."

"Listen to me, you crazy bitch. The only reason you're here is because you forced your way into my life with your lies and your obsession and your blackmail."

"I can change. I will do anything for you, Ethan. Can't you see that all this is because I'm terrified of losing you?"

"I've never been yours to lose! And there is *nothing* you could do to change that, nothing that could make me want you."

"No. No. You don't mean that, you can't. You will *grow* to love me, Ethan, you'll see."

"I'm in *love* with Angel."

"NO!" She placed her hands over her ears, shaking her head furiously. "No-no-no-no-no-no."

"I've been in love with her since the second I laid eyes on her."

"Why?" she screamed suddenly. "What the fuck has Miss America got that I haven't?"

"A heart, Rebecca! A soul! You're just a shriveled up mass of skin and bone with nothing inside but malice. She. Is. My. Life."

"You're a fool. A fucking fool. And you're wrong to love her—Christ, her own father doesn't even love her!"

The insult was the final twist of the knife to Ethan's chest, a pain he could no longer endure as the blade sank deep into his heart. Again, he went for her, screaming and cursing unfathomable words that were steeped and embroiled in anger, and once again Jackson intercepted him.

I needed to finish this.

Adrenaline pumped through my body like the devil's fuel. Never in my life had I truly wanted to physically hurt someone the way I did just then. And Jackson had only one pair of hands. "I think you'd better go, because one more word out of your filthy mouth and Jackson will let him loose, do you understand?" My voice shook with anger,

"I'll leave as soon as you give me my belongings. I want everything from the safe in my suite *and* from the safe-deposit box."

My gaze flicked to Ethan, his body shaking with pumped-up fury, his countenance engulfed in the turbulent storm of his emotions. Jackson was up close to him whispering frantically, and although I couldn't hear, I knew they would be words of reason, words to tame the battle taking place inside him.

Grabbing my purse, I tipped the contents onto the table. As well as the stuff I'd taken from the safe at the hotel, there was a large brown envelope and a selection of disks I'd found in the box at the bank. With no clue as to what was on them, I could only hazard a guess. Each had, what I supposed, were surnames scrawled over the surface, and if the contents of the envelope were anything to go by, I'd say my guess was likely to be right. And with that in mind, I was certain my curiosity would never stretch further than conjecture.

As I picked up the envelope, Rebecca's eyes turn to ice. "What the fuck are you doing?"

"Well, I'm contemplating what to give you back before I send you on your merry way. Let's see, now." I feigned perusal of the items on the table, finally tugging a single one hundred dollar bill from the stack. "Yep, I think that should do it." I tossed it at her feet. "You have your passport. All you need now is your plane ticket."

She moved with surprising speed, thrusting her hand out to make a grab for the envelope. "Give them to me!"

"What these?" I took a step back out of reach. "No, no, no. You have everything you need there to get the hell out of the States and never come back. These..." I opened the envelope and pulled out a wad of photographs, fanning them out on the table.

Her pale, insipid complexion turned even whiter, her eyes glazing as all remaining fight dwindled away. Ethan shifted, moving closer to gape at the sickening images laid out on the table, his eyes blinking rapidly as if he thought his sight must be playing tricks on him.

In the photographs Rebecca was trussed, bound, and gagged in every way imaginable. There were multiple men, all masked and engaging in brutal forms of bondage and sexual torture, using various kinds of equipment and instruments akin to those I'd seen in the trunk at the hotel.

Jackson glanced at them briefly, his expression impassive. They were probably nothing he hadn't already seen before. As for me, I'd sieved through them once at the bank, and that had been more than enough.

"... These," I continued, "are *my* insurance policy. And here's the deal you sick sack of shit: If you ever make contact with Ethan or dare to come near any one of us again—these little beauties go viral. In fact, if I so much as hear you've mentioned his name, they will not only be all over the internet, but I will have them packaged neatly into a nice little family album and have them hand delivered to your parents." Stooping, I picked up the hundred dollar bill and her passport, thrusting them into her chest. "Now you get on that plane and thank your lucky stars I was in a good mood today."

She snatched the items from my hand, her pale, withered face crumpling into a snarl. "This isn't over." She pivoted and began to walk away.

"Rebecca!" I shouted after her, shifting to make up the few steps between us. As she turned, I raised my hand and with one full force blow, slapped her hard across the face. "It is now."

CHAPTER SEVENTEEN

I gazed unblinking at the Manhattan skyline, the lights of the city on the black backdrop of the night, fuzzy and ill-defined. My thoughts were in tatters, the result of sheer mental exhaustion combined with the warm vibrations of a bourbon-buzz. The only sound in Ethan's apartment was the clinking of ice against glass as I swirled the amber fluid around and around. The third contributory factor to my inability to think clearly was that I was alone. Jackson had of course escorted Rebecca to the airport, and Ethan had insisted he go too. Unless he witnessed her physically board the plane, he would never rest, he said. In a way, I was glad he'd gone. He'd have time to process what he'd learned tonight, to work out how he felt. Sometimes you needed that, just to think without having to talk.

This evening's revelations had had a tumultuous effect on Ethan's emotions. I'd seen it in his eyes as he'd leaned in to kiss me chastely on the forehead before leaving. Like looking through a window, I'd seen how he was battling with a whole host of feelings, chasing them around his mind, trying to figure out how to feel. I'd found myself wondering how long it would take him to get around to being angry with me. I'd lied to him several times, albeit for good reason, so he *would* get around to it. I'd seen that, too.

The second they'd left, I raced to the bathroom and painfully expelled the contents of my stomach, heaving until I thought I might actually part with my stomach itself. After undressing, I'd placed every

266

item of clothing—the wig, the dress, my shoes, even my underwear—in a bag for the garbage, needing to dispose of every part of her and the day and all it symbolized.

Certain I could smell her on my skin, I'd taken a shower, cleansing my body and hair with Ethan's shampoo and bodywash, inhaling the scent deep into my lungs to purify my senses too. Just as I'd started to feel vaguely human again, something had suddenly struck me. All my things were still in their place—my toiletries and makeup in the bathroom drawer, my hairdryer, clothes and shoes in the closet, just as I'd left them the last time I was here. It was as if I'd never left, as if he'd just continued to live among everything that reminded him of me.

The realization that Ethan had refused to give up on us, even when at times it must have seemed hopeless, when I'd turned him away, refusing to see him or speak to him, made my heart swell with a surge of superabundant love. As I wandered around the place, I saw traces of me everywhere. A book I'd been reading on the table at my side of the bed, my favorite scented candles on the shelf by the bathtub, some hair pins, a bracelet, each and every single item slowly eradicating all my earlier fears. There wasn't even the tiniest vestige of Rebecca.

There were no ghosts here.

Even though I had a fine selection of clothes and lounge wear in my closet, I found myself turning to Ethan's side, and after rummaging through his drawers, finally selected one of his T-shirts, pulling it over my head. Now, contented with the knowledge that I'd smothered myself in as much of him as I possibly could without the physical presence of his body, I waited. Barefoot and wearing nothing but his T-shirt, exhausted but too edgy to even sit, I stared out of the glass wall at the night, sipping bourbon—and waited.

Finally, I heard the sound of the elevator door gliding open and then footsteps. My heart thumped frantically, and I realized I was as nervous at that moment as I'd been all day, even as I'd waited in the bank, convinced I'd be exposed as a fraudster. I was nervous about how he was going to react to what he'd discovered, how it would affect him, affect us. For a brief second, I even wondered whether I should have left, gone home to give him space to deal with his feelings.

As I heard the foyer door opening, I swallowed the remainder of my drink, the whiskey heating me from the inside with its intense, fiery burn as it slid down my throat into my stomach. The sensation dissolved in seconds, paling into insignificance as my body became suddenly ablaze with awareness, electrically receptive to Ethan's penetrating gaze.

As I turned to meet his impossibly blue eyes, they slid over me in appraisal, absorbing every detail of the scene before him: my damp hair kinking into waves as it dried, his T-shirt, the empty tumbler. He didn't look worn-out or at odds with himself as I'd anticipated. I'd considered that he might even be distant, reticent, immersed in his own thoughts. I'd even prepared myself for it, promising myself I wouldn't misinterpret it as rejection.

But I didn't see any of that.

His expression was blank, completely inscrutable at first, but his eyes were growing darker, smoldering with a riotous emotion I couldn't name. Whatever it was, he seemed compelled by it, vehemently moved by its rawness and its intensity. My eyes skimmed over him—his face, his body, his posture—trying to read him, to make sense of this... this passion that was burning from him. Was he impassioned with anger or hurt and sadness, or was it desire?

The lingering question sparked an unexpected, involuntary reaction from my own half naked body. My pulse surged, causing a rush of blood to my most intimate areas. A light sheen of sweat sprang to the surface of my skin, and the muscles of my sex contracted, making me instantly damp.

Ethan stalked toward me across the room, not with speed, but with purpose, and I felt my eyes grow large as I backed against the sheet of glass behind me. He halted just inches away from me, his breath hot on my cheek, the muscles of his face flickering beneath his skin, his nostrils flaring.

Oh God! There it was. The emotion I couldn't distinguish before was anger.

Suddenly, his lips parted, moving with a gentle tremor as if he were trying to utter the words in his head, but his mouth refused to form them.

"Fuck…!" he finally stammered, the word fading out as he crushed his lips onto mine, kissing me with an almost brutal force.

My body responded automatically, totally turned on and tuned into his. I reached up with my free hand and thrust it into his hair, pulling him in deeper as I panted against his fervent lips. He stopped, wrenching his mouth from mine, and yanking the tumbler from my hand, flung it onto the sofa. Then taking my wrists in an unyielding grip, he pinned my arms above my head.

"Don't you ever, *ever* do anything like that again!" he hissed. "Do you hear me?"

I shook my head stubbornly, my own fury blending with my arousal in an exploding impetus.

"Angel!" he roared, pressing his heaving, trembling body against me. "I fucking mean it. Don't you *dare* put yourself at risk like that! If you ever defy me in this again, God help me, I'll…"

"You'll what? You'll what, Ethan? Because if I had to do all of this again, I would. Despite the risks, the danger, the warnings. I would do *anything*. I'd throw myself under a train for us—for you. So, *you*…" I pushed ineffectively against his restraining grip "…don't *you* ever ask me not to!"

"Damn you, woman!" Releasing my arms, he pushed away from me and shrugged out of his jacket, throwing it to the floor angrily.

"I'm sorry you're upset, E—"

"No!" He cut me dead, plunging his hands into his hair with sheer and utter fury and frustration. Turning to me again, his lips parted to speak, to yell, to scold, but instead he just froze.

His dark, burning gaze shimmied down to the hem of my T-shirt. The position of my arms when he'd pinned them above my head had hoisted it up, leaving the tops of my thighs exposed and the edge of the fabric just skimming, but barely concealing the soft, pulsing flesh of my sex. The angry, salacious look in his eyes seemed to scorch my skin, leaving me damp and prickling with arousal.

"Take it off," he instructed, his voice deep and husky, still swamped with emotion.

The sudden swerve from the subject, which only a second ago seemed to embody so much magnitude, had me questioning if I'd heard him correctly. When I didn't respond instantly, he cocked a brow, his expression challenging me to refuse.

"Off," he repeated. "I want to look at you."

The look on his face and tone of his voice did not compel me to argue though. Instead, it just excited me more, eliciting a deep-down, throbbing urge to have him inside me, impossible to ignore. Defy him I might—but deny him? *Never.*

Reaching down to the hem of the T-shirt, I dragged it over my head, observing his eyes as they skimmed greedily over my body. He closed them, screwing them tight as if trying to fight the desire sweeping through him as it was me.

Then suddenly surrendering, he opened them. "Fuck!" he gasped again as he advanced toward me, his fingers already working the clasp and fly of his pants.

He pushed me against the window, the intense sensation of the ice-cold glass against my fiery skin stealing the breath from my lungs. I gasped, the effect only spurring the buzz of desire already rippling through every nerve ending of my sensory cortex. He pressed his mouth to mine, prying my lips apart with his tongue and thrusting it into my mouth.

"Fuck," he mumbled again, but this time the word was stifled by the crushing force of our kiss.

In a second, he'd gripped the back of my thigh, sliding his fingers to the crook of my knee and folding my leg around him for leverage. The throbbing heat of his cock pulsed against me as he released it from the confines of his pants, the solid hunk of flesh splaying the folds of my drenched pussy as it shoved inside me.

The breath hissed from my body, the sheer size of him an unexpected wonder as my muscles clenched in delicious delight around him. He moved with vigorous energy, each thrust delivered with no-nonsense zest, one hand buried into my hair, the other gripping my ass cheeks, fingers digging into flesh with a painful but decadent bite. Tugging on my hair, he began a trail of hot, possessive kisses along my jaw and down my neck, nibbling and suckling greedily at my skin.

"Why?" The word rasped from his throat gutturally, almost as if it had been aching inside him. "Why do you test me, Angel?"

Breathless from desire and the power of his lunge, I could barely form words. "Ethan, I…"

"I'm so fucking angry with you."

"I know…"

"And I wanted to be angry," he went on, driving his rock hard cock inside me, his breath hot against my neck and ear as he spoke. "I wanted to yell, to shout, and then I saw you and I wanted you, the sight of you making my dick so fucking hard, and then I was *furiously* angry, livid that a mere glimpse of you could banish such torrid emotions because I love you so *fucking* much." The depth and magnitude of his feelings appeared to energize him as he fucked me harder and faster, the words spilling from his mouth in one breath.

My muscles began to tense and tighten, the heat of my blood soaring to combustible heights as I neared my climax. Ethan sensed it; he knew my body well, the way my muscles clenched, the way my breathing faltered. He slowed deliberately, surveying my changing expression, my eyes demanding him deeper, faster, as I craved my release.

"No." He shook his head, his pace much slower now, depriving me of the urgency I needed to take me to the finish line. "I won't allow you to come unless you can explain why you have such a deep-seated contempt for your own safety. Why you resist all attempts I make to protect you. Convince me, make me understand, and I'll let you come," he ordered, his rhythm beginning to build again, his pace increasing, his hand reaching between us to rub my swollen clit.

I began to move my hips in time with his thrusts, relishing the overwhelming fullness as once again I raced toward climax.

"Convince me," he urged, increasing the pressure on that hot nub of flesh.

"I only did what you would have done," I gasped desperate to reach orgasm.

He froze abruptly, pulling out of me leaving me bereft and wanting. "No! Please, Ethan."

Taking hold of his swollen, pulsing cock, he began to stroke the shaft slowly up and down, his hand folded tightly around his length as he rocked back and forth into his fist. "Will I come alone, Angel?"

The act was unbearably erotic, driving my need for him, my need to come to a treacherous limit. But it was destitute of mercy. Reaching down, I pressed my fingers against my clit, the aching throb of yearning almost unbearable. Unable to quell my craving, I started to move my finger in a circular motion, my gaze fixed on Ethan's defiantly.

My actions appeared to excite him, his expression dark and wildly aroused. "No!" Suddenly, he reached out, yanking my hand away and entering me again in one swift plunge. "Me and *only* me."

"Then fuck me, Ethan." I grasped him to me, pulling myself up by his shoulders to wrap my legs around him. With renewed impetus, I writhed against him, shamelessly riding his cock.

Gripping my ass, he rammed into me with vigor, impaling me in position against the glass, and then he stilled. I tried to move my hips, to continue the momentum, but his arms were solid and strong, restraining me, his hips spreading my legs wide and pinning me firmly against the window.

No!

"Convince me," he hissed.

"Because I own you, Ethan. I will *not* share you, not any part of you. Not even as a part of someone's deranged fantasy. I meant every word when I said I'd do it all again. I will destroy anything or anybody that threatens to come between us. I would kill for you."

His eyes were on fire, his mind appearing to work furiously over what I'd said. Again, he began to move inside me with steadily-paced, deliberate thrusts. I nodded frantically, urging him on, arching into him and grinding my hips, my hands fisting into his hair.

"Yes! Yes, Ethan. You and only you." I came apart, exploding deliriously, bucking against him, frenzied and wild. The pleasure was so intense it bordered on painful.

Ethan followed, crying out my name like a prayer, his muscles tightening as he emptied himself inside me.

Blissfully exhausted, I collapsed against him, my body boneless and utterly spent. He carried me carefully to the sofa, sitting so I was still cradled in his arms, my legs around him, his cock softening but still encapsulated within me. We lay like that for long minutes, Ethan stroking my hair, our bodies sated and relaxed, stupefied with the drunkenness of our lovemaking.

"Has she gone?" I whispered against the warmth of his neck.

Squeezing me to his chest, I felt his lips brush lightly against the top of my head, his lungs finally releasing that long awaited alleviating breath. "She's gone."

We lay on our sides in bed facing each other, our legs interlaced, our eyes drooping with fatigue. We'd talked into the early hours, Ethan explaining how the journey to the airport had been traveled in silence, him riding upfront with Jackson, Rebecca alone in the back with the privacy screen firmly in place. They hadn't even made a detour to the hotel to enable her to collect her belongings, satisfactorily swayed by my reckoning that she had all she needed to get the hell out of the country.

Ethan had made use of his own ticket, by insisting on checking in so he could keep a watchful eye on her all the way to boarding time. He told me how he'd watched her ascend the steps, the door close firmly behind her, and the plane take off into the air until it was nothing but a flashing light in the distance before he'd finally felt it was safe to leave the airport. In all that time, not a single glance or a single word was exchanged between them.

As I'd anticipated, Jackson had given Ethan a detailed account of the recent events leading up to this evening on the journey back to Manhattan. Jackson had explained how I'd confronted him after spotting him leaving Rebecca's suite, and of course, the conversation which had ensued in the coffee shop when he'd revealed the details of how and why she'd been blackmailing him.

Although I wished I'd had the opportunity to explain everything to Ethan before tonight's showdown, the details of *how* she'd blackmailed Jackson was one piece of the puzzle I was grateful he'd explained himself. For one, it wasn't my place to tell Ethan about his "arrangement" with Rebecca, and two, it was only fair and appropriate that Jackson had the chance to explain himself. With it, of course, Ethan had also gained a thorough insight into Rebecca's penchant for deviant sex—the clubs and so forth. Not that the photographs hadn't been insight enough.

Jackson also confessed to helping me gain access to Rebecca's suite on two occasions, including the details of how they'd unexpectedly returned halfway through the first heist—thanks, Jackson. There'd only been so much Jackson was able to tell him about what happened after that, which had left Ethan eager for me to fill in the blanks.

So I told him everything. About hiding in the closet and using my cell to record Rebecca entering the safe and figuring out the combination. And then—after assuring him that Jia had no clue as to why, but had been happy to help anyway—how masquerading as Rebecca, we'd somehow managed to pull off the stunt at the bank.

Finally, I told him how I'd realized the incident he'd witnessed in Alistair's apartment could not have been rape. And that the real threat to Ethan, the real source of injurious material she'd tucked safely away up her sleeve, was the disk with the CCTV footage from the club. Rebecca's insurance policy, her backup plan in case all else failed.

Now, he was gazing at me, the anger depleted and replaced with sheer exhaustion. Beneath it though, I could still make out an abundance of confused emotion.

"Are you okay?" I ran my fingers through the light smattering of hair on his taut chest.

He hesitated a second and then nodded. "Feeling foolish, but I'm okay."

I frowned questioningly. "Why foolish?"

"I've spent a large part of my life believing her lies about what happened that night. I should have trusted my instincts, trusted Alistair—the man I'd known almost my entire life," he narrowed his eyes in deep contemplation, an agonizing awareness of the truth developing.

"In my head, I keep going back to those messages he left that night, trying to remember his exact words. He kept saying he was sorry, and that he'd done something stupid. I thought he was confessing to the rape, but if I'd really thought about it, analyzed his words, I would have realized that there was no way Ali would have used the word *stupid* to describe something like that. Heinous maybe, unforgiveable for sure, but *stupid*? Now I know he was referring to the sick games he'd got involved in with *her*—this fucking role-play crap. It was that which was fucking stupid, because she was crying rape and he was scared shitless. He was calling because he needed my help. Only, I didn't answer the damned phone.

"I remember the last call came in at around 3:00 a.m. I keep picturing him sitting on that fucking bridge, phone in hand, begging me for forgiveness and thinking I didn't want to know. It was freezing that night. He'd have lasted mere minutes in the unforgiving waters of the Thames. When I'd listened to those messages, I'd assumed he was showing remorse for a sick and vicious crime. But he was asking me to forgive him for letting me down, for not believing me when I tried to warn him—for killing himself. But it was I who'd made the mother of all fuck ups, me who let *him* down. If I'd just had the chance to speak to him. If I'd just picked up the fucking phone things would have been so different..." his words trailed off, fading with the weight of regret.

"You can't think like that, E. That night could have turned out a million different ways. She's a deviously smart and cunning individual. She has a deranged personality, a mind far too calculating to even begin to try and understand. She was obsessed with you, wanted you at any cost, by any means. Alistair was a pawn in her very cruel game to get to you. But even without him, she'd have found a way." I paused before continuing, hoping that what I was about to say wouldn't come across as cold and unsympathetic. "She had him fooled too, remember that. Alistair made some reckless decisions that night based on what *he* believed was the truth. He *allowed* her to manipulate him. Yes, she influenced the final choice he ever made when he climbed up on that bridge—but ultimately, *he* made it, Ethan."

He waited a beat then nodded. "I know."

"You have to let this go. Move on. Otherwise, she still wins. And I can't let that happen. I will *not* let her ruin another single minute of your life—of our lives. She doesn't get to rule our future. She might well be deviously clever, but she's not clever enough for that."

"No she's not. And she isn't nearly as clever as you are." The corner of his mouth twitched into a half smile. "You and your clever, fuckable mouth."

Feigning innocence, I gazed up through my lashes and pouted, the look dissipating quickly when I recalled how angry he'd been with me only hours before. "Do you forgive me, E?"

His hand reached up to stroke my cheek. "I can understand why you did what you did—but it was so unbelievably risky. You could have ended up in prison, or worse, if she'd got a sniff of what you were up to."

"But I didn't."

He nodded, allowing me that. "I'm sorry if it seems like I'm ungrateful for what you did. That's not it at all. There will never be enough words of gratitude to express how much it means to me; I need you to know that. I'm so proud of you, so in awe of your fearlessness and your guile. It's just that… well, I guess I'm just consumed with the what ifs and the alternative endings. Of what could have happened to you because of me. I treated you harshly before, but I needed to hear that the choices you made didn't arise from a lack of regard for your own well being. What you said… well, now I know they stemmed from a strength you've gained from loving me, and from me loving you. So yes—I forgive you. I just wish you'd talked to me before taking all this on alone. If you'd told me what you had planned—"

"If I'd told you what I had planned, you'd have bound me in chains and locked me in the attic."

"I haven't got an attic." I cocked a brow at his dryness. "Yes, you're probably right."

"No probably about it. Plus there just wasn't time. There was no way to get our hands on that disk legally. It was my only option."

A flash of contrition furrowed his brow. "Angel, about the disk and what happened that night—"

"Ethan, no. I know what happened that night, and I trust that you and Jackson made the only judgment call you could. I could have lost you that night and I never would have had the chance to know you. You did what you needed to do to protect yourself, and for that I thank God."

"How come you're so forgiving and understanding? So goddamn strong." Gently, he brushed my hair away from my eyes, his gaze examining every inch of my face. "I'm afraid I'm guilty of unduly misjudging you, underestimating you, even. The vital essence of your soul has been tested to the limit, crushed and degraded time and again. When we met, your spirit had the fragile wings of a butterfly, exquisitely dainty and beautifully formed, but delicate and so easily damaged. But now you have the wings of a graceful swan. You have strength of mind and strength of will; you're brave and amazingly clever. You're insurmountable, Angel. And I'm incredibly proud of you."

My cheeks began to flush, my lips crinkling into a reflexively shy smile. Nobody had ever said they were proud of me before. Ethan smiled back, a lopsided grin which created a perfectly formed dimple in his perfectly formed face.

"Who'd have thought you could be such a feisty, sassy little creature."

"Feisty? Me?"

"Yes, woman, feisty. And sexy as hell with it." He paused as if contemplating whether to tell me something. "I have a confession to make."

"A confession?" I hitched a brow, suddenly fascinated.

"Yes. I hadn't planned on telling you, but I just can't keep it to myself."

"What is it?"

"I watched you strutting around here tonight like some sort of gutsy lioness staking her claim to her mate. It's honestly the first time I've ever seen Rebecca thwarted. You were so in control, so sure of yourself. And despite everything that was warring in my head, despite being angry that you'd put yourself at risk, I was wildly turned on. My dick was on fire. It was so fucking hard it didn't even relent on the journey to the airport and back. It was crazy. That's why my emotions were so at odds when I returned. My brain was telling me to be angry, but my body was saying something entirely different, and I was stuck in some place between wanting to fuck you and wanting to thrash you."

It wasn't just my face that flushed now; the warm glow spread, rushing around my body and pooling at the apex of my thighs. I squeezed them together, wriggling a little, but I knew my actions had given me away when Ethan's eyes darkened knowingly.

"God, you want to fuck again, don't you?"

To answer his question, I shifted so I was sat astride him, my knees on either side of his hips. "I have a confession of my own."

"Oh?" He raised his eyebrows inquiringly.

"I knew you were stuck in that place. I could see it in your eyes. Although I knew you were angry with me, knowing you were hard for me, knowing you wanted to be inside me excited me beyond words. I wanted to inflame your fury. Incite you to fuck me hard against that cold sheet of glass until your anger faded, and we both reached that state of ecstasy that can only be reached together." My gaze shifted, gliding down over his lean body until it came to rest on his thick, veined cock lying rigid and pulsing against his lower stomach. "And now *you* want to fuck too."

In one swift move, I was underneath him, his hips locking me in place against the mattress, his hands slithering up my arms to entwine with mine on the pillow above my head.

"You're a dirty, dirty girl, Angelica Lawson."

CHAPTER EIGHTEEN

"**O**pen," Ethan instructed as he raised the fork to my mouth and gently placed the final sliver of smoked salmon and creamy scrambled eggs on to my tongue.

Chewing happily, I pulled the throw snugly around my shoulders to keep out the chill. The morning was crisp despite the warm glow from the fire pit. I couldn't remember the last time we'd cuddled up for breakfast in the comfort of the throws and beanbags on the terrace of my apartment. In fact, I couldn't remember the last time we'd spent the night at my apartment.

For weeks now we'd lived at Ethan's, calling in just briefly to mine for the mail and such. It was hard to believe that I'd worried about his apartment having too many reminders of Rebecca, and that somehow the remnants of her evil would remain embedded in the ambience of the place. Actually, the weeks we'd spent entwined in each other, post Rebecca, had proved the opposite was true. It felt like home, oddly even more so than my own. In fact, the only thing I missed was exactly this—the snug, intimate space of the terrace, the comforting warmth of the fire pit, the cozy faux fur throws. Ethan's terrace was much larger and nowhere near as intimate.

I reached out for my champagne cocktail.

"Uh, uh." Ethan swatted my hand away and taking the glass, tipped the crisp, sparkling drink to my lips. "I told you, you're not lifting a finger today, birthday girl."

Smiling, I took a sip. I couldn't ever remember being this happy on my birthday.

"Do you miss it?" he said suddenly. "Your apartment, I mean."

There were times I was eerily convinced he could actually read my mind. "No. A tiny bit, perhaps. Well, just out here really," I replied honestly.

"Yes, that's what I thought." His lips quirked into a crooked, impish smile.

"Remind me again why we stayed here last night?"

"Always so eager, Miss Lawson. You'll have to wait and see."

"I don't like surprises," I muttered petulantly.

"Oh? Have you had many?"

"Not of the pleasant variety, no."

"Then how do you know you don't like them?"

"I'm guessing."

"Well, stop guessing and finish your breakfast, we have a very busy day ahead."

"Doing what, exactly?"

"All will be revealed in due course." He glanced at his watch. "Now stop talking and get naked."

"Naked?"

"Yes. I want to fuck you," he said in a low, gravelly voice with just the right amount of coercion.

"Again?" I gasped. "You're insatiable, Mr. Wilde."

Ethan shifted from his position, burrowing his way in from the bottom of the throw and reappearing at the top so that he was lying on top of me, his face inches from mine. He thrust his hips, the thick bulk of his erection beneath the material of his lounge pants applying the perfect amount of pressure to my already ardent sex.

"Yes, I know." His lips grazed enticingly over mine. "I think it has something to do with you turning twenty-nine. I didn't know I could possibly be any hotter for you, but Christ, the big chap just won't calm down."

"So I see," I teased, tilting my pelvis and pushing up to meet his insistent bulge.

He began to wriggle out of his pants, kicking them away before yanking his sweatshirt up and over his head. "I think we should see how many times we can fuck in the final year of our twenties. And then for every year of our thirties we have to beat the record by the amount of our age."

"Sounds like a fun plan." I lifted my arms as he peeled off my—his—T-shirt, my only item of clothing. "Our individual age, or combined?"

"Christ, woman, are you trying to kill me?"

"What? In the first year it would only be like, what...? Adding one point... something more fucks to the total of each week. Would you prefer we round it up or down?"

"Neither. The 'point somethings' could be lots of fun." He settled between my legs, his mouth sliding over my neck and lapping gently at my earlobe. I tilted my neck to present myself to him more fully.

"Oh? Why, what might the 'point somethings' involve?"

Shifting slowly to my mouth, he began to nibble at my lower lip, pulling it softly through his teeth. "Well, they could involve me fucking this *very* beautiful, *very* sassy mouth."

Suddenly, his hand parted my thighs, his fingers finding the plump, juicy flesh at the summit and sinking into me as he massaged my clit with the pad of his thumb. Groaning, I quivered from his touch, my arousal coating his fingers instantly.

"Or I could do this." Ethan's lip curled into a satisfied smile. He was pleased with my response. "Fuck your luscious pussy with my fingers until you're dripping with your own slick pleasure."

Oh God!

Sliding in a second finger, he increased the pressure, the tempo quickening as he curled them deliciously inside me. I began to move against his hand, urging him deeper into me.

"By the time we hit our mid-thirties," he continued, "the 'point somethings' could even involve this."

Abruptly, he was gone, his head dipping below the throw, his fingers leaving me wanting. But only briefly. Moments later, his warm breath fluttered gently over my very damp sex, the contrasting sensation to the chilled air of the morning making me shudder with exhilarating pleasure. His nose brushed lightly against my clit, and I knew he was inhaling me. It was a wildly intimate gesture, one I knew drove him crazy and the knowledge had me arching into his mouth. Responding desirously, he claimed me, burying his tongue inside me, lapping and licking luxuriously at the creamy juices of my arousal.

My body was alive with ecstasy, a current of pure, delectable pleasure unfurling through my singing veins. Spreading my legs wider, I pumped my hips, writhing brazenly against his greedy mouth. I exploded, coming violently as I gasped and groaned his name, my fingers clawing at the warm leather of the giant bean bag beneath me, helpless in my desire.

As my body bathed in the glow of my orgasm, Ethan reappeared, his face flushed with desire, eyes hooded and hungry. The throw slid away as he pushed to his knees, exposing our naked bodies to the open breeze. Evidence of my arousal shimmered in a fine sheen around his mouth, and his tongue snaked out to lick the remnants from his lips.

"Your pussy tastes as sweet as fucking honey, baby," he growled, kneeling between my legs and taking his huge, pulsating cock in his hand.

The image was like throwing fuel on my mellowing embers, an instant explosion of hot, luring seduction. His posture was bold and strong, a godlike specimen, almost crude and primitive in his natural masculine state. The muscles of his toned chest expanded and contracted rhythmically, in time with his heaving breaths. His hips swayed gently as he presented his impressive, swollen cock like some sort of exhibit or symbol of his superior prowess. Everything about him exuded his state of arousal, his entire body a brazen display of his raw, inherent need for me.

"Fuck me," I begged breathlessly.

"With pleasure." He guided his cock to my aching entrance and sank balls deep inside me.

The breath hissed from my body as it opened up, accepting the physical extent of him, stretching and clenching in a riotous, overwhelming influx of pleasure. Crushing his lips to mine, he claimed me, his tongue gliding into my mouth, licking and devouring. We moved in time, our bodies blending in harmonious ecstasy and our minds lost to a world known only to us.

Jackson was waiting by the Cadillac Escalade when we finally emerged from my building at almost lunch time. His eyes were gleaming with mischief, and I couldn't help notice the conspiratorial nod he exchanged with Ethan as he stifled the smile tugging at the corner of his mouth.

"Morning, Jackson," I gushed merrily.

"Good morning, Miss Lawson. And may I wish you a very happy birthday."

I grinned at the formality of his greeting. Jackson and I had become firm friends since our collaboration in the Rebecca drama. We shared a sense of camaraderie unlike any I'd experienced before. A bit like the kind of kinship one would expect to share with a brother or sister, the kind I'd missed out on with Adam and Aaron. Jackson had no family to speak of, or many friends for that matter, at least not in New York. We were cut from the same cloth in many ways, not least because we both worshipped the ground Ethan walked on. If we'd formed an alliance under different circumstances, one that was separate to his employment with Ethan, I had no doubt that we would become the best of friends. But the code of ethical conduct always remained firmly intact whenever Ethan was present. Jackson, I think, was always acutely aware of overstepping the mark.

Ethan believed in an appropriate line of distinction between employee and employer, in order to sustain a high level of proficiency.

Although, it always came with a deep mutual respect between the two. So, despite the turbulent episodes of drama they'd unavoidably endured together, and their obvious, almost brotherly connection, their relationship remained fundamentally professional. I respected Ethan's principles, and so always tried to adhere to them whenever he was around. Although he'd never acknowledged it, I could sense he was aware of mine and Jackson's rapport. But Ethan understood that I'd never had the privilege of many close relationships, and for that reason, I believe he chose to turn a blind eye.

"Thank you, Jackson," I replied with a similar formality as I climbed into the back of the SUV.

On the seat was a black gift box neatly bound with a silver ribbon. Smiling, I set it on my lap, my eyes narrowed in simulated rebuke as I turned to Ethan sitting next to me. I was about to scold him for spoiling me—he'd presented me with an exquisite Cartier clutch purse in silver-colored goatskin and several boxes of ludicrously expensive, very sexy lingerie already this morning—but his expression implied the package was as much of a surprise to him as it was to me.

"Don't look at me, I know nothing about this one," he said, shrugging.

Frowning, I glanced back down at the package and noticed a tag poking out from under the ribbon. I tugged it free and read.

To Angel, from Jackson.

Oh.

Looking up, I found a pair of eyes staring at me from the rearview mirror. They were crinkled at the edges, a sign that he was smiling, then flickered warily to Ethan, who had the vaguest smile teetering at the edge of his lips. Ethan nodded once to Jackson and turned to me, his smile widening in approval.

"Well, open it, then," he urged, his tone filled with amusement.

I pulled on the ribbon excitedly and lifted the lid. Inside was a scarf the color of a smooth, subtle misty gray and made from the softest, most elegant cashmere. Printed along the edges were Om peace symbols and what I recognized as Hindi Sanskrit writing. It was beautiful.

"I wasn't entirely sure what it is they represent," Jackson said, his brown eyes scanning mine for a reaction in the reflection of the mirror. "The symbols, I mean. But I kind of guessed peace and harmony and... Well, it's what I wish for you, and I thought it was pretty, so... Well, I hope you like it."

My eyes began to glaze as I gazed back at him through the mirror, and I had to blink quickly several times to stop my vision from blurring. The gesture had touched me immensely, not specifically the gift itself—although it was exquisite—but what was intended by it, the significance of what it represented.

Many casual, flippant remarks had been made in conversations with Jackson about my family and my miserable childhood when we'd been stuck in endless traffic or sharing a coffee at his favorite "caff," as he called it. On occasion, I'd even mentioned my mom, which was weird, because apart for Ethan, I'd never really discussed her with anyone. At the time, I didn't think he'd taken much notice, but the warmth in his eyes when he'd told me the intention behind the gift— *It's what I wish for you*—suggested there was far more to this man than the beef and brawn and his thick-skinned, indifferent exterior. A lot of thought had been put into this gift.

I was familiar with the Om symbol and recalled that it had captured my attention, initially, because of its apparent symbolic relation to the four stages of consciousness. Those being: awake, sleeping, dreaming, and—my favorite, of course—the transcendental state. A state I'd spent a large part of my life yearning for—a state where the mind could discover peace and serenity. So the gift held far more meaning than Jackson would even realize.

"Like it?" I beamed a smile at him. "I totally freaking love it. Thank you, Jackson." I cast a glance at Ethan and registering his lenient mood, decided to take full advantage.

Unlocking my seatbelt, I moved through the cab of the SUV and leaning into the driver's compartment, folded my arms around Jackson's shoulders, hugging him tightly. He patted my hand gently and began frantically checking his mirrors, his face flushing with a combination of unexpected pleasure and embarrassment.

Ethan's smile waned marginally, his brow arching as he shook his head with minor disapproval. "Seat belt, Angel."

I did as I was told and buckled up, *my* smile fixed firmly in place. Nothing was going to ruin today.

By the time we reached Ethan's apartment, he seemed edgy, apprehension evident in the way his teeth worried his lower lip, and the way he stretched his neck and rolled his shoulders. Not so much in the tense, stressful fashion that I'd witnessed at other times, but more restless, fidgety, excited perhaps.

"What are you up to?" I asked as the elevator slid to a halt. We stepped out into the foyer, the familiar scent of the place embracing me with a warm, welcoming homecoming sensation. The feeling I used to get when I went home to my apartment.

"Nothing, wait and see," he said, patting his pockets and looking suddenly perturbed. His gaze drifted to Jackson's gift box in my hand. "May I borrow your lovely scarf for a minute?"

I frowned in confusion, but handed him the box anyway. "Be my guest."

Placing the box down on the vintage console table, he removed the scarf and shifted so that he was behind me. "Close your eyes," he instructed.

Flinching nervously, I angled my head to look at him over my shoulder. "Why? What are you going to do?"

"Just do as you're told."

Amused by his tone, I relaxed and held the scarf to my eyes while he tied it loosely at the back of my head. When he was satisfied that I couldn't see a thing, he held my hand and guided me through the doors into the lounge. We walked in what seemed like a straight line toward the vast windows making up the far wall and halted. Slowly, he turned me, my sense of direction telling me I was facing the wall, which apart from an exquisite piece of abstract art, I knew to be bare. What on Earth was he up to?

"Ready?" Ethan asked quietly.

Shifting my weight to one leg, I clasped my hands nervously in front of me, unsure as to what I was readying myself for. "I think so."

The first thing that struck me when Ethan untied the scarf and my vision focused was color—an immense array of vivid color melding into what was usually a black and white oasis.

A huge glass case had been set into the wall, at least eight feet long and four feet tall. My jaw dropped open as I stepped closer, my mind absorbing the wonderful, vibrant vision before me. Swimming happily amongst a beautiful structure of rocks and caves and coral were fish—lots of fish.

"Meet the cast of *Finding Nemo*," Ethan chuckled as he watched my beaming smile threaten to split my face in two. "Well, most of them, anyway."

"Ethan, it's… oh my God, it's perfect," I squealed with childish delight. "*This* is why we couldn't come home last night."

His expression shifted, his exuberant smile fusing with the warm swell of love that now filled his startling blue eyes. Nodding, his gaze flickered back to the tank as a luminous flash of orange-hue sped through one of the swim-throughs.

"Here he is," he said, lightly pressing the pad of his finger to the glass to indicate the striped orange clownfish. "Angel, meet Nemo. He's the smaller of the two clownfish; Marlin, of course, is the larger one." He pointed him out. Suddenly, he lowered his voice, as if he were afraid of being overheard. "He's not actually Nemo's biological father, but there's no need for the little guy to know."

I laughed and then gasped excitedly as I spotted the vivid blue tang fish swimming heedlessly through the corals. "Dory!"

"Yes, dear Dory. Not part of the 'Tank Gang,' I know, but there was no way I was leaving her out."

"She *actually* looks scatterbrained, bless her."

"Speaking of scatterbrained," he said, pointing to a damselfish. In the movie, Deb the damselfish was a confounded creature who adorably mistook her own reflection, believing it to be her sister, Flo, who sadly didn't actually exist. "I decided it was probably best to get a Deb and a Flo, save the poor thing from a life of delusional misconceptions. Only I have no idea how to tell them apart, so I suggest we call them both Deb-Flo."

"Deb-Flo?"

"Well, I thought it sounded better than Flo-Deb."

"Mmm. Yes, I suppose it does—slightly. Peaches!" I said, spotting the pinky-orange sea star stirring the sandy bed at the bottom of the tank.

"Jacques the Cleaner Shrimp is in there somewhere too," Ethan said, "but I'm afraid, Bloat the Puffer has been ostracized, far too aggressive apparently; he'd have eaten Jacques and Peach for supper. And Gil isn't the real thing either. By all accounts, the Moorish... something or other, would find it hard to survive in a tank environment, the most comparable was a butterfly fish."

I shook my head in complete and utter wonder. I felt wildly happy, almost to the point of giddy, and my jaw began to ache with the strain of smiling. Balling my hands into fists, I pressed them into the hinge to massage the muscles.

"You look happy," Ethan said, gazing at me.

Squealing, I placed my hands in front of my face to hide my silly, relentless smile. It was a childish gesture, really, an instinctive reaction to my overexcited giddiness.

Ethan's expression changed, his brow furrowing with vague perplexity.

"What is it?" I asked.

As if trying to decipher something in his mind, he shook his head. "I don't know. I just had a peculiar sense of déjà vu. Just when you hid your smile behind your hands, all cute and shy like that... Like I had a glimpse of a memory of some kind... Never mind, look, there's Gurgle and Tad and Bubbles."

"Bubbles, my bubbles," we shrieked, simultaneously mimicking the yellow tang that had a peculiar obsession for bubbles, thus the name.

"I love them. I love them all." I flung myself at him, folding my legs around his waist. "It's the best gift *ever.*"

"Good," he laughed, cupping my behind to support me. "Though hearing your sexy laugh is actually the best gift ever. I love seeing your face light up like a small child at Christmas."

The *small child at Christmas* reference warmed my insides, making me smile. They were words he'd used once in a text he'd sent me in the early days of our relationship, when he'd been excited about our first real date.

Grabbing his face, I kissed him. "It's all because of you. You spoil me."

"I'm allowed to. You're mine. I can do whatever I want."

The knowledge suddenly thrilled me, and I wriggled against him excitedly. That's when I noticed the photographic art on the walls. The abstract art which usually did an exuberant job of adorning the walls throughout the apartment were gone—bar the odd one here and there—and in their place was an assortment of black and white photographs. All of which were my work.

"What...? When did you...?"

"They look amazing, don't they?" Ethan lowered me back to the floor and took me by the hand to lead me closer. "I love every single one of them. It's like gaining a glimpse of the inner you and the emotional journey you've traveled when I look at them. They make me feel closer to you."

I stared at the photographs on the walls, the images all from different collections, all depicting different moods, different emotions, different stories. "Ethan you don't have to…"

"Don't have to what?"

I paused, meeting his eyes cautiously. "You don't have to champion my work just to please me."

"Is that what you think this is?" He didn't wait for a reply. "Angel, you have no clue how talented you are. I chose these pieces because they are beautiful, and because they are part of you. They allow me to see the things you see, and feel the things you feel."

Most people would just see an image, I was certain. An image that may or may not evoke an emotion. If it did, usually they were memories or a stirring of feelings that were pent up inside their own souls, just waiting to manifest themselves. But Ethan saw much more than that. He saw into *my* mind and *my* soul as clearly as if it were a window.

Ethan smiled broadly as he continued. "*And* because they are absolutely right for this apartment, for my home. They are my personal choice. The only thing in this entire apartment I've had any say in, actually—well apart from the aquarium. When I bought this place, I was still living in London. I worked with an interior designer via email to kit this place out—she sent me her ideas, I approved them. Until you came into my life this was just an apartment, the place I currently lived. But when you're here, it feels like home. I want to put *our* personal stamp on it. I want it to represent us."

Us?

"Yes, of course. Sorry." Suddenly I felt bad for putting a dampener on something he was clearly thrilled about.

"You don't have to be sorry."

I shrugged. "So. Interior designer, eh? Here was me thinking good taste was yet just another thing you had a natural flair for."

"I have impeccable taste, Miss Lawson. Take a look in the mirror."

I smiled shyly.

"Angel?" he said, looking suddenly nervous. "Before, when you saw the aquarium and you realized it was the reason we didn't come back here last night—well, you called it home."

"Did I?"

"Yes." He took a breath. "Does it feel like home?"

Uncertain of what he wanted me to say, but knowing categorically how I felt, I offered him a barely perceptible nod.

"I want you to move in with me—properly—permanently."

"What…?" The suggestion completely threw me off balance. "You mean give up my place?"

"Well, yes," he shrugged. "You could sell it. Or not. Keep it if it makes you feel better, but pack all your belongings, move out and move in here—live here. I want this to be your home. Everything I have is yours anyway, part of your future at some point in time. Why not now?" When I didn't answer immediately, he continued his pitch. "I want to be with you, baby. All the time, with nothing to separate us, especially not bricks and mortar. I asked you if you missed your place this morning and aside from the terrace, you said you didn't. We're here most of the time anyway."

He was right, of course. I had said that. And I'd felt it. My place hadn't felt like home for a long time, not properly, not like it had. It was this place that felt right—like home. I hadn't even questioned why he'd had the aquarium installed here instead of at my place. It hadn't crossed my mind. It had felt right.

My heart thudded excitedly in my chest, like I was about to embark on the thrill of my life. I opened my mouth to speak.

"Wait." He held up his hand to halt me. "Let me show you something before you decide." Grabbing my hand, he tugged me through the lounge to the terrace doors, pushing them open and waving me through.

I glanced at him questioningly and stepped outside.

On to *my* terrace.

CHAPTER NINETEEN

A portion of Ethan's vast terrace had been sectioned off, using an array of beautiful pot plants and decorative garden panels to make a cozy enclosed area. A fabulous fire pit took center stage, surrounded by giant waterproof beanbags on one side and a luxury half-moon garden sofa on the other. Just off to the side was a giant cantilever umbrella, an ideal canopy to either shade from the sun or shield from the rain. In the corner was a large hammock, and in the opposite corner a double sun-bed. There was a narrow pathway flanked by mature shrubs, which led to a more formal, though still snug, eating area. The entire space was lit with warm, intimate lanterns and the result was a sequestered, romantic retreat. Aside from the spectacular view of Central Park and the few welcome additions, such as the lovers' sun-bed, it was an almost perfect mirror image of my terrace.

Ethan observed me closely, waiting patiently for my reaction as I strolled around in stunned amazement. The terrace was the only part of his apartment that I hadn't fallen instantly in love with the moment I first saw it. It had felt too big, too open. It didn't entice you to want to curl up under the stars and make love, as we had many times on the terrace at my place. But now? Now the space had been transformed beyond recognition. And it had all been done in a day.

I gazed across the terrace at the most beautiful, most wonderful, thoughtful man in the entire world. The Cartier purse had been an extravagant luxury, a gift beyond the imaginings of most girls' dreams. The lingerie had been exciting, a gift of intimacy and secrecy and shared sensual pleasures. But this—the terrace, the fish, the photographs—this was meticulously attentive, a carefully considered gift derived from a deep-seated, pure and reverent love.

Ethan had zeroed in on everything that was dear to me. He knew that my apartment had been my only real home, the first time I'd ever felt secure and comfortable in my surroundings. And so he'd recreated the part of it that I treasured the most, the very thing that had made my home my haven. By displaying my work on his walls, the thing that most reflected my state of mind, he'd embraced my ever varying and often delicate psyche. And then the fish. Animation, of course, was my somewhat lowbrow, guilty pleasure, or—as Ethan had once alluded to—maybe a way of holding on to the child in me, because she'd never really been discovered or never really embraced. Seeing some of those beloved characters alive and swimming in my very own aquarium brought me the kind of pleasure only he would know could be possible. He'd cosseted me, brought my wishes to life for me, here in his home—my home.

Without wasting a second more, I flung myself at him again, kissing every inch of his startlingly handsome face. He grabbed me, folding his arms around my waist and spinning me around, his laughter filled with joyous relief.

"I take it that's a yes, then?" he stuttered through suffocating kisses.

"Yes, yes, yes," I cried. "It's perfect. You're perfect. Everything is perfect. Thank you, E."

"Pfft!" He waved his hand modestly. "It was nothing, just a few old bean bags and some potted plants."

"Oh, it's far more than that and you know it. It's the best birthday I've ever had. It's better than all of them put together, in fact. I always hated birthdays; they were always so dull and disappointing. But now…"

He sealed his lips over mine, a slow, devouring kiss that made me melt into his arms. "Every birthday will be perfect from now on," he whispered.

"Excuse me, Mr. Wilde, Miss Lawson." Jackson was suddenly standing in the doorway. "You have guests arriving."

"Guests?" I asked, surprised.

Ethan pulled a face as the sound of heels *click-clacking* over the ebony floor, and Abby's musical voice sang out to the terrace. "Where is the birthday girl?"

"Motherfucker," Damon's smooth tones ensued, his voice now familiar and comforting. "That is one hell of an aquarium, dudes."

Ethan and I exchanged grins. "We're out here, guys." Ethan moved behind me, snaking his arms around my waist, a typical territorial gesture of his, but especially when Damon was around. I placed my hands across his forearms in a mutual display of ownership.

"Happy birthday, Angel." Abby smiled sweetly as she stepped out on to the terrace and then her mouth opened wide with surprise when she saw the transformed space. "OMG, this is super awesome."

"You guys *have* been busy." Damon appeared behind her, glimpsing the scene and hitching a disapproving brow at Ethan's hold around me. "Put her *down*, dude."

Ethan rolled his eyes and reluctantly released me. I hugged them both and we settled onto the sofa around the fire pit.

"We come bearing gifts. You first, Damon," Abby squealed excitedly.

I flushed slightly, not used to the attention my birthday was creating. "Oh, you shouldn't have, guys, really. I wasn't expecting anything."

"Nonsense, you're like family now," she breathed genuinely.

The sentiment thrilled me, and smiling widely, I accepted Damon's proffered gift, pulling on the ribbon and opening the box. Inside was a pair of red leather Moschino gloves, distinctively adorned with a gold bar across the back of the wrists displaying the symbols for peace and love. I plucked them from the box, admiring the wonderful soft leather and cashmere lining, unable to comprehend the magnitude of such generosity. "They're gorgeous, Damon. Thank you."

He grinned, looking quite relieved.

"He chose them himself," Abby added enthusiastically.

"At first, I was thinking jewelry or perfume, but then I remembered I wanted to keep my balls intact." Damon grinned as he taunted Ethan, who responded by curling his lip into a snarl. Damon goaded him some more. "So instead, I spent some time deliberating about items of clothing made from miniscule amounts of leather that Angel would look absolutely sensational in—and came up with these."

Ethan's eyes widened. "Be very careful, Bro, be *very* careful."

"Ignore him, Ethan," Abby said, throwing Damon a cursed scowl. "You're an ass, Damon Wilde."

I laughed, amused by both Damon's incessant teasing of his brother and Ethan never failing to let it wind him up.

"My turn," Abby squealed as she thrust her neatly packaged gift toward me excitedly. "I must admit, I was sorely tempted to keep them myself, so if you don't like, or they don't fit…"

"Let the girl open the goddamn gift, Abby," Damon scolded.

"Yes, sorry. Go ahead, sorry."

The second I lifted the lid, it was as if the world had just slammed its breaks on without warning, and my heart went hurtling into my chest wall with a resounding thud.

A pair of shiny red patent shoes lay in the box on my lap. The shoes of my dreams. For what seemed like minutes, I was speechless, staring flatly at the contents of the box which seemed to burn right through to my skin. For some reason, I was drawn to red patent shoes. They had this absurdly abnormal appeal to me. I'd coveted them in pictures or store windows for as long as I could remember, but I'd never relented to buy. Because while they fascinated me, they also repelled me—haunted me. Troubled the deepest, unchartered parts of my psyche for reasons I couldn't understand. They were the shoes of my dreams.

"They're Louboutins," Abby gushed in some attempt to incite a reaction.

I barely nodded, stuck in a sort of dazed, hypnotic trance. Suddenly, I felt Ethan's hand on the small of my back, the reassuring heat of his touch saturating my body to rouse me from my frozen, stupefied state.

Abby's smile had evaporated, chased away by disappointment, and I felt bad. Really bad. "You don't like them," she whispered.

I shook my head gently. "No." Then from somewhere I summoned the courage to shove down the willful, unpleasant emotions and plastered the largest smile on to my face. "I adore them, they're amazing."

She visibly melted with relief, letting out a whoop of joy. "I know, right. I knew you would love them. I told you she would love them," she said to Damon.

"I didn't need convincing, Sis. And they're an amazing match to the gloves, don't you think? I've been picturing Angel in this entire outfit all week long. Gloves and shoes—perfect."

Ethan glared for a second and then we all burst out laughing.

"I'm just messin', dude," Damon said, looking around at the terrace as if suddenly just seeing it. "Hey, this is really awesome,"

"Like I said, Damon, if you'll just listen." Abby crumpled her nose petulantly.

"It's amazing isn't it? One of my many surprise gifts from Ethan."

"Really?" Damon almost laughed. "And when did you acquire an eye for such things as design, Bro?"

"Actually, that credit goes to Angel herself," Ethan said proudly. "It's a replica of the design she created for the terrace at her own apartment. I wanted to reproduce it here so that I could lure her away." He glanced at me then, his expression a smug glow of pride. "Angel's agreed to move in with me."

"I knew it!" Abby clapped her hands. "Wedding bells soo-oon," she sang.

"*Abby!*" Ethan scolded.

"What? Just saying."

Damon congratulated us both, a genuine face-splitting grin displaying a perfect set of white teeth.

"Mom and Dad will be *so* excited," Abby said, giving Ethan a huge hug.

"Don't you go telling them anything," he warned.

"You can tell them yourself. They're coming home next week."

My cheeks flushed, the onset of nerves instantly beginning to prickle my skin. I was yet to meet Ethan's parents, and though the prospect excited me, I was also nervous beyond belief. Aside from my father and brothers, I'd never sought approval from anyone to the extent that I did from them. I knew how much Ethan's family meant to him and was desperate for them to like me.

"Really? That's great news," Ethan said cheerfully, glancing at me. He reached up to touch my cheek. "Don't look so worried. They'll love you."

"They *will* love you," Abby agreed.

"They will *definitely* love you." Damon winked. "You will be the first girl Ethan has ever introduced to them. They'll be relieved. I'm sure they think he's gay."

Ethan narrowed his eyes in his not-amused look. "You're such an asshole, Bro."

After a light lunch on the terrace, which Mrs. Hall had kindly prepared and left in the refrigerator for us, I excused myself and headed for the bedroom. Ethan and Damon were discussing business, and Abby had insisted on clearing away the dishes.

I stared at the box containing the shoes for minutes before finally lifting the lid and plucking one glorious, shiny red shoe from the folded tissue and holding it in my hand. My skin was suddenly clammy with unease, my heart battering noisily, the way I imagined it might if someone had placed a spider in my palm—with a fear that was real, but lacked any sound logic.

"They're just shoes," I said aloud but to myself.

"Angel?" Ethan called out from the lounge. "Damon and Abby are leaving."

"Coming." I placed the shoe back in the box, slammed on the lid, and shoved it on the bottom shelf of the closet.

We said our goodbyes and Damon and Abby boarded the elevator.

"Oh, I almost forgot," Abby announced, handing me a large brown envelope. "Alisha's mom asked me to give you this. She said to say that they leave for LA next weekend and won't be back until Thanksgiving."

"Okay. Thanks." I guessed from the weight of the envelope that it contained the keys to Claudia's house. Claudia had asked me to produce a carefully chosen selection of photos from the images I'd taken at her wedding and hang them in her home as a surprise to her husband. Her house in the Hamptons was surrounded by a wonderful, mature garden which led down to a deserted beach and a breathtaking view of the Atlantic Ocean. I'd felt instantly and unusually at home there and had expressed my fondness for the place several times. For this reason, she'd suggested I make use of the place whilst she and her family were away. I could peruse the best places for her art and enjoy the peaceful setting of her home at the same time.

Of course, there was no way I would do that now I was with Ethan. I wouldn't leave him for a minute, not by choice at least, but the gesture was no less gracious. "I'll drop Claudia an email later to let her know I've received it."

"Okay. Have a lovely time this evening," she said, waving as the elevator door slid closed.

I turned to look at Ethan who was rolling his eyes and shaking his head. "What's going on this evening?" I asked suspiciously.

He scrunched his brow, ignoring me. "What's in the envelope?"

"I asked first."

Ethan responded with one hitched eyebrow, an expression that I knew meant "don't test me."

"It's keys to her house."

"Why would she give you keys to her house?"

"It's nothing, just work. She wants me to hang some prints while the house is empty. Your turn. What's going on tonight?"

"Abby's got such a big mouth." He rolled his eyes again. "I've arranged to have dinner with Jia and Charley." He paused chewing on his lip and looking suddenly wary. "And Adam. I hope you don't mind."

Adam?

My lips curled into a reflexive smile. I hadn't heard from Adam all day, and I was beginning to wonder if he'd forgotten my birthday altogether. It was a relief to know it was obviously because he was in cahoots with Ethan and didn't want to ruin the surprise. Of course, I hadn't heard from Aaron or my father either, but I didn't expect to.

"Of course I don't mind. It's a wonderful, kind gesture, thank you." I reached up on tiptoes to graze his lips with a gentle kiss. "Are you sure *you're* okay with it, though? I mean, I wouldn't have minded if it was just the two us for dinner. In fact, I wouldn't mind having you *for* dinner." I tugged at his lip playfully with my teeth.

Responding with guttural groan, he cupped my buttocks, pulling me against the rigid bulge which had suddenly sprung to life beneath the denim of his jeans. "See what you do to me, you naughty girl," he growled.

"What *you* do to me," I corrected. "Of course it would be very rude of me to feast on my godlike boyfriend while our dinner guests look on helplessly. Perhaps I should have you as an afternoon snack instead."

As if in pain, he squeezed his eyes shut and bit down on his lower lip. "Stop!" Swiftly, he released me, turning me around to spank me firmly on the behind. "You're a naughty, naughty, completely insatiable girl, Angelica."

"Of course I am. I'm positively gluttonous when it comes to you. I don't think I'll ever have my fill."

"You've had enough for now. If you don't want my heart to give out, that is."

"Are you saying no?"

"Don't be ridiculous. The word's not in my vocabulary—not where you're concerned, at least. I'm saying later. I want to reserve my energy for what I have planned, and I think you should do the same. Besides,

I have some work to do. There are some calls that won't wait, I'm afraid."

"Oh, okay." I pouted petulantly. "I suppose we should pace ourselves. So, you have something planned for later, huh?"

A mischievous smirk lit up his eyes as he shrugged a brow.

Gripping his collar, I tugged him toward me, teasing him with a full on luscious kiss, before pivoting to sashay provocatively away. "I guess I'll have to wait until later, then. Shame."

"Damn it, woman." He glanced at his watch in frustration before moving to chase after me.

"Oh no!" I turned and wagged a finger at him. "You need to reserve your energy, remember."

"Are you saying no?"

"Damn straight I'm saying no," I chuckled and pointed down the hallway toward his office. "Work. Now."

"Damn it, woman."

Feeling pleased with myself, I wandered into the lounge and settled on the sofa to check out the envelope Abby had given to me from Claudia Miller. Sliding a finger under the seal, I shook out the contents. As anticipated, it included the keys to her immaculate house in the Hamptons and a note with security details, alarm codes, and the like. The note also contained further detail as to where she wanted me to hang the prints, and a reminder that I was free to stay for a few days, to make myself at home.

I grabbed my cell and drafted a quick email to say I'd received it safely, to thank her again for the offer and assure her that I'd carry out the work per instruction. When I was finished, I pulled a comfy chair up to the tank, tucking my legs beneath me to gaze at my beautiful fish and daydreaming about the best birthday I'd ever had.

It was just approaching five o'clock when I awoke with a stiff neck. Watching the fish had been mesmerizing. The calm, fluid motions of the vividly-colored creatures flitting through tiny caves and corals had relaxed me so completely I'd drifted off into a peaceful slumber. Unfurling my limbs, I stretched and pushed to my feet to go in search of Ethan.

He was molded into the contours of his huge office chair, cell phone pressed to his ear with one hand and doodling on a notepad with the other. Leaning against the doorjamb, I studied him as he appeared to listen to whatever the caller was saying, his long graceful fingers now toying with the pen as they traced slow, delicate circles around the tip. The action was as mesmerizing as the fish as they'd glided smoothly through the water, but for altogether different reasons, and oddly, I felt the muscles between my legs contract deliciously.

Tearing my gaze away, I found him watching me, his hooded eyes gazing up through long, thick lashes, the edge of his mouth curling into a knowing smile. He looked meltingly gorgeous and I found myself having to swallow hard to prevent myself from physically drooling.

"Fine." The sound of his voice suddenly shattered my trance. "It will have to be Thursday, then, but first thing. Knowing Valiente it will take all fucking day. Where is he flying in from?… Japan? What the hell is he doing in Japan?…" He raised his brows. "Hayakawa, of course, he was the other investor. He's hoping to set a precedent, I might have known. The bastard's hoping the old man will snap his hand off with his paltry offer." He laughed, suddenly. "Well, if he thinks I'm worried about the Japanese, he's deluded. Hayakawa may seem like a bewildered billionaire, but he's the most judicious ninety-year-old bastard you're ever likely to come across."

Deciding to leave him to it, I made a thumbing motion over my shoulder and mouthed, *going for a shower*. He pouted, but nodded and I wandered off down the hallway to our suite.

By seven we were ready and heading toward Eden to collect Adam, a warm sensation of nerves and excitement bubbling in my core.

Spending social time with Adam wasn't something I often did. Who was I kidding? It was something I never did, not beyond sitting having a quick drink with him at the bar in Eden anyway, and I hadn't done that in an age.

Sensing my nervousness, Ethan reached out and took my hand. "You look amazing. Try and relax."

I smiled tentatively and began to wriggle in my seat, attempting to smooth down the skirt of my dress. "You don't think it's too short?" I asked of the emerald green wrap-over dress I'd selected.

"Do you think I'd let you leave the apartment if I thought it was even remotely inappropriate? Everything you wear is too short in the sense that other people can see parts of your flesh that belong solely to me, but skimpily inappropriate it is not."

Feeling reassured, I relaxed a little. "I'm amazed you managed to drag Adam away from Eden, especially on a Sunday. I swear he's married to that place. He'll never find his Eve if he doesn't make more effort."

"He must know you're worth it." He squeezed my hand and gazed out of the passenger window, a slight frown marring his forehead as if something was on his mind.

"Was there a problem before?"

"Problem?"

"Yes, you were on the phone with someone. It sounded tense."

"Oh, it was just Alex. Nothing for you to worry about. She was just firming up the Valiente meeting—he's a slick son of a bitch. I'd keep him waiting longer, but Damon's keen to get the deal sorted before Dad returns."

Just as I was about to ask what the deal was, my cell *buzzed* with an incoming message, and I rifled through my purse to retrieve it. When I opened the message I felt my heart plummet into my abdomen with a thud, the disappointment rolling into a heavy, aching ball in the pit of my stomach: Hey, sorry it's last minute, but have to bail tonight— crisis at the restaurant. Tell Wilde thanks for the invite though, oh and... happy birthday, Sis! Sorry it's late x

"What is it?" Ethan asked with concern.

Struggling with the sudden lump in my throat, I handed him the cell.

"What the fuck?" he hissed. "He waits until now? Is this the first you've heard from him all day?"

I nodded.

"And the others?"

Assuming he was referring to my father and Aaron, I scowled and shook my head.

"Fuckers," he mumbled under his breath, reaching to grip my hand tightly.

The smile he forced onto his lips in an attempt to reassure me didn't reach his eyes, and suddenly I felt bad for him. He'd tried to do something special for me, knowing how much it would mean for me to share my birthday with Adam, and it had blown up in his face.

"It doesn't matter, E, really. It's Sunday, a busy night for him at the restaurant. It was a big ask. The very fact that you know how to make me happy and that you asked him at all, is pleasing enough. I love you for that."

This time his smile was genuine. "We'd better head for Paddy's, then," and then to Jackson, "Head for Paddy's please, Jackson."

"Yes, boss," Jackson acknowledged, swiftly signaling and swapping lanes.

"Paddy's?" I asked in confusion.

"We're meeting Jia and Charley there. I thought if it was your choice, that's where you'd go. And it's your birthday, so it's your choice."

Could this man be more perfect?

Suddenly, something occurred to me. "You know, I don't really care if Adam can't make it. It's not like I even knew he was coming until a couple of hours ago." I paused. "To be honest, no offense to Jia and Charley, bless them, but I wouldn't be devastated if they were a no-show. Everything I want and need is right here. As long as I'm with you, it's all I care about."

"Ditto." He squeezed my hand again and winked. "Well, we can keep our fingers crossed with regards to the girls, I suppose."

My mouth made the shape of an O in a mixed expression of shock and shame. "Are we awful?"

"No." He pulled me closer and poured his arm around me. "We're just in love."

Paddy's was busy, as was usual for a Sunday evening, the bar three deep in places. Ethan gripped my hand and pulled me in front of him protectively as we pushed our way through the throngs. Dylan spotted me instantly, his face lighting up as his eyes darted past the waiting customers to focus straight on me.

"Angel cake!" He shouted, clearly delighted to see me. "Wait there." Abandoning his thirsty customers, he began to make his way around to the front of the bar.

"Christ, I forgot about your fan club," Ethan muttered in my ear, his grip on my hips growing suddenly tighter. "The poor guy's so fascinated, so tuned into you, it's as if he could smell you the moment you walked in."

I tapped his hand lightly just as Dylan approached, quietly muttering, "Behave yourself."

"Angel cake, happy birthday." Dylan leaned in for a hug, but then glanced tentatively at Ethan, as if he were asking permission.

Ethan smiled his assent, relinquishing his grip reluctantly and moving to my side.

"Thanks, Dylan. How sweet that you remembered."

"Of course he remembered," Ethan mumbled quietly, so thankfully only I could hear.

"How could I forget?" Dylan proclaimed, unaware that he was reinforcing Ethan's theory.

Ethan chuckled beside me. "You remember Ethan." I quickly

reminded Dylan of my boyfriend's presence.

"Sure." Dylan reached to shake Ethan's hand, who responded politely, but I suspect, from the way he gritted his teeth, a little harder than was necessary. My berating glare warned him it was not a pissing contest.

"Let me get you guys a drink, save you the hassle of the bar."

"Thanks, Dylan, that would be great. I'll take a beer." I nudged Ethan, whose rigid glare looked as if he were considering refusing the offer.

"Beer's good," he finally said.

Dylan patted us both on the shoulder and turned to make his way back behind the bar.

"What the hell?" I poked Ethan in the rib sharply.

Wincing, he thrust out his lower lip in a sulky pout. "I can't help it. I hate it when guys are so tastelessly blatant about how much they want you."

"E, aside from being a good host and a good friend, Dylan doesn't do anything blatantly."

"Bollocks. He was practically dribbling. Are you sure you two have never—"

"I'm certain, I think I'd know. Nothing has ever happened between us, I assure you."

"Hmm," he grunted. "Maybe not in reality, but in his imagination he's been there many times, I can assure *you*." He paused to touch his fingertips to the bridge of his nose, his eyes closing briefly as if something horrendous had just occurred to him. "Oh Christ, the bastard is going to jerk off about you later and there's not a damn thing I can do about it."

"Ethan!" I punched him in the arm. "He does not think like that about me."

Just then we were interrupted by a dark-haired young boy, no more than ten years old and far too young to be in a bar. He thrust a couple of beers at us, turned to me and said, "Dylan said I should give these to the sexy lady. Are you her?"

Flushing awkwardly, I glanced at Ethan who replied to the boy, "Yes, that's her. Tell Dylan... thanks." He eyed me smugly over the top of his bottle as he took a sip. "You were saying?"

"*What* were you saying?" Jia suddenly appeared at my elbow. "Happy birthday, bitch. Sorry we're late."

"Ah, Jia," Ethan said. "Angel was just refuting my suggestion that she might be Dylan's masturbation fantasy. What do you think?"

"Totally. He's been boning you every damn night since the day he met you, bitch. You know that." She turned to Ethan. "Not in the literal sense, obviously."

Ethan nodded, smiling with dissimulation to conceal his irritation. I think he'd rather hoped she'd disagree with him.

Speechless and exasperated, I shook my head at them both. "Where's Charley?"

Just then she appeared from somewhere behind Jia, alerting me to her presence first by rasping a painfully hoarse sounding cough, and then by wishing me a happy birthday in a voice which sounded as if she smoked fifty a day.

"Thank you, Charley, but without being rude, what the hell are you doing here?"

"I thought I was..." She paused to sneeze. "Invited."

"Yes, but you're sick." I stared at her puffy, glazed eyes and her feverish skin. "I can feel the heat coming off of you from here. You should be in bed."

She shrugged helplessly.

"I said she didn't need to come, but she insisted," Jia offered unsympathetically.

I glared at her pointedly. "Jia, Charley needs to go home, she looks really sick."

She hesitated for a beat before saying to Charley, "Do you want me to get you a cab?"

Charley shrugged again.

"No, Jia. You need to take Charley home and look after her. Jackson can take you." I turned to Ethan. "Jackson can take them, right?"

"Sure," he said without hesitation and took out his cell. "I'll give him a nudge."

"Fine." Jia forced a smile.

"You can stay if you want," Charley rasped in a voice that had me reaching to rub an imaginary ache from my own throat.

Jia looked as if she were considering the idea until I shifted my foot, putting all my weight on her little toe.

"Ouch," she grimaced. "I mean, as if. Like I'd let you go home alone."

Ethan and I exchanged a look. "Jackson's here." He nodded toward the door and we made our way outside.

"I feel awful. I've ruined your night," Charley sniffed.

"Nonsense, it's just my birthday. We can do it anytime."

She nodded and practically crawled into the waiting SUV, mumbling something about the vehicle being more plush than her entire apartment. Jia was gaping at the step up to the vehicle, probably wondering how the hell she was going to haul her tiny frame inside the car while trying to remain graceful.

Ethan rolled his eyes and grabbing her by the waist, lifted her as if she were weightless and planted her inside the car. She gasped in horror, appearing to be unsure whether to slap him or thank him, and finally deciding on the latter.

Folding his arms around my waist, we watched Jackson pull away from the curb. "Well, I suppose we should be careful what we wish for. Poor Charley."

"Oh God, you don't think we wished this on her do you?"

"Don't be silly. I think Charley was sick long before you hoped they were a no-show."

"Yeah, you're probably right. I can't believe Jia even considered coming out with her in that state. I'll be having words with her about it."

"Mmm, I'm not sure altruism is Jia's strong point."

"No," I agreed. "And this I should know." Something told me we wouldn't be seeing much of Charley from here on in.

"So…" Ethan turned me to face him. "I suppose we should brave another beer as our table for five is now a table for two and our ride has just disappeared into the night without us."

Glancing over his shoulder into the busy bar, I pondered our options. The prospect of further speculation into the mucky thoughts that may or may not go on in Dylan's apparently sullied and contaminated mind somehow didn't appeal. "I've got an idea. How would you feel if we canceled our dinner reservations altogether?"

Ethan's brow creased into a skeptical frown. "Go on," he urged me to expound.

"There's a family run Italian restaurant only a block from here—Lucia's—they make the most amazing pizzas. What do you say we grab a couple, go home, curl up in front of the fire and feed one another?"

A wicked smile slithered on to his perfect mouth. "I'd say that's a fucking amazing idea. Do I get to peel you out of that bloody dress before I feed you?"

"I thought you liked the dress?"

"I do, I'd just prefer to see it strewn on the floor next to your perfect naked body while I feed you with amazing pizza. That way it doesn't matter if I happen to spill a bit. I'll be able to simply… lick it off."

A sensual shiver ran down my spine and curled up inside my groin with the thrill of his promise. "What are we waiting for?" I asked, biting down into my lower lip hungrily, although it wasn't the prospect of pizza that had my taste buds drooling.

"You're a dirty, dirty girl, Cinderella."

CHAPTER TWENTY

By the time we emerged from Lucia's with enough pizza for Jackson, he'd returned from the trip with Jia and Charley and was waiting outside by the car.

"I hope you can handle spicy," I said, thrusting a pizza box into his hands. "Extra jalapeños on yours, on Ethan's advice."

He took it from me, his eager eyes lighting up. "Sounds perfect, thanks."

I don't know what it was that made me glance over his shoulder into the window of the bistro across the street, but something did. You could call it sixth sense, but it was as if someone had summoned me, called out my name, begging me to look up and see.

Sat at the table in the window was a family enjoying dinner together.

My father's familiar posture, the way he arranged his shoulders and arms in that irritating, excessive superior way of his, hands clasped under his chin as he chuckled at something the woman next to him was saying, was what I saw first. Across from him sat Aaron, a sad, pathetic duplicate of his father, even down to the sly, smug way his shoulders shook when he laughed. And then Adam.

The heavy aching ball of disappointment that I'd felt earlier was now a burning, perfidious poison. Toxic treachery.

"What is it, Angel?" Ethan's gaze followed mine across the street. "What the... Motherfuckers! Get in the car, Angel."

"No." I glanced at him. "Let's go and say hello." I darted out into the road, weaving through the traffic which had halted for a red light ahead.

"Angel, wait." Ethan was behind me as I pushed through the door of the restaurant, anger radiating from his very pores.

Once inside, I hesitated, gripping hold of Ethan's blazer sleeve to ensure he knew I meant every word of what I was about to say. "Let *me* handle this. Please."

His expression was dubious but he nodded, and I continued into the restaurant, stalking purposefully up to their table.

My father spotted me first, his expression a picture of surprise before carefully replacing it with condescending amusement. "Ah, yes. Angelica." His tone, when his tongue rolled over my name was an implication, as though I was something akin to a stubborn stain on his shirt which he just couldn't shift.

"Oh yes, so it is," Aaron jumped in. "Good job you spotted that, Dad." He tapped his menu with his pointy finger. "I was just about to give her my order."

The two burst into laughter, and I mentally held Ethan back, praying that he'd hold it together as he fidgeted with a palpable rage behind me. Ignoring the derisive sneers from my father and Aaron, I turned my icy cold glare on Adam. I expected nothing from them—but him?

"I thought there was a crisis... at the restaurant?" I spoke with quiet accusation.

Adam's face was burning with what I hoped was shame, his eyes darting around my face as he floundered for a viable excuse.

"One time, Adam... One time."

"Angel, I'm sorry... I couldn't... I had to... it's Monica's birthday." His eyes fluttered to the woman across from him and then helplessly down to his lap.

"Hi there," the woman seemed to lean forward, wiggling her manicured fingers in some semblance of a wave. "Well? Is someone gonna introduce me or what?" Her voice was high-pitched, evidence of a southern drawl in the way she curled and prolonged her words.

Tearing my gaze from Adam, I turned to the woman, who I now

knew to be Monica, certain that I'd seen her somewhere before. Then it came to me in a flash. She was the same busty blonde who'd been clinging to my father's arm at Claudia Miller's wedding.

Monica seemed to draw on the same conclusion when she suddenly said, "Aren't you the photographer from that wedding we attended in the Hamptons—?"

"This is my sister, Angelica." Adam's voice interjected to enlighten the blonde.

"Sister?! Jesus, Harley, you have a daughter? Well aint that something," she breathed theatrically. "You sure are a pretty little thing."

My father shrugged a non-committal brow. I ignored him again, blinking to focus on the woman. She was petite, older than I'd first imagined, maybe late forties, early fifties—too young for him, nonetheless. She was attractive—in a heavily made-up sort of way, but her face wasn't the thing clamoring for my attention.

My gaze was pulled almost magnetically to the heart-shaped diamond pendant which lay perfectly in the hollow at the base of her neck. I gaped transfixed, my mind working frantically through possible explanations for what I was seeing, but arriving at only one conclusion.

Monica suddenly squealed, her fingers flying to her neck to finger the fine piece of jewelry. "Isn't it to *die* for? Harley... your daddy got it for my birthday. He has the best taste, don't you think?" She turned and gripped my father's grinning cheek between her fingers, tugging at it affectionately. At the same time, she caught sight of Ethan. "Oh, who's this?"

Ethan moved closer to me, his trembling hand touching me gently at the small of my back in a silent request to let him handle it from here. Anger radiated off him in waves as he chomped at the bit to be unleashed, but I wasn't ready to relinquish control of this situation yet.

My glare shifted to my father, his grin settling into a smug challenge, daring me to dispute Monica's naïve assumption. I narrowed my eyes at him in disgust, his certitude that I wouldn't cross him only serving to bolster my determination to do just that.

Averting my eyes from his sickening face, I glared again at Monica. "You're wearing my mother's pendant." I spat the words at her viciously.

In an instant, her smile vanished, humiliation flaring on her cheeks as she lowered her chin and stared silently at the table in contemplation of what I'd said. Both Adam and Aaron glared across the table as they waited for my father to contradict me, to deny he'd given something precious of my mother's to his most recent fling.

"Dad?" Aaron finally said, searching for something to prove my erroneous accusation. My father ignored him, his smug smile now an impassive line. "If she's telling the truth, Dad, by rights that pendant should be mine."

"It's mine," I hissed at him in horror.

"Yours? You don't deserve anything of hers. You've got your memories, what the fuck have I got? Nothing! *You* made sure of that."

"Memories? What memories?" I gasped incredulously. "I've tried every day of my life to remember her—"

Monica stood suddenly, muttering for us to excuse her and fled toward the rest rooms.

"And did you give your mother much thought today, Angelica?" my father asked, his accusatory eyes narrowing on me. "Well, did you?"

I didn't answer him.

"After all, today would be the day she spent sixteen hours pushing you from her body."

I gaped, half in horror and half in disbelief. I knew nothing of how I'd entered the world, not even the time of day I was born.

"I watched her writhe in agony as you tore through her, destroying her beautiful body." My face began to burn with the venomous implication of his tone. And then he delivered his final blow. "You almost killed her *that* day too."

Ethan flew past me, gripping him by the collar of his shirt and lifting him out of his seat, the force of his advance upsetting the table as he hissed and growled in seething anger. Glasses toppled and crashed to the floor and the room went silent as all eyes turned on us.

"Give it your best shot, Wilde," my father spluttered, his face growing red as Ethan tightened his grip.

"It'll be the only shot he gets," warned Aaron with an unconvincing confidence.

"Best shot?" Ethan's words grated laboriously past his anger, delivered with the menacing threat that was without doubt intended. "I will fucking *kill* you, you half-wired piece of shit. You've spat your last bit of poison at her, you motherfucker. If you ever lay eyes on her again, you cross the fucking street, you leave the fucking restaurant… the city, but don't you ever even glance at her…"

Panic suddenly welled inside me, the meager dregs of my relationship with my family—albeit sad and vastly lacking—slipping from my fingers. I grasped at Ethan's arm, pulling with all my weight. "Please, Ethan. Please stop!"

For a second, I thought he couldn't hear me, too consumed by his own anger. And then suddenly he released my father, dropping him with repulsion into his seat like a bag of rotting garbage. He turned to me, his eyes raging with an unmanageable storm. "Stop?"

I nodded, my trembling hands reaching for him in the hope he'd understand. "Please. I don't want this."

"You'd do well to listen to the girl," my father straightened his shirt and tie and picked up his menu. "Now if you don't mind, we were about to order."

With that, I turned and quietly left the restaurant. Jackson was waiting on the street outside, his face full of question and concern as he opened the rear door, and taking my trembling hand helped me into the car. Then he turned back to the sidewalk, speaking briefly to Ethan who'd followed close behind me before climbing in to driver's seat.

Ethan leaned into the car, his hands resting on the edge of the roof. His complexion was pale, gray almost, as the rage retreated and confoundedness settled in his eyes. "Why? Why did you stop me?"

For seconds, I hesitated, knowing he wouldn't accept my answer, but my mind wouldn't work, and panicking, I blurted out the worst thing I could have said. "I told you to let me handle it. It's my fight."

The look on his face was as if I'd just turned the light out in his world, and with a single nod to Jackson, he pushed away from the car and slammed the door.

"What...? Where are you going?" I clambered for the door but my seat belt, which I couldn't remember fastening, jerked me back with force. Before I could release it, Jackson had pulled out into traffic. "No, Jackson, wait! What is he doing?" Turning in my seat to afford myself a view out of the rear window, I watched helplessly as Ethan disappeared into the distance. "Jackson, please, you have to stop the car."

"Sorry, kiddo." His pained expression was plain to see in the crinkling of his eyes through the rearview. "It'll be okay. Just let him calm down."

I lay in bed in the dark, the only light, aside from the moon shining through the vast window, came from my cell phone in the palm of my hand. Tapping the screen, I watched, hoping and praying as it connected to Ethan's cell for the eighteenth time tonight that he would answer. But for the eighteenth time I reached only his voicemail. I hung up. There was no point in leaving a message; I'd left a half dozen already.

Sometime later, I awoke suddenly from a half-sleep, my blurry eyes fighting to focus in the muted light. Ethan was sitting in a chair watching me, his slumped, dejected form weary and motionless.

Relief at the sight of him flooded me like a tidal wave. "Where have you been?" I asked, pushing up on my elbow.

He shrugged. "Walking."

"And drinking?" I could smell the bourbon fumes from where I lay.

"'And drinking.'" He nodded once.

"Did you...?"

"What? Go back in the restaurant and murder your father in cold blood? No, but I should have."

Choosing to ignore the comment, I asked, "Why did you abandon me?"

His eyes shot up with incredulity in his forehead. "Why did I *abandon* you? You *pushed* me away, Angelica. Your fight, remember?"

"I didn't mean it like that," I snapped, annoyed that he just didn't seem to get it.

"Oh? How did you mean it?"

"I meant that... it just has to be me who makes that call. I'm not ready to shut the door on them completely. When I am, I will. I felt like you were taking that decision from me."

"The way you took the decision of how to handle the Rebecca situation away from me, you mean?"

The remark cut me to the quick, not sure of what I should make of it. "You were too close to that situation to make the right call. I did the right thing, you said so yourself."

"Yes, right on both counts. I was too close—you did the right thing. Because you could see the full picture clearly, and my view was distorted. The same is true in this situation, except of course for the role reversal."

"You can't possibly compare the two, Ethan. She was a blackmailing psychopath, he's my—"

"Father?" He finished my sentence, shaking his head in frustration. "You credit him with far more than he deserves."

Standing, he moved to the bed to sit on the edge, but he didn't touch me. "You're blinded by the word. *Father.*" He scoffed at the word as he shook his head. "You've been waiting your entire life for him to live up to the name, to be your supporter, your protector, to be proud of you. To accept you and love you—to be your friend. How long are you prepared to wait, Angel? How many times is he going to kick you to the curb before you give up hoping for something that is never going to happen? You say you're not ready to close the door on them, but they slammed it in your fucking face long ago."

The words burned into my soul as I whipped over on to my other side, scooting away from him to the center of the bed to cover my ears. I didn't want to hear anymore. Ethan continued nonetheless.

"I'm sorry my words hurt you, but you need to hear them. You were wrong to ask me to stay out of your fight tonight—it was like asking me to stand by and watch while they beat you half to death. And I can promise you, as long as I live and breathe, it will never happen again. But I can't stop him from damaging you further if you refuse to help yourself. You're dangling over a precipice and clinging on by your fingertips in the hope that he will save you. But he's not coming, Angel."

"Let me be," I whispered hoarsely, my words struggling past the anger and unshed tears.

A few moments passed before I heard him sigh with defeat, the mattress shifting as he stood to leave. "Fine. I'll let you be, Angelica. But know this. When you fall—I'll be there to catch you."

His final words were like a train hitting me full force in the gut, the wind forced out and leaving me unable to speak or even breathe. Reaching out, he stroked my hair tenderly, then turned and was gone.

Shame rushed through me like a poison invading my veins with such venomous self-repulsion that I held onto my breath, depriving my body and brain of oxygen, punishing myself in the only way I could think of. Finally, when I thought my lungs would burst, I gasped, sucking in greedy gulps of air until I began to sob. My body shook with anguish, until eventually the convulsions subsided and slowed to a soundless weep.

But I wasn't weeping for me or for the void in my soul left by my toxic family. I was weeping for the only person in my life that had ever come close to filling it. No, he'd more than filled it. He'd flooded it with an abundance of overwhelming love and affection far beyond anything I'd dared to imagine could exist. Today—my birthday—was evidence alone of that. He'd done everything to make my day special and I'd flung it back in his face simply because he'd tried to protect me.

Why? What kind of heartless bitch does something like that? And how would I ever undo it?

Forgive me, Ethan. Forgive me, Ethan. Forgive me, Ethan.

The words were a prayer, a repetitive incantation inside my head, over and over, until finally, I slept.

My eyes were screwed tightly closed, if not as a shield against the icy-cold wind that was battering against my face, then because I was too afraid of what I'd find if I opened them. The noise was almost deafening, the whirling sounds of the wind like the engines of a jet, as it whooshed and swirled around me. And from somewhere below came a terrifying, booming, crashing sound, which seemed to grow louder with every dramatic pound of my heart.

The sensations engulfing every nerve ending in my body were beyond painful, and far more likened to torturous agony. Something wet and cold was against one cheek, the texture as sharp as shards of glass as it embedded itself into my skin, each infinitesimal movement more excruciating than the last. Every muscle in my body was cramping and burning with spasmodic convulsions in an effort to brace itself into some unnatural, contorted position. The joints of my fingers were locked into place, my fingers curved into a claw-like position as they seemed to clutch at the same sharp, wet, scratchy substance that lay beneath my face.

Aside from the noise and the fear and the pain, the only other thing my senses were chillingly alert to were the words of warning resounding in my head... Don't let go.

Suddenly, I was drenched, the shock of freezing cold water slapping painfully against my back, causing my eyes to spring open involuntarily.

And there before me was the unforgiving horror of my situation. I clung to a steep, rugged rock face, the skin on my cheek scraping painfully, once again, as I tightened my grip. Ahead there was nothing, just empty infinite space and below, the violent, booming explosion was deafening. Needing to seek the source, I summoned all my courage and lowered my chin. I stared in terror at the waves below as they crashed turbulently against the rocks, their threat as merciless and real as the licking flames of a blazing fire, and their only promise—an abyss and an endless, unfathomable hell.

Desperate to get away, I shifted my gaze upwards to where my fingers clung to the craggy, uneven rock, the cadaverous nooks and cavities only deep enough for the space my fingertips already filled. My foot positions were similar, my toes digging into inadequate spaces as I held on for dear life.

Suddenly, there was noise above—voices, and the skin on my cheek tore and burned as I strained my neck to see. I felt a surge of hope as I glimpsed the faces of the three men standing at the top of the precipice, and gathering all my strength, I called out to them. "Dad! Dad! Adam! I'm here, I'm down here. Can you hear me? Dad?"

Nothing.

I tried again, my voice straining with all my might against the raucous calamity around me, but still nothing. They just couldn't hear. Then I noticed the smirk on Aaron's face, an uneven, derisive simper he didn't even attempt to hide, and I realized with dread that the reason they hadn't answered wasn't because they couldn't hear. Their deafness derived from choice. They were deliberately closing their eyes to my danger and my impending death.

"Please!" I called out. "Please, you have to help me. Why? Why won't you help me?"

Their attention was suddenly diverted to a commotion just behind them, and I watched as the faces of two ferocious, grimacing spotted beasts shifted into view. They began to fight, warring in a vicious bloody battle over something I couldn't discern, a bone, maybe, or a small animal. They jerked and tugged at the thing they battled over, drooling mouths and snarling teeth clamping over it, as they leaned back on their haunches, pulling and yanking in a brutal tug-of-war.

Suddenly they lost their grip, the object breaking free as it was tossed into the air, spinning and somersaulting, until the physical force of gravity won out. It hurtled at speed toward the ocean, skimming the edge of the cliff and down, down, down. There was nothing I could do except watch in horror as it headed straight for me, the shape and color materializing before my eyes the closer it became.

The shiny red shoe hit me full-force in the face, the searing pain causing me to finally lose my grip. My finger nails burned, tearing from my fingertips as I scrambled helplessly at the rock, and then I was falling. My piercing scream filled the air as I plunged toward the crashing waves below and my inevitable death. My body felt broken as it hit the freezing water at force, the speed and strength of the waves sucking me under and stealing my final breath.

My first thought was to brace myself against the shock of the cold, but suddenly I was aware of only warmth. With my eyes tightly closed, the sensation was like being enfolded in a heated, fleecy blanket and all around me was peacefully silent. I opened my eyes trying to understand, and realized I was immersed in the bluest ocean I'd ever seen. Surrounding me was a mass of delicately colored corals, and swimming among them were a variety of strikingly vivid fish.

A shoal of tiny orange ones suddenly dispersed, and from the midst there came the most wonderful sight. Ethan swam toward me, his beautiful, perfect features filled with utter benignity, and then I became conscious that I was still falling, sinking deeper and deeper into the unknown. My lungs were burning, the fire tearing through me, and with sudden finality, I realized there was no air left—no time left. I'd used up every last drop of both, and the light began to fade.

Ethan's arms were suddenly around me, and just as I thought I couldn't bear the pain in my chest any longer, he spoke to me.

"Angel, look at me."

I fought to focus on his moving lips, listening to the words he appeared to utter so effortlessly.

"Breathe, Angel. I've got you. You can breathe now."

"Angel! Angel, breathe goddamn it, breathe!" Ethan's voice roused me from my hell.

Strong, warm hands shook me by the shoulders and the pain in my chest was worse than excruciating. I heaved in a breath and a sharp, cold rush of air charged into my lungs, inflating my chest as it welcomed it eagerly.

"Angel! Oh, baby, thank God."

The raw fear and relief in Ethan's voice was thick and tangible, and the sudden need to reassure him felt vital. Unable to speak yet, I reached out for him, grasping him to me with a wild and frantic desperation.

Forgive me, Ethan. Forgive me, Ethan. Forgive me, Ethan.

The truth was suddenly so lucid, the knowledge which my heart had refused to accept, now as real and solid as the guilt that came from denying it. Just as he said he would, Ethan had been there to catch me. He'd plucked me from the evil claws of the savage nightmare that had engulfed me only moments before. That in my dream had been a few moments of terror, but in reality, had been a lifetime of hell. It was time to slay my demons.

Ethan held me in his arms as I sobbed inconsolably—my rock, my love, my salvation. He held me until the residual ache of betrayal and rejection suddenly retreated, leaving my body like a demonic possession finally relinquishing my soul.

And at last, I was free.

The End

ACKNOWLEDGEMENTS

First and foremost my thanks go to my husband and daughter whose endless help and support has been essential to my wellbeing, tremendously comforting and so very valued. Thank you – I love you, I cherish you, you are my world.

Thanks to Maxann Dobson at Polished Pen for her editing skills and words of encouragement, and James Ramsey for being the final pair of eyes.

Thank you to Paula Radell who does an amazing job of promoting me and my books from thousands of miles away. I truly don't know what I'd do without you.

To all the amazing bloggers who work tirelessly to help authors promote their work. Thank you for taking a chance on my books; reading, reviewing, promoting and generally helping me make the leap from Bound for Hell to Bound for Salvation. I thank each and every one of you who got involved, but a personal mention goes to Kerry-Ann at Kez's Korner, Katy at Slut Sistas Book Blog and Jen at Two Sassy Chicks.

Finally, to my readers who make this all worthwhile. Thank you, thank you, thank you!

ABOUT THE AUTHOR

Kendra Leigh fell in love with words and reading from a very young age. She was captivated when Enid Blyton whisked her away to the magical lands at the top of the Faraway Tree with Moon-face and the rest of the gang. Now, of course, she has more of a fondness for chocolate, cheese, and hot men in suits - not necessarily in that order. Kendra devotes her life to her devilishly handsome partner, scandalously beautiful daughter, and cute as hell Shih-Tzu. She believes in love at first sight, and as well as writing and reading, Kendra has a passion for great movies and brilliantly written TV. Bound for Salvation is her second book and book two of the Bound Trilogy.

You can contact Kendra Leigh at:

Email: Kendraleighwrites@outlook.com
www.kendraleighauthor.com
www.facebook.com/KendraLeighWrites
www.goodreads.com/book/show/25147174-bound-for-salvation
Twitter: @KLeighBooks

To receive heads-up alerts on upcoming releases, cover reveals, teasers and giveaways, please subscribe to my newsletter at www.kendraleighauthor.com.

If you enjoyed reading **Bound for Salvation**, please consider leaving a rating and a review. Read on for a glimpse of what's in store for Angel and Ethan with the synopsis for book three in The Bound Trilogy, **Bound for Nirvana**.

Bound for Nirvana

Paradise can turn to hell in a heartbeat...

Angel once believed she was destined for a loveless, hellish existence. Now she willingly gives her heart to Ethan Wilde, the man whose love mends her broken soul a little more each day.

Ethan knows Hell is no place for an angel, especially not his Angel. He's sworn to protect her at any cost and would willingly sacrifice his soul to save hers.

When Ethan's past threatened to destroy them, they fought their way through a living hell, emerging stronger than ever. But yearning for the peace she craves - her nirvana, Angel continues to paper over the cracks of her troubled childhood.

Until a twist of fate forces her to confront a lifetime of buried memories and betrayal.

What happens when the worst nightmare you've ever encountered is the one you wake up in?

When the past comes face to face with the present to reveal a web of dark secrets and cruel lies?

Can Angel and Ethan find their happy ever after, or will they be forever Bound for Hell?

Bound for Nirvana

Book 3 of The Bound Trilogy, by Kendra Leigh

Relentlessly sexy. Emotionally deep. Tangled, twisted, intricately woven love story with romance and suspense. For readers 18 and over due to explicit sexual content.